Deep Blue Sea

By Tasmina Perry

Daddy's Girls
Gold Diggers
Guilty Pleasures
Original Sin
Kiss Heaven Goodbye
Private Lives
Perfect Strangers
Deep Blue Sea

Tasmina Perry

Deep Blue Sea

headline
review

First published in 2013 by HEADLINE REVIEW
An imprint of HEADLINE PUBLISHING GROUP

1

Cataloguing in Publication Data is available from the British Library

ISBN 978 0 7553 5852 6 (Hardback)
ISBN 978 0 7553 5853 3 (Trade paperback)

Typeset in Sabon by Avon DataSet Ltd, Bidford-on-Avon, Warwickshire

Printed and bound in Great Britain by Clays Ltd, St Ives plc

Headline's policy is to use papers that are natural, renewable
and recyclable products and made from wood grown in sustainable forests.
The logging and manufacturing processes are expected to conform
to the environmental regulations of the country of origin.

HEADLINE PUBLISHING GROUP
An Hachette UK Company
338 Euston Road
London NW1 3BH

www.headline.co.uk
www.hachette.co.uk

For Sheila Crowley and Wayne Brookes
And Chris Hemblade who is much missed

Prologue

Twenty years ago

'Who is she?' screamed her mother from downstairs. For the past twenty minutes, from the moment Rachel Miller had come home from swimming practice and been ordered to her room, she had been unable to hear the precise contents of her parents' argument. She had closed her bedroom door intentionally, not wanting to pick out the abuse and accusations, but there was no mistaking that her father was now being confronted. 'And don't lie to me.'

Rachel had known this argument was coming. It was almost as if she had been able to feel it in the air, like a brewing storm.

It hadn't always been like this. There was a family photo downstairs on the TV cabinet that said otherwise. Mum, Dad, Rachel and her big sister Diana, all crammed together on the sofa downstairs with big toothy smiles, arms wrapped around each other as if they would never be apart. You could almost hear the laughter and the cries of 'Cheese!' Or had that all been a lie too?

Somehow, somewhere down the line, it had all gone sour. The bickering over little things, stupid things. Resentments growing into arguments, rows growing into all-out war. There had been a particularly bad confrontation before Christmas; voices so full of hate and fury that Rachel had gone to her bedroom and prayed for it to stop.

And in some ways her prayers had been answered. The rows diminished, only to be replaced by a hostile silence, a constant tension in the house that was like the drip-drip of a tap, splashing one drop at a time until the bath finally overflowed.

Rachel reached over to her bedside table, scrabbling round in the drawer for her new compact disc player, her fingers stabbing at the buttons to switch the thing on and drown out the noise. She crept under her duvet, pulled her knees up to her chest and stuck her nose into her copy of *Just Seventeen*, which had been returned to her that day after a week of confiscation by Mr Stephenson when she had been caught reading it in double physics.

'Rach?' She jumped at the sensation of the headphone being pulled away from her ear and looked up to see her sister standing by the bed next to her. She hadn't seen her since school and was relieved to see her.

Diana had the room next door – a bigger one than her own, with pink and white Laura Ashley wallpaper that was covered with pictures of Matt Dillon and Christian Slater – but they often bunked in each other's rooms when their parents rowed.

'I should have stayed out,' said Diana quietly, pulling back the duvet and creeping in next to her sister.

'Where have you been?' asked Rachel, happy to be talking about anything else.

'Paul's.'

Paul? Rachel's eyes widened – for the moment, everything happening downstairs was forgotten. Paul *Jones*? Diana had been at his house? Paul Jones was the king of Meersbrook Comprehensive, the resident heartthrob; dark eyes peering out from under a floppy fringe, captain of the football team. He even had a motorbike. Every girl in the school was a little bit in love with him, and Rachel – in secret, in her dreams – was a lot in love with him.

'Is he . . . is Paul your boyfriend now?'

Diana shrugged her slim shoulders. 'I'm just going with him.'

Rachel nodded, trying to appear casual, although her mouth was dry and her stomach felt hot. What did 'going with' someone mean exactly? She was pretty sure it was kissing. Proper kissing on the mouth with tongues, the thought of which still freaked her out a little bit. But she was going to be thirteen next week and she was curious to know for sure.

'Is it easy?'

2

Diana smirked, one eyebrow raised.

'Is what easy?'

'Kissing.'

Diana laughed. She had a pretty laugh; everything about Diana was pretty, it was so annoying. But Rachel knew Di would never laugh at her, she was never unkind.

'I've never really thought of kissing as easy or hard,' she said. 'But it's fun.' She caught sight of Rachel's furrowed brow. 'Don't worry, you'll get the chance soon enough.'

She smiled, and Rachel felt a little of her jealousy ease. It wasn't Diana's fault that Paul Jones fancied her instead of Rachel, was it? If she was Paul, she would have probably picked Di too.

There was a loud crash. It sounded like the whole dinner service hitting the floor.

'What are they rowing about anyway?' whispered Diana, moving closer.

Rachel was always surprised at how small her sister's voice was. People expected Diana to have a big personality, perhaps because of her beauty and her popularity with the cool crowd, but she was quiet, sensitive, sitting for hours with those stupid romantic books she liked to read.

'I don't know. Dad was already here when I got home.'

Who is she?

Rachel was not a stupid girl. She had picked up on the suggestion by her mother. Her father had found somebody else, somebody else to love. But she didn't want to tell Diana that. Not tonight.

'I hate it,' said Diana. 'I hate the shouting.'

'I know,' said Rachel quietly, putting her arm around her sister.

People often mistook Rachel for the older Miller sister. It wasn't just her height and her big feet, which had finally come in so useful for swimming. Diana looked like a doll compared to her.

They could hear the noise of a door slamming shut. The two girls glanced at each other; they both knew it had been the sound of the front door.

'He's gone,' said Rachel. It was out of her mouth before she had time to think about it.

3

'Gone?' said Diana, a note of panic creeping into her voice. 'How do you know? What do you mean, gone?'

Diana scrambled out of the bed and ran to the window. Rachel didn't need to hear the car engine gunning away to know he had left them. Sometimes she just knew things: knew what people were thinking, what they were going to do. She didn't like it much, it made her feel like a storybook witch.

'Rach, do something!' screamed Diana, her eyes flooding with tears, her beautiful solemn face as white as a ghost.

Rachel puffed out a small breath, trying to convince herself that things would start getting better from now on – just the three of them.

'We should see if Mum's okay,' she said finally.

She took her sister's hand, knowing that she had to keep calm, keep strong, because she had a funny feeling that her mum and her sister weren't going to.

'Let's go and see if we can help sweep up the pieces.'

1

'So who's up for climbing Everest?'

Diana Denver glanced around the table, not sure which of her guests had said it, which friend had thrown down the gauntlet. It could have been any of the men sitting at the neat round of twelve, even a couple of the women. Their friends were like that: accomplished, ambitious, competitive. It wasn't money, it was the alpha mind-set: bigger, better, higher. Two weeks scaling the Himalayan giant was the equivalent of most people's rock-climbing at Center Parcs.

'Well I'm in,' said Michael Reynolds, her husband Julian's close friend. Diana knew Mike was winding them up – he was three stone overweight, not to mention a world-class bullshitter – but she was immediately concerned that it would only encourage Julian. Climbing a mountain was not what he – not what *they* – needed right now.

Michael leant forward in his chair. 'No, I mean it,' he said, his eyes sparkling. 'Everyone thinks it's so hard, but I've been reading up on it and it is actually quite doable. Just takes a bit of determination.'

Julian sipped his Armagnac, letting the amber liquid roll around his tongue before he finally spoke.

'I'm not sure,' he said, to Diana's great relief. Her husband was an adventurer at heart. He had trekked across deserts, motorbiked across continents, but it was all done, as was everything in his life, with great consideration, planning and thought. 'I just think it's too busy these days.'

'Too busy?' laughed Michael, knocking back his own brandy. 'It's not the ski lifts at Verbier we're talking about here, Jules.'

Michael's wife Patty swatted him on the arm. 'Well I think Julian's right. So many people want to do it, they're even running corporate trips up to Base Camp these days. It's like the adventure equivalent of a Birkin – you have to put your name down years in advance and pay through the nose for the privilege.'

Everyone began to laugh as coffee cups were refilled by Diana's fleet of caterers. The glorious smell of arabica beans mingled with the scent of honeysuckle and roses. Diana had been unconvinced about moving the party into the garden, but when numbers had necessitated five tables of twelve, outgrowing the available space in their dining room, there was nothing else for it.

'Jules doesn't need to go to the top of the world,' added Bob Wilson, a fund manager, distinguished by his unconvincing hair weave. 'You're already there, aren't you, Denver. Say, is it true the company's buying Jura Motors?'

Julian gave a low, slow smile. As CEO of the Denver Group, one of Europe's biggest and most valuable conglomerates, he was used to fending off rumour, speculation and shameless mining for information from their investor friends. 'Don't believe everything you read, Bob. I think we've all learnt that the hard way.'

He reached over and took Diana's hand, resting his fingers over hers on the table. She felt all eyes land on her, which made her feel a little uncomfortable.

'Speaking of the Himalayas, I think it's time to go and check out the vodka ice luge my wife has had sculpted. I've been promised it's not in the shape of Michael's penis,' added Julian with a wink.

'Shame!' shouted Patty, as the guests stood up and dispersed around the gardens.

Diana smoothed down the lightweight white wool of her shift dress and gave a small sigh of relief that the dinner had been a success. Pastis, her favourite caterers, had come up trumps again. She had personally selected the menu herself with Dan Donnell, the company's head chef. There was king crab, liquorice pannacotta in the palest of blue, and she had been particularly proud of the canapés – miso-glazed prawns and scallops – soft, delicate little bites. Certainly she hadn't seen anything left on anyone's plate; always a good sign among gourmands like these.

The garden also looked ravishing. Julian liked to refer to the detached four-storey Notting Hill villa as their 'London crash pad' – their main home was now Somerfold, a beautiful three-hundred-acre estate in Oxfordshire – but the garden was still impressive for this part of town, where multi-million-dollar homes usually had to make do with a communal garden square. Tall poplars framed either side, with a sloping lawn to the centre and a kidney-shaped pond full of koi reflecting the fairy lights strung from every bough and bush. In the balmy early summer evening, it was like a Victorian schoolgirl's vision of a fairy grotto – which was exactly the effect Diana had been hoping for. She had been nervous about entertaining after all this time, but the night, so far, was going down a storm.

'Oh, darling,' said Patty, approaching her on the terrace. 'It's gorgeous out here. I don't know why you don't spend more time up in town.'

Diana looked down at her glass. 'Oh, I much prefer the country nowadays. I feel so hemmed in in the city,' she said, not entirely honestly.

Patty gave a gentle smile and touched her arm. 'Of course,' she said. 'I do understand. But we miss you, you know.'

Patty was being kind – and of course, she *did* understand; Patty and Michael knew all about Diana and Julian's 'problems', as they were ever-so-politely referred to. But the truth was, Diana had been relieved to move out to the country three years ago. She had never felt entirely at ease in the sort of circles Julian so loved: the bankers, the industrialists, the gilded elite, exactly the sort of people he had invited this evening. Which was why she had insisted that this, their first appearance on the social scene in six months, should stay small and intimate, if you could call sixty friends and colleagues and a five-course dinner small.

Diana and Patty walked down to a raised seating area over-looking the pond and turned to watch Julian, Mike and a group of the men talking enthusiastically about chartering a chopper and yomping across Nepal.

'Don't they ever get bored of that macho grandstanding?'

sighed Patty. 'Climbing Everest indeed. None of them can find a space in their diaries for a round of golf, let alone an expedition to Shangri-La.'

Diana giggled.

'More to the point, none of their wives would stand for it,' added Patty with a sigh. 'I want flip-flops on my feet on holiday, not crampons.'

She gave Diana a reassuring tweak. 'Are you having a good time, darling? I'm so glad you're, well, out and about again since . . . all the trouble.'

How we love our euphemisms, thought Diana. In the long months since 'all the trouble', she had come to realise how hard people in her world found it to discuss real issues. Stillbirth, miscarriage: it was all too serious, too real for these people. *My child died inside me*, she thought. *Why can't you say it?* But she knew Patty was only trying to be kind. And besides, tonight wasn't the time to be dwelling on the past. Tonight was a time for laughter and happiness, looking to the future, not the past.

'I won't pretend the last year was one of my all-time favourites,' she said, 'but I promise I won't hide away in the country the whole time.'

'I'm glad. Because we miss you,' said Patty gently.

Diana was grateful for her words. Even though Patty was at least fifteen years older than she was, she was one of the few wives on the circuit she felt she could talk to. She was a ferociously bright and successful woman – on the board of a Swiss bank – but she didn't wear it on her sleeve. She and Michael, who headed up an influential hedge fund, were a financial power couple. So much so that they divided their time between a mews in Belgravia, a manor house in the New Forest and an eighteenth-century villa on the shores of Lake Geneva. No one mentioned that Patty was from an ordinary background in the north, because it didn't matter; she was one of them now. Diana wished she could pull the same trick. Not a day had gone by since she married Julian when she hadn't felt judged for where she had come from.

'You should go back into this professionally,' said Patty.

'Back into what?' Diana had let her thoughts wander again. It was getting to be a bad habit recently.

'Event planning, darling,' said Patty. 'Isn't that where you started?'

'Hardly. I was temping at the Denver Group and I got roped into organising the company's summer party.'

The temp that got lucky, she thought to herself. That was what the bitchy wives and girlfriends said about her with ill-disguised jealousy. *The temp that bagged the boss.*

'You should start your own business,' said Patty. 'Seriously. I'd hire you in a heartbeat. We don't entertain quite like we used to, but we could certainly use some of the fairy dust you sprinkle on your parties.'

Diana gave her friend a playful half-smile. 'Did anyone ever tell you that you are very bossy?'

Patty's eyes sparkled. 'Yes, and I don't take no for an answer either. Ask Mike.'

Diana had always envied Patty and Michael their relationship. Uniquely in their circle, it seemed, they appeared to actually like each other's company. They bickered endlessly, of course, always making jokes at each other's expense, but there was an unmistakable feeling of warmth and respect between them. They just seemed happy together.

'Patty, I can't think about starting a business right now,' said Diana. 'I have a child—'

'Charlie is a teenager,' interrupted Patty. 'A teenager who is at boarding school.'

'Okay, but I want to get pregnant again. You know how difficult it has been for us. I don't need any stress.'

'That's what everyone said about my sister when she was going through IVF. Give up work, relax, it's the only way to get pregnant. Instead she gave up IVF, went back to work and, hey presto, she had a daughter at forty-two.'

'So you're saying I should get a life?' said Diana with a wry smile.

Patty inclined her head towards a group of three women gossiping by the French windows.

'No, I'm saying that you don't want to turn into one of *those* women.'

Diana had been thinking the same thing. Dressed in a uniform of high-end labels, their hair and nails primped and polished, their eyes constantly monitoring their husbands and each other, these women were trapped in an endless cycle of one-upmanship. Yes, they had shoes and bags and Italian marble work surfaces in their architect-modelled Kensington homes, but they lived their lives on a privileged hamster wheel and in a state of constant anxiety. She looked at the hard-faced blonde standing next to Greg Willets. Greg was one of Julian's oldest friends, a successful investment banker who treated girlfriends like fast food.

'I see Greg has a new lady-friend,' said Patty, pursing her lips. 'Where do you think he met this one? A massage parlour?'

'Patty!' gasped Diana.

'Come on,' smiled her friend. 'Greg is an ordinary-looking man with an extraordinary-sized bank balance. A woman that blonde and gym-toned wouldn't be with him if he was a bin-man, and do you think Greg is looking for a career woman or an intellectual equal?'

'She could be a high-flying lawyer for all we know.'

'If she is, I'll eat Greg's Ferrari,' snorted Patty.

Diana held her tongue. For one thing, Patty was probably right; Julian's single friends tended to date former models and glamorous PRs, not brain surgeons. And for another, she was in no position to criticise those girls, because the truth was, she was one of them.

She accepted a top-up to her glass of champagne from the waiter. She had been sober all evening, but what the hell. Patty was right: it was time to start enjoying herself.

'I envy you and Michael,' she said suddenly.

'You know what the secret is to making us tick?' Patty said sagely. 'We're both *busy*. We have enough money to stop working tomorrow, but we choose not to because we want to stay interesting.'

She motioned over to Greg Willets's blonde. 'These girls get chosen because they seem to be good wife material: attractive, unchallenging, good enough in bed. They get married, they run the house, they go to the gym, shop. And you know what happens? They get boring. So their husbands, who aren't totally stupid – not even Greg – they get bored, especially when their wives start losing their looks and their perkiness. So they upgrade. I mean, is that all they have to look forward to?'

'I thought you were supposed to be cheering me up,' frowned Diana.

'Oh, I don't mean *you*, darling. You and Julian, it's different.'

Diana glanced over at her husband, who was laughing at something Michael had just said.

'Is it?'

Patty turned to look at her meaningfully. 'Yes, it is. He *adores* you, Diana. Seriously. I know it hasn't all been plain sailing for you, but Julian loves you. And don't take this the wrong way, but you're most certainly not a trophy wife.'

Diana burst out laughing. 'That's supposed to be a compliment, is it?'

'Damn straight it is,' said Patty, holding her gaze. 'And that's what I've been saying all night: you're too bright to do nothing. Get out there, set up an events company, get a job. It'd be good for you. And good for your relationship too.'

Diana nodded, but Patty's words seemed alien to her. She had never been told she was bright. Beautiful, exquisite, yes. But brainy? It was her sister who was the brain-box. The whip-smart, ruthless one who would be good at business. *Too ruthless*, she thought, stamping out an unwelcome memory.

'Promise me you'll think about it,' said Patty.

'I'll think about it.'

'Do. Because Julian has his faults, but he's a good one. Speaking of which, I had better go and rescue my husband from that woman's tits, because if he keeps staring at her cleavage, I fear he's going to fall in.'

It was gone midnight when the party finally broke up. Diana left Julian at the front door, lingering on the step saying good night to the last stragglers, and walked back through the house into the dining room. The caterers had almost finished up, tables dismantled, crockery, linens, glassware and food miraculously cleared away into the van parked on the street.

She stood at the French windows that overlooked the gardens, and took a moment to admire the scene. The fairy lights were

11

still twinkling like a thousand shining Tinker Bells. In fact, *Peter Pan* had been the inspiration for tonight's theme; Diana had happened upon a copy of the book her son Charlie had left behind in his room. He was thirteen now and in his first year at Harrow; children's stories, however classic, were not the sort of thing a self-conscious teenager would want in his dorm. It was an old copy – fifty or sixty years old, ragged and worn – but it had particular resonance for Diana, as she had bought it from a junk shop during her first year in London, when she had arrived with no money, a twelve-month-old child and nothing more than her looks and a determination to better herself.

She turned. Julian was standing in the doorway, the first three buttons of his shirt undone, and it made her heart jump.

He was a handsome man. Not perfect, of course: his dark eyes were perhaps a little too close together, his lips not quite full enough, his nose a little too strong, but beauty was more forgiving in men, wasn't it?

'Hey,' he said, stepping over to her and putting his arms around her. 'Why so sad? I thought it went really well tonight.'

She relaxed into his embrace, leaning her head against his shoulder. She loved his smell, his touch. When she was in his arms, she felt she could do anything.

'Why did you marry me?' she said softly.

'What?' he exclaimed with evident surprise.

'Answer the question,' she said, turning to look into his eyes.

He took a moment to reply. 'I chose you because you are kind and beautiful. And I asked you to marry me because I fell head over heels in love with you.'

'Good answer.' She smiled playfully, feeling completely re-assured by his answer. 'So no climbing mountains, okay? Forget busy – it's *dangerous*.'

'But what about Base Camp?' asked Julian seriously. 'It would be amazing, and we could take Charlie with us.'

'He's almost fourteen,' scoffed Diana. 'Next summer all he's going to want to do is go to Ayia Napa with his friends.'

'You underestimate our child, Di. I think it would do him good to go on an adventure.'

Our child. It had taken her a long time to think of Charlie as theirs, but Julian had never treated him as anything but his from day one. She thought of Patty's words: *Julian has his faults, but he's a good one.* He *was* a good one. Yes, there had certainly been dozens of reasons not to marry Julian Denver. Most of them were tall, leggy and blonde, like half the women she saw around Notting Hill. Diana knew there would always be women who would bat their eyelids and roll their hips, and she knew it would always be tempting for a man like Julian who liked sex, liked women and had the looks and money to attract them. Diana had been brought up to believe that men were unfaithful, and she had gone into their marriage knowing that there was always a risk that someone might get their long claws into her husband – that he might even welcome it. On that score, of course, she had been proven right, but they had got through it, pulled their marriage back to stable ground, because she believed that they loved one another.

'I love you,' she said quietly, voicing her thoughts out loud.

'What's brought this on?' he said, lifting her chin. 'I've been watching you all night, I thought you were having a good time. You sure you're okay?'

'Yes, yes, I'm fine. And you?'

She'd known tonight was going to be hard. Julian had been quiet all week, and she'd wondered if he was anxious about the party, as she had been. But at least people had been discreet about their absence from the social circuit.

He nodded and pulled her closer. As she leant against his warm body, Diana felt a flicker of lust which was sudden and unexpected. The past eighteen months had almost extinguished their sex life, except for the solitary purpose of getting pregnant again. Two miscarriages and the horrible trauma of the stillbirth had not made her feel sexy. It had made her feel like a failure.

And yet tonight she felt a lick of desire, a flicker of promise.

Tonight she wanted to make love to him. Not just because she wanted his child, but because she wanted him.

She tilted her head and kissed him softly on the lips.

'So are you coming to bed?' she murmured.

'You go up. I've got something to do first.'

She tried not to let her disappointment show. In her mind's

eye, she had seen him unzipping her dress right here in the doorway, peeling off her lingerie as he backed her into the dining room, finally pushing her back on the table, sweeping aside the imported silver . . .

'Sure. But don't be long, okay?' she said.

As he walked into his study, he stopped, turned back.

'I love you too,' he said with feeling. 'No matter what.'

The bedroom was warm after the garden, the deep white carpet soft between her toes as she kicked off her shoes and unpinned her hair. Catching a glimpse of herself in the dressing-table mirror, even she could admit how lovely she looked: petite and slim, with long dark hair that fell between her shoulder blades. She unclipped her brand-new Sabbia Rosa half-cup bra, which under any other circumstances would be just too lovely to take off.

For the first time in . . . well, a long time, Diana could feel the heat of desire spreading through her until even her fingertips were tingling. Peeling off her thong, she slipped into bed, turning off the bedside lamp, loving the feel of the crisp sheets on her skin, sliding her long legs back and forth. She felt so aroused, one hand slipped up to her breast, feeling the nipple rise to the touch.

Come on, Jules, she thought, imagining his strong arms around her, his lips on hers. *Put down that bloody phone, come upstairs.* She stretched her arms above her head, feeling warm and more relaxed than she had in ages. The last thing she thought was: *maybe I shouldn't have had that champagne.*

When she woke, the bed next to her was empty. *Julian?* she thought sleepily, reaching out to touch his side. She opened her eyes, and wondered where he was. Perhaps he had gone to the bathroom to get a glass of water – he often got dehydrated after he'd been drinking – but no: the sheets on his side felt cold and unslept-in.

Diana closed her eyes, but she was unable to fall back to sleep. Inhaling sharply, she rolled on to her side and squinted at the small digital clock by the bed – part of some expensive but never-used Bose system Julian had installed last Christmas. *04:37*.

Lifting her head towards the en suite, she saw there was no

14

crack of light in the doorway, no sign of anyone in the room. Nor were his clothes over the chair where he usually put them after undressing for bed.

Where is he? she thought crossly. Surely he wasn't still working?

Feeling groggy, she propped herself up on the pillow, her mind running through the possibilities. He could quite easily be on a call. But there were other possibilities, darker thoughts that were also easy to believe. Diana swung her legs out of the bed and reached for her robe. She had gone to sleep thinking how much she loved her husband, but she still had to be realistic. She was the wife of a billionaire, a man who had barely touched his wife sexually in the past six months. Julian was a catch to end all catches; why wouldn't she suspect he was up to his old tricks? She walked out on to the landing and cocked her head, listening. Nothing.

Stop it, Diana, she said to herself. Where did she expect him to be? On a Skype call to a secret mistress? In the garden on a booty call with a hooker? They had put all that behind them; they'd had to. How was a marriage to survive if there was no trust? She almost laughed. Eighteen months of marriage counselling after Julian's 'indiscretion' and where had it got her? Standing by her bedroom door, imagining him having some late-night tryst under her nose?

She padded down the stairs, all her senses alert.

Compared to Somerfold, their west London home was almost small, but at night it seemed cavernous. She was too practical a woman to believe in ghosts, but there was still something unsettling about walking through an empty house lit only by the dim light from the early grey dawn leaking through the windows. She stopped on the bottom step and held her breath, hoping that she would detect some sound or movement to indicate where her husband might be.

'Where the bloody hell are you?' she whispered, her disquiet turning to irritation. She turned on a downstairs light and walked through the dining room and across to Julian's study, half expecting to find him jabbering into his phone, scrolling through columns of financial hieroglyphics on his computer screen. It

15

wouldn't be the first time: it was late morning in the Far East, early afternoon in Australia, and Julian seemed to have business interests in every corner of the globe. But not tonight. The room was dark, with only a half-empty whisky glass sitting on his desk to show he had been there.

Something about that glass made prickles pop out on Diana's arms.

'Julian?' she called, moving through the house, switching on lights, opening doors. She was actively worried now. Had he gone out? But why would he, at this time of night? And anyway – how? He had certainly drunk far too much at the party to drive.

The car, of course. She had to check on the car. She went to the back door and slipped on the first footwear she came to – Julian's scuffed-up old walking boots, which felt cold and over-large on her bare feet. She fumbled the keys into the lock and stepped out into the garden, the fairy wonderland of the party now cloaked in dark shadows and strange shapes. It was cold, and a light frosting of dew had settled on the lawn. *Keep going*, she told herself, clumping along the path that led towards the large brick garage at the back of the grounds. *If his car's gone, then you'll know.* But know what, exactly?

The door to the garage was closed but unlocked. 'Julian?' she called as she poked her head inside. She could make out the outline of the two cars that they stored here – her own silver Range Rover runabout and Julian's dark blue Mercedes, which at least meant he hadn't driven anywhere.

Now she was puzzled. Shaking her head, she resolved to call him on his mobile and then go back to bed. She closed the garage door and turned back to face the house. It was then that she noticed a crack of light from one of the lower-ground-floor rooms.

It was a part of the house she rarely went to. There was a utility room down there, an overspill dressing room, and a small, sparse library – they had moved most of their book collection to Somerfold – where Julian kept his drum kit and collection of vinyl. She hurried inside and took the stairs to the basement. Like the rest of the house it was still and silent, but down here, it made her feel especially anxious.

16

She pushed open the library door and stepped inside. The room was in semi-darkness, bathed in low silvery dawn light from a gap in the curtains. As she turned to look for the lamp switch, she gasped in disbelief at the sight in front of her. Julian was kneeling slumped on the floor, a noose attached to a bookshelf tied around his neck.

She didn't even hear herself scream.

2

'So how did that feel?'

Rachel Miller squeezed the water from her dark hair and looked sideways at the handsome Canadian standing beside her on the boat.

'Incredible,' he grinned, unstrapping his air tank and putting it down on the deck with a clank.

'You know this is the second best dive site in the world after Cairns,' said Rachel.

The man raised his eyebrows. 'Yeah, I think you told me that when I made my booking.'

'I just like to remind people,' she teased, giving him her most flirtatious smile.

'I think I'll go downstairs to change.'

'I hope you haven't peed in your wetsuit,' she shouted after him.

He looked back at her quizzically, and as the split-second chemistry between them evaporated instantly, she cursed her lack of grace.

Just as well, she smiled to herself, before taking a slug of water from the bottle beside her. It was unprofessional, *verboten* even, for instructors to fraternise with the clients, although playful banter with good-looking men in wetsuits was definitely one of the perks of the job. She wiped her damp, salty brow with the back of her hand and sat down with a contented sigh. Today's diving group had been her favourite kind: young and up for fun, plus they were all PADI-certified divers, so she had been able to take them out to the more interesting dive sites that surrounded the Thai island of Ko Tao. Out by Shark Island they had seen

18

batfish, barracuda, spotted rays plus shoals of angel fish and all sorts of coloured coral and sponge. There were certainly worse ways to earn a living.

'Hey, Liam.'

Rachel looked up at the sing-song voice and the accompanying giggles: three of her clients, pretty gap-year students who had switched from damp wetsuits to skimpy bikinis and were loitering on deck watching her business partner Liam hard at work sorting out the swim fins into the right buckets. She could hardly blame them; Liam was tall, blond and muscular from leading daily dives on the reef. Still, it didn't do to encourage that sort of thing.

'Everything all right, girls?' said Rachel, walking over as Liam disappeared below deck.

'I can't believe you get to work with him every day,' whispered the most attractive of the trio.

'That's my husband you're talking about,' said Rachel evenly.

'Seriously?' gasped the girl. 'Oh God, I didn't know, I'm sorry.'

'Just kidding,' laughed Rachel. 'However, he is my business partner, which means that for an extra fifty bucks I can make him strip down to some really tiny Speedos. What do you think?'

Just then Liam reappeared, triggering gales of laughter from the girls.

'What's so funny?' he asked.

'Nothing,' chuckled Rachel. 'Nothing at all.'

The boat chugged back to Sairee Beach, Ko Tao's main landing point and the base for the diving school. As the island came into view, Rachel couldn't help but smile. Even though she had lived there for almost three years, she was still captivated by its sun-washed beauty. Ko Tao lacked the dramatic karst scenery of Thailand's Andaman Sea islands, but it was still Paradise, boasting long stretches of white sand, lush forest and crystal-clear waters.

Sairee Beach wasn't even the prettiest side of the island. On days off, Rachel would jump on her battered moped and head into the Robinson Crusoe territory of the island's quieter east coast, where palm trees stooped over the sugar-white sand and the air smelt as if you had fallen into a bottle of frangipani-scented cologne. 'Not a bad place to have your office,' she whispered to herself.

Slowly the smile drifted from her face. She might be in Paradise now, but there was a time when she'd thought she was in hell. In another life, and a million miles from this spot, Rachel had been a journalist, associate editor on London's *Sunday Post* and not yet even thirty. She was flying: at the top of her game and feted in all the capital's smartest watering holes. And then the sky had fallen in. The phone-hacking scandal had swept through Fleet Street like fire through dry wood; Rachel had barely had time to draw breath before she was shown the door. First she had been put on leave, and then summarily dismissed. Just as she had thought it couldn't get any worse, she had been arrested and her flat searched.

Thanks to a good lawyer, she had escaped prison, but overnight she had become a pariah, a newspaper Icarus who had flown too near the sun then crashed and burned.

So she had come to Thailand. No, *fled* to Thailand was closer to the truth. At first she convinced herself that it was just a much-needed holiday, a time to lie low and regroup. She had always loved the sea and was drawn to Ko Tao by the diving. But then she met Liam, a fellow fanatic who wanted to set up a dive school. And slowly, very slowly, she had felt her life pick up.

She was snapped out of her thoughts as the boat bumped against the pier and Liam nimbly jumped out and began to tie it off.

'Tell all your friends,' said Rachel as she helped the divers down to the weathered planks. 'Though July is our busiest time and I'm making no promises I can accommodate them even if they say they're friends of yours.'

'Bye, Liam,' cooed the girls, waggling their fingers and their behinds as they walked off into the village.

'We're not that busy, are we?' said Liam out of the corner of his mouth.

'I like to keep an illusion of being in demand. Just like you, in fact.'

'What do you mean?'

'What do I mean?' laughed Rachel. 'You didn't notice those girls coming on to you all day?'

'No, I was too busy watching you flirting with the beefy Canadian.'

'I don't flirt with the customers,' said Rachel with mock-offence.

'Rach, you *always* flirt with the customers.'

She put a hand on her hip.

'If I did – and I'm not saying I do – you have to admit it's good for business. We're almost booked up until the end of the season.'

'So you're flirting for my benefit?' he replied drily.

'You know sometimes I think you should have stayed a lawyer.'

She liked to tease him about his life back in England, as it seemed so removed from the laid-back beach bum he so resembled now. The short scruff of stubble, the sun-bleached dirty blond hair and the dark tan that brought out the bright blue of his eyes all said 'surf dude', and yet in Liam's former life he had worked for a Top Five commercial legal practice – a rising star who had given it all up on the verge of being made a partner. She had never probed too hard about what had made him swap the brogues for the Havaianas, but she had often wondered if there was any more to it. A breakdown, or a relationship gone bad, perhaps? But then maybe he had just hated it. It was so easy for the offspring of successful white-collar parents to become funnelled into 'respectable' professions, only finding out too late that the rat race wasn't for them.

'And why should I have stayed a lawyer?' he said, his voice calm and level. He was an expert at winding her up by never getting wound up himself about anything.

'Because confrontation is your middle name.'

'Says she.'

'Call a truce, Rumpole, and buy me a drink. We need to talk.'

'Sounds ominous,' said Liam, pulling on his shirt. 'Better make it a double.'

They went to one of the bars at the quieter end of the beach and Rachel took a wicker table outside with a view of the sea. The evening throng had not yet come out to play, but she still knew plenty of people in the bar and she didn't want to be overheard.

Liam returned with a bottle of Kingfisher and a Fanta. Rachel took long, eager sips, grateful for the clinking ice. It was past five o'clock and the sun was beginning to sink, but it still had to be thirty-five degrees at least.

'So how many bookings have we got tomorrow?' she asked.

'Party of eight on the learn-to-dive package. Honeymooners and some of their friends, I think.'

'Well, *that's* another marriage that's doomed before it starts,' said Rachel dismissively. 'Taking your friends on honeymoon. Who does that?'

Liam looked at her as if he were observing a small, disobedient child.

'They got married on the island. If a bunch of mates have come all the way to see you get married in Thailand, you're not exactly going to shove them on a plane as soon as you've said "I do". Or isn't that the way you work, Little Miss Sunshine?'

Rachel shrugged and finished her drink.

'I just wonder why some people are daft enough to spend fifty grand shipping all their friends and relations out to Thailand when they could buy a sports car or a loft conversion or something.'

'You're such a romantic,' he grinned.

Her eyes challenged him across the candlelight coming from the small hurricane lamp on the table.

'Just because I happen to think that weddings are a mug's game? Marriage is an antiquated institution and if you believe otherwise you are a romantic *fool*.'

'But of course you'll be happy to take their business. Talking of which . . . you wanted to discuss something.'

Rachel took a breath. 'You know that we're rushed off our feet and it's not even July? Well, I've been thinking.' She paused, not sure how he would react. 'I've been thinking that we should expand.'

Liam lifted his beer and took a thoughtful swig.

'Well? Say something,' she said nervously.

'I've been thinking the same thing.'

'Really? Great!' She leaned forward. 'Listen, I heard last night that the Sunset Bungalows are up for sale. Now you know as well as I do that they're in one of the best spots on the whole island, it's like a stone's throw from the main drag, and if we can do them up . . .' She was dimly aware that she was babbling, and as she spoke, she caught a glimpse of herself in the mirror behind the bar and almost laughed out loud. The last thing she looked like was a businesswoman. Her dark hair was cut into a choppy bob, her thin vest showed off a tattoo of a dolphin and, frankly, her wide-eyed enthusiasm made her look more like a madwoman than Karren Brady. Even so, Liam looked intrigued.

'Jim's selling up?' he said, rubbing his chin.

'Moving back to New Zealand.'

'How do you *know* all this stuff? I only spoke to him yesterday and he didn't mention anything to me.'

Rachel grinned. 'I keep my ear to the ground.'

'Old habits die hard, huh?'

'We should buy them,' she said determinedly.

'The bungalows?' said Liam, frowning. 'I admit they're in a good position, but we run a dive school, Rach. What do we want with a load of bungalows?'

She put her glass down. 'They'd be *part* of the dive school, Liam. That's the beauty of it. We could position ourselves as the premier dive resort on the island, selling dive packages along with accommodation. Just think how amazing it could be: we'd provide cool little boho-chic crash pads, along with food, diving tuition and a PADI certificate thrown in. We'd clean up in this part of the gulf. I think we should set up a free-diving operation too.'

'Now there's a big surprise,' he teased.

Rachel supposed she deserved that one: free-diving was her latest obsession. And it *was* an obsession, it had to be; free-diving wasn't for the faint-hearted. Diving without oxygen tanks to see how deep you could get, your lungs burning, the pressure hurting your ears, pulling at your limbs. It was dangerous and a little bit crazy, but to Rachel it was like an addiction. She had been taking instruction for the past year – diving in the deepest part of the gulf every time she could – from a mad Frenchman called Serge, and had almost got her teacher's certificate.

'I thought you came to Thailand for a simpler life,' said Liam.

'I did, and I found it, but this seems like too much of a good opportunity. Come on, Liam, don't say you're not tempted.'

'Tempted in a masochistic sort of way.'

'Just think about it . . .'

He paused for a moment, as if he was weighing up what she had said.

'Even if we were prepared to take it on – and I'm not saying we should – how could we afford it? A plot that size, with twenty bungalows and beach access, it's got to be fifty million baht minimum.'

Rachel pulled a face. It was the one stumbling block to her plan.

'I was kind of hoping you might have some savings,' she said hopefully. 'Come on, you were a hotshot lawyer.'

'Not *that* hotshot. And I'm enough of a lawyer to know there are restrictions on foreigners owning property in Thailand, and they're pretty strict about the legislation.'

'Well Jim managed it, and he's a Kiwi. Come on, I'm sure your huge legal brain can find a loophole.'

He was laughing gently, shaking his head.

'What's so funny?' she asked, inordinately cross.

'Oh, just that you come all this way to escape from something, but the truth is, we all bring it with us. You can't get away from it, can't get away from what we are.'

'And what am I exactly?' she replied quietly, unsure that she wanted to hear his reply.

'You're ambitious, Rach.' He held up a hand before she could interrupt. 'And there's nothing wrong with that. I just thought you wanted to take your foot off the gas.'

'I'm not like you,' she said softly. 'I didn't choose to give it all up.'

She stared out at the dramatic sunset, which was pouring ribbons of peach and purple light across the water.

'Well, at the very least we should take on another member of staff.'

'I'll drink to that,' he said, holding up his beer bottle and clinking it against her glass. 'We've certainly got more work than the two of us can handle at the moment. Do you have anyone in mind?'

Rachel nodded absently, distracted by her phone buzzing in her pocket. She gestured towards the bar and held up her empty glass to Liam as she lifted the phone to her ear.

'Hello,' she said, but there was only a crackle at the other end. 'Anyone there?'

There was a pause, and then a voice. A voice she hadn't heard in years. It made her heart pound and her lips dry.

'Mum?' she said, trying to sound more casual than she felt. 'How are you?'

Another pause.

'Can you talk.'

Not a question, Rachel noticed. A demand, impatient and impersonal. Sylvia Miller was thousands of miles away, but she still had the power to make her daughter feel ten years old.

'Of course,' she said, looking at Liam before standing up and walking out of the bar and down on to the beach.

'What's up?' she said, knowing how lame it sounded. She just didn't know what to say. It had been such a long time since she had spoken to her mother.

'Julian's dead.'

Just like that. No preamble, no build-up: *boom*. Just like her mother. Unconsciously, Rachel drew her hand to her chest as if she was trying to hold herself together.

She couldn't process it. He was dead? How?

'What happened?'

'He . . . he took his life yesterday.'

By now Rachel's head was spinning. This was absurd.

'He killed himself? Julian?' She was shaking her head. 'Why?'

'Why would anyone take their own life?' said her mother bluntly.

'No, I mean what happened? Was he depressed? Was he having problems? What?'

'No. He was happy. *They* were happy, no thanks to you.' Her mother's voice was quiet, the undercurrent of bitterness unmistakable. The jibe wounded her – as intended.

Rachel exhaled deeply. 'How's Diana?'

She realised what a stupid, futile question it was even before the words had left her mouth.

'She'll be fine,' said her mother. Rachel could imagine her disapproving expression, her meaning clear: *she'll be fine without you*.

'How can she be fine?' she pleaded.

'Do you really care?' Sylvia Miller's tone was emotionless.

'Of course I care.' Her voice was disappearing into a croak.

She stared out at the sea, which was darkening to navy in the dusk light, and forced herself to stay strong.

'How did he die?' she asked quietly. 'Who found him?' For a moment, she was a young journalist, back on the beat, asking difficult questions, doorstepping, intruding into people's grief, asking the questions that had to be asked to get the story.

'Diana found him in the basement of the London house. He'd hanged himself.'

Rachel shut her eyes, imagining her sister making the discovery, but it was too grim to form a proper picture. 'When's the funeral?' she asked in a more even voice.

'We don't know yet. Julian's parents are organising it. I expect there will be procedure to follow. Lots of people to get there.'

'So is Diana with you?' she asked, trying another tack.

'I'm staying with her at Somerfold. Charlie has come home from school, of course. The family are rallying round. We are all being there for one another.'

Rachel gripped the phone harder.

'I want to come home,' she said suddenly. 'I want to be there for her too. Like I always was . . . before.'

Her words were stuck in her throat. She held her breath, waiting for her mother to speak, willing her to invite her back into the fold, to share their grief, to help in whatever small way she could. The silence told her that wasn't going to happen.

'I've got to go,' said her mother in a brutally cold and efficient manner. 'I just phoned to let you know. I thought you should know.'

'Mum, don't—'

But Sylvia had already hung up.

Rachel stared down at the phone. Her feet seemed to be welded to the sand but her mind was whirling with questions. It didn't make sense. It was the same feeling of stunned disbelief that she had felt as a teenager when Princess Diana had died. Some people seemed immortal. Some people simply didn't, couldn't die. Julian was one of them.

Julian Denver. Sometimes it was hard to even remember his face. But she could vividly remember what he was like. Brooding, seductive, a little bit frightening.

She shivered, recalling those final words.

If we ever see or hear from you again . . .

Her family still hated her, that much was clear from the brief conversation she had just had with her mother. And Julian's death would do nothing to help repair that.

She sank down on the sand, feeling the cold graininess through her shorts, and rested her head softly on her knees. The evening air was a heady cocktail of sea salt, hibiscus, and green curry wafting from the nearby restaurants. But she was oblivious to it all.

A few moments later she heard scuffed footsteps on the path behind her.

'You okay?' asked a familiar voice.

Rachel stumbled to her feet. She glanced at Liam, then shook her head. 'I have to go,' she said, trying to push past.

'Hey,' he said gently, his large hand on her shoulder. 'What's wrong?'

'That was my mother,' she said finally. 'Julian, my brother-in-law? He committed suicide yesterday.'

She tried to say it as matter-of-factly as she could, but it came out wrong: breezy, light-hearted, as if she didn't care. *Which is probably what everyone thinks.*

'Oh Rach, I'm sorry,' said Liam, giving her arm an awkward squeeze.

'I'm fine. Really. Just leave me.'

A few spots of rain started to fall. Thunderstorms came quickly here, but Liam didn't move, and reluctantly she met his gaze. She saw the concern in her friend's eyes and it made her breath stutter.

'Come on, Rachel, you know you can talk to me.'

It was true: Liam was the one person in Thailand who knew everything. He knew about why she had come here, knew why she didn't want to go back. And he knew that Diana and Julian were not the whole reason she had come to Thailand, but they were the reason it had been so easy to do so.

The rain spots were getting bigger, harder now. The sky was dark but she could make out black storm clouds overhead. Her T-shirt began to stick to her body as Liam pulled her under one of the palm trees that fringed the beach.

'Listen to me,' he said. 'You should go home.'

'Liam, they hate me. I'm the last person they're going to want to see at the funeral.'

'Maybe, but maybe now is the time to say sorry.'

Rachel shook her head. 'He's dead, Liam. It's a little bit late for that.'

'It's never too late to pay your respects.'

'Well they're going to think it's a bit rich coming from me.'

There was a long pause.

'Do you want me to come with you?'

She looked up into his blue eyes. For a moment they connected absolutely with hers, and the unspoken frisson that had existed between them from the night that they had met, a frisson that mostly lay dormant, showed itself once more.

She shivered, and told herself it was the cool wind that had blown in suddenly off the sea.

'You'd do that?'

'I think it's important you go, but I know it won't be easy for you. If it were me, I'd want a bit of moral support.'

'But we'd have to close the school, and we're so busy. We can't do it,' she said.

'Look, if there was ever a time to close the school and go back home, it's now.'

'Why? Out of guilt?' replied Rachel too harshly. 'My sister doesn't want me there, my mother doesn't want me there, and Julian would not have wanted me there either. The greatest respect I can pay him is not to go. If I do, people will immediately start talking about me and the reason I left. A funeral's supposed to be a time to remember the good things about people, isn't it, not to rake over old scandals.'

'Rachel, do you want to rebuild your relationship with your sister?' asked Liam simply.

She tensed, immediately defensive. Liam knew her too well. He knew what she wanted, more than anything. But she was also convinced of her reasons to stay away from England.

'You have to go back,' he pressed.

'The rain is getting heavy,' she said, looking away from him. 'I should really be going home.'

3

The Peacock Suite had a beautiful view of the lake; that was the reason Diana loved it. That, and the fact that it was the quietest room at Somerfold and in the most distant wing of their Oxfordshire home. It was here she liked to sit, her chair pulled up in front of the enormous windows, alone with her thoughts, gazing at the water. But today the curtains were closed, with just enough light from two small lamps to make out what she was doing. No one could see into the room, but even so, Diana felt better doing this unobserved.

Taking a deep breath, she tipped the contents of two Selfridges bags on to the bed. It was quite a collection: papers, notebooks, letters, receipts, photographs. She had spent the morning gathering it together from desk drawers, filing cabinets, even jacket pockets around the house, but slowly, unobtrusively. She didn't want to raise any more eyebrows. After the police had finished with their endless questions, her mother had driven her straight to Somerfold as Diana wasn't sure she ever wanted to see the house in Notting Hill again. Predictably, both her mother and Mrs Bills, the housekeeper, had been fussing around her, watching her every move. In fact, when Mrs Bills had found her poking around the library that morning, she had dispatched her to bed with herbal tea, as if she were recuperating from a mild case of flu. She meant well, of course, they all did. Presumably they must be secretly wondering about her state of mind, perhaps even imagining that she might try to 'do something stupid', as Sylvia Miller so subtly put it. But Diana had no intention of doing anything like that; in fact her mind was unusually clear and focused. That was why she was standing here in the dark, looking at this pile of letters. She *had* to know; that was what was keeping her going. Julian was dead – it was hard enough to grasp that idea – but he hadn't been hit by a car or killed in an air crash, some senseless random event. He had taken his own life. There had to be a reason. *Had* to be. So it followed that somewhere there would be something that gave a clue as to why.

She picked up a photograph and looked at it. It was an old Polaroid, the white border yellowed and the colours slightly smeared, but it was clear enough: a group of students on a yacht. Julian was instantly recognisable in the middle of the group, with his foppish hair, shy grin and Operation Raleigh T-shirt, and Diana had to look away, her heart jumping. *Jules, how could you? How could you do it?*

Feeling overcome, she sat down on the blue silk coverlet. *It's just the lack of sleep*, she told herself. Julian had been gone for almost forty-eight hours, and in that time she had not slept for a second. It hadn't been out of choice – she was desperate to escape from this living hell, to close her eyes and shut it all out – but sleep just wouldn't come. Lying in the dark, the empty space beside her, she couldn't let her mind rest, her eyelids wide open, like some medieval torture designed to send her mad. And in those horrible, endless hours, she had gone over everything, examining every event, every word, every look between her and Julian through the past few months, searching for evidence of cracks, strains in their marriage. Things she might have said or done that could have driven him to some secret, hidden despair; things she could have said or done that might have made a difference; things that might have kept him alive. *What if, what if, what if* . . . The possibilities were endless and the nagging questions utterly futile. The guilt pressed down upon her, the frustration of simply not knowing making her head spin. Her body was weak with exhaustion, her mind stretched taut from chasing in circles. She had heard that people had died from lack of sleep, and lying there staring at the crack in the curtains, she hoped it would happen to her.

She turned back to the pile and ran her hands over the papers and photographs, half hoping to draw some sort of insight through touch alone. Shaking her head, she realised that she had met a dead end with this collection of stuff. She walked to the window, wanting to feel some light on her face, and pulled the curtain back just enough to see her son Charlie kicking a football across the grass near the lake. For a moment she almost didn't recognise him – since Christmas he had grown inches and was now a long, loping figure with a shock of tawny hair. How he reminded her of Julian. They weren't related by blood, of course, but they did say you could grow to resemble the people you were closest to, didn't they?

'Darling? What's all this?'

Diana turned, startled by her mother's voice. Sylvia Miller was a handsome woman in her late fifties, her ash-blond hair cut into a long bob, her body lithe and toned from the Dukan Diet and too much yoga. You would never guess that this woman had once been a working-class divorcee living in a terraced house in Devon. Sylvia looked born to the grandeur of Somerfold – more so, Diana had to admit, than herself.

'What are you doing with all these papers?'

'Nothing,' said Diana, quickly crossing to the bed and gathering them together. Her mother stooped and picked up a letter that had fallen on to the floor. Diana was relieved to see that it was a bill; nothing personal, nothing useful. But she could also see that Sylvia had immediately grasped what her daughter was doing.

'I really think you should leave this alone,' she said, handing the bill to Diana.

'I'm just spring-cleaning.'

Her mother raised a sceptical eyebrow. 'I think you should come downstairs and eat. Mrs Bills has made some chicken soup and a batch of madeleines that look ravishing.'

'I'm fine up here, honestly.'

'Best if you come. Liz just called. They're ten minutes away.'

Diana nodded. It was another reason why she had spent the morning sifting through drawers and cupboards; something to take her mind off the fact that the preliminary inquest into Julian's death was being held at noon. She had had no desire to be there, and Liz, Julian's older sister, had assured her that there was no need for her to be and had gone in her place. Diana knew she could not have faced it, but it was just one more item to add to the long checklist of things to feel guilty about.

'How did it go?'

'Liz said it all went as expected,' said Sylvia soothingly. 'It was just a formality today.'

Sensing her daughter's disquiet, she walked across and ran her hand up and down Diana's arm.

'Come on now, you've got enough on your mind without worrying about things like that.'

'I know. You're right.'

She sat down on the bed again and looked around the suite.

'You know, Julian used to call this the row room,' she said softly. 'I used to come and sleep in here sometimes when we'd argued. It was always over little things. A bit like you and Dad.'

Julian and her father: the two most important men in her life. Now both dead.

'Every couple on earth argues, Diana,' said Sylvia. 'It's silly dwelling on things like that.'

The trouble was, Diana couldn't do anything else, turning over every row and disagreement: had that been what had made him so unhappy? Had he really been so dissatisfied? She thought of how she and Julian had moved here four years ago, after the scandal. Diana had always associated moving house with moving on. They had decamped from Sheffield to Devon after her parents' divorce; from Devon to London after her unexpected pregnancy. It was her own version of wiping the slate clean, except with removal vans and storage boxes. They had bought Somerfold hoping to make a fresh start, hoping to rebuild the trust in their marriage. Hoping to start a family. And actually, the row room hadn't been used very much; they'd both made an effort to get along better, and eventually, day by day, their so-called 'perfect marriage' had clicked back on track. *Or had it?*

'I wish we could have a row right now,' she whispered, feeling the tears well up. 'I'd give anything to hear his voice. But it's just one of those things that's never going to happen again. I'll never see his face, hear his laugh, feel him next to me in bed . . .'

Her words started to falter. All the emotions that she'd been holding in were finally spilling over the dam.

'Why?' she said, her voice swallowed up into a sob.

Sylvia sat down next to her and held her tight as Diana's tears soaked into the soft crêpe of her mother's top. Somewhere inside, Diana felt some small relief that she was finally crying. She knew from the death of her father ten years earlier that grief was unique and it never happened the way you thought it should. Back then, she had been unable to stop crying for days, whilst her sister Rachel, who so often wore her heart on her sleeve, had been like stone.

There was a quiet knock at the door. 'Mr Denver and Elizabeth have arrived,' called Mrs Bills from outside.

Diana grabbed a handful of tissues from the bedside table, blew her nose and wiped the tears away from her face. She glanced at her reflection – not good. Her skin was so pale, no one could miss her reddened eyes. *Well, they'll just have to lump it,* she thought wearily, standing and allowing her mother to lead her from the room.

Ralph and Elizabeth Denver were standing in Somerfold's wide entrance hall as she descended the staircase. Ralph moved towards her, his limp more prominent than she remembered, the lines on his face deep. Once such a vital man, Julian's father had been one of the UK's richest and most dynamic businessmen, until he had been partially paralysed by a stroke two years ago, forcing him to scale back his duties at the Denver Group and allow Julian to take over as CEO. Diana had not seen him for months. Under pressure from his wife Barbara, they now lived between their estate in Barbados and a villa in Provence. 'You deserve a rest, Ralph,' Barbara would say. 'Julian can handle everything.' Diana wondered if she remembered those words now.

'How are you, my dear?' asked Ralph, looking into Diana's eyes. It was easy to forget, wrapped up in her own grief and confusion as she was, that Ralph was Julian's father and had to be suffering deeply. And yet he had managed to attend the inquest . . .

'Bearing up,' she replied. She forced a smile across at Elizabeth, who nodded in acknowledgement.

'That's good to hear.' Ralph squeezed her arm affectionately. Diana had always liked Julian's father. He was powerful and, by

34

reputation, ruthless in business – Diana supposed you didn't get to build up and run the Denver Group without some steel in your soul – but he had always been polite and welcoming to her, which she could not say for everyone. Elizabeth, for one. Julian's sister had always given the impression that she regarded Diana as an interloper and a gold-digger only interested in the family's money.

'It's a difficult time for everyone,' said Elizabeth, her expression still. The Denvers were not exactly old aristocratic money, but in three generations they had transformed themselves from successful soap-makers to a global conglomerate, and Elizabeth was every inch the rich heiress. Tall, elegant, clever, she was just as likely to be found giving her views to the *Economist* magazine as she was to be seen on the party pages of *Tatler*. She had grown up within the corridors of power and expected things to go her way; and they usually did. She was also very much an eldest child. She was a year older than Julian, and had almost a decade on Adam, the youngest Denver child, which Diana thought had always given her a quiet, controlling dominance in the family. Even Julian had been reluctant to take her on when she had a bee in her bonnet.

'Shall we go through?' said Sylvia, taking charge, leading them into the drawing room and calling for Mrs Bills to bring through the coffee and madeleines.

'So how was it?' prompted Diana anxiously. 'The inquest, I mean?'

'Busy,' said Elizabeth.

'Busy?' She looked at her sister-in-law and wondered how she could be so cool and in control.

'An awful lot of media interest, unfortunately,' said Elizabeth, folding her arms across her body. 'I'm going to have to get the communications team to work a little harder to contain it. It's very . . . unhelpful.'

Diana saw Ralph flash a look at his daughter, and Elizabeth shrugged.

'Well it's *not* helpful. Not good for the family, for the company. At least the police say the death is not suspicious. Which is the main thing.'

'Not suspicious?' said Diana with surprise. 'What's not suspicious about the death of a man who was talking about climbing Everest just a few hours before he killed himself? Don't they think that's worth considering?'

'Diana, please, don't do this to yourself,' said Ralph gently. 'I know it's hard to understand, we're all struggling with it, but it won't do you any good to keep torturing yourself.'

'But I can't stop thinking about it,' she said, sitting forward. 'I just can't understand it. Life was good. Julian was happy. And the business? Business is good, isn't it?'

She looked directly at Elizabeth, who was on the senior management team of the Denver Group.

'Yes, it is. But no one knows what's going on in someone's head. Who can say what was upsetting Jules? There were the pregnancies, for example.'

Diana noted how careful Elizabeth was to avoid the words 'miscarriages' and 'stillbirth'. No one wanted to be reminded of more death.

Even so, she knew her sister-in-law had a point. Two miscarriages in eighteen months had been hard enough, but then to follow that with the horror of the stillbirth . . . their shared joy of carrying Arthur to twenty-four weeks only to discover that his heart had stopped beating. Diana had been forced to give birth to him and then bury his tiny body, and it had almost destroyed her. A life snatched away before it had lived. And yet through it all, Julian had been her rock, holding her hand, smoothing her hair, telling her it would be all right. He had seemed strong, so strong. Had that all been an act? Had it hurt him as much as it had hurt her? Would she ever know?

'Was there anything else?' asked Sylvia, looking at Ralph. 'Did the coroner say anything?'

'Apparently the post-mortem examination showed no signs of a third-party involvement,' said the old man carefully.

'Third-party involvement?'

Anxiety fluttered in Diana's belly. The police had spent at least an hour interviewing her in Notting Hill. She thought it had been to get the fullest possible picture of the night that Julian had died, but had it actually been done with a different agenda?

36

Ralph held up a steadying hand. 'He said that further enquiries should take six to eight weeks, after which they'll hold the full inquest. Should be around mid-July.'

Mrs Bills came in with a tray, which she put down on the antique console table.

'So what happens now?' asked Diana, trying to calm herself.

'The coroner's office will collect information, make a date for the hearing. Some of us will have to go to court, unless the coroner thinks that's not necessary, although I have spoken to my lawyer and it's likely that you will have to give evidence,' added Ralph, glancing at Diana.

She looked away, feeling sick. The idea of it, of standing up as a witness to recount the events of that night . . . It was bad enough going over and over it in her own head, but to share it in public, to answer questions about their relationship in front of strangers?

'I can't,' she said quietly.

Ralph looked solemn. 'I have to say I agree with you. I don't know what public inquests achieve other than more heartbreak.'

'The point is to get to the bottom of what's happened,' said Elizabeth brusquely. 'Isn't that more important than some bruised feelings?'

'Elizabeth, please. We know what's happened,' snapped Ralph, his cheeks reddening slightly.

Diana frowned. 'You know? What do you mean?' she asked, catching a look of complicity between father and daughter.

'Julian's depression,' said Elizabeth flatly.

Diana could feel the slow rise of panic. 'Julian wasn't depressed,' she replied.

Ralph met her gaze. He looked crestfallen, deflated. 'Perhaps it wasn't obvious at the time, but yes, Julian had depression,' he said.

'I think I know my husband.'

Ralph looked across at Sylvia. 'Could you give me a moment alone with your daughter? Elizabeth, you too.'

Elizabeth looked reluctant, but finally she and Sylvia left the room. Ralph pushed himself up on his walking stick and came over to sit next to Diana.

37

'Julian suffered from depression,' he said softly. 'Before you.'

Diana didn't know how to react. It was as if Ralph was talking about someone she didn't know. She had always felt like an outsider in this family, and even now, even after Julian's death, she was discovering that she had been locked out of their secrets, this bond they shared. But as she looked into the old man's pale grey eyes – Julian's eyes, she realised – a little cloudy from tears, she knew that there was no unkindness in his words.

'There was a period during his time at Oxford when Julian found it difficult to cope,' said Ralph. 'Our doctor put him on antidepressants – only for a short time, but it alerted us to the fact that he was prone to dark spells.'

'But if he was struggling, I would have noticed,' said Diana. 'I mean, he hasn't been like that since he's been with me.'

'That's true,' nodded Ralph. 'I'm no expert on psychiatric illnesses, but I believe the weakness was there.'

It was unbelievable. She could see why the family would keep quiet about Julian's so-called 'weakness', but why hadn't Julian himself told her?

Ralph seemed to read her thoughts. 'No one knew about it except Julian, myself, my wife and the family doctor. Even Elizabeth and Adam were left short on the details. We never wanted it to come out because we always knew he would be CEO one day and we didn't want anything to jeopardise that. You know how jumpy shareholders can be.'

'But I just don't believe he was depressed,' said Diana, feeling utterly bewildered.

'Please, Diana,' said Ralph, touching her hand. 'Don't.'

'Don't what? Question my husband's mental state? Why shouldn't I? Because you're telling the truth, or because you don't want any more publicity?'

She saw his face harden.

'It is the truth. But you're right, we certainly don't want this all played out in public. Both for the business and for the sake of Julian's memory.'

Diana wanted to object, but she held her tongue. Perhaps Ralph was right after all. Dead was dead. Nothing anyone could do or say would bring Julian back to life. And no, she didn't want his name dragged through the mud. The rational side of her, her head, was telling her all that, but her heart was saying something else, that something was wrong, that even if he had been depressed, Julian would never have left her and Charlie. Not without saying something, giving her a sign. Something, *anything*. Her heart just wasn't satisfied.

'I don't want this inquest any more than you do. But I want to know why he did what he did, and I'll do anything to find that out.'

'Sometimes things happen that we just can't make any sense out of,' Ralph replied quietly.

'I have to know,' she whispered.

Ralph looked at her for a long moment. 'Don't be afraid to admit you need someone,' he said finally. 'Someone who can help.'

Diana gave a sad laugh. 'I don't think you can get around grief. You can only go through it.'

'But there are people to help you do that. Professionals.'

She had the sense that she was being led down a path she didn't want to follow.

'I just want to take one day at a time.'

Ralph nodded in comprehension. 'Elizabeth is sorting out the funeral,' he said, his voice taking on a more officious note.

'Is Adam back from New York?'

'He flew back last night. He'll be helping Elizabeth.'

Diana felt a moment's conflict. She knew the Denver family were taking over, and yet deep down she wanted them to.

'The coffee will be getting cold,' Ralph said finally, calling Sylvia and Elizabeth back into the room.

4

During her days as a student and as a journalist, Rachel had been an enthusiastic drinker. Not an alcoholic. Who considered themselves one of those unless you had made the first steps towards AA? No, she just thought of herself as someone who loved everything about alcohol. The taste of it. The sensation of fiery liquid sliding down her throat, the giddy promise of how it would make her feel. Besides, in her profession, a bottle of wine after work went with the job. You had to drink to be one of the gang, plus it was exciting hanging out at celeb events, glugging the free vino and catching all the gossip – and working with a hangover was perversely just part of the fun.

She had also found alcohol an escape from the various low points of the past fifteen years. The death of her father, her estrangement from her sister, toxic relationships with both boyfriends and colleagues. But when she had become embroiled in the phone-hacking scandal, she knew that either her drinking would escalate to help her cope with the fear of imprisonment, or she would have to stop it in its tracks in a bid to get some part of her life back under control. She had become sober in two weeks through willpower alone, and in the three years since, she hadn't let a drop of alcohol pass her lips.

But tonight, at her apartment on a quiet drag in Sairee village, Rachel didn't care about getting her life under control. Tonight she had bought a six-pack of beer from the minimart across the road and was already halfway through the third bottle. Tonight she wanted to feel carefree, merry, drunk, and to forget her problems for just a couple of hours.

Although she had lived here for almost three years, her

40

apartment still had the look and feel of a holiday flat. It was small, cheap, with whitewashed walls unadorned with pictures or photographs, a small sofa, a stack of books in the corner and a double bed in an alcove behind a mosquito net. Rent was low in this part of the world and she could have afforded a bigger, more luxurious place, but sometimes, in her darker moments, she wondered if she had chosen to stay here as a sort of penance for what she had done in the past.

There was a table by the window where her laptop was glowing like a big, unblinking blue eye. It had been Rachel's day off, but earlier that afternoon she had made the fatal mistake of doing an internet search on her brother-in-law. Typing in 'Julian Denver death' had brought up thousands of news stories, each one seeming to salivate over every salacious detail. It shouldn't have been a surprise; after all, the story had that potent mix of celebrity and suffering that the modern press seemed to thrive on. Not that there was much to read.

. . . Witnesses say that the 41-year-old CEO of the Denver Group was in good spirits on the night of his death . . . rumours of depression . . . family request privacy at this time . . . funeral will attract celebrities and statesmen . . .

Underneath all the speculation about the circumstances, there was little in the way of facts, but those facts that there were had been enough to make Rachel reach for the beer. The preliminary inquest had already been and gone, and the funeral was being held today.

Glancing at her watch – and taking into account the time difference between Thailand and London – she reckoned that it must be happening about now.

She slumped back on the sofa and took another swig of beer. Why hadn't she listened to Liam? Why hadn't she gone? Even if she had just been able to watch the burial from a distance, pay her respects, make her apologies . . .

She hadn't even spoken to Diana. At least a dozen times she had picked up the phone to call her sister, but each time something had made her put it back in the cradle. Cowardice, probably. Instead, she had written a letter; she *had* been a journalist after all, a writer, a woman of words. Surely she could express her

41

feelings of guilt, regret and sympathy much better on the page? Yet that single side of A5 had taken two hours to write – something of a record for someone who could bash out a front-page splash in less than twenty minutes. And she knew that, given the efficiency of the Thai post and Royal Mail, it was almost certain that Diana still wouldn't have received it. So her sister would have buried her husband without knowing how sad and sorry Rachel was, and how desperate to make it up to her.

'She's going to think I'm a heartless bitch,' she muttered as her mobile started to ring.

It was Liam, and she knew immediately why he was calling.

'Hey, it's me. Are you on your way?'

'Shit,' she muttered, grabbing her purse and sprinting for the door. 'Yeah, I'm almost there,' she lied.

'Rachel, you've already missed the first interview.'

'Sorry, something came up. Hold the fort for me, be there in two ticks.'

She ran out of her first-floor apartment, down the stairs and on to the street. She glanced at her moped: too risky. Besides, the bar was only five minutes away from her flat, three if she really legged it.

Bloody Liam, she thought, as her flip-flops slapped against the cracked concrete of the path. *Why did he have to arrange the interviews for today?*

Of course he had arranged them because Rachel had asked him to, because she wanted to expand the business, take on more staff.

She could feel the beer swirling around her stomach like washing-machine water as she ran the last hundred metres, dodging the holes in the road and the open drains, the stray dogs and the tourists ambling through the warren of alleyways.

Please God, don't let me puke on the new instructor, she thought as she finally reached the bar and tried to catch her breath. At least Liam had chosen the venue well. Harry's Bar was away from the main drag, sandwiched between a laundry and an internet café, discreet, hidden, with just a small blue neon sign and a Tiger Beer advertisement to announce itself. It was unlikely anyone would spot them there; wouldn't do for the competition to know that they were planning to step up their business. She spotted Liam at a far table, laughing with a blonde. Not just blonde. Attractive and blonde, with a pink-cheeked, girl-next-door beauty that put Rachel immediately on edge.

Liam spotted her and waved her over.

'Sorry I'm late,' she said as she took a seat next to him.

'No problem,' said Liam, a little tight-lipped. 'This is Sheryl.'

Rachel stretched across the table and shook her hand.

'We haven't met, have we?' she asked.

Sheryl smiled. Perfect teeth. Rachel suddenly needed another drink and signalled to Jin, the waitress, for a beer. She didn't look at Liam, knowing that he'd disapprove.

'No, I've only been in Ko Tao two weeks,' replied Sheryl. That would explain why she and Rachel hadn't bumped into each other before on this small, intimate island.

'Where were you previously?'

'Port Douglas, I've got three years' experience at one of the top diving schools on the reef. I got my master instructor certificate last year,' she added in her lilting Australian accent.

Rachel was impressed but didn't want to show it.

'So what were you doing before you got into diving?'

'I worked in marketing.'

Rachel nodded in recognition. When she had first arrived in Thailand, she had thought she would be an oddity out here. After all, she was thirty, making her at least ten years older than the gap-year students who came for the full-moon parties. But she had been surprised to find the place full of people like her: girls who had swapped BlackBerrys for backpacks and were trying to find another way to live.

'So how many dives have you logged?' she asked, not waiting for Liam to chip in. This was what she was good at. Interviewing people. Asking questions. Finding the cracks . . .

'Well over a thousand. I've been diving since I was ten.'

'What about night-diving?'

The Australian nodded. 'It's all in my CV: wrecks, inland waters, even did a few cenotes out in Mexico last year.'

The waitress arrived with a beer and Rachel put the bottle to her lips. 'So how would you deal with a particularly difficult

43

customer? I mean, say you're already out at sea and he starts kicking off?'

'I'd be polite, I guess,' said Sheryl. 'But if he started to be dangerous, I have a brown belt in aikido, so I guess I'd be able to handle it.'

Rachel turned to her colleague. 'What did you put on the advert, Liam? "Wanted: Wonder Woman"?' Her smile couldn't disguise the tartness in her comment.

They chatted for another ten minutes before Rachel wound the interview up. Sheryl clearly wanted to stick around, but Rachel was not in the mood. When the Australian girl had left the bar, she ordered two more beers and settled back in her chair.

'What the hell was all that about?' asked Liam.

His mood had soured, which took her by surprise. Liam was always so laid-back, nothing seemed to get to him, but right now he looked decidedly irritated with her.

'I didn't like her,' said Rachel defensively. 'She was a bit too full of herself, a bit wobbly on the technical questions too.'

'As if she really needs to know the distance in sea miles between Ko Tao and Ko Pha Ngan.'

'I happen to think that's an important question. What if the boat got stuck out there with no fuel and we had to swim back?'

'Perhaps we could float back on a raft made from your empty beer bottles,' said Liam crisply. 'How many have you had anyway?'

'Don't be ridiculous,' said Rachel, holding her bottle to her chest defensively. 'This is only my second.'

'Second? Rach, you don't drink.'

'And tonight I'm drinking,' she replied with petulance.

'Why?'

He looked at her with concern, but she glanced away.

'Why not. And you're not my babysitter, or my AA buddy, so please, just leave it.'

'Have it your way,' he said, raising a hand.

Rachel shook her head. 'If you're going to be like this, then I'm going home,' she said, standing up.

'All right.'

She wanted him to plead with her to stay, but clearly he wasn't

44

going to. She imagined Super Sheryl waiting outside, ready to slip in as soon as she had gone, and hesitated.

'I should walk you back,' said Liam, downing his beer. 'Don't want you falling over, do we?'

But as they stepped out into the evening air, their moods seemed to soften. It was impossible to stay annoyed in this part of the world, at this time of day, when the lights from the cafés and restaurants were glowing like fireflies in the dusk and the dying light of the day cast everything in a flattering bronze blush.

'Sorry,' she said after a few moments. 'I didn't mean to . . . I've just had a lot on my mind over the past few days.'

'I know. And you don't have to deal with it alone. You know that. You definitely shouldn't be dealing with it with booze.'

'It's just tonight,' she said quietly.

He knocked his hip into hers playfully.

'Good.'

They walked to the beachfront. Rachel strained her ears to listen to the hypnotic *swoosh-swoosh* sound of the tide, her favourite noise in the world, the best part of living so close to the sea.

'So what did *you* think of Sheryl?' she asked cautiously.

'She was great. I think her marketing experience could be useful too.'

'You mean she's pretty,' replied Rachel, not wanting to admit to either Liam or herself that Sheryl was the perfect candidate.

He gave a low, slow laugh.

'Yes, she's good-looking, but that's great for business. You've shown that.'

'So you think I'm pretty?' she teased, suddenly feeling self-conscious that she had said it.

'Who do *you* want to hire?' he said, avoiding the question.

'Well, I like Jeff from Blue Ray Diving. I know he wants a change from there. I saw him yesterday and mentioned that we should fix up a drink to discuss him joining us.'

'Jeff's great,' he agreed. He looked down in thought. 'I guess we could always take them both on.'

'Both?' she said with surprise. 'We can't afford both of them.'

'I have savings,' said Liam casually.

45

'I thought you said we couldn't afford it when I was talking about the Sunset Bungalows.'

Liam laughed. 'We were talking tens of millions of baht for the bungalows, Rach. I'm talking about bankrolling a couple of low-wage instructors until we get the cash flowing. Not quite the same.'

They were walking along the beachfront, and in the distance Rachel could see the Sunset Bungalows.

'Look, there they are, winking at us. Let's go and look at them.'

'What bit of "we can't afford it" don't you understand?' he chuckled.

'Just a peek,' she said, taking his hand and tugging him along the sand.

'A quick look. And then you're going home, before you fall over.'

'I'm not drunk,' she laughed, feeling suddenly happy and heady.

She ran ahead of him, and then turned round to beckon him to go faster. He squinted in the soft sunset light and smiled at her, a long, slow killer half-smile that made her heart gallop. The same gallop she had felt the night they had first met. The night after she had arrived in Ko Tao, a little lonely, here for just a couple of days of diving before heading onwards to the next Paradise island. Liam had been the only other Westerner in a tiny back-street café, and when they'd both ordered the same fifty-baht curry, he'd leaned over and joked that they would both have dysentery by the morning. Not the most romantic first line, she had to admit, but when he was that good-looking, who cared.

Rachel had hoped they'd be sharing a bed the next morning rather than a case of food poisoning, but the night hadn't panned out that way. Instead they had talked until dawn, about life and broken loves and the possibilities facing them both. Until that evening with Liam, Rachel hadn't been sure what she wanted to do with her life, which direction to turn. But as the sun had risen over the bay like a cantaloupe melon, she knew she wanted to stay here and have a lifetime full of nights like this.

'I'm going to stay and become a diving instructor,' she'd announced.

'Sounds like a plan,' he'd said, raising his beer.

'You want to join me?'

She remembered how fast her heart had been beating. A recognition that she didn't just want to stay on Ko Tao, but that she wanted him to stay too.

'Okay.'

And it was as simple as that. They had begun the business the next day, and she had suppressed any romantic thoughts about Liam with the same ruthless efficiency she applied to growing their diving school. For all the banter between them, the possibly imaginary undercurrent of something not entirely platonic, it was the easiest relationship of her life. They complemented each other. He was the brake to her gas, her kindred spirit, and together they had discovered another way to live at the other end of the world.

She watched him break into a jog to catch up with her and took a sharp intake of breath to compose herself. They were at the Sunset Bungalows now, close enough to see the rickety sign made from a pair of coconuts. Close enough to hear low jazz music coming from one of the huts. Close enough to see the shimmer of the bright blue swimming pool peeping from behind a gardenia bush.

'Why do I get the feeling you're about to hijack me?' he mused, drawing up alongside her, so close that his forearm brushed against hers.

'Come on, can't you just see the sign over the door? The Giles-Miller Diving Resort,' she said dramatically.

'It won't fit on the coconuts. Besides, it's not very catchy.'

'All right,' she said, looking down at the sand. 'What's your favourite shell?'

'The whelk.'

Rachel barked out a laugh. 'We can't have that!'

'Why not?'

'The Whelk Diving School? Not very glamorous. I was thinking something like The Pink Conch.'

'The Pink Conch?' laughed Liam. 'Is this a diving school or a gay bar? Are you sure you're not drunk?'

'No,' said Rachel, turning towards him. 'Smell my breath.'

She took a step forward so that their faces were inches apart and the space around them seemed to contract until it was just the two of them standing together, breathing the same jasmine-scented air. And then, without thinking about it, she was kissing him. His lips felt warm and soft against hers, like a piece of a jigsaw slotting perfectly into place, and he tasted delicious. Of sun and salt, a taste that was both familiar and exotic. And as she felt him respond, pushing his body against hers, she felt a warm rush of desire, happiness, relief wash over her. A relief that it was *sorted*. That she wouldn't have to feel threatened by pretty girls in bikinis or sexy diving instructors ever again. Because they loved each other and finally he was hers.

'Now I know you're drunk,' he said as he slowly retreated from her.

'You think I have to be drunk to kiss you,' she smiled, looking up at his deep blue eyes.

'No . . . Look . . .'

Her instincts began to twitch. His move away from her was more deliberate this time. Like a cold slap across the face. She knew what was coming and she didn't want to hear him say it; those awkward, pitying words telling her that this was a bad idea. He'd let her down gently, of course. She was drunk, emotional; they worked together. But what he really meant was that he didn't like her like that. Not enough. It was the only reason why something hadn't happened between them before now.

She felt her back stiffen and she steeled herself. She wasn't going to let him crush her. Not tonight. Not this week when her mind was all over the place about Julian and Diana.

'I know, I know. This is not a good idea,' she said, taking a step back in the sand and pre-empting his next words. 'I lied. I've had about five beers and I'm just feeling a bit emotional . . . I'm sorry for taking it out on you. '

'I wouldn't quite call it taking it out on me,' he said quietly. His gaze met hers and she felt a swell of emotion as strong as the tide. *Tell him you love him*, cried a little voice in her head. But already her barriers, her protective shell had gone up. She knew the only way out of this was with a joke.

'Promise you won't do me for sexual harassment,' she smiled, wrinkling her nose, staying strong, hard, impervious.

'Come here,' said Liam, drawing her into a deliberate hug. Her face was squashed into his shoulder, and she smelt the same sun and salt on his T-shirt that she had tasted on his lips a moment earlier. She knew it was like a forbidden fruit, something that she had tried but would never again enjoy.

For a few moments they didn't speak. She would have given anything to climb into his head and find out what he was thinking, but she didn't have the courage to risk it. Sadness made her shudder.

She could feel his breath on the top of her hair and knew it was too dangerous to stay like this.

'Thanks for being my friend. Promise you'll always be my friend,' she said, listening to his heartbeat through his chest. Fearing any further intimacy, she pulled away from him and slapped his back three times, as if she was sending someone off on to the football pitch, hoping that it gave out the right message of platonic forgiveness. 'I'd better go home and get my secret hangover remedy ready.'

'I think we should talk,' he said, his eyes searching hers.

'Liam, there's nothing to talk about.' She was good at making her voice sound casual. 'I just want to go home.'

'Then I'll walk with you.'

'No, no, it's fine, honestly. We'll talk about the staff thing tomorrow, okay?'

She turned and fled before he could reply, feeling her cheeks burn, wanting to cry, wanting the ground to swallow her up, but most of all wanting him to call her back.

But when she got to the bend in the beach and turned back, there was only an empty space where he had been.

5

The funeral was to be a private affair. Under the circumstances, it was the best thing for everyone – at least that was what Julian's father had said. 'Let's keep it quiet, Diana,' he'd told her. 'No fuss, no press, do what has to be done without people peering over the wall with their camera phones and long lenses.' Of course, they would hold a more formal memorial service at a later date, when the fuss had died down and the Denver PR machine had had a chance to work on rehabilitating Julian's image. Plus it would give all those global statesmen and business leaders time to clear their diaries to pay their respects. That was the important thing, wasn't it? Everyone wanted to remember Julian the way he was: perfect husband and son, a formidable force in business, the life and soul of every party. Apart from that last one, perhaps.

Diana looked out of the window of the black Mercedes limousine that was taking herself, Charlie and Sylvia to the funeral. It had been decided that the service should take place at the church in the village adjacent to Ralph and Barbara's estate on the edge of the Cotswolds. It was a beautiful fifteenth-century honey-stone building with medieval stained-glass windows and wisteria climbing around the door, but Diana couldn't help but think that she had let things run away from her. She could hardly complain if Elizabeth and Ralph had taken control of the arrangements – someone had to do it, and she just couldn't get her brain to function properly; it was like she was being held back by a thick fog. But as they approached the church, she began to panic that the service would not be the sort of occasion that Julian would have wanted. She had sent Elizabeth a list of

50

names – friends, people from his climbing club, the manager of a record shop he loved to visit in Notting Hill – but she had no idea if they had been invited. She suspected not.

'You all right, Mum?'

Charlie was sitting opposite her in the car, looking deceptively grown-up in a black suit and tie. He had confided that he had cut his own hair for the occasion – which had been one of the few things to make Diana smile all week, although her mental note to take him to the hairdresser's for a proper cut had been forgotten.

She nodded enthusiastically. A little too enthusiastically, reminding her that she was still hung-over. Without the arrangements for Julian's funeral to occupy her, she had sought distraction in Somerfold's magnificent wine cellar. It had been easy to liberate a few bottles of good Chablis without her mother, Charlie or Mrs Bills noticing, and that final one last night had not been a good idea. Diana didn't drink. Eighteen months earlier, during the 'big push' for a child, she had recruited the services of Danesh Sitri, a macrobiotic practitioner, who had encouraged her to cut everything from alcohol to gluten from her diet.

Someone else she had disappointed.

There was a curve in the road ahead of them, and Diana could see the hearse stopping outside the church gates. They had been relegated to the second car and had to wait a few moments as the Mercedes carrying the Denver family came to a halt.

'Are you sure you can do this?' She sat up and touched Charlie's knee.

'So long as the other pallbearers aren't four feet tall.'

Sylvia shot her grandson a disapproving look, but Diana just smiled, grateful that Charlie was intuitive enough to know not to let things become too sombre.

Stepping out of the car, she felt her whole body prickle, and she had a sudden urge to just run away.

'Diana.'

She spun around at the sound of a familiar baritone, for a split second expecting to see her husband calling her name. But it was only Adam, Julian's younger brother. He stood there, as

51

handsome as his sibling, but a little taller and a little darker in every sense. He was something of a black sheep in the family; either a breath of fresh air or a layabout playboy, depending on your point of view. Right now, she had never been more disappointed to see anyone's face.

'Are you okay?' he asked.

At that moment Elizabeth marched through the church gates and began ordering everyone around, directing pallbearers, guests, even the vicar.

'I feel like a spare part,' Diana said quietly, noticing that her sister-in-law had ignored her.

'You're the most important person here.'

'That would be Julian,' replied Diana, glancing over at the hearse.

Her breath faltered, the sight of the spectacular spray of red and yellow flowers almost knocking her sideways. She didn't want to look at the coffin, but it was impossible not to be drawn to the gleam of the polished wood, the shine of the gun-metal handles.

'We should go in,' ordered Sylvia, slipping her hand into Diana's as Adam leant forward.

'I'll look after Charlie,' he whispered, and Diana nodded gratefully in return.

The church was packed, a sea of faces; some she recognised, others she had no clue as to who they were. It had been the same on her wedding day almost seven years earlier, when everyone had been smiling encouragement at her as she walked down this very aisle in her Caroline Castigliano dress the colour of a South Sea pearl. But today all she could see were dozens of wan, sympathetic smiles and sombre, apologetic expressions.

She could feel her pulse quickening. Diana hated being under the spotlight. It was precisely the sort of occasion that Julian would have guided her through. In the early days of their romance she had laughed and called him Professor Higgins. Whenever she felt out of her depth – when she didn't know what to do or say, when she was stuck at a party with an interminable bore, or at the Cheltenham flat races being patronised by someone who guessed she was not part of the horsey set – Julian was always there for her. They didn't even need a secret code. He would always know when to step in, when to leave. Today she needed him more than ever. And today he wasn't here.

She took her seat in a front pew and studied the order of service. An operatic aria sung by a world-famous soprano, readings by a Cabinet minister and a senior ambassador, the sermon by a vicar who was new to the church and whom Diana had met only briefly. It was all beautifully choreographed, but if Diana hadn't spent the entire hour in a grief-stricken haze, she would have recognised that there wasn't a great deal of Julian's soul in the service. Only the eulogy, read by Charlie, a brave boy walking to the lectern to become a man, struck such a powerful chord that even the captains of industry were reaching for their handkerchiefs.

By the end of it Diana felt almost too weak to stand, and when Adam and Charlie, who had been on either side of her during the service, got up to lift the coffin, she had to be helped out of church by Elizabeth and Sylvia like two stiff sentries.

Two generations of Denvers were buried in the grounds of St Michael's church. The graveyard was overflowing, but the family had apparently purchased a parcel of surrounding land to ensure that they could all rest in peace together.

It was a warm, sunny morning that half made Diana wonder whether Elizabeth's money and contacts had been able to wangle the weather. There was a low breeze that infused the air with the smell of honeysuckle and roses. They walked behind the coffin to the grave, Diana dodging the patches of grass to avoid her heels sinking into the soil. Only close friends and family had been invited to watch the burial, but there was an enormous trail of mourners behind her – clearly this congregation did not consist of the sort of people used to being excluded from anything.

There was a row of chairs for the family at the graveside. Diana sat down, hot in her fitted black Balenciaga suit, fixing her eyes on a point on the ground. After a while, her gaze wandered to the crowd of people assembling around her. There was no one here from the climbing club.

Across the coffin she could see Patty Reynolds smiling sadly at her. Her husband Michael, one of the pallbearers, retreated to a spot next to his wife, and as he clasped her hand, Diana felt a sharp stab of injustice that the Reynoldses could share their grief together. In fact she felt envious of all Julian's friends around her. Today they would be sad. Today they might even cry. But tomorrow they would all go back to their normal lives, and that was something Diana could never do.

Why are we here? She almost wanted to ask everyone the question out loud. *Why was he taken away from us?*

Behind Patty she could see a face she didn't recognise, but one that stood out because of its obvious beauty. Blond hair, fine-boned features.

Someone knows something . . .

The phrase was going over and over in her mind as the casket was finally lowered into the ground and the vicar said a few last words.

Charlie led her away, although the walk to the car was slow. Everyone wanted to stop and offer their condolences, but Diana just wanted to get out of view. As Charlie moved away to talk to Adam, she began to feel dizzy and undid the top button on her silk blouse, which had started to claw at her neck.

The Mercedes was in sight when a tall blonde woman approached her. Diana saw immediately that it was the woman who had been standing behind Patty. Up close she was quite beautiful, although she was doing what she could to disguise her looks. Her pale hair was tied back and her face looked free of make-up, not that anyone with such remarkable bone structure needed war paint. Diana did not know the woman, but she recognised the look in her eyes: grief.

'I'm sorry to approach you like this. I don't think we've met before.'

'We haven't.'

'I'm Victoria Pearson. I'm so sorry . . .'

She'd heard the words a hundred times in the past ten minutes. The last thing she wanted was to hear them again, but she knew the woman was just being polite.

'I'm an old school friend of Julian's,' Victoria continued quickly.

'I thought Harrow was an all-boys school,' replied Diana. It came out more curtly than she'd intended, but she felt suddenly threatened.

'A turn of phrase,' the other woman said awkwardly. 'We go back a long way. Twenty years, which makes me feel rather old.'

Diana did the sums in her head. Julian had left Harrow twenty-three years ago, which didn't make them school friends.

She felt on heightened alert. Her mind searched the photographs she had spent hours and hours going through. Had this woman featured in any of them? She couldn't be certain.

'Had you seen each other recently?' She offered the question as casually as she could, but her stomach had begun to turn over.

'Not in a year or so.'

'Strange we haven't met.'

'He was a wonderful man.'

Diana's heart was thudding. Who was this woman? How well had she known Julian? Suddenly she had to know everything. She began to feel faint. The sun was directly overhead and seemed to be burning her head. She held an arm out to steady herself. The world seemed to spin, and like a dull noise travelling through water she heard a voice calling for help. Her knees started to buckle, but before she hit the ground she felt two arms catch her.

Without looking up, she began to sob, deep gulps of breath and noise so loud they didn't sound as if they came from her fragile body.

'Easy, easy, easy.' The familiar voice was soothing and the arms around her felt strong.

'Take me out of here,' she whispered, as Adam helped her to her feet. She knew that people would be watching her like some stricken caged animal.

'It's okay. The car is just here,' he reassured her, guiding her into the Mercedes.

She sank back into the leather seat, glad that the blacked-out windows had shut out the world. Adam followed her and slammed the car door behind them.

'What happened back there?'

Her eyes were like two thin slits, barely open wide enough to see him.

'Who was that? Who was that woman?' she stuttered.

55

Adam looked confused. 'Victoria. A family friend. What the hell did she say?'

'Nothing, nothing at all.' She screwed her eyes shut and pressed her fingers against her temples. 'I can't cope, Adam. I'm going mad.'

'You're not going mad. You have lost your husband.'

She opened her eyes and looked at him through her tears, and for the first time noticed how pale he was. It was a standing family joke that Adam was always tanned and sun-kissed from somewhere glamorous, but today he looked as drained as she knew she did.

A sharp rapping on the window startled her and she turned to see her mother's face pressed up against the window.

'Can't we just get out of here?' she whispered.

'I was going to say the same thing,' he replied as he instructed the driver to take them back to his parents' house.

6

Hanley Park – the *main* house, as Barbara Denver liked to call it – was just a couple of miles away from the church, although the actual boundary of the property was practically next door. Diana had always thought of the Denvers' collective portfolio of homes as a set of Russians dolls, a series of ever-larger properties each designed to make the last one appear small. Hanley Park made Somerfold look like a doll's house. One of the biggest estates in the entire country, it was just a shade smaller than Castle Howard, with the same grand and chilly beauty – a slate-coloured dome that soared up into the sky and vast baroque-style gardens designed to impress the highest of society. In the 1940s it had been used as a military hospital and still had room to spare, before it was sold to an American entrepreneur and finally to Julian's grandfather, which made it, by the skin of its teeth, an ancestral family seat.

Quite why anyone needed a property this size was beyond Diana, although she recognised the irony in even thinking that. Growing up, she had always thought their three-bedroom house in Ilfracombe was perfectly sufficient for the Miller family, provided she wasn't allocated the box room, and yet she had twisted Julian's arm to buy Somerfold.

As the car proceeded down the avenue of lime trees she watched Hanley Park get bigger and bigger. She knew it wasn't the ideal place to seek refuge. Diana just wanted to curl up somewhere warm and cosy, to pull a soft blanket up to her chin and sink into a silent, untroubled sleep. But coming here was better than staying at the funeral. On the journey over, Adam hadn't discussed her panic attack any further. She couldn't even make sense of it herself. But her cheeks were still hot from the embarrassment of it all.

The car stopped outside the impressive pillared entrance. As her foot crunched on to the gravel drive, a fleet of butlers appeared from nowhere, like genies from a lamp, clearly anticipating the arrival of the first guests for the wake. Adam straightened his thin black tie and waved them back inside.

'Thank you,' whispered Diana, grateful that Adam had read her mind that she wanted absolutely no fuss. Behind them they could hear another car speeding down the driveway. She tensed, and knew she should have insisted on being taken back to Somerfold rather than the closer Hanley Park.

'This will be Elizabeth's event planners come to tell me off for running away. Tell me you've got a secret passageway we can escape into.'

Adam put his hand on her shoulder in reassurance.

'Funnily enough, there's a priest hole in the kitchen. It takes you to the catacombs beneath us and comes out by that woodland over there. I used it plenty of times when my mum and dad were on the war path.'

Diana managed a smile at the thought of the young, mischievous Adam Denver, whose boyhood and teenage antics were the stuff of family legend. Flushing his nanny's slippers down the toilet, poking beehives to extract his own honey, taxiing his friends to the pub on a tractor liberated from the estate's farm.

'Do you think there's time to make a run for it?' she grimaced.

'Not in those heels. Come on, let's get inside,' instructed Adam.

They made it as far as the entrance hall, resplendent with huge vases of lilies, before they heard a car stopping on the gravel. Diana sighed with relief as Charlie ran through the door towards her.

'Mum, what happened?'

'It's fine, Charlie. Really . . .' she began.

Without hesitation her son hugged her as tightly as he could. The gesture took her by surprise. Charlie was now of an age when any affectionate contact with his parents was decidedly uncool. He must have been concerned about her to have her practically in a headlock.

Adam returned from the drawing room and handed her a whisky.

'Drink that,' he ordered.

'I'm not going back to school,' said Charlie suddenly, breaking away from her and meeting her gaze levelly. Since starting boarding school, he had become increasingly headstrong. Julian said it was his burgeoning confidence, but Diana was convinced he had the Denver genes if not the Denver blood.

'Of course you're going back. Granny and I are driving you there tomorrow.'

'How can I leave you like this? You fainted. You can pretend that everything is all right, but it obviously isn't.' His voice was loud, firm, protective. 'I'm staying with you. School's almost finished anyway.'

'You've got three weeks left of term,' she said feeling some maternal steeliness returning to her body. 'Besides, there's your exams.'

'Stuff exams.'

'Charlie!'

'Uncle Adam. Tell her that exams aren't important.'

'You don't want to take a leaf out of my book,' said Adam sheepishly.

'Please tell her.' Charlie looked across at his uncle, willing him to back him up. They didn't see each other very often, but they always got on like a house on fire when they did. Diana would have preferred that her son hero-worship a less mercurial member of the family; Adam sent wholly inappropriate birthday and Christmas presents – a gift-wrapped gold Dunhill cigarette lighter had arrived when Charlie had turned thirteen – but right now he was the only ally they had.

'I think you should listen to your mother. She always knows best,' he said, shooting Diana a look of complicity, and she was grateful for his support.

The front door swung open again and Sylvia Miller walked into the house, her lips pressed into a thin burgundy line.

'You just ran off!'

'I didn't run off. I had to get away.'

'What on earth happened?'

59

'Charlie, come and help me make sure there's enough food and drink,' ordered Adam.

'It's a wake, not a party,' the boy replied quietly.

'Charlie, go with Adam,' said Sylvia. She wanted to get to the bottom of what had gone on.

They moved into the study and shut the door. It was a glorious room, flooded with light, which bounced off the leather-bound books. Diana leant back on the huge mahogany desk, waiting for her mother to interrogate her.

'I know this isn't easy for you . . .' said Sylvia finally.

'But what?' said Diana, sipping the whisky. 'You know this isn't easy for me but I shouldn't just run away from my husband's funeral like that?'

'You gave Victoria Pearson the fright of her life. We all care about you. We're here to help you get through this. But you can't just be rude to people and then collapse, and expect us not to ask questions about whether you should see someone. A doctor, a counsellor.'

'I was not rude to Victoria Pearson,' Diana said quietly.

'Barbara said she heard a few sharp words between you. What was that about?'

She had to tell someone. The words were bursting on her lips and she just needed to hear that she was being ridiculous.

'I don't know. I just thought . . . I just thought Julian might have been having an affair with her, or something.'

'An affair? With Victoria?' said Sylvia incredulously.

'It's not so hard to believe, is it? Look at her. Elegant, beautiful . . . and she looked so upset.'

'Diana, I don't know how you could think such a thing . . .'

Diana gave a low, soft snort. Of course it was easy to believe that Julian was having an affair. They'd had sex just once or twice since Christmas, since they had lost the baby. Both had been awkward and painful experiences which Julian had treated with his usual diplomacy, making all the right noises about 'easing ourselves back into it'. She had counted her blessings that she had such an adoring, supportive husband, but deep down she wondered if his patience, his understanding had a darker truth. That he was simply getting his sex elsewhere.

'It would all make sense,' she said, voicing the fears that had been nagging at her since the day he died. 'Julian didn't kill himself for nothing. Something drove him to it. A feeling of the situation being out of control, guilt, I don't know, but it wasn't something that he could talk to me about.'

'And you think he had a mistress?'

'Perhaps,' she whispered.

Sylvia hesitated before she spoke again.

'But he had had an affair before,' she said softly. 'He dealt with it. You both dealt with it. That wasn't the sort of thing that would have made him do what he did.'

Diana tipped the entire contents of the whisky glass down her throat as fat tears began streaming down her cheeks. She could feel them making rivulets down her thicker than usual make-up.

'I could see people at the funeral thinking, speculating what drove him to it. Drugs, marital problems, financial ruin, another terrible scandal that would have dragged him back into the papers . . .'

'Diana, you're being paranoid,' Sylvia scolded.

'No I'm not. No one said anything, of course. They are far too polite for that. But it's human nature, isn't it? To wonder.'

She clasped the empty crystal tumbler to her chest. It felt cold through the thin fabric of her blouse.

'So imagine how it feels for the person who knew him better than anybody. Or who ought to have known him better. Imagine how it feels for me, wondering what could have been so wrong in our perfect lives, wondering what I could have done differently, wondering if I could have saved the man I loved.'

Her mother came over, took the glass out of her hand.

'You couldn't have done anything differently. Depression isn't a rational thing . . .'

'So Ralph told you he was depressed?'

'And you don't believe him?'

'There's another reason, I know it,' she whispered through bursts of sobs.

'And if there is, the inquest will find it out,' said Sylvia calmly.

'No they won't.'

Her mother looked as if she was beginning to lose patience.

61

'You should sleep this off. Barbara's doctor can be here in twenty minutes with one phone call. I believe temazepam is very good . . .'

'I want to see Rachel,' Diana said quietly.

'Rachel? What does Rachel have to do with this?'

'Everything.' She could hear her sister's voice in her head, the voice she hadn't been able to shake for the past few days. 'Rachel would work out what went on.'

'Oh yes, she's good at that,' said Sylvia sarcastically.

'It's what she does. Finding the truth.'

'And the truth hurts,' said Sylvia, curling her lip. She put both hands on Diana's shoulders. 'Listen to me. Getting through the next few months is going to be hard enough without turning it into a witch-hunt.'

'It's not a witch-hunt. I want to know what happened to my husband. I *need* to know.'

'Leave it, Diana. For Charlie's sake, if nothing else.'

'This *is* for Charlie. For Julian. For me.'

Sylvia stepped away and shook her head.

'And what happens if you involve Rachel? Say she finds some hidden reason why Julian committed suicide. Then what? Then she sells it to a newspaper and causes you and the family more pain. Is it worth it? It's certainly not going to bring him back.'

'But at least I would know,' Diana whispered, with more assurance this time. She blotted her eyes with the palms of her hands. 'I have to go before people start arriving.'

'Where are you going?'

'Back to Somerfold.'

'Darling, don't be ridiculous. Mr and Mrs Bills are here. Charlie and I have to stay. Go and sit upstairs quietly if you really can't face it.'

'I have to go home, pack my bag and get to the airport.'

'The airport?'

'I'm going to Thailand.' Her decision was made. 'I'm going to see Rachel.' For the first time in a week, something finally made sense.

7

Rachel held her breath and looked up at the surface of the sea, just a haunting, glittering silver circle above her. She never knew how many shades of blue there were until she started free-diving. Fifty metres below the waves was the entire spectrum of her favourite colour: dark navy, ultramarine, deep sapphire, even a flash of cornflower if a fish flicked its tail. Down here, she was at peace, only her heart beating slow and steady in her ears, completely in control of everything. No phone calls, no emails, no distractions. Just it and her. Man against nature – or rather Rachel against her lungs. Because free-diving was diving without equipment, no regulator in your mouth or air tank on your back, you stayed down as long as the last breath you took would allow. And right now she could feel the burn increasing as the oxygen ran out. For a moment she considered just letting go of the rope and drifting off into the sea. How long would she last? A minute, maybe two? Everyone had a limit. Without warning, an image of Julian Denver popped into her head. Had he reached his limit? Had Julian just decided to let go of the rope?

Rachel kicked for the surface with her wide monofin – kick, kick, stroke – and was suddenly bursting through into the air, liberated from the water's cold clutch, filling up her screaming lungs, gasping and clutching at the side of Serge's boat. And there he was, his creased eyes smiling down at her.

'You're getting too good for this pond,' he laughed, tapping his watch.

She took his hand and allowed herself to be pulled up on to the deck.

'Bravo,' he grinned, clapping wet hands together. 'Three minutes two seconds.'

His accent was still thick after two decades away from France. Serge Bresson had come to Thailand as a competitive diver in the eighties. Something of a character on the circuit, he had got within twenty feet of the world record. 'Feet not metres,' he always added with a mischievous smile. But he had been mentoring Rachel's diving with the same enthusiasm and eccentric energy he had brought to his own attempts, making her believe that one day, free-diving could be more than just a hobby for her too.

Right now, however, it was all she could do to lie back on the wooden boards and try to suck enough air into her body. Lack of oxygen made her feel weak, like a rag doll waiting to have life breathed into her.

'Take it easy, don't rush it,' said Serge gently. 'Let that body of yours remember you're not a fish, eh?'

Eventually she sat up and took off her weight belt and goggles, letting them thump on to the deck. She was holding a small tag that indicated how far she had travelled down under the water.

'Sixty metres!' she gasped with triumph.

Neither of them spoke for a few minutes. Breaking sixty metres for a constant weight dive – descending into the water down a long vertical line – was something of a milestone for Rachel. Only forty years earlier, this had been a record-breaking depth, although the world champions today went much deeper.

'You know, I think you're ready to do this competitively,' said Serge thoughtfully.

'Oh, I don't know,' said Rachel, her breath slowly regulating. 'Just think of all that training. All that yoga.'

Serge waved a hand dismissively. 'You can swim sixty metres down without yoga. People work for years to train their breathing to the extent you can do naturally.'

'Well, I like it that way,' said Rachel, rubbing her hair with a towel. 'I'm doing what comes naturally. Plus I have a lazy streak.'

'Maybe. But you also have talent.'

Rachel wasn't exactly sure why she was being so resistant; she had certainly thought about entering competitions, and her ambition had to go somewhere. *Ambition.*

Last night, her ambition had been focused on buying the bungalows, turning them into a dive school and resort – but look where that had got her. She had grabbed Liam in the sand outside those bungalows, taken a chance on them being together, fulfilling her dream together, and it had backfired spectacularly.

She gazed towards the island as Serge started the engine on the long-tail boat, wondering where they would go from here. Could they just forget it had happened? Was it that easy?

'So come on, *ma petite*, what is really stopping you?' said Serge, fixing her with a shrewd look as they made a lazy half-circle and began heading back towards the beach.

'Well, there's the diving school for one. I'm a fifty-fifty partner with Liam and he's not going to like it if I start swanning off to the Cayman Islands or Greece for twenty weeks of the year, is he?'

Serge gave a Gallic shrug. 'So take a minority share. I hear you're hiring new instructors anyway.'

'Where did you hear that?'

'Come on, it's a small community. Nothing is a secret here.' He raised his eyebrows meaningfully, and for a moment, Rachel had the horrible feeling that the Frenchman knew everything about her disastrous seduction of Liam.

'How old are you, Rachel?'

'Thirty-three.'

'Still young enough to reach top-flight competition. And in addition to that, you are beautiful.'

She felt herself blush. Not many people told her that.

'Seriously, I may be old, but I'm not dead,' continued Serge. 'I notice, and so will sponsors. It is different from when I was doing the sport. There is money there now.'

'It's not like being Venus Williams, though, is it?'

Serge began to chuckle. 'That's what I like about you, Rachel,' he said, wagging a stubby finger at her. 'This is why you would be a champion. Everyone else would think, "I'm not good enough to be a free-diving champion," but not you. No, you think, "*Merde*, I won't earn as much money as the world's most famous tennis player."'

Rachel couldn't help laughing along.

'You make me sound totally mercenary,' she smiled, wondering vaguely if Serge had heard the rumours, if he knew what she had done back in London.

'Not mercenary, no. I don't think the money is so important to you, but the titles, that is what you want. Besides, being a free-diver is the best job in the world. Think about the places you would go, the people you would meet. Have you been to the Philippines?'

She shook her head. She remembered that Diana had been there years ago, just after she had started seeing Julian. Where had she stayed? The Amanpulo, that was it. She had made it sound like Paradise, a heady blend of beach butlers, watermelon mojitos and yoga pavilions.

'I'll think about it,' she said.

Serge grinned as he guided the boat towards the pier.

'You think it is nice here, but you will never see sand as white or water as clear as in the Philippines.'

'Serge, I said I'd think about it.'

'I tell you what I think,' he said with a mischievous smirk. 'I think you are a little bit in love with Liam.'

Rachel's mouth dropped open. 'Don't be ridiculous.'

Serge threw up a hand. 'What is so ridiculous? You are very cute together and I have seen the way you look at him.'

'Serge, he is my friend, my business partner.'

'So. Make it more. If that's what's stopping you, then it's simple, no?'

Rachel shook her head, squinting at the long jetty stretching out into the pale green water.

'You Frenchmen. All you think about is affairs of the heart.'

'So? What else is more important?'

But Rachel wasn't listening; she was staring at a figure standing on the pier. She recognised her even before she could make out her face. It was her shape, so familiar, and her long dark hair, glinting in the sun like liquid chocolate. For a moment, she was tempted to tell Serge to turn the boat around, but he had already seen the woman.

'Ah ha! I think I have some business,' he smiled. 'A pretty one too.'

'She's not a tourist,' said Rachel with a flutter of panic. 'She's my sister.'

8

Thailand suited Rachel, Diana could tell that immediately. Standing on the strange banana-shaped boat, her younger sister seemed spotlit by the sun, highlighting a body that looked slim and toned, her dark hair slicked back, her skin glistening with beads of silvery seawater. *She just looks so . . . alive*, thought Diana, with a spike of envy, as the boat bumped gently against the pier and the driver cut the engine. Her heartbeat slowed as her sister came closer and closer, her features sharpening until Diana could make out her expression of anxious bemusement.

'Hello,' said Diana. She put one foot in front of the other and propelled herself to the end of the jetty, where Rachel stepped off the boat barefoot. 'Have you been swimming?'

It was the only thing she could think of. On the twelve-hour flight to Bangkok, she'd agonised over what she would say to her sister after four years of silence, rehearsing over and over again her first words, hoping to come up with something clever and grand. But standing here, she just felt mute and stupid. She took a deep breath and swallowed warm, clammy air. What could you say to a woman you had effectively banished, to whom your last words had been hateful and angry?

'Free-diving,' said Rachel finally. She wasn't smiling; in fact there was no trace of emotion on her face.

'Free-diving? What's that?'

'Going as far under the sea as you can without an oxygen tank.'

'Oh, like pearl divers?'

'But without the pearls,' said the man from the boat, but Rachel shot him a look and he walked on ahead of them up the pier.

68

'Why are you here?' asked Rachel when he was out of earshot. She said it quite neutrally, but Diana recognised a tiny flicker of anxiety. Rachel always put a brave face on any difficult situation, but Diana knew her too well to miss her signs of fear.

'I . . . I just want to talk. There's no one else I can talk to.'

It sounded lame, Diana knew that. But it was the truth, and it was the reason why she had flown halfway around the world. Rachel probably hated her guts. Diana herself had spent months, years blaming her sister for the problems in her marriage. But right now, Rachel was the only person she wanted to talk to.

'Do you mind if I change first?' said Rachel. 'There's a café just there.' She pointed down the beach to a bamboo-covered shack with tables on the sand.

Diana walked over and ordered a Sprite, sitting under an umbrella and slipping her sandals off as her sister disappeared into a wood-slatted shower cubicle. She was tired and anxious herself, but the view of the sea soothed her. She had been to Thailand before – to a luxury villa on Phuket that came with the biggest infinity pool she had ever seen and a massage team that had dispensed the most exquisite four-hands massage. But this place was something else. Raw, luscious and uncommercialised. Julian had always been so proud of his architect-designed office, with its white carpets and its view over the city, the Shard, the London Eye and beyond. He had called it 'the most incredible office with the most incredible view in the world', but right now, looking at the bone-white sand and the jade ocean beyond, Diana thought that he had miscalculated.

Her sister had landed on her feet, she told herself with a trace of bitterness. The taxi driver had driven her from the ferry arrivals straight to the Giles-Miller Diving School office in Sairee village, and had refused to take a fare after Diana had told him that Rachel was her sister. 'Rachel Miller, she good people,' he had said in halting English. She had been even more surprised when she had met a tanned, sexy man in the office – apparently the Giles part of the partnership – whose eyes had opened like saucers when Diana had said her name and asked where she could find Rachel. The protective way he had spoken about her sister had made Diana wonder what the exact nature of their relationship was. If Giles was her personal as well as professional partner, then Rachel was even luckier than she'd thought.

'Are you alone?'

Diana looked up, startled. She had been so lost in her thoughts, she hadn't noticed Rachel approach.

'Yes, I came on my own,' she said.

'Where's Charlie?'

'Mum and Adam took him back to school last night.'

'Boarding school?'

'Harrow.'

'Figures,' said Rachel, pulling up a chair, but only perching on the edge, as though she might jump up and run at any moment. 'Do the rest of the family know where you are right now?'

Diana stopped a frown. She had left Hanley Park before the Denvers had arrived, leaving Sylvia and Adam to cover for her.

'They know I've come to see you. They weren't exactly thrilled about it.'

Rachel just nodded. Diana didn't doubt that her sister felt awkward, but she could still be fearsome, formidable, even when she was cornered.

'Is business good? I believe you have a diving school.'

Their words were brittle. That easy familiarity that had always existed between them had completely disappeared.

'Business is great.' Rachel nodded. 'We train three hundred PADI-certified divers a year and we're gearing up to expand, open up a whole resort.' She tilted her head. 'But you didn't come here to run a credit check on me, did you?'

'No, look, Rach . . .' Diana began, but her sister had turned to speak to a waiter, rolling off long sentences in fluent Thai. Evidently she'd said something funny, because the waiter beamed as he scuttled back to the shack.

'What's so amusing?'

'I told him you were a tourist, so to go easy on the chillies.' A trace of a smile pulled at her lips. 'I guessed you'd be hungry; haven't been long-haul in a while, but I don't remember aeroplane food being that exciting, even in first class. That okay?'

Diana felt her shoulders relax. Perhaps this wasn't going to be as difficult as she'd thought.

'Look, Diana, I'm so sorry about Julian.'

Diana blinked hard, unable to get any words out.

'I thought it was better that I stayed away from the funeral,' continued Rachel. 'Even though I wasn't there, it doesn't mean I wasn't thinking about you.'

'I know.'

'Did you get my letter?'

'You wrote to me?'

'You know me: I work better in print.' Rachel grimaced. 'Or perhaps not . . .'

Diana felt a sudden overwhelming desire to tell her sister everything, although not without some trepidation. Back in Britain she had been convinced that helping her out was the very least Rachel could do. But now she was here, was it right to ask her to give up her pocket of Paradise, to return home to investigate a crime that wasn't even really a crime? To help her with her grief? To find answers Diana wasn't entirely sure she wanted to hear?

She owes you, she reminded herself.

'I need your help,' she said finally. She almost felt a physical pain just saying it. She had spent years hating her sister. In those insomniac hours and days after Julian's death, she had pinpointed the exact moment when her dream life with her husband had started to sour. And it was when her sister had chosen her career over her family by running a four-page exposé on Julian's extramarital affair. 'I want you to find out why Julian killed himself.'

Rachel jerked back. 'Isn't that what the inquest is for?'

'The inquest is to find out what happened – I already know that. I want to find out *why* it happened.'

Rachel stared at her for a long moment.

'Why me?'

'Because you were the best at what you did.'

'Di, I wasn't exactly—'

'It wasn't a compliment,' said Diana flatly. 'As a journalist, you were unscrupulous, underhand and completely unprincipled.'

'That's not entirely fair,' Rachel said, averting her eyes.

Diana leant forward. 'Yes, Rachel, it is. You almost destroyed my life for the sake of a story.'

Her sister glanced up. She was picking her nails, a habit she had kept from her teenage years; it was her only tell that she was nervous or upset.

'You've come an awful long way just to insult me.'

'I didn't come to insult you,' replied Diana. 'I'm just being honest; I want a journalist who has what it takes to get to the bottom of a story, who has the stomach for a fight. And that person is you. You stop at nothing; nobody knows that better than me. And I need you to find out why he did it.'

She could feel tears beginning to prick at her eyes, but she was glad that she had finished her speech.

Rachel just sat there, staring at her. *Oh God*, thought Diana, *I've pushed her too far. Been too heavy-handed. I've come all this way and I've screwed it up.*

Then slowly her sister reached across the table and put her tanned hand on top of Diana's. Rachel could be stubborn, dogmatic, unyielding. But right now, as the sun set in long golden ribbons behind her, she looked truly remorseful.

'I'm sorry, Di,' she said. 'I really am. I shouldn't have . . . done what I did.'

Diana could only nod. She could still remember the moment she had realised her life was going to fall apart; it was as if someone had taken a photograph. She had just returned to their Notting Hill home from a morning yoga class when the telephone on the stand by the stairs had rung. It was a reporter from the *Post* asking if she had any comment on the story they were running the next day. Julian was having an affair, they said. They had pictures, an interview with the young woman, shots of the pair of them leaving a hotel. Diana had actually been calm, coolly declining to comment. Because she just didn't believe it. For roughly sixty seconds, she had utter, unshakeable faith in her husband. Sixty seconds, because the moment she put the phone down, it rang again – and there was Julian, his voice shaking, saying that it had meant nothing, that Diana was the only woman he had ever loved: all the clichés. And she had just stood there in the hallway, the receiver held loosely in her hand, knowing that things couldn't get any worse.

Julian had called the lawyers. Diana had called her sister.

Rachel was associate editor of the newspaper, for goodness' sake. Surely she had the power to stop the story?

But she didn't answer her calls. Or return her messages. Finally Diana had gone round to the *Post's* Docklands office and cornered her as she had left the building.

It's out of my hands, was all she could say. Out of her hands that she had destroyed Diana's marriage, humiliated the family, humiliated Julian.

She could feel her hands trembling despite the heat.

'I didn't try to stop the story,' said Rachel quietly, letting Diana's hand go. 'I don't know why. Ambition, wanting to be accepted, greed.'

'You could have tried . . .'

'It wouldn't have made any difference.' Diana had heard her excuses before. 'It was a great story for the *Post*. They were always going to run it, regardless of what I said or did. I had no real power. But yes, I should have done what I could to stop it. For that I'll always, always be sorry.'

Diana's eyes narrowed. How could she just say *I'm sorry* and expect everything to be all right again?

'That world I lived in, it's vicious and selfish and completely unconcerned with anything except getting the story,' added Rachel.

'Which is why I am here talking to you,' replied Diana. She had injected obvious ice into her voice, wanting her sister to be under no illusions that she was enjoying this reunion. 'All I am asking is for you to do what you do so well. I want you to stop at nothing – nothing – until you find out the truth about Julian.'

'But I've changed,' said Rachel. She noticed that her hand had clenched into a fist on the table. 'I've changed and that's why I can't help you. Not in the way you want.' Her voice softened. 'This is my home now, and this is who I am. I deal with wetsuits, boats and the sea, and I spend my days making people happy, as far as I can. That selfish, ruthless reporter is dead, Di. I want to help you, but if you want to investigate Julian's death, then talk to the police. Hire a private detective. I can give you names. I'll support you all the way, and if you need a break from England, then you can come and stay with me. This place heals people.

There are worse things you can do than come to Thailand for a little while.'

'I don't want to stay a minute longer with you than I have to.' Diana disliked the feelings that were coursing through her. Hatred, anger, frustration. This was her sister and she loved her. *Had* loved her until Rachel had betrayed her. It had been the betrayal, almost as much as her exposé of Julian, that Diana had never been able to get over, that had made her feelings run so deep.

'You owe me, Rachel,' she said fiercely. 'You almost destroyed my marriage, and now I'm asking for something to make up for that.'

It was a minute before either of them spoke. The waiter came with two sweet-smelling curries and, detecting an atmosphere between the sisters, hurried away again.

'Why do *you* think he did it?' said Rachel.

Diana inhaled the scent of her curry, picking out the lemon grass and coconut, and somehow it soothed her like a balm.

'I don't know. I genuinely haven't got a clue,' she replied more calmly.

'But were there problems? In Julian's life, I mean?'

Diana lifted an eyebrow. 'You mean in our marriage, don't you? You'd love me to say yes, wouldn't you?'

'Not at all. Quite the opposite.'

'You think our marriage had problems. And yes, your newspaper story exposed the fact that it did. But we worked on it, we mended it. We were happy, I think.'

'What about work?'

'Everything seemed fine. No major upheavals in the company, anyway. I'd have heard.'

Rachel nodded, her face serious. Diana knew that look; her sister was thinking, turning over the possibilities – and she was fairly sure that Rachel's mind was already racing ahead. She was smart like that. Rachel never took anything at face value; she saw conspiracy everywhere, especially after she had begun working in Fleet Street. She always said there were so many stories of corruption and manipulation going on behind the scenes, stories that for legal or political reasons they couldn't print, that the only logical response was to assume everything was dirty.

'You knew Julian,' said Diana. 'You know he wouldn't do something like this.'

'I haven't known him for a long time.'

'But even if he was suicidal, wouldn't he have given a hint?' said Diana, refusing to give up. 'He was talking about climbing Everest two hours beforehand. And why not leave a note or something?'

'Not everyone who commits suicide leaves a note.'

'Not many. You know that.' She could feel her voice faltering. If she couldn't persuade her sister to help her, even after she had layered on the guilt, reminded her how much she owed her, then what hope did she have of finding out the truth? Because Rachel was the only person she trusted to do it. She was the only one she had ever trusted. Rachel had been her rock. When their father had left them, she had been the one who kept the family together – sorted out the bills, the domestic chores, whilst their mother had fallen to pieces. And when Diana had got pregnant with Charlie, after a stupid, drunken holiday one-night stand, Rachel had convinced her that her life was not over. That she could still achieve her dreams and ambitions; she would just have a baby to take along on the journey. Julian and Rachel hadn't always seen eye to eye, but that was because they were so similar in so many ways. Strong, accomplished. Dependable. More than that – they were the two most brilliant people she knew.

Diana took a deep breath in a final attempt to make her change her mind.

'Look, you're convinced David Kelly was murdered. Same with Princess Diana; you never believe the official line on anything.'

'And look where it got me.'

'Exactly. And you still believe that Malcolm McIntyre was guilty, don't you?'

Diana knew it was a low blow, but she was desperate. Malcolm McIntyre was the flamboyant businessman Rachel had been chasing when she was caught on the phone-hacking charge. She

75

had been convinced he was involved in a sex ring and had set out to prove it with methods that had got her arrested.

'That's different,' said Rachel icily. 'I knew he was dirty before I started. I just got too . . . close when I was looking for evidence to back it up.'

'But this is my Malcolm McIntyre, Rach. I know Julian's death is wrong somehow, I *know* it, it just doesn't add up. And I need the evidence to back it up. That's all.'

Diana squeezed her eyes shut, not knowing what else to say, her heart feeling leaden with defeat.

'You know the flights out of Bangkok are pretty busy this time of year.'

Her sister's comment made her sit up straight.

'You might be forced to pay for a first-class ticket,' added Rachel.

'I think I can manage that.' Diana swallowed.

Her sister took a mouthful of curry. Her whole mood had changed. A switch had flipped, and dynamic, unstoppable Rachel was back. Diana almost grinned with relief.

'All right, tell me exactly what happened at the party,' Rachel said. 'Don't leave anything out. Start with the guest list – no, start with the invitations; whose idea was it, yours or Julian's?'

Diana let her breath out. Her sister was coming home. She hoped it would be worth it.

9

'You're going to need warmer clothes than that.' Liam was standing in the doorway of her bedroom as Rachel threw a bunch of T-shirts into a holdall on the bed.

'Well it's all I've got. I haven't exactly kept up with the latest fashions in Soho.'

'Are you sure you really want to do this?'

As soon as Diana had gone back to her hotel on the island, Rachel had phoned Liam for a summit meeting, explaining everything that had happened in the past few hours: Diana's visit, her plea for Rachel to return home with her.

'I thought you were all for me going back to England. Go and make up with your sister before it's too late, isn't that what you said?' she added sharply.

Rachel knew she was being unnecessarily harsh, that Liam was only concerned for her well-being, but she was taking it out on him because the answer was: no, actually she wasn't at all sure she wanted to go back to England. And yet she had allowed herself to be emotionally blackmailed, allowed Diana to make Julian's death seem like a story waiting to be unravelled. Once she had got over the shock of the news, Rachel's first thought had been that something felt wrong about his suicide. That Diana thought so too only sent prickles of macabre curiosity around her body.

She picked up a hot-pink vest top emblazoned with the words *Keoni's Tiki Beach*, then threw it back on to a chair. Liam was right about that too: she wasn't at all prepared for going back to England, clothes or anything else. She sat down on the edge of the bed and let out a long breath.

When she glanced up, she saw that her business partner was watching her. They hadn't seen each other since the night at the beach. It had been his day off immediately afterwards, and the embarrassment between them now was palpable.

'Look, Liam, I have to do this,' she said. 'But I can only do it if it's all right with you.' She looked at him, almost willing him to forbid her to go, give her some excuse to tell Diana. And of course, she wanted him to miss her. That more than anything.

But Liam just shrugged.

'Of course it's all right, of course you should go. Just . . . how long do you think you'll be?'

'Two weeks. Maybe three.'

'Well, Sheryl can start tomorrow and Jeff can start in a week.'

Rachel felt panic rise in her throat, instantly imagining Liam and Sheryl alone on the boat, Liam stripped to the waist, Sheryl in her skimpy bikini. Even worse was the idea that they might share the same intimate banter and mutual flirtation she herself had with him day in day out. *Please don't*, she thought, looking at him miserably.

She reminded herself that she had no claim over her business partner. Liam had never had a serious relationship in the entire time that they had known one another, and the few flings that he had had – the particularly beautiful tourist, the sexually confident, slightly slutty American barmaid – Rachel had kept discreet tabs on, using every ounce of her journalistic know-how to assess their threat. In any event, Liam had always given the impression that they were nothing serious, and secretly Rachel had considered this to be a good sign. A sign that Liam was actually hopelessly in love with her and, like herself, was just waiting for the right opportunity to declare it. But since their kiss on the beach, as painful as it was to admit, Rachel was no longer under any illusion that he was interested in her. More worryingly, now that the issue of their relationship had been confronted, now that they had finally, categorically clarified that they were 'just good friends', she wondered if Liam would quickly move on and find a proper girlfriend, rather than a business partner it was easy to spend his evenings with.

'Great,' she said, pasting on a false smile, 'Sheryl starts

tomorrow. That's just great.' She zipped up her bag with finality. It was probably a good thing to put some distance between them. 'Well, I suppose that's that, then.'

'You *are* coming back?'

'Of course I'm coming back,' she said lightly. 'Why do you say that?'

'Because I think you miss it,' he said, pushing his hair away from his forehead. 'Running around chasing down stories.'

'I'm not chasing a story,' said Rachel. 'I'm trying to help my sister get closure.'

Was she? Was that it? Or was Liam right: did she really have an itch still needing to be scratched? Deep down, she was scared. Over the past three years, she had managed to push all her memories and feelings about her life on the newspaper into one dusty corner of her mind, locking it away – she hoped for ever. But now, now it was all coming rushing back. She had been associate editor of London's *Sunday Post* when a sting involving a senior-level banker and a prostitute had been a front-page splash, leading to a spike in circulation. It had put fat-cat-bashing back on the menu and the editor, Alistair Hall, had wanted more of the same – the newsroom had been in an arms race to see who could get there first. Rachel had been aware of Julian's unfaithfulness and she had hated him for it. Infidelity ruined lives, destroyed families – she knew that better than anyone. That had been her motivation; she had always maintained that, although she had been unwilling to spell it out to Diana. When the news team had brought the story of Julian's infidelity with an eighteen-year-old model to conference, the daily meeting they had at the paper to discuss the stories, she hadn't fought to kill it. Short-term pain for Diana would mean a happier life in the long run. Or so she had tried to justify her actions to herself.

Liam was looking at her as if he wanted to say something.

'What?' said Rachel, all thoughts of newspapers forgotten. She had the sense that he wanted to talk about that night, about the kiss. She was conflicted. Part of her needed to know for sure that he wasn't in love with her, that the kiss and the subsequent rejection hadn't been some big misunderstanding. The other part didn't want to inflict any more pain or rejection.

But it had been two days ago, two days she had spent trying not to speak to him, and now it seemed the moment had passed.

'Just don't go getting used to it again,' he said. 'I know how much you loved that life, and it's so easy to get sucked back in.'

'Don't be silly. When you go back to London, I don't notice you chomping at the bit to stay.'

'The difference between you and me is that I chose to leave.'

He paused before he continued. 'I just think part of you wants to go back, permanently. You've never tried to put proper roots down here.'

She looked around at the sparsely furnished apartment and admitted that he had a point.

'Listen, if you want me to stay, you only have to say . . .'

'No, I want you to do the right thing,' he said. 'And I think it's the right thing to go with Diana. But I do want you to come back.'

'I'm going to have fun,' she said, with a playfulness she didn't feel. If he thought she was going to be depressed about his rejection of her, he had another think coming. 'Have fun, do a bit of snooping around, catch up with old friends, snog a few unsuitable men, and then I'll come back.'

'Don't have too much fun . . .'

How dare he? she thought, grabbing her bag and making for the door.

'Don't worry about me,' she said, brushing past him, their arms touching, a crackle of electricity passing between them. 'Don't worry about me at all.'

10

Diana's body clock was all over the place. She had been tempted to spend the night in Bangkok; the city had some of her favourite hotels and shopping centres – the delicious spa at the Sukhothai, the rooftop restaurant on the Lebua with its views right over the city – but she was desperate to get back, for the sake of her mental well-being if nothing else. The lack of sleep was starting to have an impact on her body; she was getting headaches and feeling spaced out. If Rachel hadn't been by her side, she wasn't sure she would have been able to find the right gate at the airport. All she could think about was her lovely soft bed at Somerfold – if she could only make it there, everything would be all right.

It wasn't far now, at any rate. Mr Bills had met them at Heathrow, and the car was now sweeping through the Berkshire countryside, the green hedgerows and trees soothing after the overbright and crumbling urban sprawl of Bangkok. Diana certainly felt calmer here, although she wasn't exactly sure that was a logical response: there were going to be awkward questions to answer when she arrived with her estranged sister. She looked across at Rachel, dozing with her head back on the seat. They had hardly spoken since they had left Ko Tao; Rachel had seemed preoccupied with something. Perhaps she was simply worried about coming back to England. Three years was a long time, and must have seemed even longer to someone who may well have expected to stay away for ever. That was a strange thought now that Rachel was sitting only inches away. For so long Diana had expected the same thing; in fact had wished to never see her sister again. *Was I too hard on her?* she wondered. No, what Rachel had done had been spiteful, selfish and unforgivable. And yet

81

here Diana was, inviting her back into her life. Not forgiving her, not that, but she was certainly pinning all her hopes on her little sister. She supposed it was simply a measure of how desperate she was.

'Where are we?' murmured Rachel, squinting out of the window. 'This isn't Notting Hill.'

'We're not going there. We're going to Somerfold.'

'The country place?' Diana thought she said the words with a trace of sarcasm, but perhaps it was just sleep. 'Will Mum be there?' she added.

'No, she's up in London for a friend's birthday.'

Diana could see the relief on her sister's face. They both knew their mother was unlikely to welcome Rachel with open arms. Sylvia Miller had always been a world-class grudge-bearer; she had refused to mention their father's name from the day he had walked out, had even refused to go to his funeral after his death from cancer. There was little chance she would welcome her younger daughter with open arms, especially as Diana had defied her by going to Thailand to fetch Rachel. They would have to meet at some point, of course, but Diana was content to avoid that moment for the next couple of days at least.

'I bought something for Charlie,' said Rachel, rooting in her tote bag and pulling out a large teddy bear dressed in a T-shirt emblazoned with the words *I ♥ Thailand*. 'I picked this up at Samui airport when you went to the ladies'. What do you think?'

'He's a bit old for that,' Diana replied, trying not to smile. 'If you'd got him the new iPod I think it'd be more his style.'

'Well, it's the thought that counts,' Rachel said, looking a touch put out. 'Perhaps we can all do something together at the weekend?' she asked more hopefully.

'I told you. He's at school.'

'Doesn't he come home on Fridays?'

Diana shook her head. She could see her sister's disappointment. Charlie and Rachel had always got on like a house on fire. A closet tomboy, Auntie Rachel had taught her son how to ride a bike and do all the rough-and-tumble boy things like climbing trees and building dams.

'Well, I'll send it to him,' she said. 'Maybe he can tell his mates he went to Thailand for a full-moon party.'

They turned off a country lane and through a set of gates on to a long driveway. To the left was the lake, and set on a low hill overlooking it was Somerfold. Diana sighed with relief at seeing her home.

'Bloody hell,' said Rachel, sitting forward. 'Is this it? It's massive!'

Diana realised that her sister would never have seen or possibly even heard of their country home.

'How big *is* it?' gasped Rachel, her face practically squashed against the window.

'Probably a bit too big,' said Diana modestly, although she was pleased at her sister's reaction.

'How many staff do you need in a place like this?'

'The minimum, although it's nice to have people around, to be honest.'

'I bet you've got a live-in gardener and everything.'

'Phil and his wife Sue live in a cottage near the stables.'

'Stables!' laughed Rachel. 'Do you have a sexy groom in tight jodhpurs?'

'Depends on your point of view, and anyway, Jessica only works part-time.'

They almost giggled, a trace of their old good-humoured banter poking its head above the parapet. As the car pulled up at the front door, Mrs Bills stepped out. A formal dresser, she was wearing her usual pale grey skirt and blouse.

'A female butler?' whispered Rachel as they got out, crunching on to the gravel.

'Mrs Bills is the housekeeper,' said Diana. 'Her husband David has been kind enough to drive us from the airport,' she said, smiling towards the front seat.

'It's like bloody Downton Abbey.'

'Pleased to meet you, Miss Rachel,' said the woman, taking their bags. 'I've put you in the Lake House. Would you like me to show you the way?'

'The Lake House?' said Rachel, turning to Diana. 'Aren't I staying here?' There was disappointment on her face, not just because she was being sidelined to an outbuilding, but because of what it really meant: she was back, but she wasn't being *welcomed* back.

'I thought it would be a better place for you to work,' said Diana, feeling suddenly guilty. She found herself wanting to justify her very deliberate decision to keep Rachel away from the main house. 'It's much quieter and tucked away. Julian used to go out there when he needed a clear head.'

Rachel nodded, but was clearly unconvinced. 'That sounds good.'

'Let's go inside first,' said Diana. 'I'll show you around quickly.'

Diana would have been lying if she'd said she wasn't enjoying the open-mouthed wonder on her sister's face as they walked into the grand entrance hall, through the drawing rooms and around the gallery and library on the ground floor. Much of the Georgian grandeur was still in evidence in the tall windows and roof mouldings – Diana was particularly fond of the plaster eagles swooping from the ceiling rose in the ballroom – but she had worked hard with an interior designer to make the place feel softer, more welcoming, by adding more modern furniture and deep cream carpets underfoot.

'It's mental,' smiled Rachel, flopping down on to a leather chesterfield in the living room. 'It's a long way from Charleville Street,' she said, referring to their old Ilfracombe home. 'It's like the Queen has just left the room.' There was no sense that she was mocking; just delight and excitement at the size and luxuriousness of the surroundings. *Perhaps people really can change*, thought Diana, reaching over to the walnut coffee table, where Mrs Bills had left a steaming cafetière, two porcelain mugs and a plate stacked high with home-made biscuits. 'Seriously, Di, this house is beautiful. I prefer it to Julian's parents' place. It's grand but still a home. How the hell did you find it?'

Diana paused before answering. She wasn't sure she wanted to get into all this right now, but she supposed the time had come for complete honesty.

'An agent found it for us. We bought it after the scandal, because we couldn't stay in London. We needed to get away from that social scene, partly because the party invitations dried up overnight – people in our circle really don't want your misfortune rubbing off on them. And partly because, well, I wanted Julian out of temptation's way.'

She watched her sister lower her head in shame. She wasn't sorry that she was making her feel awkward.

'The fallout from the story was difficult. Photographers following us for months, sly gossip in the press, the fact that Julian's name became synonymous with sleazy businessmen.'

'You've made your point,' said Rachel with quiet defiance. 'But it wasn't all down to me. Julian had the affair. With an eighteen-year-old girl. You can't do things like that and expect there not to be consequences.'

Diana looked away, conceding the truth in what Rachel had just said. She had imagined this confrontation over the years, imagined making her sister feel sorry, really desperately sorry and ashamed for what she had done, but she felt no victory now the moment was here. Both Rachel and Julian, the two people she had loved most in the world, had been wrong. It didn't make her triumphant to dredge it all up – it just made her sad.

'Are we ever going to get over this, or am I just wasting my time being here?'

'Is that why you're here?' replied Diana. 'To make amends? To make yourself feel better?'

'Partly,' she admitted.

'I should show you to the Lake House,' she said, wanting to change the subject.

Rachel picked up her rucksack and they went out of the main door of the house, Diana leading her left down a gravel path, past the swimming pool, gleaming like polished tanzanite in the darkening day.

They turned a corner and the lake was in front of them. When a land agent had been commissioned to find the Denvers the perfect country house within commuting distance of London, they had been inundated with dozens of beautiful properties, but Somerfold had stood out from the start. A contrite Julian had allowed Diana to choose the property, and it was the lake that had swung it for her. Diana had always loved the water. Not in the way that Rachel did – Rachel the water baby, the superb swimmer – but she found it soothing. After her parents' divorce, when they had moved to Ilfracombe to be near her mother's sister, she had taken long walks along the cliffs and it had helped her deal with her new life, just as she knew that the lake would help her adjust to life in the countryside.

A building on stilts jutted out into the water.

'Wow,' whispered Rachel, pausing to admire the view.

Diana had to admit it was impressive. Built out of slate and cedarwood in sleek architectural lines, it had been a labour of love for Julian bringing it to life.

'It used to be the old boathouse. It was falling down when we bought the place, so Jules wanted to renovate it. He demolished it and rebuilt it from scratch. He loved it, although the truth was, he wasn't around enough to use it.'

'I thought you said you bought Somerfold to get Julian away from London. To keep him here.'

'That was the plan. But he worked so hard, so late, that it just wasn't practical for him to come home every night.'

She didn't miss her sister's fleeting distrustful expression.

Pulling a key out of her trouser pocket, Diana pushed it into the lock and opened the door. She hadn't been in here for weeks, and there was a slight smell of dust and damp.

'It's been a bit neglected, I'm afraid,' she said, opening a window to let in warm, sweet-smelling evening air.

'That's what happens when people work too hard,' replied Rachel. She said it absently, but Diana got her meaning.

The door opened on to a wide living space. It had a grey modular sofa, a television, and a beautiful oak desk overlooking the lake, and they could see the sun setting over the water through the floor-to-ceiling windows.

'The balcony runs around the perimeter of the house. It's lovely to sit out and watch the kingfishers and herons,' said Diana, pointing to two Adirondack chairs outside.

'I bet you can dive straight off into the water,' said Rachel, her eyes wide in pleasure.

'I think it's deep enough,' confirmed Diana, knowing that she was too timid to try it herself but imagining her sister jumping in and cooling off.

'Where do I sleep?' asked Rachel.

Diana pointed to the left.

'There's a bed through here. There's cooking equipment and a fridge over there,' she said, pointing to the opposite end of the house.

She watched Rachel running her hand over the bookshelves and realised, quite bitterly, that she had inadvertently put her sister in her perfect home.

'So how do we start this?' she asked finally.

Rachel flopped on the sofa and crossed her legs.

'It's a bit like police work, I suppose,' she said, flinging her head back with tiredness. 'You've seen it on the TV, haven't you? They get a big board on the wall with photos and lines linking people and events. That's pretty much how you start an investigation, although without the board.' She gave a wry smile. 'Journalists are more into scrawled notes on the back of receipts, but it's the same principle. We want to build up the fullest picture of Julian's life we can.'

'Of course,' said Diana, feeling uncomfortable. She knew she would have to be open and honest with her sister, but she hadn't appreciated how awkward it would make her feel.

'Tell me we've got coffee in this place?' said Rachel, standing up and walking to the tiny galley kitchen.

Diana had thought that Thailand might have calmed her sister down, but she was still like an alley cat – constantly restless, constantly on edge, as she had always been as a child.

'This is a great place to start,' Rachel shouted. 'You say he used to work here? What sort of work?'

Diana shook her head. 'I don't really know. He didn't discuss business with me. But there's a couple of filing cabinets in the other room. They're locked; I tried, but I've no idea where the keys are.'

'We can get your driver to break them open. He looks brawny enough.'

Rachel walked through with two mugs of coffee. Mrs Bills must have stocked the fridge, thought Diana, noticing that her sister had a Kit Kat sticking out of her pocket.

'I need to know everything else. Home life, sex life, family life, social life. And I'll need you to put me in touch with anyone who can fill in the rest, like someone who can tell me what projects he was working on at the company.'

'Okay,' said Diana. 'I think I know who to ask.'

'Good. I'll need to speak to as many people who knew Julian as I can. His colleagues, his friends, particularly any close friends, the ones he'd tell his secrets to.'

Diana looked doubtful. 'Men don't have those sorts of friendships.'

'People know more than they think they know,' she said through slurps of coffee. 'Besides, I need to start somewhere. I'll have to go through his personal stuff too. Photographs, bank statements, receipts . . .'

'I've already done that; it's all in a box at the house. I went through his drawers, his pockets. I didn't see anything suspicious, though.'

'Good, but I'll have to do it again. And I'll need access to his computer.'

Diana blushed as she realised she didn't know the password to her husband's computer – in fact she couldn't even have said for sure how many he had. Did he have a personal laptop as well as his company one? Would he have kept it at the London house? Did the police take it? Why didn't she *know* this stuff?

'I'll try,' she said haltingly. 'But I really don't know much about the company.'

'I appreciate this all seems a bit weird to you,' Rachel said soothingly. 'But we need to look into everything, however small or irrelevant it seems to you. And most importantly, I need you to *tell* me everything. No secrets, no holding back because you think something is too personal or embarrassing.' She looked at Diana. 'Are you absolutely sure you want to do this?'

Diana nodded, but in truth she wasn't sure. Who would expose every last detail of their life to anyone, let alone to an unscrupulous sister? Whose marriage could stand up to that sort of scrutiny? And yet for the past few minutes she had felt a strange swell of relief. She had hoped that this was what Rachel would do – grasp the problem by the scruff of the neck and start shaking – because no one, not the police, not her family, not even the press, seemed interested in doing anything about her husband's death. Taking it seriously; taking *her* seriously.

'Yes, let's do it,' she said. 'I *have* to do it, Rach. I won't be able to rest until we do.'

Rachel took a deep breath and nodded towards the big desk. The setting sun was bright orange now, spilling deep golden light all around them, so that she felt as if they were floating in a summery equivalent of a snow globe.

'Tonight we sleep and tomorrow we talk,' she said. 'We'll get to the bottom of this, I promise you.'

Diana forced a smile and turned to leave. That was exactly what she was afraid of. She had to get to the truth – she *had* to, or she would go mad – but she had the unsettling feeling that the truth was the last thing she wanted to hear.

11

Rachel looked out of the window of her black cab, craning her neck to see why the taxi had stopped: another red light. *Bloody London*. The streets outside were dark, the lights of the shops and restaurants shining off the rain that had suddenly hammered on to the roof of the cab five minutes earlier and had just as suddenly stopped. *Just like being home*, she thought. In Thailand, rain came without warning, pouring down so hard it left tiny footprints in the wet sand. But out in the tropics, after ten minutes everything would be dry, the whole storm forgotten. Here, despite it being the height of summer, they would be splashing through puddles until midday tomorrow. The thought of the beach inevitably made her think of Liam. What was he doing right now? She glanced at the digital clock next to the cab's meter – she really should get a watch – 9.12 p.m. Liam would be fast asleep. *Alone, hopefully*, she thought, then wished she hadn't, forcing herself to focus on the meeting instead.

Rachel had arranged to meet Julian's PA, Anne-Marie Carr, in the hope of getting some background on Julian's movements in the week prior to his death. The woman had been decidedly chilly on the telephone, and it was only when Diana had confirmed that Rachel was acting on her behalf that she had reluctantly agreed. *I hope the old battleaxe gives me more than my sister has*, she thought as the cab finally cleared the lights.

Rachel had tried to interview her sister that morning, but had come away with virtually nothing of any use. Despite her pep talk the night before about the importance of openness and co-operation, Diana had persisted in presenting a picture of a perfect marriage. According to her, both she and Julian had been blissfully happy in every department; not even the problems with

90

her pregnancies had cast a shadow over their sunny lives. Rachel supposed that for now she had to go along with it – she couldn't reasonably expect Diana to tell her the unvarnished truth straight away – but it was frustrating: she felt as if she hadn't got off the launch pad.

Maybe I'm not as good at this as I thought I was, she reflected, watching a single raindrop make its way down the streaked window. One thing was for sure though: however much she had tried to tell herself otherwise, Liam had been right when he suggested that she missed this dirty, cluttered, unfriendly city. Thailand was beautiful, it was exotic, it was Paradise. And yes, right now it felt more like home than here. But there was something about London: it thrummed with energy, the sense that anything could happen on any street corner at any moment; it was *vital*, that was the word. That was why she had come here in the first place: London was where things happened. At sixth-form college, one of her teachers had taken Rachel aside and told her – to her utter surprise – that she stood a decent chance of getting into Oxford or Cambridge. She had gone through the motions and was even offered a place at Trinity Hall, but she had never had any real interest in riding round some half-dead jumped-up tourist trap on a bicycle. She wanted the bright lights, the sounds and smells of the big city. So she had gone to UCL to do an English degree, landing in the capital just as Cool Britannia and Britpop were making it the epicentre of everything.

Rachel hadn't paid much attention to Joyce and Chaucer; instead she had spent her time at the Coach and Horses in Soho, the middle of the epicentre. One evening she had got talking to a guy called Simon who worked for artist Darius Cooper, the controversial leader of the New British Art Movement. According to Simon, who was clearly trying to impress Rachel into bed, Darius never did any of his own work; instead he picked paintings and sculptures from a group of promising students who were then sworn to secrecy as he sold the works to galleries for hundreds of thousands, giving the students a minuscule cut of the proceeds. Drunk and giggling, Simon had let Rachel into Darius's studio in then-unfashionable Shoreditch, where three of his artists were hard at work. Two bottles of vodka later and the students were all happy to tell her the details of the scam, even offering to pose for pictures.

By ten the next morning, Rachel had written an exposé entitled 'The Great Art Swindle: How Darius Cooper Lied To The Nation'. She took it straight to London's *Daily Post*, where she talked her way into the news editor's cramped office. The story ran the next day with the *Post*'s chief reporter's byline attached, but Rachel was up and running, trawling the bars of Soho and Camden for scurrilous gossip.

A few weeks later, she scored again with a story about the singer in a squeaky-clean girl band. Rachel had happened to see her entering a toilet cubicle in a nightclub with a notorious drug-user. Bribing the toilet attendant to close the ladies' for an hour, she had called a friend doing a PhD in chemistry, who had rushed down with the necessary solutions and swabs to test the top of the cistern for cocaine. The positive result had been enough to create the headline 'Pop Poppet in Drugs Quiz' – and to get Rachel back into the news editor's office, this time with a job offer. Her timing was perfect: the *Post* was low on female reporters. Besides, while there was no way the new breed of Britpop stars were going to talk to gnarled old-school hacks, they were happy to swap gossip with a pretty, street-smart girl who could match them drink for drink. Rachel quickly discovered that the newspaper was a true meritocracy: they didn't care who you were as long as you kept the stories coming in. And the more stories you brought in, the higher and faster your promotion. She quit university and joined the *Post*. Within six months she had moved over to the Sunday edition as deputy features editor; within a year, she was running the showbiz desk. She had certainly been right about London being the place where things could happen.

'This it, love?'

The cab had pulled into Finsbury Square, right on the edge of the City. The railed garden in the centre of the square was dark and locked, but the lights were still on in most of the buildings towering over it. *The city that never sleeps*, thought Rachel with a smile.

'Yes, just over there, the one with the steps.'

The entrance to the Denver Group HQ was large and imposing,

complete with marble pillars and three receptionists in headsets, even at this late hour. Rachel was given a security pass and shown to a lift, which opened and chose the floor without her having to touch a button. *Impressive*, she thought.

A tall, austere-looking woman met her as she stepped out on to the eighth floor. She was much more the old-school secretary rather than the more glamorous and dynamic MBA-wielding personal assistant favoured by the rich and powerful these days.

'Anne-Marie?' said Rachel, offering her hand.

'You're late,' said the woman, turning on her heel.

Charming, thought Rachel as she followed her along a corridor past glass-fronted offices, some empty, others occupied by people peering intently at screens or jabbering into telephones.

'In here, please,' said Anne-Marie, holding open a door to a small office. Rachel sized her up as she took out her notebook. Late fifties, possibly single – no ring, anyway – certainly hostile if her expression was anything to go by. She wondered idly if Diana had demanded that Julian hire a secretary who was impossible to find attractive, even for a womaniser. She tried not to smile at the thought.

'Well, thank you for speaking to me, Ms Carr,' she said.

'You can dispense with the niceties, Miss Miller,' said the woman. 'You are only here because Mr Denver's wife specifically requested that I co-operate with you.'

'I am only trying to find out the truth about Julian, Ms Carr,' said Rachel as pleasantly as she could.

'I imagine that's what you said to yourself the last time too. You've got a nerve, you know that? Do you know how much damage you did to that family?'

Rachel nodded slowly. 'It's why I'm here. To try and make amends.'

The secretary's expression clearly communicated that she was sceptical about whether that was possible.

'Can we go into Julian's office?' asked Rachel. She wanted to see his personal space.

'Very well,' replied Anne-Marie disapprovingly.

She led Rachel to a corner office that was as big as her entire flat in Ko Tao. It had floor-to-ceiling windows through which the City glittered with dots of light and shadow.

'I've started packing,' she said more softly. Rachel noticed the pile of boxes along one side of the room. The contents of the desk remained untouched. She could see a photo of Diana in a silver frame; one of Julian, Diana and Charlie in another. There was a copy of the *Economist*, a stack of Post-it notes, and a bottle of water by the phone. A desk waiting for its owner to return.

Anne-Marie blinked hard, as if shutting out emotion.

'So,' she asked more briskly, 'what do you want to know?'

'You sat outside his office twelve hours of every day. How did he seem in the weeks leading up to his death?'

'You mean did he seem suicidal?'

Rachel nodded.

'If he had done, I would have alerted somebody to that, of course. But he didn't seem any different. A little stressed and short-tempered sometimes, but that goes with the territory with this job. Sadly I was not privy to his inner thoughts. Who knows what made him do such a thing.'

'So he didn't seem down or upset by anything?'

'The day of the . . . incident, he came into the office as normal. There was nothing particularly out of the ordinary. He was a little distracted, perhaps. Then again, he had his wife on the phone a lot about the party. Julian never really enjoyed socialising in the way that his siblings do.'

'So he wasn't looking forward to the party?'

'I never said that.'

Rachel tried a different approach.

'Julian and his team were doing a great job at Denver, weren't they?'

Anne-Marie couldn't hide a small smile at that.

'Julian was always too modest to blow his own trumpet, but he was doing a good job considering . . .'

'Considering what?'

She looked thoughtful. 'Well, like many companies you see around the City, the group had been affected by the recession.'

'I was under the impression it was doing well.'

'It is, considering the climate. I'm not an accountant or an

94

analyst, but the mood around here has been buoyant. I put that down to Julian. He was a good leader.'

Another small smile.

If I didn't know better, I'd say you were a little bit in love with my brother-in-law, thought Rachel. *Anne-Marie, you dark horse.*

'Why do you think he did it?' she asked.

'I've no interest in gossip,' Anne-Marie said quickly, but Rachel could see that she was becoming emotional.

'Anne-Marie, please. You must have known him as well as anyone.'

'I don't know what pushed him over the edge. What I do know is that he was doing an incredibly high-pressure job and perhaps all it took was the tiniest of things.'

'What do you mean?'

'You might think differently, Miss Miller, but Julian was a very decent man. Let me show you something,' she said, standing up and beckoning Rachel to follow her into a side room stacked with files and boxes. She pulled a cardboard storage container off a top shelf and placed it on the table. 'This is only a small sample,' she said, taking out a sheaf of papers.

'What are they?'

'Letters to Julian. Or rather, to the CEO of Denver Group. Complaints, gripes, suggestions, even proposals.' She pulled one out and handed it to Rachel. It was written in red ink, a scrawled angry hand, and it began 'Dear Blood-sucker'.

'We used to get a lot of this on the newspaper,' said Rachel. 'People with too much time on their hands.'

Anne-Marie pursed her lips at the mention of Rachel's previous career. That was a misstep, thought Rachel, cursing herself.

'Not all of these letters are from attention-seekers,' Anne-Marie went on, her tone noticeably less warm. 'In fact, many are genuine.' She pulled out a thick file and opened it on the table.

'All these are complaints about a helipad that serviced some of the more remote Scottish islands. Denver owned the heliport and were closing it down; someone in management believed it was no longer viable since North Sea oil has begun to run out. There are people here accusing Julian of destroying their lives, their communities, their relationships. Some are quite vitriolic; others are just downright heartbreaking. He's even had death threats. You know, Miss Miller, if Julian had been murdered, there would be hundreds, if not thousands of suspects in these files. But he always tried to do his best for them.'

Rachel frowned at her. 'He knew about these letters?'

'He got someone on the team to answer every single one of them.'

'*All* of them?' said Rachel incredulously.

'You know, we get all these hotshot business school graduates in here: Harvard, Stanford, INSEAD. And they all want to be CEO. They see the prestige, the money, the power, and they think that's all there is to it. Yes, Julian Denver was wealthy, but I wouldn't have swapped my position with him in a month of Sundays.'

She put the letters back in the box.

'You see, Miss Miller, to be a really great CEO you have to be tough. Thick-skinned, ruthless, but not in the way you think – stabbing people in the back, insider dealing, all that. Yes, Julian could do that too if the situation required it, but it's much harder to have to make unpopular decisions; you have to be able to lay off a thousand people before Christmas and then sleep easy at night.'

'Do you think that bothered him?'

The woman shook her head to indicate her disapproval.

'Do you really believe any of these questions will bring him back?' she asked, her face set in stone. 'What good do you imagine it will do?'

'It will set his wife's mind at rest.'

'Really? Is that what you think?'

'Don't you? Honestly, Ms Carr, if you know some—'

'Honestly?' spat the secretary. 'What would you know about honesty? Mrs Denver is a decent woman and I agreed to speak to you for her sake, but if you care for your sister at all' – the woman's expression suggested she didn't believe that for a moment – 'then you will go back to wherever you came from and drop all this nonsense right now.'

'Please, Anne-Marie,' said Rachel, 'I only wanted to—'

'Good night, Miss Miller,' said the woman, walking to the door of the office and holding it open. 'I trust you can find your own way to the lift.'

12

Diana had never been to a shrink before. Sometimes, in the early days of her marriage to Julian, when she had felt so excluded and lonely, she had considered it, had even looked up a few numbers. But something had stopped her; the shame of it, probably. Not that there seemed to be much stigma about it in the circles she mixed in – women in Kensington and Notting Hill talked quite openly about sessions with their therapist. It was as if they were talking about popping down to the Cowshed Spa for a massage, and perhaps that was the way they looked at it: a soothing session for a tired or stressed mind, in exactly the same way you'd give physio to a knee injured during a spinning session. But Diana wasn't like those women, she didn't come from their world; she'd grown up in small-town Devon. If you had problems there, you went to friends and family; if you needed anything more, well, there was always the loony bin.

This isn't the loony bin, thought Diana. This was a discreet Edwardian house on a leafy street in Highgate, the sort of private clinic that had a brass plaque on the door, the sort of place where wealthy people came to get the very best care. There were leather sofas and big pot plants in the corner of the waiting room, which was decorated in subdued Farrow and Ball – Elephant's Breath, she recognised – and Colefax and Fowler, designed to make rich women feel at home, she supposed. She looked up from the month-old copy of *Country Life* she had been pretending to read. The only other person – patient? – in the waiting room was a pretty woman in her early thirties. Well-dressed and groomed, she was using one of her perfectly manicured nails to pick at something on her Chanel skirt. *Pick, pick, pick*; she kept doing it until Diana had to look away. *Am I like her? Am I just obsessively picking at something that isn't there?*

'Diana Denver?'

She looked up. 'Olga Shapiro,' said a woman standing by the door. 'Would you like to come this way?'

Dr Shapiro was younger than she had expected – prettier too, with long blond hair and a pencil skirt that showed off her figure – but she had come highly recommended. The consulting room was a surprise too: vaguely Swedish, with a modernist grey sofa and an oval mustard rug, a big splash of colour in the middle of the room.

The therapist sat in a chair opposite Diana and tilted her head.

'Not what you were expecting?'

'I was imagining a life coach sort of thing,' said Diana. 'More New Age. Or maybe something Dickensian. You know, full of books and dust and photos of philosophers on the walls.'

'Would you be more comfortable in those surroundings?'

'No, not really,' said Diana, feeling as if the analysis had already begun. 'It's just this seems a bit more formal, like a real doctor's. A bit too . . . medical.'

'And if it's a real doctor's, then whatever is troubling you must be really serious, is that it?'

Diana gave a nervous laugh. 'Yes, something like that.'

'Well, let me put your mind at rest. I'm not here to judge you or assess you or trick you into saying anything, I'm just here to listen. So let's have a chat, talk about what brought you here and take it from there. You should see if you like me first, see if we hit it off. No pressure, okay?'

Diana nodded, relieved. She had thought that sitting in the therapist's chair would be like awaiting Stasi interrogation under a hot and unyielding spotlight.

'All right, do you want to tell me how you're feeling?'

She looked down at her hands. 'Well, I lost my husband ten days ago. So I'm not feeling too great, as you might imagine.'

'Grief is one of the hardest emotions to predict, actually. There are lots of different ways people experience it, but it does tend to go through stages. How are you feeling about it right now?'

'I feel . . . mad.'

'Mad?'

'No, not insane or anything,' said Diana quickly. 'I mean in the American sense, you know? Angry, but not only that. I'm frustrated and irritated and I just can't seem to get my head around it.'

Olga Shapiro nodded. 'It's only logical that you're going to be overwhelmed with emotions at a time like this. You can't expect to be able to process it all in the space of a week. May I ask how your husband died?'

'Suicide; at least that's what they're saying.'

'I see. And you don't agree with that assessment?'

'I don't know. Really I don't. There are too many questions and there shouldn't be. Death is supposed to be a full stop, isn't it, an end, but it doesn't feel like that. I can't get closure and it's sending me mad. I can't sleep, I can't stop thinking about it. It's like a treadmill of mental torture.'

'You don't feel as if he's really gone?'

Diana hung her head, not wanting the woman to see the tears that were forming.

'I can't accept what has happened because I don't understand it . . .'

She choked off and the doctor handed her a box of tissues with a kind smile.

'I've had two miscarriages and one stillborn child in the last two years. All that death – or absence of life, whatever – it's very hard to take.' She looked up, her eyes pleading. 'Is it me? Have I done something to make it happen?'

Olga Shapiro did not react.

'Did you go and see someone about it?'

'No.'

'Why not?'

'I thought I could cope. My husband was very supportive.'

She felt a surge of panic. The walls of the room were closing in on her, unwelcome pressure bearing in from every side.

'I don't really want to be here,' she admitted in a faltering voice.

'Then why are you?'

She puffed out her cheeks, willing herself to stay in control.

'My father-in-law insisted I see someone. I had an episode at Julian's funeral. A panic attack. Then I went to Thailand. They think I ran away.'

'And you didn't?'

'I went to see my sister.'

'So you don't think you need professional help?'

'I don't want to be put on more pills. After my baby died, I was given medication by my doctor to help me sleep. I didn't like how it made me feel.'

'I'm a psychotherapist, not a psychiatrist. I'm not here to dispense pills. We just talk.'

Diana looked at her with a sense of disappointment. Ralph and Barbara Denver hadn't tried to disguise their unhappiness that she had left the funeral under such dramatic circumstances, and she had only agreed to seek help as a way of pacifying them. But even though she was here under duress, she had secretly been hoping for a miracle cure that would free her from the intensity of her grief. She wondered whether she should just stand up and walk out of the door, then told herself that she would only get out of this session what she put in. If she was going to circle Olga Shapiro in wide, distrusting circles, then this trip to Highgate would only be a waste of time.

'I don't like myself right now,' she whispered, hoping that the relationship between doctor and patient really was private.

'Why not?' Olga Shapiro did not react with any surprise, and Diana felt reassured by her calmness and the orderly surroundings that seemed to help make more sense of the world.

'I'm looking into his death. Myself,' she said quietly. 'I thought it would make me feel better, I thought it would make me feel empowered, as though I'm finally in control. But I think it's actually making things worse.'

'Worse?'

'I feel so guilty,' cried Diana. 'What do you think it says about me, about my relationship with my husband? It's as if I'm saying I didn't trust him, like I'm looking for evidence, secrets he kept from me.'

'Do you think he kept secrets?'

She nodded. 'He's been unfaithful before now.'

'Do you want to tell me about it?'

She told the therapist about how she had discovered Julian's infidelity, seeing it on the front page. But she left out the part about her sister's involvement. That was a story for another day.

'Was it a surprise?'

Diana shook her head ruefully. 'I didn't want to believe it, but deep down I think I'd been expecting it.'

She remembered Rachel telling her once that it was her instinct that made her a good journalist – and perhaps that instinct ran in the family. Yes, she had known Julian was cheating. Not just with the eighteen-year-old model he had been caught out with either; her instinct told her there were others. Although none since the scandal. Even though they'd worked at their marriage, she had still kept her eyes open for evidence of marital guilt – credit card entries for jewellery or roses, text messages – cursing her paranoia when she found nothing suspicious.

'You know, women were even flirting with him at our wedding reception. It was as if the fact that he was now married was just a minor irritation . . .' She felt the tears running down her cheeks again.

'We should probably keep today's session quite short.'

'No, sorry. I haven't been too bad with the waterworks so far. I guess it's talking about it that set me off.'

Olga waited while Diana wiped her eyes and blew her nose.

'You *should* talk about it. Is there anyone else you can share this with? Your sister, perhaps.'

'Maybe,' she said softly. It had been hard to tell Rachel any of this when she had probed. She hated admitting her weaknesses.

'I always find it's useful to surround yourself with people who make you feel better about yourself,' continued Olga, as if she had detected an undercurrent of difficulty between the siblings. 'Spend time with people you like. Think about who makes you smile.'

'My son,' said Diana. 'But he's at boarding school. I think that's the best place for him right now.'

'Couldn't you arrange for a day out of school? Might be good for both of you.'

Diana nodded. It wasn't a bad idea at all.

'Is there anyone else?'

A face came into her head, so vividly that it was impossible to push it out.

Adam Denver.

'Well, there is someone, a . . . a friend,' she said vaguely. She wasn't about to share everything with this woman, and she wasn't at all sure how a psychologist would interpret her desire to see her brother-in-law. But then why not? Adam understood better than anyone what she was going through, and more importantly, he was fun. She could do with a bit of that right now.

'Great, then go and call your friend as soon as you leave my office. Make a date. Take a drive. Fly a kite. Smile.'

Diana nodded, avoiding the doctor's eye. She felt sure that she had blushed. 'Thank you, Dr Shapiro,' she said, standing up and picking up her clutch bag. 'I'll do that. I really will.'

13

Rachel stood in the kitchen at the Notting Hill house and closed her eyes. It was late morning and sunlight flooded into the room, the trees in the garden casting sinewy shapes on the marble worktops, but Rachel tried to push all that from her mind and picture the house as it was on the night of the party. She imagined laughter and the clinking of expensive crystal. She imagined beautiful women in designer dresses and the alpha males in *Mad Men* suits, all of them feeling pleased with themselves. All except one. Julian Denver had known that under that glittering surface something was wrong, very, very wrong. But what was it?

She opened her eyes as the kettle huffed and clicked off. God, she needed coffee. There was a shiny Gaggia machine standing on the side, but she didn't have time for that, so she made a cup of double-strong instant and walked towards the stairs.

Rachel had been in Diana's London house since eight that morning. She could have slept here, of course, but she wouldn't have felt comfortable. She wasn't squeamish – she couldn't have been a tabloid reporter if she had been – but even so, she didn't want to spend the night with Julian's ghost. Instead she had checked into a hotel in the West End, taking the tube to Notting Hill after breakfast. She was glad she had. Even now, with the sun slanting across the stairs, the house felt cold, empty and depressing.

Stop being such a wuss, she scolded herself as she walked into the master suite. She had started her search of the house on the ground floor, methodically working her way through the kitchen, two reception rooms, dining room and study, checking drawers, bookshelves, even down the backs of chairs. It hadn't taken that long. It was not a cluttered house and it was easy to spot that this was no longer Diana and Julian's main residence. It had a masculine vibe, compared to the floral whimsy of Somerfold; Diana had confessed that it had been mainly Julian's London crash pad, underlined by the fact that it had a full-spec media room and an extensive wine cellar. Rachel didn't know a great deal about fine wine, but she felt sure there was enough good stuff down there to buy most of Ko Tao. The reality was she had come here looking for a reason why a man would take his own life, but all she had found was a thousand reasons why he shouldn't.

She stopped at the doorway of Julian and Diana's bedroom, hesitating before she went inside. As a journalist, she had spent most of her professional life snooping round, sniffing for stories, doorstepping widows, peeping over walls. But somehow this was different; it felt like she was trespassing, somehow stepping into her sister's private world.

She walked softly over to a glass dressing table by the window. It was hard not to compare it with the rickety old desk from Diana's youth. That had been laden with magazines and cheap lipsticks. This was a far more pared-down and luxurious space. There were a few items of make-up – a blusher, a Chanel mascara – lying on one side, and a pair of Julian's cufflinks in a little glass tray, just sitting there waiting to be put on. Had he decided not to wear that particular shirt? Would it have made a difference? Or maybe it was all meaningless, just fading footprints on the beach.

She felt her mouth curl down with sadness.

'You need to toughen up, my girl,' she told herself. Perhaps three years swimming with the fishes had softened her more than she knew.

She put down her coffee, tiny brown spots of liquid spilling on to the glass surface. She rubbed at them with the edge of her T-shirt, knowing that her ferocious scrubbing was just an outlet for her frustration.

She had interviewed Julian's secretary, searched both the houses, and what had she come up with? No insights into how they lived, no telling details about Julian's state of mind, no evidence of his supposed troubles. But what had she expected? Prescriptions for antidepressants? An address book packed with secret assignations?

Still, there had to be something. *Had* to be. She took a deep breath. She did not want to let Diana down. Not again.

'What do you see?' she muttered, sweeping her eyes around.

She walked over to the small dressing room at the side of the bedroom, predictably dominated by Julian's clothes, and ran her hand along the line of suits. No surprises here either: sober, well-cut, almost certainly Savile Row, no bright colours or checks. His shoes were polished, with little wear to the leather; a row of identical white shirts were ironed and ready to go. It was bland, colourless and unexciting.

Still, Rachel had worked on the tabloids long enough to know that what happened under the surface of supposedly straight-forward lives was often very strange indeed. Husbands with double lives as transvestites, students who were covert hookers, the cuddly TV presenter who was a wife-beater, the very macho movie star who liked effeminate boys. But their secrets always had a way of leaking out, because however careful they were, they always left clues: receipts, voicemails, letters. Someone, somewhere had always seen something. But what?

She went back into the bedroom and opened the bedside cabinet. There was a literary paperback – unread, no bookmark – some lip balm and a box of condoms still in their cellophane. Rachel made a mental note about that one, not relishing the thought of asking Diana detailed questions about her sex life. Unopened condoms might not mean very much at all, or they could be significant. Were Julian and Diana having sex? Presumably – Diana had struggled with conception, but that suggested they were trying. In which case, why the condoms? Rachel blew out her cheeks. Was that all she had? A jangling sense that something was wrong about an unopened packet of condoms? It was pretty thin.

She was so lost in thought that she didn't hear the front door open, and the footsteps were almost at the top of the stairs before she looked up.

'What the hell are you doing?'

Rachel's heart gave a lurch.

'Mum,' she said, startled.

Rachel rarely got nervous, but her mouth was dry and her heart was hammering. She had been dreading this confrontation ever since she boarded the plane in Thailand, and now it was here, catching her unawares.

Sylvia stayed silent, as if she was waiting for Rachel to reply to her question.

'I'm here . . . Diana asked me to come. She gave me the keys,' Rachel said, feeling quite dumbstruck.

Sylvia Miller twisted her mouth disapprovingly.

'You're here to *help* her, presumably.' There was no trace of any maternal warmth in her words. Her mother had always had an edge. She was a difficult woman to live with; much as Rachel hated to admit it, she wasn't exactly surprised that their father had left her for another woman.

'Did she tell you that?' she asked, assuming there was no point in lying.

'There had to be some reason she went careering off to Thailand.'

'She needs me,' said Rachel, wishing the ground would open up and swallow her whole.

'Well, it's not helping.'

'I think that's for Di to decide.'

Sylvia turned on her daughter angrily. 'Diana is a grieving woman half out of her mind, imagining all sorts of ridiculous things; she needs reassurance, kindness, not a reporter snooping around looking for reasons to make her more unhappy.'

'I'm her sister, not a reporter.'

'You could have fooled me,' Sylvia replied acidly.

Rachel wanted to strike back, to set her mother straight, put her side of the story, but something made her stop and look at Sylvia Miller for the first time. *She was looking old.* She hadn't seen this woman in over three years, but it looked as though she had aged ten. No one else would think that, of course; her mother had certainly made the best of herself: well-tailored clothes, blow-dried and coloured hair, and whatever treatments were de rigueur that month; it all added up to an image of elegance and

106

quietly wealthy self-confidence. But Rachel could see beyond the mask, could see that she looked tired, worn out. What had made her that way?

'Aren't you going to say anything?' Sylvia goaded.

Rachel blinked hard, trying not to show that this was upsetting her. Deep down, all she wanted was for her mother to ask how she was, ask about her new life in Thailand: did she enjoy her new job, had she found anyone to love, did she have good friends, a nice life? Questions that showed that a mother cared about her daughter. But she knew those questions were never going to come.

'Anything I say will just slide off like water off a duck's back,' she replied quietly. 'You've made up your mind about me – and about Diana too. What's the point in discussing it any further, because you are never going to get past this.'

'*Past this?* You betrayed your sister, your brother-in-law. You were the one who cut yourself off from the family.'

Her mother's remarks toughened her.

'If anyone almost destroyed their marriage, it was Julian. I didn't try to cover his tracks, no, but he was going to get caught out at some point, and somewhere in all the mess and finger-pointing at me, all that got forgotten.'

'You still don't accept any blame, then?' said Sylvia with ice in her voice.

'Yes, I do. And I was reminded of it every day in Thailand, when I saw families playing on the beach, when you didn't answer my calls on Mother's Day, when I was lonely at Christmas. But I never once heard you blame Julian.'

'He was a good man,' Sylvia said quietly.

'He was good to *you*. He got you that flat in Bayswater, sent you to couture with Diana, gave you use of the villas . . .'

'So you think he bought me?'

'Money talks,' she said, looking away. 'It always does.'

Words that had been on the tip of her tongue for so many years were ready to tumble out of her mouth.

'I've always been a disappointment to you, haven't I? No matter how hard I tried, what I did, you never quite *got me*, did you? What is your problem with me, Mother? I mean, seriously.

I know you've always given all your attention to Diana, but what's wrong with me? Why have I always disappointed you?'

A million memories came flooding back. How Diana's mediocre school reports were rewarded with ice-cream sundaes for 'good effort'. How Sylvia would slip Diana twenty pounds to buy something new to look pretty for a date. How she would drive her thirty miles to a pop concert, when Rachel had to get the bus and a train to swimming galas because they started too early. Diana's surprise pregnancy had been a small setback, but Sylvia had been instrumental in deciding that her daughter and grandson should move to London to better themselves, and had even found a thousand pounds to help them make the move.

Part of Rachel was expecting her mother to deny the obvious favouritism that had always existed in the family, but Sylvia had never been a woman to keep her feelings hidden.

'You could have been so much more,' she said finally. 'Look at Diana. Yes, she had looks, rather than smarts, but she was clever enough to know how potent that was. She wanted to make the best of herself, so she went out and found herself a good husband. But you? Running around town half drunk, spreading lies about decent people . . .'

'That's it?' asked Rachel, almost relieved that Sylvia had voiced her thoughts. 'That's why you're so angry? Because I didn't marry some rich banker and get a big house in Kensington?' Her eyes were filling with tears and she brushed them quickly away. 'Because I'm not beautiful and vulnerable and attractive to alpha men like Diana is?'

'No, I'm angry because you tried to take away what Diana had, because your jealousy for your sister ruined their marriage. If you hadn't been so bloody selfish, perhaps Julian would still be alive.'

'I did not have anything to do with Julian's death – and any problems in their marriage were there before the *Post* published a word.' She could feel herself trembling, not sure if she was trying to convince her mother or herself.

'We'll agree to disagree then, shall we?' said Sylvia, turning for the door and leaving without another word.

14

Rachel hadn't smoked in a long time. Not since the nineties. Not since she had interviewed a sixty-year-old woman with emphysema who had seen a packet of Marlboro Lights poking out of her bag and had told her with the brutality of someone who didn't have long left in this world that she was a stupid, stupid girl for killing herself. But standing on the pavement outside one of the City's most fashionable power-broking restaurants, the fix of nicotine from some hastily purchased cigarettes felt very good indeed.

She glanced at her watch, wondering if she could while away any more time out here. Lunch with one of Julian's old friends was the last thing she felt like after her confrontation with her mother, but it was all arranged, space made in Greg Willets's busy diary. She couldn't turn back now, no matter how much she wanted to.

A taxi stopped by the pavement in front of her. The door opened and an elegant leg swung out, its high heel hitting the concrete with a brusque tap.

'Hello,' said Diana flatly. She looked exquisite. Wearing a pale pink knee-length dress and grey shoes, her dark hair pushed off her beautiful face with two tortoiseshell clips, she could have been a Russian tsarina on a royal visit.

She looked her sister up and down, and Rachel could tell in an instant that she disapproved. After all, Rachel was still in the same clothes as yesterday. Black jeans, a white T-shirt, ballet pumps, all of them a bit tired and smelly.

'The restaurant has a dress code,' Diana said awkwardly.

'Well I didn't know we were going to be coming to places like this when I left Somerfold yesterday.' She threw the stub on to the ground, twisting it into the tarmac with the sole of her shoe.

'You should have borrowed something from the house,' Diana said, snapping her clutch bag under her arm.

'I didn't like to take anything without asking.'

'That makes a change.' She smiled, her expression softening.

Inside, they were directed to a lift that took them at speed to the seventeenth floor. Diana took off her grey leopard-print pashmina and gave it to Rachel.

'Put that on.'

'Is this a makeover?'

'Hardly. But it might get you past the maître d'.'

They stepped out into the restaurant, which was packed, humming with the lunchtime crowd, and were shown directly to their table.

'You know Mum dropped by at the house,' whispered Rachel as they threaded through the dining space. She watched with grudging admiration the way her sister negotiated the crowd, nodding at friends, pausing every now and then to exchange a word. Diana had always been so reserved, so unsure of herself in loud public places, but here, she looked right at home.

'I plead guilty on that one,' said Diana, stopping momentarily. 'I thought it was best you two spoke to each other as soon as possible. I got the impression that Mum was avoiding you. Did she give you a hard time?'

'Not as hard as Greg Willets is probably going to give me,' muttered Rachel, seeing Julian's old friend sitting in a prime seat by the window.

Greg Willets stood up and came round the table to kiss Diana lightly on the cheek.

'How are you?' he asked her sombrely.

She nodded with a wan smile. 'Greg, you know my sister Rachel,' she added more brightly.

'Of course,' he said, ignoring Rachel's smile and proffered hand. He reluctantly sat down opposite her, glaring at her.

'I have to say, this is something of a surprise,' he began, raising his finger to summon the sommelier. 'Where have you been? Costa Rica, wasn't it?'

'Thailand,' said Rachel, taking a quick swallow of the water that had already been poured for her.

'Yes, I knew it was somewhere a long way away. Had to be, didn't it?'

There was a small embarrassed silence.

'All right, you two, play nice,' said Diana, stepping in. 'I know you have your differences, but we're all here for the same reason, okay?'

'Sorry, Di, but some of us have long memories.'

'Greg, I know Julian's friends haven't got a very high opinion of me, but I'm here to help.'

He held up his hands in surrender.

'Fine.'

He opened the wine menu and pointed out something to the sommelier.

'Is red okay with the pair of you? I suppose we should try and make this as civil as we can.'

Some years earlier, Diana had tried to fix Greg and Rachel up. They had gone to a villa in Ibiza and it had been all couples, the obvious hope being that the two singles on the trip would get together by the end of it. But they hadn't connected. Greg was apparently popular with the ladies, but despite his high-flying job in the City, Rachel hadn't found him remotely attractive, and the feeling had been mutual.

'Thanks for your note,' said Diana, softening the atmosphere.

Greg looked at Diana as though she was a wounded little bird. She had always had that effect on the opposite sex. She had obvious beauty, but it was something else as well, perhaps a soft vulnerability that made any red-blooded male want to protect her. Rachel had tried to analyse this response a hundred times over, because it was not one that she herself had ever provoked in a man. Perhaps Diana made even the most beta of males feel more alpha.

'So,' he said, shutting the wine list. He turned his gaze to Rachel and she could feel his expression hardening. 'Help . . .'

'Rachel has been asking people close to Julian a few questions,' began Diana diplomatically.

'Why?'

Diana put her manicured hand on the table. 'Greg, we went through this on the phone . . .'

He looked as if he didn't approve of what they were doing. Another one.

'You were Julian's close friend. Did you even suspect—'

'Suspect?' he said incredulously. 'Rachel, I have spent the last ten days going over it in my head, cursing myself, wondering why none of us spotted anything. I was there at the party the night he died. We talked about going surfing to Maui, coming to my place in Monaco this weekend . . .'

'So how long have you known Julian?'

'I was his best man. Two young blades, knocking around the City. I worked at the Denver Group fresh out of uni. I started the same day as Julian.' He puffed out his cheeks. A crack in his alpha-male armour. He looked as if he might start to cry, but then the waitress came to take their order and granted him a reprieve.

'I spoke to Julian's secretary. She thought he might not have been handling the pressure of being CEO very well.'

Greg thought about the statement for a minute.

'She's right that being CEO of the Denver Group is a big, big job. Not many gigs bigger, in fact. I mean, do you know how vast the company has become? We're talking seven different divisions. Motors, finance, food, agribusiness, hotels, pharmaceuticals and chemicals, steel. With one man at the head of it all. Who wouldn't feel the pressure when put in charge of all that? But Jules was born for it, literally. He was prepared, and he had a lot of support from the board.'

'Well I haven't spoken to any of the executive committee yet.'

'Good luck with that,' he said thinly. 'Your paper's little story could have cost Julian his job.'

Rachel looked down at the notebook she had pulled out of her bag, staring at the blank pages, wondering if everyone in Julian's inner circle was determined to give her a hard time. She had known this wasn't going to be easy, known that she would need her tough skin to steel her for the job, but she hadn't quite appreciated how wretched the last few days would make her feel. It was tempting to make a run for it, head to Heathrow and get the first plane back to Thailand.

'So, was there any part of the business that was causing him particular trouble in the weeks before his death?' she asked briskly.

'Possibly, but nothing he shared with me.'

'But you were close. Julian valued your opinion,' said Diana, her voice almost a plea, a cry for help.

Rachel knew a little about Greg Willets. He had been a hotshot at Lehman Brothers before it had gone under. Instead of being devastated, he had gone on to set up his own boutique investment house. She had heard him once talking about becoming the new Goldman Sachs. It was a big ask, but Greg Willets was the sort of man you'd bet your last dollar on. The sort of man a high-flyer like Julian would want as a sounding board.

'Look, we talked about stuff, but there was only so far Jules would go. After all, I'm in finance, investment. He was always professional about not telling me too much stuff.'

'And he didn't have any problems with the business in that last week?'

'Not that he mentioned, no.'

'If you'll both excuse me, I'm just popping to the ladies'.'

Good for you, thought Rachel. She had been worried about talking frankly in front of Diana, but clearly her sister understood the need for privacy. She watched Diana disappear from the dining room, then turned to Greg.

'All right, you have about four minutes to tell me anything that you don't want Diana to know.'

Greg snorted. 'Ah. So the subterfuge begins again.'

'I'm doing a job here . . .'

'I believe that's what you said last time.'

'Three minutes,' said Rachel flatly.

Greg held his hands open and sighed. 'All right, ask away.'

'How happy was the marriage?'

'Happy enough, considering.'

She ignored the jibe. 'Was he seeing anyone?'

Greg's expression clouded. 'No.'

'I know you don't like me being here, but there is absolutely no point in me talking to you unless you are honest with me. Was he seeing anyone?' she repeated.

'I don't know,' he said, taking a sip of his wine then meeting her gaze. 'And if I did, I wouldn't tell you.'

Rachel sat forward. 'Come on, Greg, I need your help. This is for Diana. What do you know? Anything.'

'I don't know,' he repeated more firmly.

'Well, speculate.'

He looked suddenly uncomfortable. His eyes flicked in the direction of the ladies'.

'Two minutes,' said Rachel quietly.

'I don't want you repeating this to Diana, and I don't want to read about it in the *Sunday* bloody *Post*, all right?'

Rachel gave a terse nod.

He hesitated, and took another sip of wine. 'We met in Washington a few weeks ago. We were attending the same economic forum. When we go to these things, Davos, TED, we try and stay in the same hotel, make it social . . . We went for dinner with some friends. Julian left early. I was walking back to my hotel, the Four Seasons, which was where Julian was staying as well, and I saw him with someone.'

'A woman?'

'Blonde, pretty, young. I think he saw us – actually, I'm pretty sure that he saw me, because they both scuttled off in the opposite direction.'

'Who was she?'

'No idea. I waited for Julian to mention it, but he didn't, so I assumed he didn't want to discuss it. What happens in Vegas and all that.'

'Could it have been someone from the conference?'

Greg looked doubtful. 'Perhaps, although she looked a bit too young and too beautiful for that.'

'Just his type then. Could she have been a hooker?'

'Hooker? You've got such a high opinion of him,' he said sarcastically.

'I'm not naïve, Greg. I've been to conferences like that; the hotel bars are full of them. Escort girls,' she said pointedly.

'Yes, she could have been an escort girl,' he conceded.

Rachel glanced over towards the loos, checking that Diana was not on her way back.

'So did he use them? Prostitutes – sorry, escorts?'

'Come on, Rachel.'

'Greg, this is important . . .'

'I don't know. Perhaps. I gather things weren't electric in the bedroom department at home.'

'How do you know?'

'A few things he said. Besides, it figures after everything that Diana had been through recently. The babies.'

'So the marriage wasn't back on track?' She looked at him sharply. What was he trying to imply? She let it slide, using the awkward silence between them to do the work – an old journalist's trick. Leave a space and let the subject fill it.

'They worked really hard on it, I'll say that much. Beyond that, I couldn't say.'

'Can't say or won't say?'

Greg's expression hardened. 'I think I've told you more than enough already, considering what you did. More fool Diana if she thinks she can trust you with what you find out.'

'Look, Greg,' began Rachel, but he just smiled and pointed behind her. Diana was making her way back across the room. As Greg stood up, he bent to whisper in Rachel's ear.

'Watch your step, Rachel Miller,' he murmured. 'Diana may have forgiven you, but Julian had a lot of friends, and we've all got long memories.'

'Is that a threat?'

He turned his mouth down into a 'what, me?' expression.

'Everything all right here?' said Diana as she approached, looking back and forth between them.

'Of course,' said Greg. 'We've kissed and made up, isn't that right, Rachel?'

Rachel forced a smile. 'Absolutely,' she said.

'Was Greg any help?'

'Yes, yes, a great help.'

But she wasn't at all sure. In fact, she was pretty sure she'd achieved nothing beyond making Julian's friends hate her even more.

15

In a third-floor gallery at the V&A, Diana stopped to admire the painting in front of her. She knew that it wasn't particularly fashionable to like watercolours. She had been on the society scene long enough, met enough dealers, been encouraged to buy enough expensive modern art pieces to know that they were the poor relation of the art world. But there was something about these paintings that soothed her – their soft lines, luminosity and dreamy colour palettes – and this particular landscape, a night-time scene of Venice that had drained the city's life and vibrancy and replaced it with grey melancholy, seemed to reflect her mood perfectly.

'How are you?' asked a voice behind her. She felt a hand on her shoulder and spun round to see who it belonged to.

'Adam, you scared me,' she said, bringing a hand up to her chest. She was surprised to see him, even though they had arranged to meet in this very spot.

'Lost in thought?'

'Something like that.'

'I'm a bit late. Sorry.'

He kissed her lightly on the cheek, and as she drew close to him, she could see that he was out of breath, as if he had been in a rush. She wondered where he had been, what he'd had to leave, feeling suddenly quite selfish that she had called him that morning and asked to meet. She had done it immediately after her session with Olga Shapiro, not wanting to procrastinate, feeling the importance of seeing him quite acutely, not realising, or perhaps caring, that it was a Friday night and he almost certainly had better things to do with his time than see his grieving sister-in-law.

'No, no, I was late myself,' she lied, not wanting to reveal that she had arrived at the museum an hour early. After leaving Greg and Rachel in the City, she had wandered around Knightsbridge for a couple of hours, browsing but not seeing the pretty clothes in Harvey Nichols, succumbing to brief moments of normality as she wandered aimlessly around Harrods, only to remind herself that her husband was dead which made her feel ashamed and frivolous for even being there. The museum had felt like a more restful and sombre place to sit it out and wait for Adam.

'I didn't know this place was open at this time.'

'It's not that late.'

'It's late enough. I feel like Ben Stiller in *Night at the Museum*,' he smiled.

'Well now you know. You can bring all your girlfriends here for Friday-night date night.'

'What girlfriends are we talking about here?' he said, loosening his tie and fastening his gaze on to hers.

'Come on, you must have some Victoria's Secret model tucked away in London,' teased Diana, reminding herself that she was under instruction to try and smile this evening.

'Are you saying I have a type?'

'I read *People* magazine.'

'You must be confusing me with someone else,' he said idly.

'Portraits are just through here,' she said as they reached the end of the gallery.

'Do you come here often?' he grinned. He had a good smile. Sincere and broad. The two Denver brothers looked a lot alike, the chief difference being that Adam smiled more. In his smart suit, he looked like a mischievous best man at a wedding about to play a trick on the groom.

She ignored his teasing reference to a chat-up line.

'I love this place. When I first moved to London, I didn't have any money, any direction. I lived in this cold, damp flat and I used to bring Charlie to all the free places where we could keep warm. The V&A was one of his favourites. I know kids aren't supposed to like museums, but he was fascinated by all the silver and twinkly things.'

'Something in common with my mother, then.'

Diana giggled. Barbara Denver was rumoured to have a diamond collection to rival Elizabeth Taylor's.

A sixty-something couple shot a disapproving look at her laughter.

'Are we not allowed to talk in this place?' whispered Adam.

'Some people think not.'

'Quiet places always make me nervous,' he said, glancing around at the Old Master oils. 'Particularly when we have all these eyes staring down at us.'

'Let's go somewhere else then,' she said, feeling a dart of complicity between them.

'How about China?' he said, running his finger down the directions board and picking one at random. He put his hand on the small of her back and directed her downstairs towards the T. T. Tsui gallery, housing all the museum's Far East artefacts. It was noisier down here. There was a pop-up bar in the foyer and an African band were playing something vibrant. Usually it would have represented everything Diana loved about London, but tonight it didn't feel right. How dare all these people be having fun, enjoying life with a drink and an exotic soundtrack when she was still reeling from Julian's death, still trying, but failing, to get her head round the idea that she would never see her husband again?

'So how long are you staying in London for?'

For the past two years Adam had been based in New York, after he had taken up the role of president of the Denver Hotel Group. Julian had described it as the perfect job for his brother, who had struggled to find a niche for himself in the family company. Considered too irresponsible for a main board position, he had drifted around the outskirts of the company, doing event organising, PR and communications, until he had been seconded to the hotel division and found his groove. Twelve months earlier, Julian had told Diana with some pride that profits in Adam's new division had increased by twenty-three per cent.

'A while. Possibly permanently.'

'Permanently? You're leaving New York? Leaving the hotel division?'

'I can work from Europe for now. It's not a problem.'

'But I thought you loved it in New York. You have that lovely house.' He had just bought a beautiful brownstone in Brooklyn Heights, with views right over Manhattan, and no one would have enjoyed New York's party scene and pretty girls more than Adam.

'I do, but Dad says I'm going to have to step up to the plate.'

'CEO?' she said with surprise.

'A comedown from president, I know.' Another smile. 'But there's been a Denver at the head of the company since it was founded eighty years ago, and Dad wants it to stay that way,' he continued with none of his usual verve and swagger.

'Do you want it?'

'I could never replace Julian.'

'I didn't mean that . . . I just always got the impression you never wanted the job.'

'I don't. Not really. Besides, Elizabeth is gunning for that gig, is probably lobbying the executive committee as we speak, none of whom are going to take me particularly seriously even if my father has a majority voting share in the business and suddenly goes mad and wants to give me the job. But, you know, maybe I need a project. I don't mean the CEO's job, but something big to get my teeth into. Something to help me forget.'

For a moment Diana forgot about her own grief and thought about Adam and Elizabeth; siblings were often overlooked in favour of partners and parents in the condolences pecking order.

'What are you in town for?' he asked more cheerfully, clearly wanting to change the subject.

'I went to see Greg Willets with Rachel.'

'How is he?'

'He sent me a lovely note.'

'I bet you've had a lot of those.'

'But seeing him today made me feel a bit sad.'

'Why?' asked Adam, looking puzzled.

Diana knew it was the chance to articulate the feelings she had had at lunchtime with someone she trusted.

'I worry that I'm not going to have an excuse to see people like Greg for very much longer, and I hate that, because I know that the second I stop seeing Julian's friends, his colleagues, stop talking about him, is the second he really dies.'

'Then keep seeing them, keep talking about him,' replied Adam fiercely. 'No one wants him to fade away. We won't let him.'

'It's going to be hard keeping plugged in when I'm at Somerfold.'

'Then you should come to London more often. Move back here. You've got the house in Notting Hill.'

'I'm not moving back to that place.'

Adam nodded, comprehending her feelings for the spot where Julian had ended his life.

'You know the company has a couple of apartments. For executives. I could set you up there with one phone call. I'm in one, in fact. They are quite nice. Just off the King's Road. Hey, we'd be neighbours.'

'But it wouldn't be my home,' said Diana, though she had to admit to herself that it sounded quite a nice idea. 'Home is the best place for me right now.'

They both decided they needed a drink, and went into the café. The place was full of pretty, arty-looking girls, who gave Adam discreet second glances as he stood in the queue buying their two cups of coffee. Diana doubted they recognised him from the society pages, but there was something about him that made you want to look twice. He was certainly not as good-looking as Rachel's diving colleague in Thailand, or as poised and elegant as Julian. Perhaps it was the way he filled out a suit, the glint in his eyes that promised fun, his easy, flirtatious charm as he talked to the waitress. He caught her looking at him and she glanced away.

The café was busy and it was a warm evening, which made sitting outside even more tempting. The gardens looked quite lovely. The summer sky was beginning to darken, casting long shadows around the courtyard, but light spilled out of the museum's long windows, turning the central reflecting pool a thousand shades of bronze and gold.

Many of the tables around the perimeter were occupied. Adam found a single iron chair and took it to the edge of the water, beckoning Diana to sit on it, and then crouched down on the step by her feet.

'Good cake,' he said, tearing into a slice of banana loaf. 'Want some?'

She shook her head and sipped her coffee.

'I don't want to hear it,' pressed Adam, forcing her to take some. 'Cake is one of life's great pleasures.'

As the sleeve of his jacket brushed against her bare leg, she shivered. She closed her eyes and thought of Julian. The morning after his death, she had found an old, unwashed T-shirt of his, one that had been recently worn and had not yet been through the laundry, and she had slept with it until it no longer smelt of him, but of her own perfume, soap and sweat. It was one of a few things she had done to try and feel connected with him – looking at old photographs, listening to his favourite CDs – but right now, through physical contact with his brother, she felt closer to her husband than she had been since his death.

She opened her eyes and returned to the present. For a moment they were both quiet, as if they had run out of conversation.

'Julian taught me how to swim,' said Adam finally. 'How to sail, how to tie a slip knot. Did you know I tie really good knots?'

'He taught me a lot too. Too many things to even mention,' she said, feeling her eyes well with tears. She touched Adam's shoulder. 'Thank you for being so good to me at the funeral.'

He nodded, as if the memory of that day was just too painful.

'When's the memorial service?'

'Six weeks' time. Elizabeth is after St Paul's.'

'Cathedral?'

'Where else?'

'Julian would have hated that.'

'Clinton will be invited. And the Beckhams.'

'But he'd have liked that,' she smiled. Her husband had been a huge football fan, and considered Clinton a great political hero, despite his indiscretions.

'How's Rachel?'

'You know she's back in London . . .'

'Good news travels fast.'

'I need to know why he died.'

121

'I know. She's good,' he said quietly. 'Besides, if the last two weeks have taught us one thing, it's that life's too short to bear grudges.'

She was grateful for his words. Everyone else had made her feel as if she was wrong or weak or plain idiotic for welcoming her sister back into her life.

'I'm sorry for calling you this morning.'

'Sorry? What on earth for?'

'When I said I had to see you. It was a bit dramatic. Sorry if I worried you; it's just that I went to see a therapist this morning and she said I should be around people that make me smile.'

'Is that an insult or a compliment?' he asked, looking up at her.

'Oh, it's a compliment.'

He hesitated. 'I'm glad you rang. Just being here with you makes me think that Julian is going to come walking through that door any minute.'

'It's a good feeling, isn't it, for the few seconds before you realise he's not.'

He slapped his palms against his thighs and stood up.

'Apparently it's my mission to cheer you up, so why don't we do something about it? Maybe we should go clubbing.' He said it as if the idea had just presented itself.

Diana laughed. 'I haven't been clubbing since the nineties.'

'So what? Do you want to?'

'My therapist said I should do fun stuff, but I'm not sure that clubbing is entirely appropriate. Or what the doctor ordered.'

'Did she have any suggestions, because I'm all out of ideas about how to feel better.'

'She said we should go fly a kite.'

'That might cause terrible problems on the Cromwell Road,' he laughed.

She watched him glance at his watch.

'Do you have to be somewhere? It's the fourth time you've looked at your watch in the last ten minutes. Hot date?'

'No.'

'*Adam.*'

'There's nothing.'

'Tell me.'

He looked at her with the realisation that he'd been caught out.

'All right, there's a meeting at the Mandarin Oriental . . .'

She looked at her own watch. They hadn't even been here an hour.

'Then what are you doing here still? Go,' she said, waving her hand frantically.

'My assistant can handle it.'

'What's the meeting?' she pressed.

'Qatari investors. I might be buying some hotels off them.'

'You can't blow them off.'

'I can,' he replied unconvincingly.

'I should be going home anyway.'

'You sure you don't want to go clubbing?' His face was as soft and apologetic as a naughty puppy's.

'No.'

'Dinner?'

'No.'

It was so tempting to say yes. She didn't fancy clubbing or dinner, but right now all she wanted to do was sit by this pool and watch the ripples and feel the warmth of someone besides her who knew exactly what she was going through, and who cared enough to drop whatever he was doing to come and see her.

'In which case, do you mind?' he said, already straightening his tie and smoothing out the creases in his trousers.

'It's been good to see you, Adam.'

He kissed her cheek and she noticed how good he smelt.

'We'll do it again, all right?'

'I'd like that very much indeed.'

16

Rachel sat on the train and smiled to herself. A twenty-something couple sitting opposite her started kissing, then pulled apart and giggled, their eyes locked, oblivious to the people around them: happy and in love. She caught the expression of a City gent standing peering down at them: the curl of the lip and the roll of the eye. A few years ago, Rachel knew she would have thought the same, but things had changed since then. A lot of things. She closed her eyes and thought about that night in Thailand, her lips on Liam's, the smell of him, his hot breath on her skin.

Yeah, a lot of things have changed, she thought, opening her eyes. *And not all for the better.*

She was glad the day was almost over. Meetings with both her mother and Greg Willets had left her feeling raw. She wanted to see a friendly face. Not that she was guaranteed that at the other end of her journey. Rachel hadn't seen Ross McKiney in three years, and they hadn't parted in the best circumstances; she wasn't at all sure what sort of reception she would get.

She got off at Clapton station, squinting in the early evening sun. Across the road was a fried chicken outlet, a minimart and a booth proclaiming 'We unlock all phones'. This was not the fashionable part of the East End, made hip by art and music or gentrified by the presence of the Olympic Park, and given that it would be getting dark soon, it was a little scary.

Come on, Rach, she scolded herself, stealing a look at her A to Z. She'd walked around the back streets of Bangkok; this was Beverly Hills by comparison. Following her map, she came to an estate, a mixture of sixties terraces and tower blocks that made her quicken her pace, and within a few minutes she was outside an end-of-row house with a wonky gate and a rusty motorbike in the tiny front yard.

She knocked, and as the door creaked open, a ball of fluff slid out of the house, brushing past her leg. Ross McKiney stood in the door frame in jeans and an old jumper.

'You have a cat.' Rachel smiled at her old friend.

'Things change. You know that, look at you. Hair, short?'

'Men don't usually notice that sort of thing.'

'I'm just your typical metrosexual,' he said as his face slowly creased into a smile. He reached out and pulled her into a hug. 'Come on into the palace,' he said, ruffling the top of her hair.

She followed him inside, blinking in the gloom.

'You'll have to excuse the mess, maid's day off and all that.'

It was a small living room, dominated by an overlarge Dralon sofa. It had the air of having been recently – and hurriedly – tidied, but no amount of hoovering could disguise the peeling wallpaper and the faint smell of cat pee. Rachel felt awkward standing here in his private space. No, not just awkward, guilty. Over the last three years, she had barely spoken to Ross McKiney, despite the fact that they had once been such good friends. She had written to him several times in jail, and had begun emailing him when he was released. Both types of communication were rarely answered. For months there would be nothing, then long, unpunctuated, rambling replies talking about things and people she had never heard of. She looked at her old friend; his hairline had receded since they had last met, his mouth scored with heavy smoker's lines. Six months in prison had aged him by ten years at least. She wondered how she might have looked now if she hadn't had such a good lawyer.

'Sit down,' said Ross, and Rachel perched on the edge of an armchair. 'Nice tan, by the way. What on earth possessed you to leave Paradise?'

Rachel laughed, and felt herself relax a little. She and Ross had been close once – as her favoured investigator and fix-it man, he had worked side by side with her on dozens of stories. He was ex-forces, off-the-book intelligence; he could extract computer files, obtain criminal records within the hour and had a hotline to the most ruthless paparazzi. He was like a cut-price James

Bond, but you'd never know to look at him. Broad nose, broader Midlands accent and a bit flabby around the middle, he looked like someone's dad at the school gates.

'All will be revealed if you want to put the kettle on,' she said, relaxing back in the chair. 'Got any Kit Kats?'

As Ross disappeared into the kitchen, Rachel got out her notebook and pen. She would have been happy to spend time laughing and joking – you didn't sit for hours in a car staking out some politician's house, fuelled by Lucozade and packets of prawn cocktail crisps, without developing an honest and easy friendship – but she knew that Ross would want to get straight down to business. He had always been no-nonsense; that was why he had been good at his job. In fact, when Rachel had seen him that day in court, before he was sentenced for phone-hacking – her newspaper's phone-hacking – he had just shrugged. 'Well, at least I'll be able to catch up on my knitting,' he had said.

Ross was a pragmatist; he knew someone had to go to jail for the scandal, but that didn't mean it wasn't hard for him. Rachel had spent the last three years wishing she could have done something more to help him. Wishing he hadn't been a scapegoat, not just for her, but for many others in the industry who hadn't merely known what he did, but had condoned and encouraged it. He was simply a contractor, someone the newspapers paid to do the leg-work on stories: surveillance, covert photography and, yes, phone-tapping. He was there to incubate the investigations, flesh them out; without private investigators, many stories would just remain as rumours.

Ross came back into the room and handed her a steaming mug.

'Listen,' said Rachel, 'I just wanted to say—'

'I know, I know.' He shrugged. 'You feel guilty, it shouldn't have been me, you wish it hadn't turned out the way it did.' He shook his head. 'I know, but it's all water under the bridge now, okay? I don't blame you.'

'I just wish that more of the bastards had suffered . . .'

She didn't want to name-check any of the senior journalists and management – they both knew who they were. The ones who had demanded juicier scoops to boost the paper's circulation, who were reckless about how stories were got hold of, but who had been quick to raise their hands in disbelief and say that they had had no idea that their staff had broken the law and phone-hacked to get their information. Who had been paid off with hefty retirement pots or shunted upstairs to escape the scandal when it had come home to roost.

'But they didn't, did they?' said Ross. 'And it wouldn't have made me feel any better if you'd gone down too, hand on heart, Rach. So let's move on, okay?'

He took a Kit Kat out of his pocket and threw it towards her.

'Have your sugar fix, then you can start to tell me about Julian.'

'How do you know this is about my brother-in-law?' She hadn't told him on the phone.

'I do still read the papers, Rachel. Julian Denver commits suicide, two weeks later you appear on my doorstep; it doesn't take Sherlock Holmes to put two and two together.'

'Diana asked me to find out what happened.'

'He killed himself, didn't he? Your sister doesn't suspect foul play, does she?'

Rachel shook her head. 'No, but she wants to know why. According to Diana, he was happy, looking forward to the future. Things happen for a reason, especially things as awful as suicide, and she's angry and sad and bewildered that she doesn't know what that reason was.'

'And she doesn't trust the inquest to find out.'

She nodded, knowing that an investigator as experienced as Ross would be able to fill in the gaps. They had both attended inquests in the name of work, and knew that open verdicts were quite regularly recorded in cases like this, which was often both heartbreaking and frustrating for the families concerned.

Ross looked thoughtful. 'What do the police think?'

Rachel hadn't had time to see the investigating officer in person yet, although she had spoken to an Inspector Mark Graham on the phone. 'Straightforward suicide, no reason to think otherwise,' she confirmed. 'The house had CCTV surveillance – no one came in or out, only Julian and Diana in the house.'

He looked at her, eyebrows raised.

127

'No, Ross. They don't think she killed him either.'

'She'd have enough motive,' said Ross cynically.

'Ross, this is my sister.'

'Okay, okay, just saying,' he said, raising a palm. 'You were the one who always insisted on looking at every angle on a story.'

'This isn't a "story". Julian was my brother-in-law. It's personal. I want to know why he did it too.'

'Mind if I get something stronger?' he said, pointing at his tea.

'Not for me.'

She watched him get up and go to a small drinks cabinet. He pulled out a bottle of Scotch and poured himself a measure. He had always been a big drinker, but that was almost half an IKEA tumbler full of neat Famous Grouse.

'How's life treating you, Ross?' she asked when he sat down.

'A spell in jail doesn't exactly help one's employment prospects . . .'

'Have you found anything?'

'Couple of shifts behind the bar at the local pub, plus I was thinking of signing on for a course to retrain as a plumber, although you wouldn't believe how expensive college fees are for mature students.'

'Well, I might be able to help you out there.'

He looked at her with interest.

'I need help,' she added. 'Help to find out what was going on in Julian's life. Money is no object. Diana will pay a generous fee, plus any expenses . . .'

'Well, it's not as if my diary's full.'

Rachel grinned.

'Tell me what you know,' he said, leaning forward and resting his elbows on his knees.

'Aren't you going to ask how much I'm paying you?'

'It'll be more than my pub shifts, believe me.'

She ran her finger down the foil of her chocolate bar and began to tell him about the past forty-eight hours, finishing her story at around the same time as he had drained his Scotch.

'So you've not got much then,' he said flatly.

She frowned. 'I thought the woman in Washington was interesting.'

'Most likely a hooker. Especially if he wasn't getting much sex at home. A leopard doesn't change his spots and all that.'

'Even if it was a hooker, it would show there were cracks in the marriage.'

Ross scoffed. 'Men like Julian don't have affairs because there's something wrong with their marriages. They have sex with other women because they can.'

There was a few seconds' silence as Ross seemed to turn things over in his mind.

'So what do you think, Rach? Your instincts were always pretty sound.'

'I think he was weak, for a start. He had an eye for the ladies. Plus I think that the CEO role at Denver Group was a big, stressful job and maybe he just buckled under the pressure. He'd been groomed all his life for it – what if he couldn't handle it?'

'I'm no rich guy, but I've spent enough time following them around and I've never seen much mental weakness. They all think they're God's gift.'

'He did suffer from depression when he was at university,' said Rachel.

'Twenty-odd years ago?' Ross pulled a face. 'No disrespect to your sister, but that sounds like someone trying to find a convenient reason, not the real one.'

Rachel looked at her friend, heard the passion in his voice. There was more colour in his face, and his hands were moving around excitedly. It was as if he was coming alive before her eyes.

'So what is the real one?' she asked.

'That their marriage was horrible? Maybe *she* was screwing around on *him*?'

'Ross!'

'If you're going to do this properly, you need to examine all the possibilities, not just the ones that you feel comfortable with. It's the only way to get to the truth. Then all you have to work out is what to tell your sister.'

'What do you mean?'

'Diana wants resolution, not the truth,' said Ross plainly. 'Don't put her through any more pain.'

'I think you've missed this,' she said finally.

'No, I've missed you, Rachel Miller. Even if you do drive me round the bend.'

'I've missed you too, you old goat.'

'What do the family think?'

'I haven't talked to them yet, but Diana seems to think they are blaming the depression. She doesn't really believe it, but secretly I think that's the answer she wants to hear.'

'Well she's not going to want to hear that he killed himself because their marriage was so bad. No one wants to hear that. So where do you want me to start?' asked Ross.

'Check out this woman in Washington.' She reached into her bag and pulled out a fat envelope. 'You should also look through these. Copies of Julian's bank statements from various accounts. I want you to see if I've missed anything.'

'What did you find?'

'Apart from my astonishment at how someone can spend £4,650 at a cigar shop, there were a couple of interesting things.'

'Payments to a Washington lingerie store? A transvestite brothel?'

She laughed. 'Wouldn't that make life so much easier?'

'Well, if we're settling in, I'd better get myself another drink.'

'Ross, go easy.'

'You sound like my ex-wife.' Ross had separated very shortly after his imprisonment and divorced twelve months later.

'How is she?'

'Okay,' he replied without conviction. 'Getting ready to move to Cape Town. She's got married again; they're all moving out there.'

Rachel frowned. 'That guy Phillip? She's only been with him two minutes.'

'Try two years.'

'But what about the kids?' she said, glancing at a picture of two teenagers on the TV cabinet. 'Don't you have any say in it? She can't just take them to South Africa, surely?'

'Sure, I could object. I could spend the money I don't have on lawyers' fees, but the truth is, Phillip's a nice guy. Good job, stable, everything Kath's always wanted. And, well . . . the kids don't like coming here. You can't really blame them, can you?'

His expression wasn't bitter, just sad, like a man defeated. She wondered if this was the right time to tell him about her life in Thailand. How she had turned things around, made a new life for herself without the people she loved in it.

'Do you want to talk about it?' she asked.

'I want to work,' he said simply. 'Work gets you through.'

She could only nod in agreement.

They sat down at his cramped dining table and Ross cleared the piles of magazines and papers to make a space. Dark had fallen while they were talking, so he switched on an old anglepoise lamp, reminding Rachel of the newsroom late at night when she had burnt the midnight oil for a story.

'Let's have a look,' said Ross, bending over the statements.

Rachel pointed to an entry she had underlined in black ink. 'This is one that jumped out at me. A payment to Flypedia, the travel booking company, on one of his credit card bills.'

'Why is that unusual?'

Rachel had given this some thought. 'Well, why was he booking flights himself? He travelled a lot, but there's hardly any other payments to anything travel-related. Diana told me that Denver Group have a travel agency and everything went through that, not his personal account – besides which, the company has a private jet; why not just use that?'

'Family holiday? Romantic mini-break for him and Diana?'

Rachel smiled. 'Men never book holidays, Ross, it's always the wife or girlfriend. Anyway, Diana told me they use a concierge service. Look: there're dozens of payments to them.'

'You're right.' He frowned. 'This one does seem random. Maybe he had to book something himself quickly.'

'Exactly – but it feels like an off-the-books payment, doesn't it?'

'Hack's instinct – it doesn't leave you, does it?' smiled Ross.

Rachel swiped playfully at his arm, but she couldn't help but feel excited; it was like slipping back into something comfortable, something natural. When she had first started in print journalism, she honestly couldn't imagine herself doing anything else. From the very first second she had barged into that newsroom, she had

131

just known this was what she wanted to do for the rest of her life. Even though she had spent more than a year running errands, making coffee and getting shouted at, she had loved every second of it – listening to the news desk, watching a story unfold, seeing the team jump into action when a news item was streamed through from Reuters or a tip-off. News was her drug and she had forgotten how much she loved it.

'If we could access his travel account, we could find out what this money is for,' she said. 'It's a few thousand, so it's probably flights. What we need to know is where to, and who for.'

She glanced up at Ross. They both knew what she was asking. He had been to prison for something very similar.

'Invasion of privacy of a dead man,' he mused. 'Where does the law stand on that these days?'

'His wife has asked me to do this,' said Rachel hopefully.

'Doesn't make it right.'

'Since when did you get all moral?'

'Not a question of morals, Rach. It's a question of what my probation officer will make of it.'

'Sorry, Ross, if it's going to put you in a difficult position . . .'

'Don't be daft,' he laughed, opening his laptop. 'I went to a prison packed with white-collar criminals – it was like going to the Open University for computer crime. Learnt an awful lot of new tricks. Used to have a team of hackers on speed-dial. Now I'm pretty sure I can do it myself.'

She grinned, beginning to feel a spot of headway.

'In which case, I had better leave you to it.'

17

Diana turned the dial into the red, feeling the water get hotter and hotter as it ran down her back. She twisted it again, her skin prickling in the now-scalding water, staying under the jet for as long as she could stand. Then she spun the tap in the other direction, all the way into cold, letting the icy torrent hit her, forcing herself to stay there for a moment longer. Finally she switched the shower off and bolted for the towel rail, wrapping herself in a fluffy robe.

The shower trick was something Rachel had taught her, some Scandinavian theory of how hot then cold could reset the body when you were feeling sluggish. Of course, Rachel had used it to combat hangovers, but Diana supposed the principle was the same. She could certainly do with a jump-start these days. She had always been an early riser, up with the lark to tend to Charlie or go to a gym class, but since Julian's death, she was finding it harder and harder to get up in the morning. Even on the days when she had spent all night awake, going over her thoughts and memories in the bed that was suddenly too big for her, it was easier to stay under the covers when daylight broke. Today it had been ten thirty before she could bring herself to crawl from beneath the duvet, and as the day stretched ahead of her like a dark, gaping hole, it was very tempting to creep back again.

She jumped at a thumping on the door.

'Diana!' Her mother put her head into the bathroom, her voice high-pitched with irritation. 'Mrs Bills has been calling you for five minutes. You have a visitor. Adam Denver.'

Her body was still goose-bumped from the cold shower, but she felt a shimmer of warmth at the mention of his name.

'Adam's here now?' she asked, feeling suddenly panicky. 'Get rid of him. I'm practically naked.'

'Well get dressed,' her mother whispered back. 'I can't very well send him away now, can I?'

Diana hurriedly smoothed her hair back and wrapped her robe tighter, then stepped into the bedroom. She gasped when she saw Adam standing in the doorway.

'Is this a bad time?' he asked, looking embarrassed.

'No, yes. No,' she stuttered. 'Of course not.'

'Perhaps I should wait downstairs?' he said.

'We'll grab some coffee,' said Sylvia. She touched him on the arm, and Diana realised, with horror, that she was flirting with him.

'Is everything okay?' he asked, keeping a respectful distance at the door. He glanced at Sylvia, who took the message to leave the room.

They listened to her footsteps getting softer and softer down the stairs.

'I'm sorry about running off yesterday,' he said when she was out of earshot.

'You had a meeting.'

'I don't want you to think I abandoned you . . .'

'Don't be silly. I hope you've not driven all this way to apologise for that.'

'No, I've driven all the way here to see if you'd like to come for lunch.'

'I should probably get dressed then.' She smiled slowly.

'Yeah – I'm not sure how well white towelling would go down on *Vogue*'s best-dressed list.'

She felt her cheeks colour.

'Shoes. Wear running shoes.'

'Where are we going? The athletics track?'

'It's a surprise. I'll see you downstairs in ten minutes.'

Diana pulled on some jeans, a short-sleeved bottle-green cashmere top and a pair of trainers.

'Where are you two heading off to?' asked Sylvia with evident curiosity.

'Apparently we're going running.'

134

'In *cashmere?*' said her mother with surprise.

It was late morning and the sun was climbing in preparation for another warm day. Diana couldn't remember an unbroken string of sunny days like it, and whilst she knew that the weather would never be able to shift her grief, the feeling of the sun on her face was a good one. Of strength and of hope.

'How were the Qataris?'

'We've got a deal.'

'Then I'm glad we didn't go clubbing.'

Adam's car was parked on the drive. It was a beauty, one that Julian, with his own collection of vintage Ferraris, had himself coveted. A 1960s convertible Aston Martin. Diana considered it a James Bond car and always thought it suited its owner perfectly.

'I thought you had this shipped to America.'

'No, it's been at my parents'.'

'It's beautiful,' she said, stroking the silver paintwork.

'There's no better way of getting from A to B than in this baby,' he grinned.

'So where's B?'

'I thought we'd drive to the coast. Figured some sea air might do us good.'

'The sea is quite a long way from here, you know,' she said, climbing into the passenger seat.

'Well I haven't got any plans for the rest of the day, unless you have.'

They took the back roads to the coast, threading through south Oxfordshire, Wiltshire and down into Dorset, through quaint, gorgeous countryside that Adam described as Hardy country. The roof of the car was down so that the sun warmed Diana's shoulders, and the wind blew her hair out in a ribbon behind her head and rattled around their ears so that they did not need to talk.

Perhaps it was what they both needed – time out to clear their heads. It was good to get out of the house, somewhere far away, some place that Diana hadn't been before, unconnected with memories of Julian. She was loath to admit it to herself, but she had not lived a very big life since she moved to Somerfold. The house was enormous, but her horizons had compressed to a very small and confined space. The renovations had taken up the first eighteen months of her time there, but when they were completed there had been very little to occupy her time, other than trips to a Pilates studio in Henley, a photography course in the village and the occasional visit to London to see friends who all seemed to have moved on with their lives since she had left Notting Hill. The irony that she had left London to live a more fulfilled life, only to have it replaced by a gilded cage, wasn't lost on her.

After two hours, they stopped at a pub on the outskirts of Abbotsbury. Diana's face cracked open with a smile as she saw the glittering sea in front of her.

'The coast,' she said with glee as she looked out over a long finger of shingle.

'There's nearer coastline to your house, but nothing as special as this,' said Adam, opening the car door for her with impeccable manners.

'Where are we?'

'Chesil Beach,' he said, guiding her into the beer garden. 'I'm going inside to order. What do you fancy?'

'You choose,' she said, unable to tear her eyes away from the vista. It was quite perfect. To the left, the garden overlooked green fields striped with yellow shale which curved away from them over the rolling hill, dotted with farm buildings and meandering cattle; while in front of her the English Channel sparkled silver in the sun.

No wonder the place was so busy, she thought, her eyes scanning for a place to sit. It was past one o'clock on a summer Saturday, and the garden was already full. She spotted a wooden table away from the crowds and sat down as Adam brought out a jug of Pimm's complete with chunks of fruit.

'It's like a giant swimming pool,' she laughed, looking up and down the coastline.

'It's a lagoon.'

'How do you know about this place?'

'I went to boarding school a few miles down the road.'

'I thought you went to Harrow.'

'They expelled me,' he said cheerfully. 'The first of many.'

Diana only knew the broad strokes of Adam's tearaway youth. It was not something the family liked to dwell on, not something that fitted in with their usual success and order, and as she sat with him at their rickety table overlooking the coast, ready to hear his story, she realised that the two of them had had very few heart-to-hearts, spent very little time alone, even though the brothers had been quite close.

'How many schools did you leave?' she asked, pouring Pimm's into a glass.

'Three.' He grimaced.

The waitress came and put two club sandwiches on the table, and Adam waited until she had gone before he spoke again.

'You know I always wanted to be like Julian. Strong, capable, accomplished. He was a few years older than me. Too old to be my friend, so he became my hero. I wanted to be like him so much, but when I realised I never could, I must have subconsciously decided to be everything he wasn't. It was a philosophy that kind of got me into trouble.'

'You're very alike. I always thought that.'

'I don't think anyone else has ever shared that opinion.'

'You're more alike than you realise. Kind of different sides of the same coin.'

'My parents don't agree with you.'

She knew what it was like for a parent to have a favoured child. In their family it had been her, a state of affairs she had struggled to understand, struggled to accept; until the scandal, she had always felt a deep sense of guilt about it.

Not wanting to think about that, she tipped her head back and let the sun shine on her face.

'This place is amazing. I can't believe I've never been here before.'

'Never?' he said disbelievingly.

'I've been missing out.'

He gave a soft snort. 'You know, since Jules died, I've been thinking a lot about all the things I haven't done, all the things I want to do. Is that selfish?'

'No. It's only natural to think about your own mortality.'

He looked deep in thought.

137

'So what's on your bucket list?' she asked, picking at some lettuce. 'What are the things you've always wanted to do? Compared to most men, you've probably done a lot. Driven a Bond car. Slept with a *Sports Illustrated* cover girl . . .'

He didn't deny it.

'There's loads of stuff I've not done. I know I've got money, and that's great, but I just haven't got my arse into gear to do things.'

'Like what?'

'Take a motorbike across Asia.'

'Then do it.'

'Fly to the edge of space. Maybe in one of those F-14s or Russian MiG jets. Pretend I'm Maverick in *Top Gun*.'

'Surely you know Tom Cruise. He might be able to sort you out.'

'I want to see a volcano erupt, camp in the Arctic – you know, man versus nature. I want to free-dive.'

She opened her mouth to tell him that this was one of Rachel's great loves, but stopped short of revealing it. It had often occurred to her that Adam and her sister would be a good match, and she had thought about subtly setting them up. But every time, she had found some excuse not to. True enough, in those early days she wasn't even sure that she liked Adam. He was self-confident in a way that made her feel inadequate, with a reputation as a commitment-phobe, and her sister did not deserve a man like that. Or secretly, deep down, did she not *want* her sister to have a man like that? A man even more handsome and charismatic than her own husband. Was that an unspoken truth between sisters? That you wanted them to have the best of everything so long as it wasn't better than yours.

'And I want to get married. Have a family,' added Adam, polishing off his sandwich in just a handful of bites.

That one nearly knocked her off her seat.

'*You're* broody?'

'It's pure ego,' he teased. 'It's just what the world needs – Adam Denver mini-mes running around brightening the place up. What about you?' he added more softly.

138

She shrugged and smiled, wondering why she had never played this game before. After all, she and Julian had had the money to do whatever they fancied.

'See Ayres Rock at sunrise. Get a degree. Go to a lap-dancing club.'

He almost spluttered on his Pepsi. 'You're a dark horse . . .'

'Rachel lived in Soho for a while. She always used to make it sound so exciting. She knew all these crazy people. Sometimes I think I need a walk on the wild side.'

'You might find it's overrated.'

She felt exhilarated by the conversation. For just a few moments life was full of possibilities once again, and there seemed an urgency about it.

'Is that it?' he asked after a few moments.

There was one thing she wondered if she would ever do, but she didn't dare voice it aloud.

She wondered if she would ever recover from the death of her husband, if she would ever meet anyone new.

'That's it,' she said, wiping the corner of her mouth with a napkin.

They talked for another twenty minutes about Adam's latest hotel purchase from the Qataris – a string of grand dame hotels in some of the world's top cities – and as he spoke, Diana wondered why the Denvers had been so quick to dismiss him as the family clown.

'We should go,' said Adam when they had both finished their food. They got back into the car and drove along the coast through the village of Charmouth, taking a turn up a steep hill shaded on both sides by oak and poplar trees. It was a glorious day to be out in the country and a perfect day to forget your troubles and just be, thought Diana. Not worrying about yesterday or tomorrow, no inquest or investigation, just driving through beautiful scenery with someone she liked.

As she glanced across at him, watching him concentrating, observing his hands on the wheel, the same strong hands and lightly tanned forearms as Julian, she realised that the day was beginning to feel more like a date. The thought was unwelcome. It felt traitorous and wrong. And yet if she squinted, if she allowed herself to get swept away by the moment, it was like going back in time.

Back to her first date with Julian, an occasion that still brought a smile to her face. She had insisted on meeting him in Highgate Village. At the time she had been living with Charlie in a small flat in nearby Tufnell Park and had been too embarrassed for him to pick her up from where she lived. More particularly, she didn't want him to come inside and see the books and toys belonging to her six-year-old son. She had never denied Charlie's existence at work, but had felt it better to keep the fact that she had a child low-key. She loved her temporary admin job at the Denver Group and she didn't want to do anything to jeopardise it. Besides, she was realistic enough to know that being a single mum did not help your dating prospects, no matter how attractive men found you.

It had been a warm Saturday, much like this one. Julian had been wearing chinos and a white shirt, and she had been pleased to see that he looked nervous. She knew she was playing with fire dating Julian Denver. Not only was he the boss, but she had also heard through the secretarial rumour mill of his reputation with the ladies. He had led her to his car and she had half expected him to take her into town – to one of the flashy restaurants or hotels she knew his sort frequented. But instead they had driven the short distance to Hampstead Heath. They had sat outside Kenwood House with ice creams and gone to the Spaniards Inn for lunch, when Julian had told her all the folk tales and legends associated with the pub. How Keats had written his most famous poem here. How Dick Turpin had stopped here for a tankard of beer. How the owners – two brothers – had ended up duelling over a lover.

She and Julian had just clicked. And when he'd driven her back to Tufnell Park, without even asking her address, finally admitting that he'd looked it up on the human resources database, she knew that their fledgling romance had a future.

Much as she hadn't wanted the evening to end, she hadn't invited him into her flat. She'd played it right all day and didn't want to ruin everything by having him step on a plastic fire engine. Years later, when she knew him better, she saw that it

140

had been a clever move. Julian wasn't used to being turned down, and he loved a challenge. Diana's apparent reticence made him all the more intrigued, the one woman in London who seemed to be able to resist him. Inadvertently, she had played it perfectly.

'Here we are,' said Adam, stopping the Aston Martin in a small dusty car park on top of the hill.

Diana stood and waited for him to unload a navy nylon bag from out of the boot.

'What's that?'

'You'll see,' he said, putting it under his arm and striding ahead.

He led her up a shady path. On either side was a sun-dappled wood, bursting with summer flowers. Butterflies and insects flitted through the dusty beams of light breaking through the leaves. Ever since Julian's death, Diana had found it hard to see the beauty in things. But this was perfect.

At the top of the hill they came out of the wood and the ground fell away; they were standing on the edge of a steep drop, with a view out over the Dorset hills, and off in the distance the hazy blue of the coast.

'Look at it,' said Diana, feeling the wind on her face.

'I thought you'd like it,' grinned Adam. 'We used to run around here when I was at school. I hated cross-country. You'd come up here rain and shine, but no matter how much your legs were hurting and your lungs were crying out for mercy, this view would kind of pull you out of it.'

She watched him unzip the carrying case.

'A kite,' she said, feeling lightened.

'No idea how to use the bloody thing.'

She couldn't imagine where he had got a kite from since last night, but she was glad that he had.

He took hold of the frame and walked backwards with it, instructing Diana to keep hold of the string. When he was far enough away, he launched it into the air and Diana paid out the line, shrieking with glee as the kite soared higher and higher into the sky, dancing around the gulls, stretching to touch the clouds.

'Go on! Run with it!' he shouted, his voice muffled on the breeze. 'But stay away from the edge.'

The kite was flapping wildly, and as she ran as fast as she could, she could feel a little of her dark mood lift out of her into the air.

Finally the kite tumbled back to earth. Diana was too emotional to speak.

'We should probably be getting back,' said Adam, squinting at the sun as though he was gauging the time like an ancient mariner. She felt a stab of disappointment, and wondered where he had to run off to this time.

'The traffic will be murder.'

It was almost seven o'clock by the time they arrived back at Somerfold. As they drove past the lake, they saw the lights on at the boathouse and an unfamiliar car pulling up outside.

'Rachel must have a visitor,' mused Diana out loud.

Adam stopped the Aston outside the main entrance. He hopped out of the vehicle and opened the door for Diana.

'Are you coming in?' she asked hopefully.

'I have to get back to London.'

She smiled, hoping to mask her disappointment.

'Well, thank you,' she said finally.

'You're very welcome,' he said.

'Thank you for showing me that days don't have to be so dark.'

He stepped forward and planted a light fraternal kiss on her forehead.

'You're shivering.'

'It's cold when the sun goes down,' she said, not wanting to meet his gaze.

He said his goodbyes and she stood at the door of Somerfold until his tail lights had disappeared from sight.

18

'Bloody hell, I feel like I've come on a mini-break,' said Ross McKiney, standing in the doorway of the boathouse, casting his eyes from side to side to take it all in. 'Look at this place. It's like something from one of those posh interiors magazines.'

'Gorgeous, isn't it?' smiled Rachel, beckoning him inside. 'Although I think I'm only here because Diana doesn't want me in the big house. This is supposed to be my punishment.'

'I wouldn't mind some punishment like this,' said Ross, his eyes still wide.

Rachel shook her head. 'Anyone would think you've never seen a tree before,' she teased.

'We don't have trees where I live,' said Ross. 'Council cuts.'

'Let me open the doors,' she said, pulling back the floor-to-ceiling plate glass so that balmy evening air tumbled into the house. She was willing to bet that Ross hadn't been on a holiday in the last five years – the least she could do was make this evening as convivial as possible.

'I can't believe you've driven all the way out here,' she said, noticing that he'd had a haircut in the twenty-four hours since they had last met. He looked smart, professional, not the neglected, semi-employed hermit she had seen yesterday.

'You said daily updates.'

'A phone call would have done,' she grinned.

'You know me. I give you more bang for your buck.'

'That's what all the ladies say,' she teased, clearing the mess off the sofa so that he could sit down. 'So. I see you're driving. I have some zero-alcohol beer if you fancy one.'

'Go on. We can pretend.'

She went to the kitchen, returning with drinks and bowls of crisps and nuts. She hadn't found the local shop yet and had been subsisting on the snacks that Mrs Bills had originally left for her.

'Seen your mum yet?' asked Ross as he opened his laptop.

'Saw her the day I came to Clapton to see you.'

'So you survived the encounter?'

'Barely,' she replied. 'She's been avoiding me since I got back from Thailand. Diana engineered a meeting where she practically accused me of being Satan. She came back to Somerfold this morning. Curiosity couldn't keep her away, I bet.'

She watched Ross click open some files on the desktop.

'You've been busy.'

'I don't mess around,' he said.

Rachel gulped down her Becks Zero, anxious to see what he had come up with. She had been trying to do things the proper way – interviewing Julian's friends and colleagues, searching through his possessions – but she had yet to make a breakthrough. *By any means necessary*, she thought, looking at Ross and remembering an old maxim from the newsroom.

'So I managed to get into Julian's Flypedia account,' he said, sticking a pencil behind his ear.

'I won't ask how.'

'Here's what those payments you circled were for.' He started to read from the screen. 'One economy flight from Washington Dulles airport to London Heathrow in the name of Madison Kopek. Flight from Washington to Montego Bay also in the name of Madison Kopek. One flight London to Montego economy class in the name of Julian Denver. One return flight economy to Bucharest, Julian Denver.'

Rachel looked at him with puzzlement.

'Julian was flying economy? He was worth a few billion quid and he had a Gulfstream V. What the hell was he doing flying economy to Jamaica and Romania?'

'No idea what he was doing in Romania, but you can guess what he was up to in Jamaica.'

'A nice little assignation in the sun,' she said as her brain caught up with her mouth.

'And imagine you're well known, you've been in the papers, but you want to travel abroad without anyone noticing. If you're a high-profile billionaire like Julian, off to meet a lady friend, you just travel economy on a scheduled airline.'

Rachel whistled through her teeth, not wanting to speak ill of the dead.

'So who is Kopek? Have you tracked her down?'

Ross glanced at her. 'You can be bossy, you know that?'

Rachel smiled. It was funny how easily she and Ross had slipped back into their old working relationship. Blunt, to the point, dispensing with pleasantries, getting the job done. It felt good, she had to admit.

Ross clicked on a file, and an image of a young, beautiful, blue-eyed blonde filled the screen.

'Diana's basic nightmare,' said Rachel, knowing in the pit of her stomach that this was the woman Greg Willets had seen his friend with outside the Four Seasons.

'Not any more,' said Ross. 'She's dead.'

He pulled up another window: a small online newspaper report.

'Madison Kopek, twenty-one, a student from Maryland,' he read, 'was killed in a hit-and-run in College Park Thursday evening. Paramedics tried to revive her at the scene, but she was pronounced dead on arrival at hospital. Police are appealing for witnesses.'

Rachel read the full report. Her head was reeling as she tried to process all the information.

'So she died two days before Julian killed himself?'

'That's about the size of it.'

'Shit,' she whispered.

'Indeed.'

Rachel stood up and walked over to the window, the penny dropping with a dreadful thud.

'So let's assume Madison was a girlfriend; if Julian was in love with her, he could have been grief-stricken – that's enough of a reason for doing what he did.'

She pressed her fingertips against her temples. She had no idea how she was going to explain this to her sister, and knew instinctively that she had to protect her from it. She tried to make her mind twist the facts around to come to a more palatable conclusion.

'According to Diana, Julian seemed cheerful that night. He was talking about the future, making plans. If you were cut up about your dead mistress, how do you hide something like that?'

Ross gave a cynical laugh. 'He'd had enough practice, Rach. And anyway, if this Madison was his secret lover, who could he tell? For two days he would have had to carry all that grief, all that sorrow around on his own, keeping it locked inside.'

He bent to pull a file from his briefcase and handed it to Rachel. It contained all the information he had managed to gather on Madison Kopek. At the front were three different glossy photos, clearly professionally taken, perhaps for a modelling portfolio. She looked exactly as Rachel had imagined: wholesome, squeaky-clean beauty queen. Greg's story of Julian picking up hookers in hotel bars hadn't quite rung true for Rachel; he liked the nice things in life, shiny and new – there was nothing gritty or street-corner, even hotel-bar escort girl, about her brother-in-law. No, Madison was much more his style. And as she read, it confirmed her image of the girl. Madison Kopek was an honours student at the University of Maryland; smart and beautiful, easy to fall in love with. *What a terrible loss*, thought Rachel, *terrible for everyone involved*.

'Still, we don't know that Madison *was* Julian's lover,' she said, snapping the file shut.

'No, we don't,' agreed Ross. 'For all we know, Jamaica was some innocent business trip.'

'So why do it on the sly?' she said cynically. She could feel her frustration growing. Ross had always been uncanny in his ability to winkle out information; she had become accustomed to him knowing the answers to almost everything. 'Where now? We can't exactly quiz Madison Kopek about it.'

'At least show her photo to Greg Willets. Get him to confirm she was the girl he saw with Julian outside the hotel.'

Rachel made a mental note to do that first thing in the morning.

'And if it is her, then here's the town where her mother lives. I hear Maryland is lovely this time of year.'

19

Diana watched from the window as the car pulled away down the drive from the direction of the Lake House. Folding her arms tightly across her chest, she wondered who had been visiting her sister – in an ancient-looking Fiesta at that – on a Saturday night. She mulled over the possibilities in her mind. It was the same car she had seen arriving at the Lake House when Adam had dropped her off a little while earlier. Most likely it was an old friend or a colleague, although Somerfold seemed an awfully long way to come for just an hour – to stay such a short time suggested that it had been somebody come to deliver something. A piece of information? she wondered, feeling suddenly keyed up that Rachel was making progress with the job at hand. Curious, she pulled on a pair of wellington boots from beside the door and crunched down the gravel drive towards the lake, passing the aviary and sending up a flurry of wings and cheeping.

Usually she felt nervous wandering around the grounds in the dark. Somerfold was a lonely place without Julian and Charlie around, so much so that she had almost instantly regretted putting Rachel in the Lake House. But tonight, as a squirrel darted across the lawn, and the boathouse appeared through a gap in the trees, she felt as if she had been dropped in the middle of a fairy tale. Like many things that day, Diana suddenly saw the house in a new light. It looked magical, like a Hansel and Gretel cottage hidden in the woods. She was surprised to find herself smiling as she walked on. She did not usually look forward to her meetings with Rachel, but this evening she felt more relaxed and mellow, which she thought momentarily might be Adam's doing.

As she approached the house, she could see Rachel's silhouette on the window seat in the bedroom. Her head was bent over a book, her long legs stretched out in front of her, and Diana was struck by how serene and clever her sister looked.

She knocked gently. The door creaked open, just an inch at first, and she was met by Rachel's anxious smile.

'Hello, can I come in?'

'Of course. It's your house.' Rachel beckoned her in.

Diana frowned at the gloom inside the house. Her first thought was for her sister's eyesight, but standing here in the dark, she was also reminded of how spooky this part of the estate was at night. She wondered guiltily if Rachel was scared, if she should invite her up to stay in the main house, but then she remembered that Rachel Miller never got scared. Growing up, her courage and pluckiness was legendary among their little group of friends – Rachel was always the one to be pushed forward to do a dare, to retrieve a ball from an irate neighbour's garden. She had always been the first kid to jump off the top diving board, the first one to explore a derelict garage, pretending that she was Nancy Drew or George from the Famous Five in the midst of some intrepid adventure.

'It's dark in here,' said Diana finally. 'Can't we switch some lights on?'

'Habit.' Rachel grinned sheepishly. 'In Ko Tao, our office just has a little diesel generator. We're always trying to save electricity.'

'Do you remember at home, you'd leave every light on?' laughed Diana. 'Mum used to go mad.'

Rachel smiled. 'It's good to see you laugh, Di.'

Diana turned away. She nearly blurted out that it had been Adam who had put that smile on her face, but . . . well, she wasn't ready to think about that right now. Wasn't sure what sort of message it sent.

'Why don't you sit down and I'll go and make some tea.'

'Just hot water and lemon if you have it,' called Diana as Rachel moved out of sight. She looked around at the chaos of the cottage. Rachel had only been here a week, and already the Lake House looked like it had been sucked up by the tornado in *The Wizard of Oz*. There were socks on the floor, papers piled high on the desk and stuff hanging out of drawers. How was it possible to make such a small place so messy in such a short space of time? She resisted the urge to start tidying, instead resolving to send Mrs Bills down first thing in the morning for a swift clean.

'Builder's tea,' said Rachel, thrusting a mug into her hand. 'Sorry, I'm all out of lemons. But it's just how you used to like it.'

Diana narrowed her eyes, detecting a dig. *Chill out, Diana,* she reminded herself. *Don't ruin a lovely day over something silly.*

'I see Mum's back,' said Rachel, sipping her own tea. 'Saw her doing something strange on the lawn this morning.' She waved her free hand around in the air as if she were a wizard about to cast a spell.

Diana giggled, spraying a spot of tea on to her green cashmere top.

'That will be her t'ai chi.'

'Mum does t'ai chi?' said Rachel in amazement.

'She does a lot of things you might not recognise.' Diana smiled complicitly, for a moment enjoying the banter between them.

'Tell all.'

'There are a lot of charity committees. She's on the board of an inner-city youth ballet group, she's planning a fund-raising ball for the Tories, *and* she's taking a course in portraiture at an art college in Chelsea.'

'Bloody hell,' whistled Rachel. 'You couldn't even get her to join the PTA back in the day.'

'You should talk to her.'

'I've tried that.'

'Look, I know she can be a bit . . . inflexible at times, but don't you think we should all try and get along while we're living together?'

She was surprised to hear the conciliatory words coming out of her mouth. The last thing she'd expected was to find herself as the mediator between Rachel and her mother.

'Listen, there's a few bits of housekeeping things we need to discuss.'

Diana's eyes floated around the mess once more.

'Yes, I was thinking that.'

'Not that.' Rachel smiled. 'We need to talk about how expenses are going to work. I need to pay for a couple of flights. I'd do it myself, but booking at such late notice, we're talking over two thousand pounds, and that might be a bit of a stretch . . . well, a lot of a stretch actually.'

Diana felt disappointed that Rachel seemed so eager to revert to business matters.

'Don't worry about the money, I'll book the flights. What are they for?'

Rachel handed over a piece of paper with some hastily scribbled details written on it.

'Washington? Why do you need to go to Washington? And who's Ross McKiney? The man who just left?'

Rachel nodded. 'He's an old friend of mine. A private investigator. I thought I'd get him to help with some things. He's good, Di. Really good.'

'But why Washington?' she repeated, suddenly needing to know everything. 'Has he found anything out? Got a lead?'

Rachel waved a hand. 'We just need to go to the States to speak to some people about Julian.' She was being blasé. Overly blasé, and vague, as if she was hiding something. Diana could feel her fretfulness returning, the good mood of the day evaporating immediately.

'Who? Who do you need to speak to?' she pressed.

'I don't exactly know yet,' Rachel said haltingly. 'Ross is finding the contacts.'

Diana could feel her pulse throbbing. Why was her sister lying? She was doing her damnedest to try and hide it, but there was definitely something she didn't want to tell her.

'But if you don't know who you need to speak to, how do you know you need to go to Washington?'

Rachel gave a laugh. A nervous laugh she tried to disguise by sipping her tea.

'Diana, this is the way it works. Don't ask too many questions and I will tell you when I know stuff. I promise.'

'You don't have to shield me from anything, Rachel. The deal was I wanted to find out what had happened to Julian – that hasn't changed.'

But Rachel was equally firm. 'Just trust me, Di. Now, do you mind if I swim in the pool?' she said, standing up and looking out of the back window towards Somerfold.

'What? Now?' replied Diana, feeling confused – had she missed a part of the conversation? Why was Rachel talking about swimming all of a sudden? She got the distinct feeling that her sister wanted to get rid of her, and she certainly didn't want to talk about Washington.

'You've got a beautiful pool. I saw it when I was taking a walk this morning. I was desperate for a dip, but I thought Mum might see me and have a go, so I thought I had better ask your permission . . .'

Diana knew it was an opportunity to take a different tack.

'Okay,' she said quietly. 'Do you have a costume, or do you want to borrow one?'

'I brought one on the off-chance.'

'Well, go and get it. We can walk back up to the house together.'

As Rachel disappeared into the bedroom, Diana's eyes darted around the room. The desk by the window was a mess, a leaning tower of books and papers that looked as if it might topple at any moment.

'Do you have goggles?' shouted Rachel.

'Yes,' replied Diana, walking towards the desk and rifling quickly through the papers. There was a blue file by the laptop, held shut by elastic ribbons. She opened it and read the first piece of paper that presented itself. It was a printout of a news report about a car crash.

'What are you doing?' asked a voice behind her. Rachel stood in the doorway holding a swimsuit and a carrier bag.

'Who's this Madison Kopek?' asked Diana, wishing she'd had time to go through the whole file. She was sure that her sister had paled.

'It's just a news story, Di,' Rachel said, stuffing the costume into the bag. 'Come on, we should go before it gets totally dark.'

'Why is it here?'

151

Rachel shrugged. 'Ross left it.'

'So this girl is part of the investigation. Is it someone Julian knew?'

Rachel hesitated, as if she was taking a moment to construct a lie.

'Possibly. Like I say, we aren't entirely sure whether she's involved yet . . .'

'This accident happened in Maryland. Is that why you want to go to Washington?'

'Yes,' said Rachel finally.

'Then you must think she's significant,' Diana pressed. She felt warm. The paper was trembling in her hand. She didn't want her sister to say anything further, wanted to rewind the last two minutes and erase everything she had just learnt, and yet as she looked down at the picture on the printout, taking in the girl's blonde prettiness, she knew that Rachel had made a breakthrough, and she wanted to know exactly what it was.

The words *someone Julian knew* echoed over and over in her head. Yes, Madison Kopek looked exactly like the sort of girl Julian might have known, she thought, forcing herself to read the story once more.

'Diana, put it down,' said Rachel, walking over and snatching the page from her hand.

Diana's stomach clenched as she absorbed the date of the accident and acknowledged its relevance.

'But this girl's dead. She died two days before Julian.'

Rachel just nodded, her mouth pursed, as if she didn't want to say any more.

'Who *is* she, Rachel? What does she have to do with my husband?'

'I don't know yet,' said Rachel, her voice wobbling. 'There's a chance she might have been working with Julian.'

Diana had smelled blood and was not going to let this go.

'Working?' she repeated. 'And how closely do you think they were "working" together?'

'Diana . . .'

'Tell me what you think!' she yelled. She was surprised by the level of her own anger. No, it wasn't just anger, it was fury.

Right at that moment she hated this Madison person, she hated her dead husband and she hated her sister and her horrible, sticky web of secrets and lies.

'Diana, please,' said Rachel. 'I've only been working on this for three days, you can't expect me to know everything. These things take time.'

'Don't give me that crap,' said Diana, crumpling the paper in her hand. 'You think he was having an affair with this girl, don't you?'

'Di . . .'

'DON'T YOU?'

Rachel let out a long breath. 'It's a possibility, yes.'

'That's rubbish,' said Diana, stepping towards her sister, holding up the crumpled sheet. 'Julian was faithful. Ever since that time, he promised me. He said he'd never do it ever again, and I believed him.'

Rachel dropped the carrier bag to the floor with a thud.

'Di, please. Why did you bring me here if it's what you hadn't already suspected? You knew that something was going on in Julian's life that you didn't know about, that he didn't want you to know about.'

'I didn't think it would be another woman,' Diana lied. She began to pace around the Lake House. She felt dizzy, as if her world was turning on its axis and she had nothing to hold on to. 'Mum's right. This *is* a witch-hunt,' she said almost to herself.

'Di, come on. I'm doing a job.'

She felt powerless, out of control, and the only thing that made any sense was to turn all the anger, frustration and blame on her sister, because it was wrong to speak ill of the dead, wrong to think such a thing about her husband who was barely cold in the ground.

'Why did you hate him so much?' she said, feeling white-hot rage explode in her belly. 'Hmm? You never liked him, did you? Were you jealous, was that it?'

'Diana, this isn't helping . . .' said Rachel, but Diana could see the concern in her sister's eyes – the fear. And weirdly, it felt good, it felt powerful. She took another step forward, and even though she was almost four inches shorter than her sister and a much slighter physical presence, she forced Rachel to press back against the window.

'You hated him, why?'

'I didn't hate him.'

'Even now that he's dead in the ground, you have to think the worst of him, don't you?'

'No, Di, honestly, I was happy for you. I cried at your wedding and they were real tears of joy; you were going to have the life we never had. Why wouldn't I be happy?'

'Exactly!' cried Diana, pushing at her chest. 'Why weren't you happy? Why couldn't you leave us alone?'

Rachel barged past her, her expression changing.

'Because he wasn't good enough for you, Di!' she cried finally, her voice loud and clear as if it had been liberated from some place deep inside her.

'Why?' Diana's own tone was more anxious. She felt as if she was walking over cracked ice, as if at any moment it would break and she would plunge into the unforgiving icy depths beneath.

'Because he was a cheat, a womaniser. He always was. And men like that keep on cheating until they break you down. He wasn't good enough for you, for Charlie. And that's why I didn't fight to stop the story about his infidelity. I knew it would hurt you, but I knew that in the long run you were better off without him.'

'That wasn't your choice to make,' growled Diana, tears beginning to roll down her cheeks. 'It wasn't any of your business.'

'Well Julian made it my business,' roared Rachel.

Diana looked at her and saw that she was crying. The sight of tears glistening like a clear, cold mountain stream down her sister's cheeks made her stand quite still. Rachel never cried. But now Diana could see a deep sadness welling in her dark irises, and she knew that something was upsetting her a great deal.

'What the hell does that mean?' she whispered fearfully.

Rachel moved away, but Diana grabbed her arm.

'Answer me, what does that *mean*?'

'You don't want to know.'

'Yes,' hissed Diana, pushing her face close to Rachel's, 'I do want to know. I want to know why you think you're such an expert on my family and why you clearly have such a low opinion of the man I loved.'

Rachel's eyes burned with defiance. 'You want to know? You want to know what kind of man he was, you want to know why I wanted him out of your life?' She held her breath, as if she had a split second to turn back. 'He didn't just have sex with that model. He wanted sex with *me*. What sort of a man would try to have sex with his wife's sister?'

'LIAR!' Diana's hand flew out and she slapped Rachel hard across the face.

For a moment the world seemed to stop turning. Rachel stood there clutching her cheek.

'Why would you say such a wicked thing?' whispered Diana.

'Because it's true,' croaked Rachel between sobs. 'It happened in Italy a few summers ago when we all went away together. He was drunk, so was I. He followed me . . .'

Diana could remember that Tuscan holiday vividly. It had been the week of Julian's birthday, and they had invited Rachel along for the ride. She could picture her sister now, reluctant to join the wives and girlfriends in their poolside manicure sessions. Instead she had raced around the grounds with water pistols, organised impromptu girls-versus-boys water polo matches and regaled the dinner table with scurrilous stories about unfaithful celebrities and industry rumours from the City desk. The female guests had frowned at her antics but the men had been fascinated by her. 'I'm not like those other women,' she'd heard Rachel say to one of them, and it was certainly true.

'I think you need help,' said Diana, starting to shake, not wishing to concede that her own husband had been enchanted by Rachel. 'You're crazy, a fantasist. What did he do? Ask you for a light? For a drink? And you think that he *wanted you*.'

'It was a bit more than that,' Rachel said, looking away.

Diana felt a wave of nausea. An image popped into her head. Of Rachel and Julian, giddy on red wine, heady from the sun. She stamped the thought out before it sharpened into more painful focus.

'You had sex with him?'

'Of course I didn't. But he tried to kiss me, whispered things in my ear . . . I said no and he wouldn't take that for an answer. I almost had to kick him in the bloody balls.' She shook her head violently.

'I don't believe it,' whispered Diana.

'Of course you don't. Maybe I'm not as beautiful as you or all those other women in Tuscany, but I think Julian just wanted what he couldn't have. And he didn't care that that was your sister. He didn't care who he hurt or humiliated. I wanted him out of your life, Di, though not in this way, and I am so sorry and sad about what happened to him. But he didn't treat you the way you deserved to be treated.'

'So you were doing me a favour, is that it? You exposed him in the national press as a way of helping me out, his poor ignorant wife who needed to have all her stupid illusions shattered. Is that what you were doing?'

'Yes,' said Rachel. Her voice was barely audible.

'Well it didn't feel like it, Rachel. It felt like you were breaking my heart.'

Diana looked down and realised she was still clutching the crumpled news report. She walked over to the desk and, smoothing it out, left it on top of the file where she had found it. Then she opened the Lake House door.

'Di, please . . .'

Diana shook her head. 'I can't speak to you. I don't even want to look at you.' She turned around and walked out into the night. Behind her, she heard Rachel's voice.

'Diana, wait!'

'What is it?'

'Well, what now? Do you want me to finish the job or not?'

Diana snorted and shook her head. 'I think it's the least you can do,' she said. And she turned back towards the house.

20

Rachel had never really enjoyed air travel. Turbulence or the thought of crashing didn't scare her; it was just that she was naturally a doer, and therefore sitting still for eight hours as she and Ross crossed the Atlantic was her idea of hell.

'Why don't you just do like I do and take advantage of the bar?' said Ross, clearly enjoying the perks of business class. 'It's all free, you know.'

Rachel shook her head. She had watched her companion sink three generous Scotches already, and they hadn't even served the in-flight meal yet. Experience had taught her that it was never a good idea to drink on the plane, that your hangover always seemed to exaggerate the jet lag, or was it the other way around? Besides, she wanted to be clear-headed when they got to Washington. After her horrible row with Diana the day before, she certainly felt as though she owed her sister the courtesy of doing her job to the best of her abilities, not half-cut.

She had gone over their argument again and again since she had boarded the plane, even confessing the details to Ross, who had simply nodded and explained that honesty was invariably the best policy before suggesting she have a champagne cocktail to forget about it.

But Rachel couldn't forget about it. She had never been able to forget that hot, dusky night in Tuscany. It had been a real treat to spend a week somewhere as beautiful and luxurious as the Denvers' palazzo. It wasn't her world. Foreign trips were generally of the chasing-celebrities-around-Cannes-film-festival or press-junket type, and they had been getting increasingly rare as office budgets were slashed and she was forced to spend more time behind her desk. She could see it now, the stunning palazzo surrounded by poppy fields, olive groves and cypress trees. She could smell the lavender and the bougainvillea, taste the lobster risotto and almond biscuits cooked by the household chef, feel the warm water of the infinity pool against her sun-roasted skin as she dived through its surface. And she could hear the footsteps behind her in the darkness, tap, tap, expensive leather against cold stone, as she walked down the path towards her room, a single-storey cottage in the grounds.

She hadn't thought to ask Julian why he had followed her – after all, her cottage was some distance from the palazzo. But he was drunk, and so was she. It had been his birthday the previous day, and they were all still high from the free-flowing champagne and the furtive lines of cocaine. After a few minutes of polite chat they had both fallen silent and all she had been able to hear was the distant shrieks and laughter of those guests still around the pool, and the sound of cicadas on the warm evening air. That was when he had kissed her. Or tried to. Pressing her against the wooden door of her cottage, sliding his hand down the back of her skirt until his fingers touched the top of her thong, breathing into her ear that he had always wanted her, that no one needed to know, that it could be their little secret. He was making an offer Rachel had no doubt would have been attractive to almost any of the women at that villa: to be Julian's mistress, his bit on the side.

Instead, Rachel had kneed him in the groin and, while he was doubled up on the floor, had whispered in *his* ear, 'If I hear that you have played around on my sister ever again, I will make the pain you are in right now feel like a kiss.'

Clearly he hadn't listened – and that was why she and Ross were flying across the Atlantic to talk to the family of a girl Julian had almost certainly been screwing. What the hell was it about these men? Why couldn't they keep their cocks in their pants? Did they really do it just because they could? A combination of weakness and male arrogance that made them overlook the little detail that they were married.

She looked over at Ross. Of course, it didn't always work that way. She didn't know the whole story of his relationship, but she knew that his wife had cheated on him with the man from the local dry-cleaner's, citing Ross's frequent nights away on stakeouts as reason enough. If he had been rich, would she have put up with his absences? Turned a blind eye?

Love just didn't work the way it should, not the way it did in books and songs, anyway. She thought of Liam for a moment, wishing she had stayed – wishing he had asked her to stay. But no, like everyone else, he had thought she should go. 'Be with your sister.'

Well, that was all going so well, wasn't it?

In Thailand, Rachel had seen real poverty. In Ko Tao there was a whole fishing village made from bamboo, thatched palm leaves and rusting corrugated iron. Beyond their nets and the clothes they stood up in, those people had nothing, but, being Buddhists, they were genuinely happy to share their last bowl of rice with you. Pulling up outside the Kopek residence, Rachel certainly didn't get that feeling of forbearance and togetherness. They had picked up a hire car at Dulles airport and driven a hundred miles west, towards the Appalachians, until they came to Rocksburgh, Maryland, pop. 2,347. Growing up, Rachel had always considered America to be the most starry and glamorous of destinations. It was Disneyland and movie stars, Pacific beaches and city skyscrapers. But this was not the USA of her dreams. This was poor, neglected America, where old pick-up trucks grumbled down highways dotted with trailer parks and empty lots full of junk.

'Look at this place,' said Ross, taking a moment to study the view. 'I feel like I've stepped back in time, not driven an hour and a half out of Washington.'

Rachel had seen trailer parks in the movies before, but she had never actually been to one. Some of the plots were well tended and tidy, with the trailers themselves resembling small, shingle-fronted houses. Others were unkempt, the trailers more like the caravans from the rain-swept holidays of her childhood, their yards cluttered with rusting cars and discarded furniture. A dog – a mongrel with xylophone ribs and a foaming mouth – barked at them from the next lot, and Rachel was glad to see it was

159

securely chained up. She thought of Madison Kopek with her shiny blond hair and her college degree – the amount of ambition it must have taken her to get out of here, it was no surprise she had managed to find her way into Julian Denver's life.

Pamela Kopek's house was one of the larger properties. It was timber-fronted, with grilles at the windows, and rimmed by flower beds full of plants that had wilted in the heat.

'Do you think we should have phoned ahead to say we were coming?' said Rachel, waiting for someone to answer the door.

'It was tough enough getting her address,' said Ross. 'We didn't want to risk spooking her.'

He knocked again, but there was no answer, apart from the furious barking of the dog.

'She could be out at work,' said Rachel.

'Wait here,' said Ross, and disappeared around the back of the trailer. Rachel didn't much like being left alone here, and she looked around anxiously. She heard shouting coming from the back of the trailer, then jumped as the door rattled open. A tall, very thin woman in khaki Bermuda shorts and a vest top stood there squinting in the semi-dark. She was of indeterminate age – her hair was high-school blond, but her face was heavily lined. She looked as if she had just been woken up, and didn't seem too pleased about it.

'Can I help you?' she asked, looking at Rachel and then Ross.

Ross stepped forward and extended his hand.

'Very sorry to have disturbed you, Mrs Kopek,' he said, his Midlands accent replaced by something more royal. 'It's just we've come here straight from London and we wondered if we could impose on you for just a few minutes.'

Smooth, thought Rachel. *Very smooth*.

The woman was evidently impressed. She raised her eyebrows. 'London, you say? London, England?'

Ross nodded. 'And it is a rather private matter. We've come to talk to you about your daughter.'

Pamela Kopek hesitated. 'You knew Maddie?'

'My brother-in-law did. Can we come in?'

Pamela nodded and opened the door wider for them to step inside.

The interior of the mobile home was nothing like a caravan. From the swiftest glance, Rachel could see there were bedrooms at the far end, and a large living space, with a kitchen area, small dining table and two cheap-looking sofas. Inexplicably, there were three televisions, all tuned to different channels, all with the sound off. Pamela cleared a washing basket from the table and gestured for them to sit down.

'You cops?'

'No,' said Rachel. 'But we are here to ask you a few questions about Madison's accident.'

'Lawyers, then? Some of them ambulance-chasers? 'Cos if you is, you can stop right now. Maddie's gone, and that's all there is to it. I don't want to go stirring things up again.'

'No, we're not lawyers,' said Rachel. 'As I said, Madison was a friend of my brother-in-law's. I just wanted to say how sorry we are to hear about what happened, Mrs Kopek.'

Pamela Kopek nodded slowly. 'I think I'm going to need a drink. And call me Pam, everyone does.'

She reached behind her and pulled out a bottle, pouring some into a teacup, not offering any to her guests.

'I've lost two kids in six months, you know that?' she said, taking a drink and grimacing. 'So don't you start asking why all I want to do is sleep and drink.'

Rachel and Ross exchanged a look.

'Two kids?'

The woman nodded. 'My son Billy passed on six months ago. Things have never really gone my way, but the last few months have been more than a little bit shitty.'

Rachel gave a sympathetic nod. 'Have they caught the driver?'

Pamela shook her head. 'Not likely to now, are they?'

'What actually happened?' said Ross, interjecting. The news reports of the hit-and-run accident that had killed Madison hadn't been detailed.

'College had just finished, she'd graduated and she decided to stay back in town to go to some parties, maybe find a summer job. She was on her way home from a bar, stepped out into the road . . .'

Pamela bowed her head as if she could no longer speak.

'At least she graduated,' she said finally, her lip trembling with emotion. 'All she ever wanted to do was go to college, make something of herself. She got a full scholarship, you know. Got accepted into one of those fancy sorority houses. She was such a smart, pretty girl. So, your brother-in-law,' she added, frowning. 'Do I know him?'

'His name was Julian Denver. Did Madison ever mention him?'

Pamela shrugged. 'No, but then me and Maddie weren't so close. She didn't talk to me about her friends, let alone boyfriends. I can't really blame her. What did her ole mom ever do right? She was a clever girl and knew better than to come running to me for advice.'

She paused to take a drink.

'You know what? She never even told me she was pregnant.'

Rachel tried not to show her surprise – in any case, Pam Kopek was staring at one of the silent TVs, a tear running down her face.

'Had to hear it from the hospital, you believe that? I guess I shouldn't have been shocked. I mean, she was a pretty girl, always had a lot of attention.'

'Who was the father?' asked Rachel, scarcely daring to breathe. 'He must have been pretty devastated.'

'I don't know. She had lots of admirers, that was for sure. But I'll guess we'll never know who the daddy was.'

Rachel took a moment to steady herself.

'So Maddie didn't have a steady boyfriend at the time she died?'

The older woman shook her head, then looked across at Rachel, as if she had just made a connection.

'Your brother-in-law, was he a good friend of Madison's?'

'No, they just worked together,' said Rachel as smoothly as she could. 'Besides, he's married to my sister.'

Pam Kopek let out a laugh. 'Honey, I don't know how it works over there in England, but out here? If they're married or they're single, it don't make a whole heap of difference.'

'You mean Maddie had been out with married men before?'

Pamela looked at her wide-eyed, the effects of the alcohol kicking in.

'Who knows? But if she took after her mama, she would have done. How do you think I ended up here? Kids' daddy played away, so did I. Whole thing ended up such a mess.'

She took another slug of bourbon, spilling a few droplets on her shorts, lost to a flood of memories.

'It's getting late. We'd better be going,' said Rachel.

'Won't find any fancy hotels around here,' said Pam, without even looking at them.

'Maddie's friends. I don't suppose you have any contact details for them . . .'

'Bunch of condolence letters some of them sent over there,' she said, motioning lifelessly towards one of the televisions.

Ross went over to where she was pointing. While he copied some details into his notebook, Pamela turned and looked at Rachel more directly, as if she suddenly resented the intrusion.

'Why do you say you came here again? What is it your brother-in-law wanted?'

'Nothing,' said Rachel, sad to leave the woman alone like this. 'We just wanted to say we are so sorry for everything that's happened.'

It felt like a long way back to Washington, even if they did have a stay in the Four Seasons hotel to look forward to at the other end of it.

Rachel concentrated at the wheel of the hire car, seeing nothing but the blackness of night and the occasional pinpricks of headlights coming towards her.

'What am I going to tell her?' she said eventually, as they motored east towards the capital. Despite the conflict between them, Diana was still going to ask questions when they got back to England. After all, she had paid for the flights and hotel reservations, which had both been sorted out overnight, so that Rachel and Ross had been on a plane only hours after telling Diana that they needed to go to America.

'Why do you have to tell her anything?' said Ross.

Rachel glanced angrily across to the passenger seat. 'Ross, Madison Kopek could have been pregnant with Julian's child. How can I keep that little nugget from my sister? That's the

163

reason for his suicide right there. He was desperate for a baby. He couldn't have one with his wife, his mistress gets pregnant, and when she dies in a car accident, that's going to be enough to put anyone in a tail-spin.'

'Wait, wait, wait,' said Ross, putting up a hand. 'Stop getting emotional and listen to yourself.'

'What's wrong?' she asked irritably.

'Madison *could* have been pregnant with Julian's child,' said Ross, holding up a finger. 'We don't even know if they were in a relationship, and as Pam herself said, Madison had lots of admirers.'

'But how many of those admirers bought her two plane tickets – from his personal account – in the weeks just before her death?'

'Have you sent Maddie's picture over to Greg Willets yet? Asked him if it's the same girl he saw Julian with in Washington?'

'I emailed it over to him yesterday. He hasn't got back to me yet.'

'Then it's a good thing your uncle Ross is here, isn't it?' he grinned, pulling out the notebook he had been writing in at Pamela's. 'The names and addresses of three of Madison's closest friends. Let's track them down in the morning, because mothers don't always know best.'

21

Diana had known it might come. She had read about widows so paralysed by grief that they found it impossible to move or function, and in the two weeks since Julian's death she had felt some small comfort that this terrible fate had escaped her. But after her argument with Rachel, she had gone to her bedroom, closed the curtains, climbed into bed and not got out of it for thirty-six hours. For some of that time she had slept, but for most of it she had lain in the darkness, unable to move or speak. Grief had consumed her, seeped into every molecule of her being like a creeping fog, suffocated her with its loneliness. The worst was not over, she realised. It was just beginning. This was her new life, and it was oppressive, empty and cold. There was nowhere to run from it, nowhere to hide. She couldn't pack a bag and move somewhere different, because wherever she went, however hot and beautiful that place might be, it would follow and haunt her.

Diana wasn't sure that she wanted to die, but she wasn't sure if she could carry on living, and for now, she was happy to stay in this bedroom limbo, between a crisp sheet and a warm duvet, waiting for something, someone to tell her what direction to take when she stepped out of bed once more. She lay on her back and exhaled slowly, listening to her breath escape her body. She knew that she was no longer just mourning her husband; she was mourning the contented life she had once had, or thought she had had. It was the lies that were the most difficult thing to accept. There was the lie about her sister. Julian had insisted that he hated Rachel after her newspaper had exposed his affair. He hated her, but it was only because he had tried to sleep with her.

Madison Kopek was even more painful to think about. Diana had known her marriage wasn't perfect, but she had thought that Julian had loved her and Charlie deeply. The truth, as Rachel had so painfully revealed to her, was that he had clearly loved someone else more. Madison Kopek, with her youth and her American cheerleader beauty. The realisation that Julian had killed himself two days after Madison had died had been almost too much to take on board. The understanding that the pain of losing Madison had been greater than Julian's own love of life, his love of his family. He must have adored her so much that life wasn't worth living without her, and that made Diana feel worthless and wretched.

She heard the door open and managed to turn her head to the side to see who it was. Sylvia walked into Somerfold's master bedroom, whipped back the curtains, flooding the room with sunlight, and with equal ruthlessness pulled back the duvet, making Diana curl up into a ball.

'Mum, what are you doing?' she croaked, raising one hand to shield her eyes from the light.

'Getting you moving, darling,' said her mother breezily. 'I thought we'd walk down to the village.'

'But I need to sleep,' she said, struggling to get the words out.

'And you *have* slept. Since Saturday. It is now three o'clock on Monday afternoon, and it's time to get up.'

'I don't want to go out. I can't.'

But her mother wasn't listening. She had gone to the en suite, turned on the shower and returned to throw Diana's bathrobe on the bed.

'I expect you downstairs in fifteen minutes,' she said, in a voice that not even Diana's grief-stricken body dared defy.

Boughton was a thirty-minute stroll away from the house – most of it taken up by the long, winding gravel drive that snaked through Somerfold's grounds. Diana and Sylvia walked slowly. It had been hard not to think of Rachel as they had gone past the Lake House, but Sylvia hadn't mentioned her, instead chatting quite distractingly about a new opera that was coming to the ROH, a news item she had read on the *Daily Mail* online, an oil painting she was working on. Diana hadn't spoken, only listened. Her interest in anything seemed to have been sapped out of her, but she was grateful that her mother seemed to intuitively understand that all she wanted was background noise to stop her sinking into the quicksand of her own emotions.

The village always looked loveliest in the sun. It was one of the most picturesque places in England, with rows of red-brick cottages, an old church, a duck pond and a collection of lively pubs that competed for the local custom with a series of quiz nights, ale festivals and curry evenings.

'So where are we going?' Diana asked, watching the sun break through the overhanging trees.

'To the café by the green.'

Diana knew the one. She used to pop in occasionally when she first moved here, for bread and pastries for Charlie and Julian, and had been charmed by the couple who owned it, but her visits had dwindled, and anyway, Mrs Bills had reported that the place had gone downhill.

'I'm not hungry,' she said honestly.

She hadn't felt hungry since Julian died. Her clothes were falling off her, her wedding ring felt looser, and she didn't need to step on the scales to know that she could do with a thick wedge of chocolate cake to fatten her up.

'Well, we're not exactly going there to eat,' said Sylvia, quickening her pace.

'What *are* we going there for?' Diana asked anxiously.

'There's a meeting about the village fair. I thought it might be fun if we got involved.'

Diana turned on her heel and held up her hand.

'No. Absolutely not,' she said, feeling her pulse flutter in panic. 'I can't. I'm not up to it.'

Sylvia put a firm hand on her shoulder.

'Of course you can do it. It's good for you. It will help distract you.'

'Mum, please. It's the last thing I feel like.'

Sylvia placed her other hand on the other shoulder, so that she looked at her directly. It was a firm grip, like a vice, and Diana wasn't sure she could run away even if she tried.

'I get that all you want to do is hide away. When your father died, I felt the same, and we weren't even married any more. I didn't love him; in fact you know I probably even still hated him for leaving us like he did. But I mourned him,' she said, and for one moment Diana saw her mother's vulnerability. 'I was sad for a life lost, a father gone; sad to lose the man I once loved and still had some happy memories of. But you have to stay strong, and even when you don't feel as if you can take another step, take a deep breath and do it. Because you can. Life goes on, perhaps a different life, but you have to keep going.'

Diana found strength in her mother's words and suddenly didn't feel quite so alone. In the spirit of solidarity she wondered if she should tell Sylvia about her showdown with Rachel, what her sister had said and what it all meant, but perhaps her mother was right. It was better to look forward, not back. Throw yourself into jam-making and brass-band judging and all the things the village fair committee no doubt had in store.

The meeting had started by the time they got there. The owner of the Blue Ribbon café – Diana couldn't remember her name; Dot or Doreen, perhaps – was filling mugs from a white china teapot. The two of them managed to slip in at the back, with only a few people twisting their necks to send sympathetic looks in their direction.

Diana had received many letters of condolence from the villagers, although not many people had stopped by or approached her to say that they were sorry for her loss. Death did that. It embarrassed people. If they didn't know what to say, they would say nothing at all. They would cross the street, or look the other way to avoid you, and Diana had no doubt that as soon as the meeting was finished, most would scuttle away to avert a conversation with the recently widowed lady of the manor.

She sat back and listened as the committee debated the merits of putting bunting on the bandstand and discussed the budget available for the Punch and Judy man. In many ways it was rather soothing seeing all these people getting so involved in such small details, almost as if they were completely unaware of how easily their familiar, cosy world could unravel. Perhaps they were; Diana wished she shared their ignorance.

It took a couple of seconds to register that Mrs Beatty, the vicar's wife, was speaking to her.

'Mrs Denver, we're so pleased you could join us. We were wondering earlier if you would be so kind as to present the prizes for the flower and vegetable competitions this year, although I have to say the categories are getting a little out of control. Perhaps we can get that man from *Top Gear* to help out, the one who lives locally . . .'

'No, it's fine. I'd love to,' said Diana, feeling Sylvia squeeze her knee reassuringly.

Mrs Beatty collared them on the way out, sheltering from the sun under a pink IKEA umbrella as the committee filed out without a word. 'You should come round for tea to discuss the judging process,' she said when the three of them were alone. 'The weather's been beautiful, hasn't it? We can sit in the rectory garden and talk, and maybe sample my non-prize-winning chutney.'

'That would be lovely,' said Diana, pasting on a smile.

'We're all thinking of you and praying for you, you know that, Diana,' she added, making Diana feel a pang of guilt that she went to church so infrequently. The Reverend Beatty and his wife had written one of the most thoughtful pieces of correspondence, including a beautiful poem by Henry Scott Holland, a former canon of St Paul's Cathedral, called 'Death is Nothing At All'.

She made a decision on the spot that she would take her up on her offer.

'Can I come round next Friday?' she asked, plucking a date from the air, knowing that her diary was filled with very little.

'Looking forward to it,' said Mrs Beatty, touching her on the arm and running across the green to catch up with her husband.

'That wasn't so bad, was it?' whispered Sylvia, linking her arm through her daughter's.

'No,' she said quietly.

'I'm going to have to bully you more often.' Sylvia squeezed her arm. 'In fact I'm returning to London tomorrow. There's a piano recital at the Wigmore Hall. You should come, stay at the Bayswater flat. Perhaps arrange to meet friends. I think it would be good for you to see people.'

It was easier to nod than resist.

'Dammit,' Diana said quietly. 'I left my scarf in the café.'

She turned and returned to the Blue Ribbon, where the owner was collecting mugs from the tables.

'Just about to shut, love,' she said without turning round.

'I've only come to collect my scarf.'

The old lady's eyes opened wider when she saw Diana.

'Ah, you came back for it. I was going to pop it up to the house later,' she said, going round the counter and retrieving the scarf from behind the till. 'It was good to see you here today. I know how hard that must have been.'

'Thank you, er . . .' she replied, scrabbling around for the woman's name.

'Dot.' She smiled kindly. 'He gave you the scarf, didn't he?'

'How did you know?' replied Diana, still feeling embarrassed that Dot obviously knew all about her but she hadn't even been able to remember the woman's name.

'Panic in your eyes about losing something sentimental. Felt it myself. I remember, a year after my Ron died, a friend came round and tidied away his fishing tackle in the hall. I went mad with her and she couldn't understand why. Couldn't explain it myself, but there are some things you just have to hold on to, you just have to keep around you.'

Diana stroked the scarf absently. She hadn't considered the sentimental attachment. After Rachel's revelation about Madison Kopek, she had gone home and flung all Julian's possessions from their bedroom – shirts, shoes, a bottle of aftershave – into three bin liners, and given them to a startled Mrs Bills to store out of sight.

'You okay, love?' asked Dot.

She nodded. 'I'm sorry about Ron,' she said quietly. 'I didn't know. I remember him. He ran the café with you, didn't he?'

The old woman smiled nostalgically. 'Married for fifty-two years, ran this place for fifteen of them when he retired from his job in London. He was a pastry chef at the Savoy in the sixties, you know. His macaroons got served to Liz Taylor, Brigitte Bardot, Frank Sinatra. You must remember Ron's Chelsea buns,' she added. 'People came from far and wide for his Chelsea buns. In fact, I remember your husband liked them. He used to ride down from the big house on that beautiful horse of his. He'd tie the horse up and get a Chelsea bun for himself and a chocolate brownie for your son. Apparently you don't eat carbohydrates,' she teased.

Diana nodded, feeling a pang of regret for getting rid of his clothes. She could imagine him here, standing at the counter on those Saturday mornings he went for a ride, and wished with all her heart that she had gone with him more often. Laughed with him, eaten cake, galloped until the wind took their breath away, made him happy. *Happy so that he didn't have to go looking for it elsewhere* said an after-thought.

'It does get easier, you know,' said Dot softly. 'Grief doesn't ever go away, but it shows itself less often.'

She picked up a cloth and started rubbing down the surfaces.

'This café certainly misses Ron. He'd have hated that I've let the place get like this.'

'Don't be silly,' said Diana. 'It's lovely.'

'You think so?' said Dot more sharply. 'Try that lemon drizzle cake and tell me I don't need to change my supplier. Bloody rotten it is, but there doesn't seem much point when I'm just waiting for a buyer.'

'You're selling up?'

Dot nodded. 'I've had some good times here, but now? For the first couple of years it actually made things easier, because when I'm here I can still feel him around me. But now . . . let's be honest, the café's seen better days and so have I.'

Diana looked around the room and had to agree with Dot. It was dark and tired, and that lemon drizzle cake didn't look too appetising. It was a shame really, as it was a good space and perfectly placed to catch the passing tourist trade that flocked in at weekends. An image started forming in her mind. One in which the café was buzzing and full of life, the tables were covered in blue gingham and home-made cakes were tied up with brown paper and string.

'Don't know of a buyer, do you?' asked Dot.

'I'll keep my ears open,' mused Diana.

The bell above the door tinkled behind them.

'Are you coming?' asked Sylvia, looking a little piqued.

'We were just chatting, weren't we?' said Dot. 'Come back whenever you fancy doing it again.'

'I will,' said Diana, suddenly feeling in the mood for cake.

22

From the coffee shop, Rachel and Ross had a perfect view of Chesapeake Beach. They could see cafés, ice-cream parlours and tackle shops; they could see the marina and the white charter fishing boats chugging back to shore full of tourists and the big catches of the day. They could see the beautiful bay, with its silvery water glinting in the sun and holidaymakers milling around in T-shirts and shorts, holding wicker baskets and beach towels. They could pretty much see everything and everyone except Madison's friend Laura Dale, who worked at the water park across the road from where they were sitting. Who was due to have finished her shift at least half an hour ago, but who had not yet revealed herself.

Sighing impatiently, Rachel ordered another strawberry milkshake and a slice of key lime pie that was winking at her from under a big plastic dome. One of the perils of this sort of work was all the sitting around. In her first couple of years as a journalist, she had put on over a stone in weight from drinking in the pub and snacks and coffees whilst she was waiting around for leads. It was one of the reasons she had taken up swimming again in her mid twenties – her love of the sport had tailed off completely once she had discovered boys and gone to university, but getting back in the water had restored her slim, lean physique that was easy to pour into skinny jeans.

'Come on, come on, there she is,' hissed Ross, hauling Rachel to her feet just as she was spooning some cake into her mouth.

Across the road, a tall, twenty-ish woman with a dark brown ponytail was leaving the water park. It had taken Rachel less than a minute to find half a dozen photographs of Laura Dale on

Facebook so they didn't have to debate whether they had the right person.

Rachel had tried the direct approach, of course, calling Laura to try and arrange a meeting, but the girl had been evasive, hostile even. And so she had decided that if the mountain wouldn't come to Muhammad, then Muhammad must go to the mountain – or whatever that quote was.

They pushed out on to the street, sidestepping a moped, and crossed to the other side. Rachel had been worried they would lose the girl, but she was still there, bending over a bicycle, unlocking it from some railings.

'Hi, Laura, can we talk?'

She glanced up, startled, looking back and forth between Ross and Rachel, then her face darkened and she turned back to her task.

'Sorry, do I know you?'

'Rachel Miller, journalist. We spoke on the phone. I got your address from Pamela Kopek.'

'Pamela didn't have this address.'

Rachel didn't want to go into how Ross had tracked her down. The charming phone call to her parents, who had told him that Laura was working in Chesapeake Beach for the summer.

'Please, we need to talk,' she said simply.

'I don't want to talk to you,' Laura replied.

Rachel took hold of the handlebars of her bicycle. 'We guessed that, but we only want to ask a couple of questions about Madison.'

'Yeah, *I* guessed that,' said Laura, throwing her chain into the basket and wheeling the bike away. 'I have nothing to say.'

Rachel and Ross exchanged a look, then followed her.

'I know you must be upset,' said Rachel, trotting to keep up. 'It must be hard to lose a friend so suddenly.'

The girl stopped and turned to face Rachel. 'What do you want?'

She was sharper, shrewder than Pamela Kopek, that was for sure. But Rachel could tell that she was also a shy, gentle sort of girl – the sort that came to a quiet, relaxing town like Chesapeake Beach for the summer rather than the noisy student favourites

174

like Ocean City – and that her truculence and annoyance was because she was scared and upset.

'I want to find out about Madison's relationship with my brother-in-law.'

'Your brother-in-law? And who's that?'

'Julian Denver.'

Laura's eyes widened and she shook her head.

'I don't want to talk about this,' she said, moving away again. 'I have to get home.'

'Stop, please,' said Rachel, jumping ahead and blocking the girl's path. 'This is important.'

'Madison is dead. Leave me alone.'

'Julian is dead too, Laura. Just talk to me, please.'

Laura's expression was confused and fearful. 'Dead?'

'Two days after Madison.'

'How?' she whispered.

'He commited suicide.'

'Do you know why?'

Rachel shook her head. 'It's what we're trying to work out. Please, help us make sense of it,' she said slowly.

They retreated to a pizza restaurant across the road. Laura sat opposite them in a booth, out of earshot of the other diners. Her shoulders were hunched and she slowly sipped at the Coke that Ross had ordered for her.

'You were one of Maddie's best friends,' stated Rachel carefully.

'We were room-mates for a year at college. Stayed good friends ever since, yeah.'

'I spoke to her mum yesterday. She told me Maddie was pregnant. Did you know that?'

Laura nodded. 'I was there when she took the test.'

Rachel took a deep breath. 'Did she say who the father was?'

'Maddie wasn't promiscuous,' Laura said fiercely.

'But she *was* sleeping with Julian,' said Rachel, almost scared to say it out loud.

The younger girl nodded again. 'Your sister is Julian's wife, right? Does she know about Maddie?'

'Yes . . . no. Well, she saw the . . . No. It's complicated.'

'More than you think,' said Laura quietly. 'Maddie wasn't a bad girl, a husband-stealer. It didn't start out like that. She went to Julian Denver for help.'

'Help?'

Laura chewed her lip, as if she were debating whether to say more.

'She didn't tell me everything, but it was to do with her brother,' she said finally.

'Billy. He died recently too, didn't he?'

'Heart attack,' said Laura. 'He was twenty and he had a heart attack, can you believe that?'

'What was it? An undiagnosed heart defect or something?'

'Maybe. But Madison didn't believe that. Billy was an athlete, you see, on a football scholarship at Riverdale College. Anyway, his coach had told him he was getting too big, that he had to lose weight. Well, Billy didn't want to spend six hours a day training – who does when they're twenty, right? – so when someone told him there was a new drug he could take to control his weight, he jumped at it.'

'A weight-loss drug? What was it?'

'Rena-something. No, Rheladrex, that's it. All I know is that it was new, maybe experimental. And nine months after starting on the pills, he was dead.'

'And Madison thought there was a link?'

'She was convinced it was the drugs. She got obsessed about it, researching stuff about chemicals, the drugs industry, everything. She majored in chemistry, so it wasn't tough for her to process it all.'

Despite herself, Rachel was beginning to feel the old instincts stirring. It was probably just coincidence, a grieving woman looking for answers that weren't there, just like Diana. But even so, could there be something in it?

'Did she discover anything?'

'The drug was pretty new to the market. Maddie found that at least three other people who had been taking it had died suddenly. When she heard that, well, she started planning all this crazy stuff.'

'Crazy?'

176

Laura looked at Rachel, her eyes wary. 'She decided to track down Julian Denver.'

Rachel's mind raced ahead. 'So you're saying this drug was manufactured by the Denver Group?'

Laura nodded. 'Their pharmaceuticals division.'

'And that's why she contacted Julian – because he was CEO? What did she want? Money? Compensation for Billy's death?'

Laura looked doubtful. 'I think by then it had gone beyond that. Maddie was convinced the drug was bad and all she wanted was for it to be taken off the market. It was like a crusade for her. She'd lodged a complaint with the FDA, but very little happened. She'd spoken to some fancy lawyer in DC who said it was expensive to take on the drugs companies and there weren't enough people to start a class action.'

'So she thought she'd go straight to the top. Ballsy girl. Did she write him a letter?' asked Rachel, thinking of the boxes of correspondence that Anne-Marie Carr had shown her. Had Julian himself picked Madison's letter out of the mountain of mail?

Laura smiled sadly. 'Jeez, no. She wasn't going to wait around for that. No, she wanted to speak to Julian Denver directly. She'd read a lot of interviews with him, heard how much he did for charity, thought he might be a decent guy who would listen to what she had to say. She found out he was coming to a conference in DC, which wasn't far from college. Found out he was staying at the Four Seasons, so she hung around the bar there. And she was beautiful. She got talking to him, and I think one thing just led to another.'

'She seduced him?' Rachel said, with reluctant admiration that Maddie could have done something so brazen. It was the classic honey-pot sting. Gorgeous woman tricks powerful businessman into her confidence.

'Maybe it started off like that. She couldn't exactly accost him and demand that he take his new drug off the market. But they met up a few times, and I guess they started to like each other. The most important thing was that Julian Denver seemed to take what she was saying seriously. He said he'd look into the drug and its side effects.'

177

'How long were they sleeping together? Do you know?'

'From that first night, I think.'

'And did Julian know about the baby?'

'I don't know,' Laura said quietly. She had finished her Coke. 'I should go.'

'You can't go,' said Ross, putting his hand up to call the waitress.

'Do you think it's strange?' said Laura, suddenly looking anxious.

'What's strange?' asked Rachel, trying to meet her gaze, trying to read her mind.

'Strange that she got killed,' Laura replied, her voice barely a whisper. 'I told her it wasn't a good idea taking these people on, challenging them about a drug that was probably worth billions. But she wouldn't listen.'

'You don't think it was an accident? You think she was targeted?' said Rachel incredulously.

'I know it sounds paranoid, but when I first heard she'd been killed, I thought she might have been, yeah. But since the bad guy would have been your brother-in-law and he's dead too, I guess it's nothing like that. I wonder if he did know about the baby,' she offered softly.

Rachel kept silent.

'I'm very sad for your sister,' said Laura finally. 'Now I really have to go.'

23

He stepped out into the road, his hand raised, hailing a taxi. Diana did a double-take, jabbing at the brakes, swerving to the right, her wheel hitting the kerb, bouncing to a halt. *Damn damn damn!* A horn blared and a van driver leant out of his window, gesturing wildly.

'Bloody women drivers, shouldn't be on the bloody road!' he yelled.

Diana put her head down on the steering wheel and felt her heart thumping. Her hands were trembling violently and for a moment she couldn't catch her breath. She watched him stepping into a black cab, and as he turned to see what the disturbance was behind him, she knew that it was not him. Of course it wouldn't be him. Julian was dead. The man in the sharp dark suit was just a lookalike, and she was hallucinating.

Exhaling slowly to calm her nerves, she glanced in her rear-view mirror and pulled back out into the traffic. She knew she should have listened to her mother and allowed Mr Bills to drive her into central London, or at least got the train. Instead, she had managed to convince herself that it would do her good to drive herself – blow away the cobwebs or something like that – but she was clearly in no fit state to ride a bicycle, let alone negotiate the Range Rover through the busy streets of London.

She found a place to park, taking several attempts to reverse the car into the space. She was still shaking and her head was sore. Whiplash: that was all she needed.

She looked up at the tall Bloomsbury mews house in front of her. A short flight of stone steps led to the front door, which had a small bronze plaque next to it reading *Wilson and Nedwell, Solicitors.*

She paused for a moment to compose herself. She had known this day would come, but hadn't appreciated how nervous she would be. A week earlier, she had thought she would be able to predict the contents of Julian's will. It was something that they had occasionally discussed. Julian had always maintained he would look after Diana and Charlie in the event of his death. And whilst she didn't doubt that he would be true to his word, she was more anxious about what other provisions his will might contain. There was almost certainly a mistress on the scene. One that Julian had loved so much he had killed himself over her death. She had seen enough courtroom dramas, read enough family sagas to know that wills were often a hotbed of surprises.

Diana swung her bag over her shoulder and walked up the steps with as much purpose as she could muster. A secretary came to meet her at reception, and she was ushered to Stuart Wilson's office on the top floor. She had met the genial lawyer several times before. He was a friendly-looking man with highly coloured cheeks and a very smart suit. The very picture of a Dickensian solicitor, in fact. Diana wouldn't have been surprised to see a top hat on the old-fashioned wooden coat-stand by the door. Fitting in with the image, his office was lined from floor to ceiling with heavy leather-bound legal books, although the technology dotted around the room – the iPad, computer and plasma television screwed to the wall – indicated that this was definitely a twenty-first-century operation.

'Diana, I am so glad you came.'

'I wanted to get out of the house,' she said, appreciating Stuart's offer to come to Somerfold. 'Thank you for this,' she added anxiously. 'I don't think I could have faced one of those public readings of the will.' She imagined Julian's family all squashed into the room, Elizabeth Denver no doubt taking charge of proceedings.

'Julian wanted it this way. I think he understood the family dynamics,' he said simply.

He sat forward and passed Diana a slim bound document about six pages long. She read the cover slip. *The Last Will and*

Testament of Julian Edward Denver, dated March of that year. So it was recent, but not something hastily arranged after Madison Kopek's death. She wondered what – if anything – that might mean.

'You can of course read it in private if you'd prefer, but I thought you might prefer to go through it together?'

Diana nodded. She could already see that it was written in impenetrable legalese and that she would need the solicitor to decipher it. Besides, he had drafted the document in the first place; what was the point of her reading it in private? *Unless he really has left everything to his American mistress*, said a voice in her head.

'Yes, that's fine, talk me through it if you would, Mr Wilson,' she said, her palms beading with sweat.

If the last few horrible weeks had taught her anything, it was that she couldn't take anything for granted. Diana hadn't married Julian for his money. She had fallen in love with him, pure and simple. She had loved his patrician looks, his educated cleverness, his alpha-male poise and his power – not because of the cash he had in the bank but the confidence he had in a room, the way it felt to be at his side.

But still, she had enjoyed the financial security that life as a Denver had brought her. She would be a liar to say she did not love the exotic holidays, the money-is-no-object shopping sprees, the ability to buy her dream house at the click of her fingers. And yet here she was, sitting in a stranger's office, waiting for the axe to fall. Even from beyond the grave, Julian had the power to take everything away from her. If there was already an American mistress, why not more of them, one in every port? For all she knew, there could be love-children, each one given a share of his estate. Perhaps he had even bequeathed something to Rachel – the one temptation who had refused him. The last weeks had been so unpredictable – she knew the will could contain anything.

Her mouth felt dry as Stuart Wilson cleared his throat and flipped open his own copy of the will.

'I'll go through the nitty-gritty in a few moments, but I should probably cut to the chase, as they say, shouldn't I?'

Diana gave a tight nod.

'Well, the long and the short of it is that Julian left all his personal possessions to you, Mrs Denver.'

Diana felt as if all the air had been sucked from the room.

'I'm sorry?' she croaked. 'Everything?'

'Well, not quite,' said Wilson, licking his fingers and turning to the back page of the document. 'He has left a few specific bequests: his cars, motorbikes, some small cash payments, a charitable fund – mainly a tax loophole, that one – and a particular, important bequest for your son, which we will come on to. But in the main, yes, everything goes to you. Somerfold and all its grounds and buildings, the house in Notting Hill, all his investments here and offshore and a sizeable amount of money in a number of bank accounts, including – ah – three in Switzerland.'

He looked up.

'All as expected, I should imagine?'

Diana couldn't reply. Her head was pounding. She had gone from believing that Julian had rejected her and their family to discovering that he had, in fact, made her a very wealthy woman. She felt lower than a snake for ever doubting him. He had loved her, and the thought of it made her feel suddenly heady.

'Are you all right? You look quite pale,' said Mr Wilson, standing and going to a side table to fetch Diana a glass of water. 'I know these occasions can be emotional,' he said, handing it to her.

Diana sipped the water and handed back the glass.

'Thank you, Mr Wilson, you're very understanding.'

'Not at all, dear lady,' said the lawyer. 'Between the two of us, in the past month I have had to deal with a couple of will readings where the wife in question was left nothing at all, in favour of a nanny and a work colleague respectively. All very unpleasant. Things were thrown.'

Diana rubbed her temples. It was all too much to process. Then suddenly something pushed through the fog.

'What about Charlie?' she said. 'You mentioned that Julian had left him something?'

'Julian wants his shareholding in the Denver Group to go to Charlie.'

182

'What, all of it?'

'Yes.' Stuart Wilson ran his finger down the page, then tapped it. 'All of his Class A and Class B shares in Denver Group and its subsidiaries. Left in trust for Charlie until he turns twenty-one.'

Diana shook her head. 'He's giving it to Charlie?' Her heart felt as if it was about to burst with love.

'With you as the trustee. I'm having a meeting with Ralph, Adam and Elizabeth Denver to let them know.'

'You mean they don't already?' she asked with a surge of nerves.

'The shareholding structure of the Denver Group is complicated. Much of the voting class of shares is held in family trust. However, when Ralph Denver suffered his stroke and stepped down, he handed ten per cent of the Class B voting shares to Julian, with a provision that those shares can only be transferred to other members of the family. Whether Ralph specifically knows that his grandson is to be the beneficiary of such a valuable shareholding I don't know . . .'

'When you say *valuable* – what are you talking about here?' she asked cautiously.

'Current valuation of the Class A shares would be around £850 million. The Class B shares are potentially more valuable because of the control they allow within the company. There is also a letter of intent expressing his wish that Charlie should one day be CEO of the company.'

'He loved him. He really loved Charlie,' she whispered, squeezing her fingers so tightly together that they began to hurt.

'He loved you both very much,' said Mr Wilson, nodding.

24

DrugWatchAmerica was not at all what Rachel had expected. Hidden away on the first floor of a walk-up brownstone in the shabbier end of Foggy Bottom, that delightfully named suburb of Washington DC, the entrance was almost entirely blocked by a shoulder-high stack of boxes containing flyers advertising a rally against 'POISONING A GENERATION' due to happen in Lafayette Park. *Assuming they don't get blasted with a water cannon first*, thought Rachel cynically, grabbing a flyer and putting it in her pocket.

The inside of the office was no less chaotic – a clutter of mismatched desks piled high with more papers and boxes, the walls covered with posters and cork pinboards, everyone seeming to talk at once, either to each other or into their phones.

Megan Hill, however, was exactly as Rachel had imagined. The brains behind the consumer watchdog group 'keeping an eye on Big Pharma' had long red Pre-Raphaelite hair, wire-rimmed glasses and a floaty hippyish dress. She looked like she should be carrying a placard, but Rachel guessed that was all part of the act. Ross had researched Megan Hill, and her CV was eye-popping. The daughter of two sixties civil-rights campaigners, she had grown up on Boston's south side before crossing the Charles River to graduate third in her class at Harvard Law. She could have been earning an indecent salary on Wall Street or for one of the prominent litigation firms in Washington, but clearly the influence of her committed parents had been strong. Instead, she was heading up a cash-strapped group of liberal agitators and making waves across the cyberverse with her DrugWatch blog.

'Rachel Miller?' she said, crossing to shake hands and closing the door to her tiny office. 'You'll have to excuse the mess, we have a protest march at the weekend. It's caused quite a stir already.'

'Well thank you for seeing me at such short notice,' said Rachel, taking a seat opposite Megan.

'Are you kidding? I've been following Rheladrex since it was first trialled eight years ago. Then I get a call from a relative of Julian Denver? I'm going to cancel my own kid's birthday party for that.'

'You knew Julian?'

'Miss Miller, please. I'm the co-founder of DrugWatchAmerica. It's my job to be familiar with the CEOs of all the drug companies and their bosses above them. I heard about Julian's death,' she said more softly. 'I'm sorry for your loss.'

Rachel nodded politely. 'As I said on the phone, I wanted to pick your brains about Rheladrex.'

Contacting a pressure group with specialist knowledge of Big Pharma was the quickest way of learning about the drug. After speaking to Laura Dale, Ross and Rachel had trawled the internet trying to find the best and most convenient person to help them, and had chanced upon DrugWatchAmerica through a conspiracy theory website.

'Sure,' said Megan, sitting back in her chair. 'We've been aware of it before it even entered late-stage development. You see – and most people are surprised by this – not many genuinely new blockbuster drugs make it to market these days.'

'Blockbuster drugs?' asked Rachel. She was aware of the phrase but wasn't certain of its precise definition.

'A big, popular drug. One that generates at least a billion dollars per annum for the company that creates it. So when any potential blockbuster makes it to human trials, we tend to hear about it.'

Megan stood up and walked over to a coffee machine and poured them both a cup.

'Rheladrex is a fascinating one, because potentially it's a licence to print money. Fat inhibitors are one of the holy grails of modern science. We've got a soaring obesity problem in the USA;

it's tripled in the last thirty years. But more to the point, weight loss is the number one obsession of at least half of the US population.'

'Not only over here,' smiled Rachel. 'Name me a woman who isn't on some sort of diet most of the time.'

'Exactly. So whoever cracks the code will be an instant billionaire. It's no surprise that every drug company on earth has tried to come up with something that works. I can name several companies that tried and failed – all of them filed for Chapter 7 liquidation.'

'So there's nothing like it on the market?'

'There's lots of anti-obesity medication out there. But no magic-bullet pill for weight loss, no.'

'And is Rheladrex it?'

Megan shrugged. 'Potentially. The trials showed incredible weight-loss results. It's very new to the market so we've yet to see if it catches fire. Denver Group's chemicals division isn't a huge global player like Pfizer or Glaxo, but if they market it properly, if they manage to make this work, well . . .' she held her hands up, 'the sky's the limit.'

Rachel thought for a moment. She wasn't sure how much she could tell this woman. She needed to find out what she could about the drug and Denver's chemical operation, but at the same time she didn't want to alert a pharmaceutical watchdog group to something that might implicate Denver – and Julian in particular – in another scandal, especially as she currently had no idea of the facts.

'Did someone called Madison Kopek ever approach you?' she asked carefully.

'No. Who's she?' asked Megan, writing down the name.

'Her brother was taking Rheladrex and died of a heart attack. She was convinced the drug was to blame and was trying to find a way to get to Denver.'

Megan Hill looked at Rachel for a moment, sipping her coffee.

'Do you have Miss Kopek's contact details? I'd love to talk to her.'

'She's dead.'

'When . . . how . . .' She tailed off. Rachel could see that she had the reporter's instinct and was no doubt asking similar questions in her head as were going through Rachel's own.

'She was killed in a car accident three weeks ago.'

'Three people are dead: Madison, her brother and Julian Denver. And they all have a connection to Rheladrex?'

Rachel couldn't help but smile. 'You're beginning to sound like those nuts that populate the internet.'

'You were a reporter yourself, Miss Miller. I googled you. Isn't that what they teach you at journalism school? Consider things from every angle?'

'The angle I want to know, the angle I think you can help me with, is the Denver Group and Rheladrex. What if Madison Kopek was right? What if the drug that her brother took was dangerous? What happens next?'

'How long have you got?' scoffed Megan, standing up and pacing around her shoebox-sized office. She was like a trial lawyer performing in front of the jury. 'In America at least, complaints about a drug go through the FDA, the Food and Drug Administration. They have a division called MedWatch. The drug is investigated, then the FDA can request that a company add labelling information about side effects. In extreme cases the drug can be pulled from the market, but it can be a long process. And obviously the Big Pharma companies will fight their corner to keep their drugs on the market and protect themselves against paying enormous sums in damages.'

'How enormous can they be?'

'There was a diet drug called Fen-Phen several years ago. It was linked to heart valve problems in hundreds of patients who took it. More than nine thousand lawsuits were filed against it. Damages claims ran into the billions. There are court cases involving it still going on . . .'

'So the stakes are high.'

'It's every pharma company's worst nightmare. You spend millions developing a drug, get it to market, only to pay out billions.'

'But these drugs are tested, approved.'

'It's not an infallible system. One that has many flaws, in fact.'

'Do you know anything about the Rheladrex clinical trials?'

'Not off the top of my head. But I can find out.'

'Can you let me have what you get hold of?'

'What's it worth?' she said shrewdly.

'You've got to trust me. But I'll make it worth your while.'

Megan's phone started ringing.

'I should get this,' she said quickly.

'And I should go,' replied Rachel. 'Trials. Information. As soon as possible.'

'I'd better not be working for the enemy.'

'I promise you're not,' grinned Rachel. She was suddenly feeling more motivated to get to the truth.

25

Diana urged the horse onwards, leaning low over his neck, loving the sound of the beast's hooves thumping against the grass.

'Here we go, Nero,' she whispered. 'You can do it.'

She gripped the reins as the horse leapt the fallen tree, thrilled by the brief feeling of weightlessness as she left the saddle, almost as if time had stopped as they flew. Then they pounded down on the other side and the world shook back into motion.

'Bravo,' shouted Patty Reynolds from the other side of the paddock.

'Good boy, Nero!' said Diana, patting the colt's neck. 'We did it!'

She dismounted and led the horse over to Patty, who gave him lots of encouraging strokes on the nose.

'You're good at this,' smiled Patty wryly.

'Breaking horses in? Not really. I think it's just the mother in me. Besides, Nero's three now, he's ready, aren't you, boy?'

Patty linked her arm through her friend's.

'Thanks for coming. It's good to see you,' Diana said honestly.

Patty had arrived at ten o'clock that morning. They'd had brunch, then a stroll out to the paddock.

'Now are you quite sure you don't want to come and stay with us?'

'I'm fine here, honestly. But I wouldn't mind more gossipy breakfasts with one of my best friends.' Diana smiled, thinking how much she had enjoyed coffee and croissants with Patty that morning.

'So have you heard from the Denvers about the will?' asked Patty, looking serious.

Diana had confessed everything to her friend over coffee. Even though she had been Julian's wife, the amount of money she had been gifted in his will had shocked her, and more than anything she just wanted some practical advice about what to do with an inheritance that was as big as a small country's GNP.

'Not yet,' she said nervously. 'I'm sure I'm not their favourite person right now.'

'You and me both,' smiled Patty.

'What have you done?' asked Diana with surprise.

'I'm wresting control of Jules's memorial from bloody Elizabeth Denver.'

'You are?'

'I don't want it to be a repeat of the funeral. It should be a celebration of Julian, and I think if it's left in Liz's hands, it's just going to be another big showing-off occasion. This is about Jules, not how popular the Denvers are.'

'Thank you,' said Diana quietly. Patty had just articulated everything she had felt about the way the funeral had been handled.

'Speaking of which, you have a visitor,' said Patty under her breath.

Diana followed her line of sight and saw Adam leaning across the fence.

'Come and join us,' shouted Patty, her voice carrying on the breeze. 'Or are your City-boy shoes not up to it?'

'I think my boots are up to country life,' he smiled, swinging one leg over the fence and hopping into the field.

Immediately, Diana felt self-conscious. She had been riding for half an hour and she knew she must look terrible: sweaty, red-cheeked, her clothes speckled with mud. She quickly pushed her hair out of her face and straightened her clothes.

'I should go,' whispered Patty.

Diana felt even more embarrassed. 'It's fine. Stay.'

'I have a tennis match at two, unless you think it's going to get a bit hairy.'

'Adam? He's okay. If it was Liz marching this way, I'd be restraining you with Nero's reins.'

'Hello, Patty. Di,' said Adam, kissing both of them on the cheek.

190

Patty said her goodbyes and walked towards the main house.

'What are you doing here?' asked Diana, wiping the beads of sweat from her forehead.

Adam squinted at her in the sunlight. 'Checking up on you, of course.'

'I don't need a babysitter.' She smiled softly.

'Clearly not. I wasn't disturbing a girls' day out or anything, was I?'

'Well, I think Patty was checking up on me as well.'

'How are you?' he asked as they walked across the parched yellow field.

'Better than I was a few days ago.'

'Did you see Stuart Wilson yesterday?'

'Ah, this is what the visit is about,' she said, feeling on edge. 'You know about the will.'

'What's that supposed to mean?' replied Adam, frowning.

Diana hoped she wouldn't have to spell it out. 'I'm expecting a call from Ralph or Elizabeth any minute. I'm surprised they haven't contacted me already. Didn't the family have a meeting with Stuart after I'd been there?'

'Diana, I'm glad everything has gone to you and Charlie. Why the hell should it be any other way?'

'Does Liz see it like that?'

'Liz has funny ideas.'

Jessica, the groom, came out of the stables and took Nero's reins from Diana.

'Is that it for the day, Mrs Denver?'

'Not unless you fancy taking a horse out, Adam?'

He nodded his head in approval. 'I fancy it if you do.'

'Jess, we'll give Nero a rest. Can you bring out Audley and Casper?'

'How about Snowdon?' said Jessica. Behind the stable door Diana could see the dark nose of Julian's grey and white gelding, which had not been ridden since his death. She nodded, knowing that she couldn't carry on ignoring the poor animal.

Jessica and her assistant saddled up the two horses and brought them over to Diana and Adam, who took them at a gentle trot towards a copse on the outer edges of the estate. Diana didn't

191

want to bring the will up again. If Adam was upset at not inheriting Julian's multi-million-pound shareholding, then he was doing a good job of disguising it.

'I'm judging at the village fair,' she said with a smile. 'Biggest carrot.'

'I bet that's going to whip the residents of Boughton up into a lather.'

'Are you going to come?'

'Do you think I want to miss you manhandling vegetables?'

'You can help.'

'Keep me away from giant melons. I have a bad enough reputation as it is.'

She started to laugh. She felt guilty doing it, but it was a good, rich sound that came out of her body.

'Well, my mother forced me to get involved and I'm glad I did. I met a really nice lady at the committee meeting. She owns the café by the green. Her husband died a couple of years ago. It was good to talk to her.'

'You should make friends.'

'She's about seventy.'

'So? She's probably a better laugh than all those Notting Hill blondes you used to like having coffee with.'

'You mean the sort of women you date?' she smiled.

That world, those people seemed a lifetime ago. The charity events at various smart watering holes, the blow-dry appointments and Cowshed Spa afternoons. A conveyor belt of wives and girlfriends who would love-bomb you the minute they thought you were useful and then drop you the second you weren't. Then again, Patty's visit had only emphasised how isolated she was in Boughton. And after her showdown with Rachel, that was another female companion struck off the list.

'She could do a lot with that café, you know. It's a tatty old time warp at the moment, but she wants to sell up and I just don't think she'll get a decent price for it, the pittance she must be turning over selling a few teas and biscuits a day.'

'Sounds like a project,' he said, winking.

'Me? Become a café owner?'

'Why not?'

'Have you ever tried my cooking?'

'No. Not when the fabulous Mrs Bills is around. Does she still do that amazing beef bourguignon?'

They came to a stream. It was a lovely shady spot with a willow tree dipping into the water. Dismounting, they tied the horses' reins around a tree stump and sat on the grass.

'Tell me you'll think about the café.'

'I'll think about it,' she said, feeling secretly quite excited by the idea.

'How's Rachel?'

She knew what he was really asking. *What has she found out?*

'I don't want to talk about her.'

'Di, I thought you had got past that.'

She felt prickles of tears behind her eyeballs. Her mood swings were wild. One minute she could be astride a horse feeling that life might one day be liveable again. The next it was as if she had been pulverised by a concrete boulder.

She took a deep breath, knowing that she had to tell someone. How was she supposed to get better, move on, when the one thing she wanted to talk about was the one thing she daren't voice?

'Julian was having an affair.'

'What?' said Adam, wide-eyed. 'Recently?'

'You want to know what Rachel's been up to. Well that's what she's found out.'

'Do you believe her?'

He had chosen his words carefully. Clearly he thought it was possible.

'I called her a liar. Screamed at her,' she said, tears leaking out of her eyes. 'Truth is, yes, I can believe it.'

'*I* can't believe she did that,' muttered Adam, his face clouded with anger. Diana felt a little stir of emotion. He looked like he wanted to protect her, care for her. It was a good feeling right now.

'She had her reasons,' she said quietly.

'What?'

'You know Julian tried it on with Rachel too.'

'Tried it on?'

'Wanted sex with her. My sister. That's why she hated him.' Diana ran her tongue over her lips. 'I've been so angry the last few days. Blaming Rachel, blaming Julian's mistress. I should be blaming Julian, but I can't do that now, can I? Not now he's dead.'

She looked away from Adam. The truth was she *had* been blaming Julian and all that sorrow she had been feeling since his death had been funnelled into bitterness and a deep sense of betrayal.

Adam put his arm around her shoulder.

'Hey, hey. Stop this. I'm assuming Rachel hasn't got any actual *proof.*'

'Why, don't you believe it?' she asked, her eyes challenging his.

He looked away, and Diana remembered their conversation in Dorset when she had described Adam and Julian as different sides of the same coin. Adam had never been able to settle down, despite numerous beautiful girlfriends; he had never really been committed to one woman. The difference between him and Julian was that Adam wasn't married.

'Don't answer that,' she whispered, not wanting him to lie to her.

He put his hand over hers and squeezed her fingers.

She wanted him to hold her, to feel secure in someone's arms. He stood up and pulled her to her feet, and as their gazes locked she knew that he felt it too – a connection to the past, a connection to Julian, the person they had both loved most. It excited and unsettled her. And then it had gone, and she was glad that it had.

26

The Four Seasons hotel was in the perfect spot, with views over the city and the Potomac River. The smart lobby was milling with powerful-looking people, her suite was luxurious, and the whole place made her feel like a glamorous diplomat. Reclining on her cloud-sized pillows, Rachel flipped open her laptop, deciding that these were very agreeable working conditions and that she would quite happily move in here at the drop of a fedora.

She logged in and checked her emails, surprised to see that she had received one from the Giles-Miller Diving School, a place that seemed so far away, so long ago, it was as if it had fallen out of her consciousness.

> *Hey Newshound,*
>   *How's things over there in the motherland? Everything's going swimmingly over here (see what I did there?) and we're booked up until the end of the season. We could do with the extra pair of hands, but no rush. Let me know how it's going. Don't be a stranger and all that.*
>   *Lx*

She scanned it again, trying to work out if there was hidden meaning in any of the words. It was stupid really, there was nothing to the message, just a postcard really, but she was glad it had come. During their time together in Thailand, Liam had been the one she went to whenever she had a problem, the one she'd bounce ideas off, the one she trusted above anyone else. Right now she could do with running this whole mess past him, see what his big Cambridge brain would make of it.

'What are you looking so pleased about? Boyfriend?' asked Ross from the table by the window.

She felt herself blush, not realising that she had been smiling.

'No. Absolutely not.'

'She protesteth too much,' grinned Ross, scrolling through his own messages.

'If you must know, it's my diving partner, fishing around for when I'm coming back.'

'Good luck with that one. We could be here months.' He stretched his arms above his head, cracking his fingers and grinning. 'In fact there are some cold cases that stretch back decades.'

'I can't be here months, much as a room at the Four Seasons is much nicer than my apartment.'

The light was fading, and already Washington was disappearing from view outside the windows.

'How far do you want to take this?' Ross asked more quietly.

'What do you mean?'

'Diana wants answers. You have them. We can keep on looking, but for what? Where does this stop? As I said at the start, this is about providing your sister with resolution. It's not *All the President's Men*.'

She fell quiet, acknowledging that Ross had hit a nerve. She felt satisfied, important, just being here. She had always wanted to be a great reporter. She had started out at the more frivolous end of newspaper journalism, and although stories about cheating celebrities and benefit scams had hardly been Pulitzer prize-winning journalism, when she had exposed a truth, a cheat, it had felt good, even though she appreciated the hypocrisy that she often had to be devious herself to generate those stories. Being here, in a fancy hotel suite, interviewing people once more, piecing together bits of a mystery that so far had no sense or meaning, reminded her how much she had loved her old life. It was as if her professional downfall hadn't happened, as if her career trajectory had carried on how it had been meant to. She knew she was doing this as much for herself as for her sister, and Ross was absolutely right when he said they had to stop where Diana wanted them to.

'Look. A message from Greg Willets,' she said, opening up another email.

'Finally. What does it say?'

She scanned it quickly, paraphrasing. 'Yes. He thinks the photo I sent him might have been the blonde he saw Julian with in Washington. Quote, "Can't be sure. It was from across the road. It was dark. I'd had a drink."'

'Thanks for that,' said Ross sarcastically.

'We didn't need him anyway. Laura's confirmed the affair.'

There was a knock at the door. When Rachel opened it, a hotel employee in a smart dark suit handed her an envelope.

'What is it?' asked Ross when she had shut the door.

Rachel sliced open the envelope and flicked through the pages inside.

'Information about Rheladrex, by the looks of it,' she muttered. 'Thank you, Megan Hill.'

She lay back down on the bed, propping two pillows behind her head, and started to read.

'I'm hungry,' said Ross, getting up from his chair. 'There's a diner a few blocks away if you fancy it. Want me to go and get some takeout?'

'Sod that. Let's call up room service.'

'Are you sure? I mean, your sister is paying for all this and I'm sure she would much rather see you at the youth hostel than whooping it up at the Seasons. What if she refuses to pay the bill?'

'She's already given me cash. Besides, she knows I need the right conditions to work.' She grinned at him but secretly thought he might have a point. But remembering her sister's hard slap across the face at the Lake House, Rachel figured the least Diana owed her was a club sandwich on expenses.

'You take half of these pages,' she ordered. 'It's details of the late-stage development trials for Rheladrex.'

'Conducted by Rassalle Inc. Who are they?' queried Ross, scanning the top sheet.

'I read about this on the internet. Obviously for a drug to get passed by the FDA they have to go through layers of testing. The bulk of it used to be done on home turf – in this case

America – but in the past few years pharmaceutical companies have been doing a lot of their clinical trials overseas, often farming the job out to companies who specialise in it. They go all over the place: Africa, eastern Europe . . .'

'Cheap places, basically.'

'Life is cheap where there's money to be made,' replied Rachel cynically. 'Critics say that in some of the Third World countries used for testing there is also less regulation.'

'Look at this. Bristol, Jamaica.' Ross was already on Google Maps. 'It's about ten miles from Montego Bay. Bucharest is also listed.'

'So both of the places that Julian and Madison flew to had Rheladrex trials going on there.'

She took a swig of Coke from the bedside cabinet.

'Fancy a holiday?'

'What, now?' queried Ross.

'A working holiday. Which would you prefer? Montego Bay or Romania?'

'I think Montego Bay has better beaches,' smiled Ross.

'The words needle and haystack spring to mind, but if anyone can find out why Maddie and Julian were there and what they found, it's you, McKiney.'

Her mobile phone was buzzing furiously.

'Unknown number,' she tutted. 'They always make me nervous.'

When the caller spoke, Rachel almost fell back with shock. A smart, rich baritone; a voice from the grave.

'Rachel, it's Adam Denver.'

Her pulse slowed with relief. 'Adam, how are you?'

Ross pointed at the door. 'I'll be in my room,' he mouthed as she gave a thumbs-up.

The line was fuzzy, but Adam's annoyance was unmistakable. 'Are you a total bitch all of the time, or is it just when it comes to your sister?'

Rachel took a deep breath. He had caught her off guard with his call. She had spent most of the night struggling with the problem of whether to tell Diana about the developments in Washington, and had come to the conclusion that whilst honesty was the best policy, she was going to hang fire on telling her the whole uncomfortable truth. Having Julian's brother ranting at her only added to the confusion and reminded her that other people were involved in this – a lot of other people. People who might also be able to shed light on what was going on.

'Listen, Adam,' she said, struggling to control her temper. 'I'm only here because Diana asked me. If she's got a problem with what I'm doing, then fine. Until then, please keep out of it.'

'You want me to keep out of it?' he said. 'You'd like that, wouldn't you? Let you get on with doing more damage to my family.'

'It's my family too, Adam.'

'Really? Because I'm struggling to see why a member of this family would think it was a good idea to tell a grieving widow not only that her husband was having an affair, but that he wanted to have sex with her sister.'

'I didn't mean to,' she said, feeling her cheeks burn hot.

'You didn't mean to?' he said incredulously. 'I was with her today. She's so tight-wound, pale, nervy. She's pretending she is okay, but I honestly think she's on the edge.'

'The edge of what?' asked Rachel with alarm. 'Is she all right?'

'She will be. But it doesn't take a genius to work out that she is really, really fragile at the moment. You know, I understood why she asked you back to London. I'm Julian's brother. I want answers too. But you have to choose your moment.'

He was so bloody self-righteous, she thought, imagining his smug, good-looking face mocking her. She had a strong urge to smash her mobile against the wall, but mentally counted to ten to try and compose herself.

'I tried to be discreet. But she went snooping through one of the files.'

'Really? Knowing you, you'd have told her with the subtlety of a brick.'

'Adam, this isn't helping.'

'No, it's not.'

'I'll be more careful in future.' She couldn't believe she was actually apologising. Then again, she probably *had* told Diana too much. It had certainly not been the right moment to tell her about Julian's proposition in Tuscany. But it had been like magma inside her, burning her up, desperate to get to the surface for years. She had always felt the family had overreacted about the newspaper story, that she had become the lightning rod for all the anger and lies. She had admitted that she hadn't really stuck up for Julian when the story had been about to go to press, but she had never had occasion to explain why. She was glad her motives had been outed at last, but no, she hadn't chosen her moment with any tact or elegance.

'Good,' said Adam finally. 'So where are you now?'

'Washington.'

'I think we should talk.'

'So do I,' she said more excitedly. 'I've been trying to get in touch with you for days. You see, I'm trying to build up a picture of Julian's life before his death.'

'Rachel, we need to set a few parameters.'

She almost laughed at his arrogance, but she needed to keep him on side, for now at least.

'So when do you want to *talk*?' she said flatly.

'I have a space in my diary tomorrow.'

'Well I happen to be in Washington.'

'And I happen to have time to see you tomorrow.'

He was maddening, she thought, before reluctantly acquiescing to his demands.

Ross walked back into the room with a platter of French fries and sandwiches. But as Rachel said her goodbyes to Adam Denver, suddenly she wasn't hungry any more.

27

Harrow School was both magnificent and terrifying. When Diana had first driven up the main road of the village, she could remember craning her neck to look up at the dark stone of the buildings with their leaded windows leaning in over the road.

'This place is wonderful,' she had said to Julian, grinning in the driving seat. 'Is the school as pretty as this?'

'This *is* the school, honey,' he had laughed.

Even now, it seemed to Diana that the school had been plonked down on the hill and the rest of the village had simply grown up in the tiny spaces in between. According to Julian, that was a fairly close approximation of its history. The school buildings were everywhere – if the boys had a music lesson, say, they would walk down the high street, past the butcher's and the florist's, and in through a narrow doorway marked only by a brass plaque. The whole village was the playground, and on any given day you could see boys hurrying to class, books and folders under their arms, along with the distinctive straw boaters – 'hats', Charlie seemed determined to call them – which were part of the navy and grey uniform but were never willingly worn outside. Unusually for most educational establishments in the twenty-first century, it was also a full boarding school, which meant that the opportunities for parents to see their children in term time were limited. But the school had been very supportive and understanding about Julian's death, and had readily agreed to Diana's request to take Charlie out for the afternoon.

He was waiting in front of his house as Diana hurried up the high street to meet him. She looked at her son and her heart gave a lurch. She wanted to reach out and smooth down his unruly

201

russet hair, restraining herself when she saw that a group of students were close by and would no doubt mock him mercilessly.

'All right, Mum?' He had a teenager's reticence about physical contact with his parents, but his grin said that he was pleased to see her.

'So where's the best place for lunch around here?' she asked. As she looked at him, she suddenly realised that they were back to where they'd started. Just a single mum and her little boy trying to make their way in the world.

The days of Charlie's early childhood, when they had lived on benefits in the tiny flat in Tufnell Park, seemed a very long time ago indeed. She didn't miss the constant worry about money, the anxiety of how to juggle a job with child care, the decisions she had to make on a daily basis – should she put the heating on for the morning with the little pound-coin meter, or should she spend the money on proper nappies for Charlie?

In a strange way, though, life was simpler then. She had come to London with a dream of bettering herself, and even when she thought they would be stuck in their tiny flat for ever, she had the sense that life was out there in front of them, ready to be lived. She had never shared her sister's passion for the capital, but could admit that it seemed a place where excitement lurked around every corner. She remembered their bus rides into the West End to meet Auntie Rachel in one of her cheap and cheerful student lunch hangouts. She remembered listening to Rachel's weird and wonderful stories involving celebrities she met at the bar where she worked. People from the telly, people who seemed so worldly and glamorous it was as if they were from another universe. So many things filled her with a sense of wonder on a daily basis – the sight of Buckingham Palace at the end of the Mall, the black door of 10 Downing Street that winked at you through the iron security gates, the world-class view of the Houses of Parliament and St Paul's Cathedral as you sat on a red bus crossing the Thames.

Things were different now. Not much made her go *wow* any more. Money, opportunities, anaesthetised you from that.

'How hungry are you?' asked Charlie.

'Starving,' she lied.

'Right. Burger and chips it is. There's a great place just down here.'

'So I'm not pulling you out of anything important?' she asked, nudging him playfully.

'Just cricket this afternoon. Although the team will obviously be missing out on my ace batsmanship.'

'Can't keep you too long, then.'

'Is everything all right, Mum?' he asked intuitively.

She put on her most practised brave face. 'Everything is fine. Auntie Rachel is back from Thailand. She brought you this,' she said, pulling the teddy bear out of her Vuitton tote.

Charlie took it and just looked at it for a few moments. He had always been conflicted about Rachel's estrangement from the family. He had only been nine when the story about Julian had appeared in the *Sunday Post*, too young to really understand it, but old enough to get that his beloved auntie had done something very wrong. Something that had led to terrible teasing and bullying in the school playground. *Your daddy doesn't love your mummy*; words that had sent him home from prep school crying each afternoon.

They approached the restaurant that Charlie had recommended and went inside. It was warm and smelt of freshly baked bread. It was also quiet, and a waitress showed them to the best seat in the house, a small booth by the window.

'I'm fine, you know,' said Charlie after they had settled down and ordered.

'I know you're fine. That's why I wanted to have this conversation with you.'

'This sounds as if it is going to be rather grown-up.'

'It is.' She smiled, admiring his maturity. 'I went to Dad's solicitor this week. He wanted to tell me about the contents of his will.'

'Money doesn't matter. It won't bring him back.'

'No, it won't. But there are lots of practical things we have to sort out, much as we'd rather not. And this is one of them.'

'Did Uncle Adam get the Ferrari collection?' Charlie asked, peering up at her through his long tawny fringe.

Diana laughed. 'Yes, he did. Why? Did you want them?'

'No, but I wouldn't have minded the motorbikes,' he smiled.

His mother put her hand over her son's on the table.

'That was never going to happen; Dad knew I wouldn't allow it.'

'So they went to Adam too?'

'I'd say that was a good home, wouldn't you?'

Their drinks arrived. Charlie swizzled his straw around his glass of cola.

'So you've made up with Auntie Rachel? I thought she might be at the funeral. I was hoping she would be. You know, sometimes you don't think you need certain people, but you do.'

He was wiser than his years. Diana knew that Julian had made a good choice gifting his shareholding to their son.

'Charlie, I'm here to talk about something your dad wanted you to have.'

'What?' he asked doubtfully.

'He's given you all his shares in the company.'

There was a couple of seconds' silence.

'All of them?' he said finally.

Diana nodded.

'Voting shares?'

She looked at her son with surprise. She'd had no idea that he understood the corporate make-up of the business.

'Everything that Dad owned. They are to be held in trust until you are twenty-one. He also attached a letter of intent. It's not legally binding, but he expressed a wish that one day you become CEO of the company.'

Charlie had fallen silent.

'The reason I wanted to talk to you about it now is that I need to know how you feel about it,' continued Diana softly. 'I spoke to Adam and he maintains that he never really wanted to join the family business, that he felt obliged to do so. And I would never want you to be in that position of feeling that it's your duty.'

She thought of the Denvers – steely Ralph, frightening Elizabeth, snobby Barbara – and wondered if she always wanted to be so tightly aligned with them. But then this was Charlie's choice. Not hers.

'He really thought of me as his son, didn't he?'

'Of course you were his son,' she said, her mouth opening in horror.

Charlie looked up at her, his mellow hazel eyes taking on an edge of defiance.

'When he married you, he got me. I know he *called* me his son, but don't you think I've often wondered how he could love another man's child like his own?'

'But he did,' whispered Diana, wondering how much the thought of this had tortured Charlie.

'I know that now,' he said, his lips beginning to wobble with emotion.

'You should read this,' she said, pushing a sheet of paper across the table between them. It was Julian's letter of intent that he had attached to his will. She had read it a dozen times over since she had left Stuart Wilson's office and could memorise every word, even though it had felt as if she been intruding on a father's parting words to his son.

'I'll read it later,' said Charlie, putting it in his pocket. 'I do want his shares,' he added. 'I want to make him proud of me. I want to be the man he thought I could be.'

Diana clenched her fists under the table. She was determined not to cry in front of her son, even though this time, they were tears of happiness.

28

Rachel was feeling terrible. She had a pounding headache and her skin had that crawling feeling you get just before the onset of a three-day cold. Glancing into the window of the taxi, she was pretty sure she looked as bad as she felt. Her flying visit to Washington had been one of those classic red-eye in-and-outs that was a positive magnet for jet lag. She had been living on coffee, junk food and nerves for three days, and the return trip had been disrupted by a baby in the row behind her. What she wanted right now was a long bath and three or four glasses of red wine, not to be zooming down the motorway to meet someone who had called her a bitch the last time they had spoken.

'You have to go, Rach,' Ross had said when Rachel had explained her plan on the way to the airport. 'Adam Denver could be useful even if he doesn't know it.'

Of course, it was easy for Ross to say. Rachel couldn't help but think she had got the raw end of the deal – she was flying straight into the dragon's den, whilst he was probably sitting on the beach now sipping a cocktail.

She looked down at the phone in her lap and opened the message again. It had been waiting for her when she turned on her phone at Heathrow.

Blackbushe, midday today. I checked your flights, car will be waiting. GU17 9LQ. You'll see where. Adam.

She shook her head at the self-importance of 'I checked your flights'. He was telling her he was in control and that he knew she would drop everything to come and meet him. She toyed with the idea of leaning over to tell the driver to turn around, take her back to that hot bath and Pinot Noir at Somerfold, but she couldn't. Adam knew that, and it drove her wild. *He probably knows that too*, she thought. *That's why he's doing it.*

Rachel couldn't quite believe that she had once found Adam Denver attractive. Shuddering, she thought of all the cack-handed seduction attempts she had made over the years. She had been seated next to him at a number of dinner parties, and each time had got so drunk that she could scarcely string a sentence together, let alone dazzle him with her line in witty repartee. He'd been there too on that fateful Tuscan holiday, and during the first couple of days she had invited him to Sienna, for a walk in the poppy fields, to a wine-tasting session at a local vineyard, before a six-foot model called Carina had turned up at the palazzo – straight from a modelling assignment into Adam Denver's bed. She was older now, wiser. She wouldn't make those sort of mistakes again.

They turned off the motorway and on to a country road. Where the hell were they going? She wondered about asking the driver, but he had just tapped the postcode into his GPS, so there was no point. It was all big houses and open fields: a golf course? Funny, she didn't see Adam Denver playing golf, it was a little too parochial for him, a little too Rotary Club, especially out here in deepest Surrey – or was it Hampshire by now? And then she saw it, and began to chuckle despite herself. Of course. Blackbushe was an aerodrome, complete with a tall red-brick control tower and one of those stripy windsocks waving over the dozens of cute little propeller planes parked next to the runway.

She offered the driver a fistful of notes, but he refused to take them. The cab had apparently been paid for on account.

Adam Denver was standing by the double doors to the airport office, wearing a navy flying jacket, cream chinos and aviator sunglasses. He looked like Steve McQueen and Rachel was damn sure he knew it.

'An aerodrome, Adam?' she said, wincing as a small plane came in to land, cutting through the air with a roar.

'Nothing gets past you, does it, Rachel?' he said. 'Are you ready for this?'

'For what exactly?'

He nodded towards the runway and set off without looking to see if she was following.

'I've got some things to attend to,' he said when she had caught up. 'I thought we could kill two birds with one stone.'

'What, in that?' she said, as she saw where he was leading her. A shiny black helicopter was sitting to one side of the aeroplanes, its bubble-shaped cockpit catching the sun.

'I thought you might enjoy a ride,' he said coolly.

'I'm not some hick from the sticks who has never been in a helicopter before,' she said as Adam leant over her to strap her in.

'Here, put these on,' he said, handing her a pair of headphones with a microphone attached, then turning away to flick switches and start the engine.

Come to think of it, Rachel couldn't actually remember ever being in a helicopter, and she was secretly rather thrilled as she adjusted the earphones on her head. She glanced over at Adam as he worked, seeing the sharp cheekbones, those lazy green eyes behind the sunglasses.

'So where are we going?' she asked, raising her voice over the noise of the helicopter.

Adam reached across her and plugged her headphones into a socket so they could talk on the intercom.

'Jersey,' he said, his voice a little crackly.

'Jersey!'

'Got somewhere more important to go?'

'How long is it going to take?' she said. 'I'm on a tight schedule and I've just flown in from Washington.'

'Aren't we the busy girl?' smiled Adam, pulling smoothly on the lever next to his seat. The helicopter rose into the air and Rachel grabbed at the dashboard to stabilise herself as the ground dropped away beneath them.

She opened her mouth to speak, and for the first time Adam glanced at her. 'Why don't you just shut up and enjoy the view?'

It was certainly exhilarating flying over the English countryside, low enough to see people walking along the rivers, cows in the fields, and it was fascinating to watch everything from above, like peering into a hidden world. It was even more exciting to leave the English coast just west of the Isle of Wight and strike out over the Channel, which was twinkling in the late morning sun.

The journey took a little over half an hour, and she was quite sorry when they eventually swooped over the patchwork fields of the island. Adam pushed forward on the controls and the helicopter tilted down towards the large white H of a heliport.

They crossed to the terminal, where a man in a tie was waiting with a clipboard. 'Morning, James,' said Adam, signing something with a flourish, then jumping into a dark green Range Rover.

'You coming?' he called, leaning out of the window.

Rachel pointedly didn't ask any questions as Adam drove along the narrow lanes; she didn't want to give him the satisfaction. Instead she sat and watched the scenery pass. It was surprisingly like rural England: hedgerows, stone walls, cute little whitewashed farmhouses; they could have been in Devon or Somerset, except that all the road names were in French. Rue de la Mare, Route des Landes.

They drove into the capital, St Helier. Adam parked on yellow lines and told her to wait in the vehicle. 'So we don't get a ticket,' he said, opening the door and hopping on to the pavement.

'Where are you going?'

'In there.'

'A bank? What are you doing? Staging a heist? I wouldn't put the whole Thomas Crown thing past you.'

'If you must know, I have to go and sign some papers. I shouldn't be more than twenty minutes.'

'But what if a traffic warden comes? I don't speak French . . .' but he had already run up the stone steps into the building.

He was back in the car within ten minutes.

'Well that was an awfully long way for nothing.'

'Actually, I was just securing a loan for seventy-five million euros. Are you hungry?'

'Famished. I slept through breakfast on the plane. Those business-class beds are actually pretty comfy. But I thought you wanted to talk.'

'I do want to talk, but I thought we could do it over food.'

They crossed the island to its north-westerly tip. As they

rounded a bend, the green-blue of the sea glistened in front of them, framed on either side by the plunging sides of a headland.

'Wow,' said Rachel. 'Look at that.'

'Plemont,' said Adam. 'One of the prettiest spots on the island.'

He drove down a single-lane black-top road until it simply disappeared into a sandy turning space, fringed with yellow gorse, only the cliffs beyond.

'This way,' he said, jumping out and heading for a little footpath.

'Where the hell are you taking me now?' Rachel muttered under her breath, worrying that she was going to turn an ankle over in her city-girl heels. The thought did cross her mind that Adam could simply push her into the sea; there was no one out here to witness it, save a few squawking seagulls.

She came up beside him, standing in front of the view: the dramatic cliffs plunging into the waves, a tiny strip of yellow beach just visible below.

'This is amazing,' she said with a gasp.

'Glad you like it. I'm going to buy it.' He pointed back up the hill. 'See those buildings? Used to be a holiday camp, but it's been derelict for years. The hotel division is in negotiations to buy this whole stretch of land and build a hotel.'

'Another holiday camp?'

'Deluxe private villas, each with uninterrupted views of the headland. Can't you see it?'

'Actually I can.' She nodded. 'It reminds me a little of the Scilly Isles. I used to love going there when I was a kid. It was so exotic, but homespun at the same time. And I guess this place is more accessible than the Scillies.'

Adam nodded. 'It's less than an hour from London, five airlines fly here every day and it's the sunniest part of the British Isles by far.'

'Actually I think the Scillies holds that honour.'

'Do you have to challenge me on everything?'

'I expect you're about to have a go at me, so I thought I'd simply get a headstart.'

They walked along the headland to a small, bustling café at

the top of the cliff. They ordered two mugs of tea and some Victoria sponge, and sat on a wooden picnic bench outside.

'So,' said Adam, poking at his sponge. 'What do you want to discuss?'

'I thought you wanted to talk to me,' she said, looking up at him over her mug.

'I said my piece on the phone. I just want you to tread carefully with Diana.'

'And I will,' she said quietly. 'How is she? Honestly? I was freaking out when you said she was on the edge.'

'She feels angry, duped . . .'

'I didn't want to lie to her.'

'Not with you. With Julian.' He looked at her cynically.

'What?' she said tartly.

He didn't speak for a few moments. 'I just think you're your own worst enemy,' he said finally.

'What's that supposed to mean?'

'You had it all. You were on track to being an editor by thirty, weren't you? Beyond that the sky was your limit; you could have had an editorship in New York, a consultancy for one of the big lobbyists in DC. You threw it all away, and what the hell for? Petty revenge? One-upmanship with your big sister? Believe me, Rachel, when I say that it just isn't worth it.'

'You sound like you're talking from experience.'

He hesitated and a furrow appeared between his brows.

'I actually had a row with Jules a couple of weeks before he died. A big one. It was about this place, actually. I was adamant I wanted to buy it; Julian said it was a folly, that I was expanding the group too quickly. We said some nasty things. I didn't go to their garden party . . .' The corners of his mouth curled downwards, spoiling his prettiness. 'I wonder if I'd been there whether I'd have been able to do something, spot that something was wrong.'

'I think a lot of people have been thinking that.'

'Some people might not want you around, Rachel, but I do. I want you to find out what happened, and I agree with Di that if there is one person who can do that, it's you.'

'I wasn't expecting a vote of confidence.'

'What were you in Washington for?' he asked finally.

She sipped her tea and told him all about Madison Kopek. She told him that the autopsy had revealed that she was pregnant, and that Laura Dale had confirmed that Madison was sleeping with Julian. She asked him about Rheladrex, which he confessed he had never heard of, and told him how Ross McKiney was in Montego Bay trying to trace Julian and Madison's steps there.

By the end of the story, Adam had definitely paled.

'So what's your conclusion? You think Jules killed himself over Madison and the baby, or you're thinking something else, because you don't need me to tell you that conspiracy theories have got you into a whole heap of trouble before.'

She knew he was referring to Malcolm McIntyre, and wondered how he knew. It wasn't a secret why she had got booted off the newspaper – her arrest had been high-profile – but she wondered if he had been keeping tabs on her career.

'That wasn't a conspiracy theory. That was my Watergate. I almost nailed him, I had the evidence. It just wasn't legal.'

'Illegal evidence might as well be no evidence,' said Adam harshly.

Rachel didn't like thinking about it. Malcolm McIntyre was a wealthy businessman, society figure and heavyweight political donor and philanthropist. Rumours that he also had a predilection for young boys had been around for years, whispered in the corridors of power and in the newsrooms around the country. But no one had outed him. He'd been reported to the police many times, but each time the allegations had been dismissed. Several of his victims had stepped forward years after the abuse happened, abuse that had damaged them and made them, in the eyes of the law, unreliable. That he was also incredibly litigious made every editor in the land want to keep him at arm's length. But not Rachel Miller. She had met one of his victims, Edward, when he had called the *Post* and offered to sell his story. He was homeless, living in hostels and on the streets. He busked for money, dabbled in drugs, but Rachel had liked him, trusted him.

Edward had met McIntyre in the children's home where he had grown up, and had been offered work experience in his office, which had led to something much more sinister. His story had made Rachel hot with anger. She didn't care if McIntyre was litigious. Why should he be allowed to get away with something as heinous as that just because he could afford an army of lawyers? So she'd gone after him. She was senior enough at the newspaper by now to authorise payments to Ross McKiney, who had linked McIntyre to pimps and pornographers, but had done so by hacking into his phone. And so Ross had gone to jail, Rachel had narrowly escaped it, and with pomp and spin and legal threats Malcolm McIntyre had been completely exonerated.

'Does Diana know about Madison Kopek's pregnancy?' asked Adam finally.

'No. And I'm not going to tell her.'

He nodded in agreement.

'Do you know the CEO of Denver Chemicals?'

'Simon Michaels? I know who he is. I've met him a number of times. I wouldn't say he's a close pal.'

'Can you speak to him for me?'

'What about? Rheladrex?' he said incredulously.

'Of course. Haven't you been listening to anything I've said?'

'You've got your story, Rachel. Julian's mistress was pregnant. With his baby. A child he was desperate for. Fuck, Jules. You idiot.' He tipped his chin up towards the sky and closed his eyes.

'That's not the story. It's information. And information isn't always the truth,' she said quietly. 'It would be easy to stop here. Diana already knows about Madison. That's enough. But I want the truth, Adam. I always have.'

'And how do you know you've found it?' he asked, looking at her.

Her eyes scanned to a path that led to the edge of the cliff.

'Somehow you always know when it's the end of the road. And I just don't think we're there yet.'

'I'll take you home.'

'Will you call Simon Michaels?'

'Tell me what you want to know and I'll call him.'

29

Elizabeth Denver's house was big, even by Kensington standards. A tall double-fronted town house set just off a square only a stone's throw from the High Street, in the exclusive pocket known as the Phillimores, it seemed even whiter than the other properties, with a shiny black door that reminded Diana of 10 Downing Street. She was greeted by a maid – *not a butler?* she thought as she handed over her wrap and was shown towards the living room. *Elizabeth is letting standards drop.*

Not that anyone else would think such a thing, especially when they saw the living area. It was an expensively designed mix of styles, with deep red floral-patterned wallpaper, extravagant gold picture frames and modern furniture. The centrepiece of the room was the huge crystal chandelier, twinkling like a fallen star.

'Diana, wonderful to see you,' said Elizabeth, striding purposefully through the door. Diana had rarely seen her sister-in-law in anything but a trouser suit and a serious blow-dry, but today she was wearing a pair of cream jeans and a silk blouse. Her hair was flat and tucked behind her ears, and she wore little make-up. 'So glad you could come.'

It wasn't as if Diana had had a great deal of choice; Elizabeth had practically insisted, in her rather lofty, school-marmish way, when she had called with the invitation. 'You can't stay out there in that huge draughty house,' she had said in a tone that suggested argument was not acceptable. 'No, I will make you some comfort food and we'll have a good old chin-wag. How's that sound?'

It actually sounded hideous to Diana. She had never warmed to Julian's sister – in fact she doubted there was any warmth in the woman at all – and she was fairly sure the antipathy was mutual. When Julian had been alive they had seen Elizabeth once a month for supper, and each time she had made it seem like an interview for an MBA programme, with Diana forced to apologise for her ignorance. Elizabeth clearly felt that her brother should have made a more strategic marriage, possibly to an heiress due to come into a suitably compatible multinational business, or even some sort of minor European royalty, someone who fitted in with Elizabeth's overblown self-image; certainly not to his secretary, at any rate.

So under normal circumstances Diana would have done anything to put off her formidable sister-in-law. But things weren't normal, far from it. Julian was dead, Charlie was at school and Rachel was out playing detective. And after her meeting with Stuart Wilson earlier in the week, Diana knew that she had to face the Denver family sooner rather than later. Adam was one thing, but Elizabeth was quite another, so it was with trepidation that she accepted her sister-in-law's invitation to come through to the kitchen.

The large oak table at one end of the room was set for two, with wine goblets.

'It's just the two of us for supper, although David might join us later.' David Douglas was Elizabeth's much older husband, who had a senior job in the City. Diana quite liked him. Although she thought he would doubtless be as fierce in business as his wife, he was an old-school gent with beautiful manners and she found herself wishing he was here.

'So. How was your day?' asked Elizabeth, her voice still breezy.

'I've been to see Charlie.'

'You've been to Harrow? How nice. I must drive up there one afternoon with David. And how's Olga Shapiro? She's good, isn't she?'

Diana couldn't help frowning. Olga had not been Elizabeth's recommendation, so she had no idea how her sister-in-law knew which therapist she was seeing. Then again, Elizabeth had always made it her business to know everything. It would not surprise Diana if there was some bugging device in her car that fed all her movements back to Elizabeth's Kensington HQ. Or was she being ultra-paranoid?

Diana sat down at the table and Elizabeth slid her slender hand into an oven glove, an image that Diana wanted to capture on her phone for posterity.

'It's Consuela's night off, so I'm afraid you're lumbered with my cooking. Cordon bleu standard cuisine sadly isn't in my repertoire of skills.'

She pulled a tray out of the oven and a steaming highly glazed salmon en croute presented itself.

'Looks impressive to me,' said Diana, knowing that Elizabeth's idea of casual supper for two would inevitably involve some aspect of showing-off.

Elizabeth was an incredibly accomplished woman, but unlike many of her type and class she had no qualms about letting people know it. Educated at Yale and Stanford Business School, she had gone out of her way to be different from her brothers. She'd had a short tenure in her twenties working for Denver, specialising in the finance side, but had promptly left to set up her own business when her father had made it clear that Julian would be his heir. Diana wasn't exactly sure what Elizabeth did, but it was certainly profitable – her asset management company was worth over $1 billion in less than five years. Three years ago, her operation had been 'folded' into the Denver Group – perhaps when she had made her point to her father – and she was now a very vocal member of the board.

'So, were you surprised by the contents of Julian's will?' said Elizabeth, slicing a knife through the pastry. She looked up, her bright eyes challenging Diana's as she served the food. It was typical of her to cut straight to the chase.

'Well, Adam got the Ducatis. That wasn't too much of a shock.'

Elizabeth licked a fleck of pink salmon flesh from her fingertip and sat down.

'I thought it was only fair to let you know as soon as possible that we intend to contest the will,' she said, as matter-of-factly as if she were reporting the weather.

'I'm sorry?' gasped Diana, feeling the words stick in her throat.

'Don't take it personally,' replied Elizabeth more kindly. 'But you should understand that this is family. This is business.'

'What do you mean, *this is family*? Charlie and I were Julian's family. His wife and son.' She could feel a circle of heat pooling around her neck. She was determined not to wither, but Elizabeth had switched into full aggressive business mode.

'We accepted you into this family, Diana, but Julian was your only connection to it. Charlie is not Julian's natural son and he is not a Denver. We certainly can't allow him to be on the board.'

'Of course Charlie is his son,' said Diana, willing herself to stay strong. 'Not by birth, but legally. Julian adopted him.'

Elizabeth waved her hand as if that was a trifling legality.

'This is bigger than that, Diana. This affects the whole company. We can't allow Julian's sentimentality to undermine the stability of a multi-billion-pound business.'

'Sentimentality?' said Diana, amazed. 'Julian loved Charlie; he was his father!'

Elizabeth was clearly unmoved by this argument. Diana forced herself to think. She knew she was not as smart as her sister-in-law, she didn't have the mental nimbleness to win arguments, but she thought about Charlie's face over lunch, his quiet determination that he was going to make his father proud.

'Challenge the will. On what grounds?' she asked, battling to disguise the shake in her voice.

'Mental incompetence, of course.'

'Don't be ridiculous,' spluttered Diana.

'I spent the whole day with a very experienced team of probate lawyers yesterday and they seem to think otherwise. Julian killed himself. I hate to remind you of that detail. But he did. He had lost his mind. He was unstable, depressed, unpredictable undoubtedly. It was a very recent will and I am not convinced that he was of the appropriate soundness of mind to make it. Certainly I am aware that previous versions made proper provisions for Julian's shareholding. I believe they were gifted to Adam and myself which my lawyers are calling a testamentary promise, especially in view of all the work I do for Denver. Julian could not have done his job without me . . .'

'You're wicked, you know that,' said Diana, standing up and

throwing her napkin down on the table. Her cheeks were burning.

Elizabeth put a regal arm out to soften the atmosphere.

'I am not the bad guy here, Diana. Believe it or not, I don't want to see you and Charlie lose out. You deserve Somerfold. And if Julian wanted you to have his other investments, then so be it.' Her mouth twitched as if she didn't exactly believe what she was saying. 'But forget the Denver shareholdings, Diana. Be reasonable. Think of the family, the business. And ask yourself – do you really, honestly want it for Charlie? The profile, the responsibility? The family certainly don't want to see him fall short. There is an earlier will we suggest should be admitted to probate. In it there are plenty of provisions that will make you a very wealthy woman. Richer than you ever dreamt possible when you first arrived in London. I mean, ask yourself, how much money do you and Charlie need?'

'This isn't about the money,' Diana whispered. 'This is about Julian. His wishes. What he wanted for Charlie.'

Elizabeth gave a hard, superior laugh. 'Julian could be a fool. He let his heart rule his head. You know that more than anyone.'

'Ralph, Adam, I don't believe they would do this . . .' She had to put her hands on the table to support herself. Her whole body felt beaten and weak.

'My parents are old, as you well know, and my father is in ill health. You correctly guess that they won't want a fight, but they will, believe me, if it means protecting the company, protecting the family.'

'Is that how you see yourself now? The head of the family?' she said with as much scorn as she could muster. 'I am glad to hear that Julian's death has been of some use to you.'

Elizabeth put down her fork. 'How dare you say such a thing?' she said, making no attempt to conceal her contempt.

Diana could feel her resolve crumbling. The fog was creeping back in, ready to suffocate her.

'I'm leaving,' she said quietly.

'Fine. Go,' said Elizabeth sharply. 'Go home and think about whether you've got the strength for the fight.'

'Don't underestimate the strength a mother can find to protect her child,' Diana said as she turned for the door.

She let herself out and sank on to the stone steps outside. She could sense a presence at the window behind her, Elizabeth watching her from a crack in the curtains, but she didn't care.

Her hands were shaking as she pulled her phone out of her bag. 'Mum,' she whispered when a voice answered at the other end. 'Mum. Come and get me. I need you. And find Rachel, please. Find her and bring her to us.'

30

Rachel stood at the bottom of the steps leading to her mother's apartment for a long time, too scared to go inside, too worried about what she was going to see or hear. She had been on her way back to Somerfold in the executive Mercedes that Adam Denver had laid on for her, not wanting to admit to herself that she'd had an unexpectedly pleasant afternoon in Jersey, when her mother had contacted her saying that she had to come to Bayswater immediately. The urgency of Sylvia Miller's voice and the knowledge that her mother would rather communicate with her via homing pigeon than actually talk to her had sent a cold shiver of worry down her spine. All she could hear were Adam's words about Diana being on the edge, and despite Sylvia's reassurances that her sister was okay, Rachel had spent the entire journey into London feeling sick with fear and guilt that something dreadful had happened to her.

Finally she pressed the bell and took the long flight of stairs to her mother's first-floor flat. The door was slightly ajar, so she crept inside, using the few moments she was alone to take in her surroundings. She had been aware that Julian had bought Sylvia a property in London when Diana had first fallen pregnant three years earlier. A large lateral space with long windows that overlooked a pretty square, the property was an estate agent's wet dream, not so much a granny flat as a bribe. After his infidelity, after his betrayal of her daughter, it appeared that Julian had paid for Sylvia's forgiveness the only way he knew how – with money.

She heard footsteps from the other end of the hall and felt her pulse quicken; the last thing she felt like was another hostile reception, but instead her mother crept out of the kitchen with the quietness and solemnity of an undertaker.

'Hello, Rachel. How are you?' she said softly.

The gentle welcome almost knocked Rachel sideways and heightened her concern even further.

'Hello, Mum,' she said quickly. 'Where is she?'

'In the guest bedroom. I didn't know whether to call the doctor for a sedative.'

Her mother hadn't actually told her anything other than that Diana was upset and wanted to see her. In the car over here Rachel had been imagining all sorts of scenarios. As a child she had never been able to wait to see what happened at the end of a story, always sneaking a look at the last page, desperate to find out if Cinderella and Prince Charming got together. Of course they always did – but then that was only fairy tales, wasn't it? Look how it had turned out for Diana and her handsome prince: no happily-ever-after there.

'Can't she sleep?'

'She says she can't.'

'But she's okay?'

Sylvia nodded, her eyes closed, her lips pressed together. 'She called me from Kensington,' she said, her voice not even a whisper. 'She was sobbing so hard I could hardly hear where to pick her up from. I found her eventually. Slumped up against a wall in the Phillimores like a homeless person. I hope to God that no one saw her.'

Rachel didn't like to point out that being spotted by a west London acquaintance was probably the least of Diana's problems.

'She wants to talk to you.'

'Then you'd better put the kettle on.'

Sylvia put her hand out and touched her daughter's forearm. Rachel flinched. Sylvia had never been the most demonstrative of parents – Rachel couldn't remember being scooped up or hugged as a child – and whilst the gesture wasn't unwelcome, it certainly made her jolt with surprise.

'Thank you for coming.'

Rachel knew it was not an apology for excommunicating her

221

daughter for almost four years, but it was a peace offering, a sign that the worst was over, and she smiled back softly.

She walked down the hallway, taking slow, quiet steps. It wasn't more than ten metres to the bedroom at the far end of the apartment, but it felt like a very long way indeed. She pushed open the door and peeped inside. The room was unlit and gloomy. Diana was standing by the window, peering out. As she turned to look at Rachel, a cone of light from the street lamp outside illuminated her face. Despite its soft, fuzzy glow, Rachel could see that she was as white as a ghost, and her once glossy hair was lank around her face. Her eyes seemed to have receded a little further back into her skull, her cheekbones were sharper, her beautiful fine-boned face looked haunted.

Rachel turned a lamp on and sat on the bed.

'Do you want to talk?' she said simply.

Diana just nodded.

'Maybe we should go for a walk. This place is so close to the park . . .'

'Now?' asked Diana, wrapping her arms across herself. 'Won't it be dangerous?'

'Don't be daft. It's a warm summer night, it'll be teeming. I think there's a concert on, actually. We might even be able to buy ice cream and beer.'

'I think I'll pass on that one,' Diana said weakly.

There was a cardigan draped across the back of the chair. Rachel picked it up and handed it to her sister.

'Come on. Let's get some fresh air.'

Sylvia was standing outside in the hallway, her face racked with worry. Her eyes darted between the two women as they came out of the room.

'We're going out,' said Diana briskly.

'Is that a good idea?' Sylvia's expression indicated that she thought it was anything but.

'I think so.'

Rachel noticed how Sylvia instantly deferred to her elder daughter.

Leaving their mother's flat, they came out of the square, crossed Bayswater Road, dodging the traffic and the cyclists, and walked into Hyde Park. The distant sound of drums and guitars came to them on the breeze, muffled as if it was travelling through water.

'So how was Washington?'

'Interesting.'

'Did your friend go to Jamaica?'

'Yes.'

'Are you going to tell me about it, or am I just here to pick up the tab?'

'Why did you want me here?' asked Rachel, ignoring her jibe. 'I didn't think you'd want to see me again for a very long time.'

'Did Mum tell you where she found me?'

Rachel laughed. 'She was worried Richard Branson was going to spot you in the gutter.'

'It was so embarrassing.' She looked pained at the very thought of it. Diana was usually so elegant, so poised, she rarely had anything to be embarrassed about.

'It can't have been as embarrassing as the time I bumped into Daniel Craig in Soho and asked him if I knew him from school,' said Rachel, attempting to lighten the situation.

'You didn't?' said Diana, staring at her wide-eyed.

'He was polite. I kept pressing the point home. Asked him if he was from Ilfracombe. If he was in the swimming club . . .'

Diana giggled. It was a proper chuckle, and Rachel felt proud that she had been able to provoke that response from someone consumed with grief.

'What happened tonight, Di?'

'I went to see Liz Denver. She's going to challenge Julian's will.'

'You're kidding.'

'You know he left everything to me and Charlie. I get the houses, his investments, all his money. Charlie gets the shareholding in Denver.'

The wave of envy was unwelcome, but so palpable it almost took her breath away. Sometimes it was hard to believe that she and Diana had started out from the same point. Two ordinary girls from an ordinary town. Rachel remembered their Saturday waitressing jobs that paid two pounds an hour, half of which had to go to their mother for their keep. Those were the days

223

when a five-pound note in a birthday card meant you could have a social life, the days when ferreting under the sofa cushions for loose change meant being able to afford your bus fare. She remembered helping Diana with her GCSEs so her sister could get enough of them to move into the sixth form, because Rachel knew that education was the way to get them out of their small town and on to a bigger, more exciting stage.

She had never wanted that stage to be Diana's world. She liked making her own money, her own excitement, not just hanging off the bespoke coat-tails of a rich man she had met and married. But now it was impossible not to feel disappointed with her own lot in life. Diana was no longer just the long-suffering wife of Julian Denver; she was one of the richest women in Europe in her own right. And Rachel? Despite years of hard work, she was just a diving instructor, who couldn't afford to be anything more.

She pushed the thought away, remembering what Diana was going through. She might be a billionairess, but she was also a widow.

'So what did Elizabeth say to you?'

'She told me that she thought I didn't have the fight for taking her on.'

'Does she expect you to roll over and accept it?' asked Rachel incredulously.

'She has a point. I'm drained, empty. I can't even cry any more because it feels as if there is nothing left inside me.'

'She can't do it,' said Rachel, suddenly feeling united with her sister against a common enemy. 'On what grounds does she plan to make the challenge?'

'Mental incapacity. Testamentary promise, I don't know . . .'

'She's got no chance,' scoffed Rachel.

'Her expensive lawyers think otherwise.'

Rachel's mind was whirling. The beauty of being a journalist was that you got to know a little about a lot. Probate law was not a particular area of expertise, but she knew enough to try and reassure Diana.

'Honestly, the courts won't accept it. I don't see how Elizabeth can win.'

Diana regarded her sceptically. 'You know what's it's like. If she's got enough of a claim to take this to court, they'll run circles around us, grind us down. But I can't let her, Rach. Julian loved Charlie, his will proved that, and Charlie equally wants to make his dad proud . . .'

The two women fell silent. Usually Rachel would enjoy an evening like this: the sight of rollerbladers speeding through the park, couples lounging on the grass, teenagers shrieking and laughing as they played frisbee. But tonight she hardly noticed them.

'What should I do?' said Diana finally.

'You get a good lawyer.'

Diana looked at her sister carefully. 'The reason why you are so smart is that you know the best way isn't always the right way to do things.'

Rachel knew what her sister was implying.

'Yeah, and it almost got me sent to jail,' she said cynically.

'But if you didn't want to fight Elizabeth in the courts, what would you do?' pressed Diana.

'Do you really think I'm a criminal mastermind?'

They stopped to buy ice creams from a vendor who looked as if he was about to pack up and go home.

'I think you're smart and brilliant and resourceful,' continued Diana. 'I'd always want you in my corner even if you weren't my sister.'

Rachel gave a slow, grateful smile. She peeled the lid off her ice cream and beckoned Diana to come and sit on a bench beside her.

'If Julian didn't commit suicide, then he wasn't depressed,' said Rachel thinking out loud. 'And if he wasn't depressed, the Denvers have no chance of challenging his will under mental competence. That's as far as my thinking goes without speaking to a lawyer.'

'What do you mean, not suicide?' There was a spark of something in Diana's eyes. Fear? Hope? Rachel reminded herself that she had to tread carefully. There was no more margin for error, no room for mistakes.

'Maybe it was an accident.'

'You don't have to be kind,' said Diana suspiciously.

'It's not unheard of. Has anyone considered whether it could have been an auto-erotic accident?'

'You mean kinky stuff?'

Rachel knew she was clutching at straws, but she had to give her sister some hope, even if it was just for one night.

'The coroner's official is coming round tomorrow. He wants to speak to me.'

'Then you should ask him about it.'

'I think he is supposed to be interviewing me. Not the other way around.'

'Are you going to tell him about me? What you've asked me to do? What I've found out?'

Diana stopped in her tracks and looked at her.

'What do you think?'

Rachel gazed over Diana's shoulder, fixing her sights on a distant line of trees as she struggled with the dilemma.

'Look, we want to help the police, the coroner's office, but if you tell them what we know, what we suspect, then it's just going to give people an excuse to pack Julian's death into a tidy little box.'

'You mean Julian died of heartbreak,' Diana said bitterly.

Rachel found it hard to contradict her. Diana had brought her back to England to find answers, and Rachel had discovered a more potent reason for Julian's death than the teenage depression his family seemed to be accepting. Julian's pregnant mistress was dead. That felt like the end of the road, the reason for his suicide they had been looking for. Rachel knew how easy it would be to stop things right here. Confess about Madison's pregnancy. Diana would be devastated, but it would decrease the Denvers' chances of a successful challenge to the will. Charlie meant everything to Diana, and obviously she would want him to inherit her husband's legacy.

'Was he in love with Madison Kopek?'

'I don't know.'

They stood up from the bench and started walking back to Bayswater.

'I'm sorry about what happened the other night,' Diana said finally.

Rachel didn't respond.

'I was wrong to react the way I did. I was just hurt and angry and humiliated . . .'

'I'm sorry too. I was insensitive. I was caught off guard. I didn't think. Typical me, eh?'

Diana shook her head. 'Turns out you're a better person than my husband.' She was obviously referring to Tuscany.

'He was drunk, and men like sex,' replied Rachel obliquely.

'When you told me about Julian's mistress, I wasn't surprised,' said Diana. 'We didn't have sex any more. He was spending more and more time in London. But I always thought he loved me. To find out he might have killed himself over another woman sort of crushed me.'

Rachel knew right then that she could not tell her about Madison's baby. She had to find another reason, another answer. As Ross had pointed out on her first visit to Clapton: tell her what she wants to hear. She's been through enough pain.

'When are you coming back to Somerfold?'

'I'll come back with you.'

'Good,' Diana said quietly. 'After the coroner's visit, I wondered if you could come and look at something with me.'

'Sure. What is it?'

'There's a café in the village run by a widow. It's run-down. I was thinking of investing in it. Adam thinks I need a project, and I think he's right. I've bloody missed you, you know.'

'I've missed you too.'

'Did you ever think of calling me?'

'All the time,' said Rachel honestly. 'I have a good life in Thailand, but it doesn't feel quite right because my family isn't in it.' She looked down at the path, not wanting to admit that there was a selfish element to this story. Liam's parents, his siblings, had all been over to see him in Ko Tao. They called at Christmas, and sent parcels for his birthday. Rachel had friends with whom she celebrated her birthday, and Songkran, the Thai New Year. But she often felt lonely, isolated, without back-up. Sometimes she thought that she could free-dive to the bottom of the ocean and if she never resurfaced no one would notice or care. Not really.

'You have Liam. What's the story there? He was very protective of you when I showed up asking questions.'

'Was he?' she asked more animatedly.

Diana slid her thin arm into Rachel's, an intimate gesture that almost made Rachel stop walking; the last time Diana had touched her was to slap her across the face.

'Anyway, you've got me now.'

They both smiled and started walking back to Bayswater.

31

Rachel listened in to Diana's meeting with the coroner's officer. Not in any official way, of course – Diana had insisted that she take the meeting alone – but Rachel thought it best that she monitor the conversation, not only to check that her sister was okay, but to make sure that she didn't let slip any information to him that she hadn't told her.

She sat on the warm stone step outside Somerfold and listened intently. She had left the French windows a little ajar, but the morning birdsong blotted out much of what was being said. From what she could make out, though, Mr Nicholson, the sensible-looking man who had arrived half an hour earlier, had ruled out the possibility of auto-erotic asphyxiation. Rachel cringed when she heard Diana fishing around the subject.

'Auto-erotic asphyxiation is masturbation,' explained Mr Nicholson. 'If he was masturbating, then it's likely he would have removed some or all of his clothes, but he was found fully clothed. Plus there was no semen found in the post-mortem.'

Poor Diana, thought Rachel, hugging her knees. Poor Julian, too, being described in such cold, clinical terms.

She heard them say their goodbyes, heard him leave, and she crept into the house through the French windows.

Diana spun round, looking startled.

'Were you out there the whole time?' she gasped.

Rachel looked sheepish. 'I was just, gardening, er, sunbathing . . . Yes, I was,' she admitted.

She watched Diana lean against the wall as if all the life was draining out of her.

'Come on,' she said briskly. 'It's time to show me that café you're interested in.'

'Not today . . .'

'Yes, today. Should we invite Mum?'

'No. Just us,' said Diana, standing up straight.

'Do you have bikes?'

'Julian's Ducatis . . .'

'As much as I would love to arrive in the village at ninety miles per hour, I was thinking more like bicycles. Let me go and speak to Mr Bills.'

She found Mr Bills and asked him to bring two bikes to the front of the house. She knew she had to keep her sister moving, knew how difficult it had been for her to be interviewed today.

'Come on. Mum's having a swim. She'll be back at the house any minute.'

'It makes it seem like we're sneaking off.'

'We are,' grinned Rachel, remembering all the times as teenagers when they had slipped out of the house to meet boys or go to a party.

'How about you move into the main house?' said Diana suddenly.

'Are you sure?' asked Rachel, swinging one long leg over the Pashley frame.

Diana nodded, and Rachel felt a warm glow that she had finally been accepted home.

They were both sweating by the time they got to the village. It was a warm day. Rachel had barely run or swum since she had arrived in London and she could feel her fitness levels slipping.

'Is this it?' she asked, leaning her bike against the pub railing by the green. 'Good location.'

The café was a long honey-stone building with tired curtains at the windows. Inside, an elderly woman was transferring scones from a box marked 'Catering Pack' on to chipped white plates.

She looked up and smiled. 'I'm not even open yet, girls.'

'Dot, meet my sister Rachel,' said Diana, pushing her forward.

'Look at the colour of you,' grinned Dot.

'I live in Thailand.'

'How do you cope with that?' she asked disapprovingly. 'Two sisters living so far apart.'

Rachel watched Diana moving around the room, stroking the rickety tables. She couldn't see the potential in this place; then again, her own flat proved that she lacked the Midas touch when it came to interiors. Diana, on the other hand, had always been a wizard. It wasn't just herself she could make look pretty. Her Christmas trees were always beautifully decorated, even when she could only afford to go to the pound shop; presents were always exquisitely gift-wrapped; her home had the sort of taste and style that money alone couldn't buy. And right now Rachel could tell that she wanted to get her hands on the Blue Ribbon café.

'My sister has a proposition for you,' she said without further preamble.

Diana shot her a horrified look, but Rachel always did things with purpose once she had made up her mind to do something.

'She wants to invest in your business. She thinks it has a lot of potential.'

'This place?' said Dot, taking off her apron.

Diana's expression softened, her eyes sparkling with excitement. 'It could be fabulous, Dot.'

'Listen to her,' agreed Rachel. 'Have you ever seen that Meryl Streep movie *It's Complicated*? That fabulous café-bakery that Meryl's character owns? Deli porn, that's what it was. Diana could make this place as sexy as that.'

Dot looked as if she didn't know where to put herself. She clearly didn't see the café as in any way pornographic.

'What Rachel means is that I really would love to help you give it a facelift, bring it right up to date, back to the glory days of when Ron was still with us,' said Diana more gently.

'I want to sell the place, not bring it up to date, lovey,' said Dot. 'I could always sell it to you if you were interested, but I'm not sure you'd . . . well, with respect, I can't really see a smart lady like you standing behind a counter.'

'Which is why the two of you should do it together,' said Rachel, looking at Diana and then Dot. She remembered the days when she was setting up the diving school with Liam. They

231

had found a tiny shack by the beach and spent all weekend painting it red, white and blue. They had flyers printed, delivered them all over the island, and accosted tourists in the streets to hustle for business. They had both arrived in Thailand a little burnt-out and broken, but the diving school had brought them back to life again, and Rachel just knew that this place could do the same for her sister.

'Tell me what it was like in its heyday,' said Rachel, noticing that Dot didn't look convinced.

'Oh, it was marvellous, lovey,' replied Dot, softening. 'Everyone used to come here,' she said. 'On a summer Saturday they'd queue down the street for tables. It was Ron's recipes, you see.'

'Do you still have them?'

Dot shook her head sadly. 'Not really. Well, he had a little notebook where he'd scribble down his experiments, but I can't make head nor tail of them.'

'Do you still have it? The notebook, I mean?' asked Rachel.

Dot rummaged in a cupboard. 'Here it is,' she said, handing over a pale blue pocketbook.

Rachel flipped it open but could only frown when she saw the text. She'd had visions of being able to revive the bakery using Ron's old recipes, but Dot was right, it made no sense at all. Instead of the clear step-by-step instructions you got in cookbooks, it was a lot of scrawled letters and numbers – 'S1Y BHF BS 2pch' – with no relation to each other.

Diana peered over Rachel's shoulder. 'Do you think they might be ingredients?'

Dot shrugged. 'What on earth can "MHFP" mean?'

'Look, there's a gap between the letters, I think it's "M HF P",' said Diana, trying to make sense of it. 'Could it be "milk half pint"? Look at the next one: "B 3 O"? I think that might be "butter three ounces".'

Rachel started to laugh. 'I think you're right, Mary Berry. Check this out: "4e". That's got to be four eggs, surely?'

Dot snatched the book back, her eyes skimming over her late husband's script as though he was coming back to life with each deciphered message.

'Girls, you're right!'

'We should try and make something,' said Rachel mischievously.

'What, now?' asked Dot, bug-eyed.

'We're not doing anything for the rest of the afternoon, are we, Di?'

'You know, Ron's courgette cake was legendary.'

'Is it in the recipe book?'

Dot nodded. 'And now that you clever clogs have cracked the code, we know how to make it.'

She beckoned them to follow her into the kitchen, which was surprisingly clean and modern. She started opening cupboards, checking best-before dates on packets, and eventually declared that they had every ingredient they needed except courgettes.

'There's the village stores,' offered Diana.

Dot snorted. 'You'll have as much luck finding courgettes there as you would a designer handbag.'

'Where's the nearest supermarket?' asked Rachel.

'In Henley. About a twenty-minute drive away.'

'Maybe we'll have to try something else, then.'

'There is *one* place we could get courgettes . . .' said Dot.

'Go on. Over you go.'

Diana looked at the wall dubiously. It was only about four feet high, but there were spiky-looking bushes on the other side and her pretty Moschino dress wasn't exactly designed for mountaineering.

'Are you sure she's not in?'

'Dot says she's in Bournemouth with her grandchildren.'

'This is trespassing.'

'I'm the family law-breaker. I'll take all responsibility.' Rachel pushed the toe of her Converse into a gap in the wall, hoisting herself up. She pulled Diana up behind her, then dropped into the garden, taking a moment to savour the smells: flowers, leaves, even the grass smelled wonderfully damp from last night's rain.

Diana looked like a demure terrified doll on the top of the wall.

'Come on,' hissed Rachel.

'I don't even know what a courgette plant looks like,' Diana moaned.

'I thought you *lived* in the organic greengrocer's.' She pointed to the vegetable patch – easy to spot from the cane wigwams with runner beans twisting around them. 'Spiky leaves, yellow flowers, over there, go, go, go.'

Diana's eyes opened wide, as if she'd had an adrenalin shot. She scuttled across the garden and scooped up the contraband vegetables. When she returned to Rachel, her face was pink and radiant.

By the time they got back to the café, Dot had already assembled pots, pan and scales around her. It was Ron's old equipment, she told them as she followed his code, mixing flour, eggs, sugar and butter together. Diana got stuck in too, and Rachel took a moment to watch them. It was as if the two women were coming back to life, like watching a photo develop in front of her.

Within an hour, it was ready, a perfect slab of loaf, flecked with courgette and ginger.

'You do the honours,' said Dot. 'My hands are shaking.'

Diana divided the loaf into generous slices and they took one each on a plate.

'Go on, try it,' urged Dot.

Tentatively, Diana took a mouthful. 'It's delicious,' she said. 'I mean, really, really good. What do you think? Is it as good as Ron's?'

But Dot couldn't speak; there were tears running down her face.

'What's the matter? Is it that bad?'

Dot shook her head. 'It's perfect. It's just like Ron was here, like he'd just baked it and stepped through to the other room.'

Rachel had switched into business mode.

'You shouldn't be selling factory-made cakes, Dot. You should make your own, with Ron's recipes. Diana can get to work on the interiors and organisation and I might even have a few old press contacts to get word out about the place . . .' She could feel energy and anticipation pulsating not just within her but around the whole room.

'We could reopen on the day of the village fair,' said Diana, beaming. Rachel could feel her own smile stretching from ear to ear.

She could hear a loud buzzing noise. At first she thought it was one of Dot's kitchen appliances, before she realised it was her own phone. She stopped laughing to answer it.

At first there was silence on the other end, then a gentle snivel. Rachel realised instantly that it was someone crying.

'Who is this?' she asked softly.

'It's Kath Jensen.' For a second Rachel couldn't place the name. 'Ross's ex-wife.'

She was immediately on alert. 'What's wrong?'

'It's Ross. He's been attacked in Jamaica. He was on a job. The job he was working on with you, I think. Rachel, he's in a coma and they don't know if he is going to pull through.'

32

Rachel had expected it to be hot, of course she had: it was the Caribbean. But it was one thing to imagine it and another to feel the almost physical thump as you stepped from the air-conditioned plane and into the furnace of Montego Bay. Her body shivered as it fought to cope with the sudden shift, and her breathing increased, like it was hard to drag oxygen from the humid air. *Now I know how gingerbread men feel*, she thought. Perhaps she had been away from Thailand too long. Or perhaps she was still in shock from the news about Ross – she was torn between being desperate to get to her friend's side and dreading seeing him. No, that wasn't shock, it was guilt. There were no two ways about it: if Rachel hadn't turned up on his doorstep a few weeks ago, Ross would still have been walking around happily. Well, perhaps not happily; he was never exactly a ray of sunshine, she thought with a grim smile as she was waved through customs. A tall man in a suit was holding up a sign with her name on it.

'Miss Rachel? I am Yohan,' he said, holding out a huge hand and showing her his teeth – perfect except for one missing at the side. 'How long are you staying with us?'

'I don't know yet.'

'*Irie*,' he said, taking her bag. 'I was sorry to hear about your friend.'

'Really?' said Rachel. 'Was it on the news?'

The man let out a chuckle. 'Nah, I spoke to your sister, Miss Diana? She told me that whatever you want to do while you're in Jamaica, I should take you. So I will be your driver, your guide. And . . .' he gave her another wide smile, 'I was in the Jamaican army, so you will be safe.'

A bodyguard? Rachel felt her emotions pulled in two directions at once. The hardened hack in her bristled at the idea that she might need protection; she had faced worse things than Jamaica could throw at her. But at the same time, so had Ross; in fact, he had also been in the army, and what good had it done him? She looked at Yohan's broad back as he led her to a large black Mercedes. No, on balance she was rather glad her driver was on hand, because she was starting to think that perhaps Diana's worries about her safety weren't entirely unjustified.

Yohan put Rachel's bag in the boot and opened the car door for her.

'You want to go straight to the hospital?'

Rachel pulled a face, then nodded. 'Yes, okay. You know the way?'

He laughed again. 'Miss Rachel, I know everything and everyone on this island. I told you, you're in good hands.'

Rachel sat in the back seat, glad to be once more sealed inside a climate-controlled environment, and watched as the airport gave way to fields. Sometimes new places surprised you: Naples had been like that. Rachel had once taken a train to the city from Rome, expecting a glamorous seaside town; instead she had been confronted by endless run-down concrete tenements, covered in grime and graffiti. But Jamaica was exactly as she had imagined: banana groves and sun-blasted fields interspersed with tiny settlements seemingly thrown together from planks and corrugated iron, people literally sitting on the kerb in shorts drinking Red Stripe and Tang. And then suddenly you'd glimpse the sea and the high gates of a luxury resort, the razor wire at the top designed to keep the wealthy holidaymakers inside and on their sunloungers and the real Jamaicans out. No wonder so many of those places were all-inclusive, thought Rachel.

By contrast, Montego Bay was raw. Yes, the poverty was everywhere – dirt roads, lean-to shacks selling dusty car parts and coconuts – but it pulsated with noise and life. Even though the car's windows were firmly closed, she could hear the music: reggae and dub pumping from every opening along with the horns, the shouts, the laughter. Rachel had been to some poor parts of the world, but the mood in Jamaica was defiantly upbeat.

237

The Cornwall Hospital also refused to conform: a high-rise building in lush grounds high on a hill looking out over the sea. Apart from the ambulances parked outside, it could have been a holiday resort. Inside, Rachel was directed to the surgical unit, where she approached a nurse.

'I'm looking for Ross McKiney?'

'And you are?' She turned at the sound of a deep male voice behind her. The Jamaican man was mid forties, stocky, with that unmistakable world-weary yet tuned-in look of policemen the world over.

'Are you Detective Henry, by any chance?' she said.

The man nodded warily. 'I am.'

Rachel stepped forward and offered her hand. 'Rachel Miller, we spoke on the phone yesterday?'

'Ah yes. I have just been visiting Mr McKiney.' He glanced towards the door to the ward. 'I imagine you are thirsty after your journey, Miss Miller. Perhaps I could buy you a coffee before you go in to see your friend?'

Rachel didn't really think she had much choice, so she nodded. Besides, she needed to speak to the policeman. He led her to a lift, then down to a café with a view of the bay.

'So how is he?' asked Rachel when they were sitting at a table with their drinks.

'As well as can be expected, isn't that the phrase? You should prepare yourself, Miss Miller, he's not a pretty sight – he took quite a beating.'

He registered the dismay on Rachel's face and held up a finger.

'However, I spoke to his doctor earlier; he is expected to make a full recovery. I think he was lucky.'

'Lucky?' said Rachel angrily. 'My friend has almost been killed and you think that's lucky?'

She sipped her coffee, feeling a swell of dread at seeing Ross.

'So what happened? A tourist in the wrong place at the wrong time? I should have reminded him that this was the murder capital of the world.' She knew she was being rude about someone else's country, but she was angry and frustrated,

'Contrary to what you might have heard, Jamaica is generally a safe country,' Henry said patiently. 'We work hard to protect

238

our people and the people who come to visit us. Most of the violence you hear about in the media is by the criminal community directed at the criminal community. It is not the Wild West, Miss Miller.'

'So what went wrong?' she pressed.

'Mr McKiney was walking in what might be termed a bad area. Shack housing, a few run-down businesses, the sort of place you wouldn't want to be walking alone, even as a Jamaican. He was seen asking directions, then taking photographs with expensive camera equipment, and he was white, well-dressed . . .' He shrugged. 'He looked exactly like a lost tourist.' Henry swirled his coffee around the cheap plastic cup.

'I assume his possessions were taken.'

Henry nodded. 'Unfortunately, we have a few of these cases each year. But this one seemed different. The ferocity of the attack was unusual for a simple mugging.'

Rachel felt a sinking in her stomach. *Oh God, Ross, what have I done to you?* she thought miserably.

'Muggers, are, how do you say, opportunists: whack someone over the head, grab the stuff and run. They don't want to risk anyone seeing them, especially in a small community where they might be recognised. In this case there was more than one assailant, definitely armed. Clearly Mr McKiney fought back, but even so, if they hadn't been disturbed – a pastor visiting a sick parishioner happened to come by – I think we would be looking at a murder.'

The word seemed to hang in the air.

'Why was Mr McKiney in Jamaica, Miss Miller? I have checked out his hotel. It isn't a tourist resort.'

Rachel looked out at the view and wondered how much she should tell him.

'It does not do your friend any favours to keep secrets,' said the policeman in his thick Caribbean accent.

Rachel's mouth felt dry. 'He was tracing the movements of a friend,' she said finally. 'A friend who had come to the island with his mistress.'

'Ah,' said Henry, nodding as things became clear. 'That makes sense,' he said quietly.

'What do you mean?'

'Perhaps someone didn't want him to find anything out.'

'You mean he got scared off.'

'He was warned.'

Henry finished his coffee and threw the cup into the bin with a direct hit.

'You should go and see your friend. Call me from your hotel and perhaps we can talk more later.'

Before Detective Henry's warning, Rachel wasn't sure how she had expected Ross to look. Perhaps she would find him lying peacefully, a drip in his arm, a plaster on his cheek. Instead, she wanted to cry, he looked so beaten and broken. He was lying on his back, his arm in plaster held at a right angle, bandages around his head. His face was swollen and bruised, one eye almost closed.

She was allowed to take a seat by his bedside. She wasn't sure how long she had been there when she felt another presence enter the room.

Turning to the door, she didn't recognise the couple who had come in until they introduced themselves as Kath and Phillip Jensen.

'Thank goodness,' said Rachel, feeling suddenly less alone.

'Can he be flown home?' asked Kath.

'Not until he regains consciousness. And then, who knows.'

'We'll stay until it gets sorted,' said Phillip. 'The kids are at my mother's. Thank you for the flights over here,' he added, stepping forward with a grateful handshake.

Rachel smiled. As soon as she had come off the phone with Kath Jensen, Diana had forgotten her own troubles and sorted out immediate travel for both Rachel and Ross's family to fly to Jamaica, paying for every single expense.

Standing at Ross's bedside, Kath Jensen looked ready to cry. Rachel watched as her husband put a concerned arm around her shoulders, and remembered what Ross had said about him. He had every reason to dislike Phillip Jensen, and yet he had called him a nice guy. He had been able to see through the betrayal to the man beneath.

Rachel stayed until the nurse indicated that visiting hours were over. Yohan was waiting for her, a reassuring presence standing by his Mercedes outside the hospital.

'How is your friend?' he asked.

'We'll see,' she said, not wanting to think about it too hard. She looked at the man quizzically. 'Yohan, you said you know everyone on the island, right?'

He grinned. 'Maybe not everyone, but most people, sure.'

'So would you have any idea who did this to my friend?'

Yohan's face clouded over. 'I have already started to ask around, Miss Rachel. My job is to look after you; look what happened to Mr Ross.'

'And what have you found out?'

'Nothing yet, but I will,' he said with determination. He opened the car door. 'I should take you to your hotel,' he said quietly.

They drove out of the city past coconut and banana plantations. Deeper into the island, Rachel could see a backdrop of thick jungle that reminded her of Thailand. She wanted to ask Yohan more questions, but her body was tired, eyelids drooping. She had been on the go for over a week, with barely time for a change of clothes. She wound down the window to let the breeze on to her face, breathing in the warm air infused with salt and the smell of tropical flowers. She must have nodded off, because when she opened her eyes, Yohan was standing outside the car, grinning at her through the window.

'We're here, Miss Rachel.'

She had read about Round Hill in a magazine when she had been waiting in Virgin's Upper Class lounge at Heathrow – a delicious colonial estate just outside the city, the feature had said, aglow with a glamorous heritage that included guests of the calibre of John and Jackie Kennedy and Elizabeth Taylor, before being revamped by Ralph Lauren in recent years. The green and white awning over the entrance suggested a small house, but it opened out on to a verandah with spectacular views across a jutting headland and down to white beaches and blue sea.

Thanks again, she thought, offering her prayer up to the goddess Diana, she with her fingers on the purse strings. She felt her shoulders relax as she walked in and took her bag from Yohan.

'Do you need me this evening, Miss Rachel?'

'I'm not sure yet. Give me your cell phone number and I'll call you.'

She checked in and was shown to her room. It was cool and spacious – white linen and wood – and she fell backwards on to the bed, sighing, but she knew that if she stayed there, she would never get up again. And if she stopped moving, the emotions of the afternoon – of the last month – might overtake her. So she levered herself up and ran into the bathroom and showered, washing her hair through twice until she felt really clean. Walking back into the room, towelling her hair, her eye fell on the minibar. Usually she called ahead and requested that her room be cleared of alcohol; that was what they told you in AA – don't put temptation in your way – but she wasn't sure she would get through this without something. Moving quickly, before she could change her mind, she sat down and poured the contents of two small whisky bottles into a tumbler. She could call room service for ice, but she just wanted to feel the liquid burn down her throat; her mouth was literally watering at the prospect.

The tumbler had just touched her lips when she heard knocking at the door.

'Shit,' she whispered. She had always wondered what it would be like to have a bodyguard at your beck and call. But right now, all she wanted was to be left alone.

She pulled the door open. But it wasn't Yohan standing there.

'Liam?' she said, her voice tumbling into staccato laughter. For a moment she couldn't quite understand what she was seeing. Was this some cruel trick of the booze? But she hadn't even had a sip.

'It's me. The Ghost of Christmas Past,' he said, smiling.

'I don't believe it,' she said, throwing her arms around him. For a moment she forgot the awkwardness of their last couple of days in Thailand. She just stood there holding him, enjoying his shape, his smell, the sensation of his arms folded around her body.

'I think you'd better put me down now,' he whispered.

Rachel took a step back, just to check that what she had felt was real.

'What the hell are you doing here?' she said, for one minute feeling inordinately glad that she had washed her hair.

'Your sister called me. Thought you might need a friendly face.'

'She did that?'

Liam was trying to make light of it, breaking the tension in the room, but the fact remained that he had flown thousands of miles to be with her. Now what did that mean exactly? She turned to look at him, but he avoided her gaze. Now what did *that* mean?

'It was a military bloody operation,' he said, laughing nervously. 'Diana phoned me in the middle of the night and said I had to be in Bangkok by nine o'clock. There was a speedboat waiting for me at Sairee Beach, which took me to Samui for the first flight, then at Bangkok I was escorted through the fast lane to the private jet terminal.'

'I bet you felt like James Bond.'

'But better-looking, obviously.'

'Well don't start getting ideas above your station,' said Rachel. 'When we get back to Ko Tao, it's straight back on the scooters.'

They both started laughing, but Rachel felt like she might burst into tears.

Liam put his small holdall on the bed and walked outside to the balcony. She followed him out into the balmy night, feeling as though she was part of a dream, as if they were back in Thailand, in some beautiful villa by the sea, living together, loving each other.

'I'm glad you came,' she said finally.

Liam nodded and turned to face her. 'What's happening, Rach? I'm worried about you.'

'The potted version?' she said, knowing that she had to tell somebody everything. 'It's a story about a billionaire, a pretty college student and a diet drug called Rheladrex . . .'

33

The view was so perfect that it made her forget everything. As the town car slid across the George Washington Bridge, Diana pushed her face up against the glass, smiling to herself as the glittering palace of Manhattan appeared to rise from the blue-green river. To her, New York had always looked like the Emerald City and had the same magical possibilities. As a girl, sitting in that cramped bedroom hiding from her parents' screaming matches, she had read everything she could about the Big Apple, imagining what it would be like to actually visit the place, to see those flashing 'walk/don't walk' signs, to feel the whoosh of the air coming out of the subway, to walk up to a hot-dog stand and order a chili dog 'with everything on it'.

As they jostled their way cross-town and turned on to Amsterdam, Diana craned her neck to peer up at those boxy red-brick buildings like a tourist. Whenever she had visited New York with Julian, she had been dismayed to see him sitting in the back of the car reading the paper or flicking through messages on his phone, as though the exotic scene outside their little bubble barely registered. But of course, that was the truth. For a wealthy cosmopolitan like Julian Denver, a visit to New York was like the bus journey to work, and he had long since stopped seeing the bright red fire hydrants and the yellow taxis as anything other than street furniture. But Diana didn't think she would ever lose her wonder at this city, however often she visited. To her, it was the most exciting place in the world, a place where anything could happen.

They turned off Madison and drew up outside The Mark, the doorman offering Diana a hand as she stepped out. 'Thank you,' she said. She couldn't deny that she enjoyed this part of being wealthy, the part where people made a huge fuss over her, but she still felt slightly detached from it, almost as if someone was going to pop up any minute and say, 'Ah-ha! Caught you! This isn't *your* life, Diana Miller. There's been an almighty cock-up and you've actually got to go back to Sheffield.'

But no one did. They smiled and took her credit card and handed her a key and showed her up to a wonderful suite, tastefully decorated, with tiny fragrant soaps waiting for her by the vast bathtub. It was like some sort of conjuring trick.

But as the bellhop closed the door with a discreet click and left Diana standing facing the perfectly smooth double bed, she suddenly felt terribly alone. No Julian, no Rachel, no Mum. *What the hell am I doing here?* she thought, sinking on to the mattress.

Rachel had been distraught when she had heard the news about her friend Ross. It had made perfect sense for her to fly out to Jamaica to see him, and Diana had been glad she could make the appropriate arrangements. But when Rachel had asked Diana to fly to New York and speak to the head of Denver Chemicals, she had been reluctant. She was not a detective or a reporter. In fact she didn't really like meeting people she didn't know very well, let alone asking them difficult questions. When Rachel had told her about this Rheladrex drug, though, about Julian and Madison's connection to it, she could not help but be intrigued.

She showered and changed into a fitted black dress. It was smart, respectable, professional. She was due to meet Simon Michaels at Le Cirque – a restaurant she had been to once before and remembered as a place full of power-brokers. She wanted to be taken seriously. Her mobile phone buzzed with a text message. Picking up her clutch bag, she took the lift to the ground floor.

Her eyes scanned the lobby before she recognised the back of his head, his broad shoulders trapped in a suit, his hand thrust casually in his pocket as he killed time.

He turned and saw her. His usual greeting of a smile had been replaced by something more cautious.

'What's all this about, Di?' he asked as he kissed her lightly on the cheek.

The previous day, Diana had phoned Adam to see if he had yet made contact with Simon Michaels as Rachel had asked him to. Adam was in New York, a detail that hadn't exactly surprised her – as global head of the hotels division, it was where he had been based until Julian's death had brought him back to London. It had also felt quite fortuitous, as if the gods were finally smiling on her, as it meant she did not have to meet Simon Michaels alone.

'I thought Rachel had discussed it with you. She needs to know about the new Denver diet pill, Rheladrex.'

They walked out of the hotel on to Madison Avenue and its wall of heat and noise.

'Yes, she asked me about it. I didn't know it was urgent, though. What's so important that you've flown to New York to speak to Simon?'

'I don't know. Maybe that's what we'll find out when we meet him.'

They took a taxi to the Bloomberg building in midtown, where Le Cirque occupied a cavernous space on the ground floor. Adam knew the maître d', and they were shown to one of the best tables in the house, where he ordered two aperitifs as they waited for Simon Michaels.

Although she had met him before, Diana didn't recognise Michaels as he approached the table. It was only when he shook hands with Adam and sat down that she realised this was the CEO of Denver Chemicals.

'Thanks for meeting us at such short notice,' said Adam, turning on the charm.

'We were devastated about Julian,' said Simon, peering through his round wire-framed glasses. 'I couldn't be at the funeral, but Dave Donnelly, our VP, said it was very moving.'

They ordered food and made small talk. Simon had come from the Denver Chemicals headquarters, twenty miles away in New Jersey. Business was apparently good. Elizabeth Denver had called him a week earlier to say that a new CEO would be appointed soon and that uncertainty within the company would be kept to a minimum.

Diana had never liked Simon Michaels. He seemed oily and

246

somehow disingenuous, even in the social situations in which she'd encountered him. Maybe it was his eyes, which always seemed to be jumping around, looking for more important people to speak to, or perhaps searching for an escape route.

'Diana. How are you?' he said finally. 'I was worried about you when you called. You sounded terribly serious.' He tilted his head, which was a trick Diana had seen many senior managers at Denver Group adopt. It implied concern, and yet a slight superiority. She wondered if it was something they taught you at business school.

'Life isn't a bed of roses at the moment,' she said, which made him instantly squirm. She reminded herself that she had a role to play here: the grieving widow, scatty and a bit overwhelmed, which didn't feel too far from the truth. She wasn't going to get anything out of him by being combative. 'I was in town for a charity thing and I thought I'd pop by.' She smiled warmly. 'You'll be aware that Julian left us an interest in the company. I felt I should get up to speed with what it does and who works for us.'

Her message was clear. Julian had put the shares in trust for Charlie, but until he was of age, the voting rights and administration of those shares would fall to Diana. That made her powerful. Theoretically, she could have Simon Michaels fired – and he would know that.

Michaels looked on edge as he gave her a condensed version of what the company was up to.

'I heard about a new drug that looks promising. Rheladrex,' she said, sinking her fork into a fillet of monkfish.

Simon nodded. 'It's exciting.'

'Is it safe? We're not going to have another Fen-Phen on our hands?'

'Of course not,' said Simon, looking surprised that she had some knowledge of the business. 'It's taken twenty years of testing to get it to market. It's as safe as any drug can be, and nothing short of a miracle. I believe that Rheladrex can transform the fortunes of the company. I know that Julian was perhaps losing faith in the pharmaceuticals division, but I think Rheladrex will prove otherwise.'

247

'I always thought the pharma division was a licence to print money.'

'We get a bad press,' he said stiffly. 'People criticise us for the so-called inflated prices of drugs under patent. But do they realise how much research and development costs? How many drugs don't make it to market, so they have to be supported by the ones that do? What a small window we have, whilst the drug is still under patent, to make back those costs?'

He twirled the stem of his wine glass between his fingers.

'I know Julian wanted to sell the division, but with luck, Rheladrex can renew the faith.' He looked at Adam, trying to win him round to his way of thinking.

'He wanted to sell the division?' said Adam, as if he didn't believe a word of it.

'You don't know?' That small superior tilt of the head again. 'The pharmaceutical industry, as you may or may not be aware, is going through a period of consolidation. Denver is not a major player. Julian felt that we were better merging with one of the giants.'

'So you *were* for sale,' said Diana.

'Julian was looking for a strategic alliance.' Michaels lowered his voice, knowing that there would be people in this restaurant who would relish that piece of information. 'But I told him he was unwise to start off-loading the company now. If he sat tight, let Rheladrex shift the volume, the valuation, our bonuses, would go stellar.'

After saying goodbye to Simon, Diana and Adam walked on to the street.

'So was that worth coming all the way to Manhattan for?' Adam asked, looking around for a taxi.

'We should have asked him about Madison Kopek,' she said, feeling unsatisfied. 'Rachel said that Madison had registered her brother's death with the FDA. Perhaps she had complained to the drug company too.'

'Simon is the CEO,' said Adam patiently. 'He's not going to get involved with the detail of every complaint, and even if Madison did complain, what on earth does it prove?'

'Complaint? This isn't someone taking a leaky kettle back to customer services. Someone died, Adam.'

He looked apologetic, but didn't respond.

'You heard about Rachel's friend? The investigator who was helping her with Julian.'

'What happened?'

'He's in a coma. He got mugged.'

'You think this is all linked to Rheladrex?' said Adam sceptically.

'Julian and Madison went to Jamaica together. Rachel thought it was because Rheladrex had some clinical trials done out there.'

'Or perhaps they just went to Jamaica together.' He put his hand up immediately and apologised. 'I'm sorry. I didn't mean that.'

'Just email Simon and ask him if he's heard of Madison and Billy Kopek. Please.'

Adam sighed audibly and got out his phone. He stood on the sidewalk, composing his email. When he had finished, he put the phone back in his pocket.

'I know why you're doing this.'

'What?'

'Looking for another reason.'

Diana pressed her lips together. He was right. Rheladrex represented her way out. Julian's will proved that he had still loved his wife and child. And if Julian and Madison were simply working together to expose Rheladrex, it exonerated her husband in other ways too.

'Wouldn't you?' she said softly.

'It's too nice an evening to get morbid,' he said finally.

'Got any better suggestions?' she said, feeling her mood slip. Adam was right. She had to catch herself before she slipped into melancholy.

'How about you try and forget everything, just for a few hours? Lose yourself in a night on the town?'

She smiled and nodded. It was getting dark, and New York was becoming even more magical.

'It's your city, cowboy. Show me around.'

'The beauty of New York is that it's lots of different cities,' said Adam as they started to walk away from Le Cirque. 'We've got Chinatown, downtown, uptown, fashion New York, the art scene, the hipster scene . . . You could live in the city a decade and go to a different place every night, be a different person.'

'Give me *your* New York.'

'You mean the late-night bars and the strip joints?' he said, his dark green eyes flashing mischievously.

'I didn't mean—'

'I'm joking. You know I live over the river now. Brooklyn Heights. I am officially a bridge-and-tunnel guy.'

'So let's go there. Show me your manor.'

Diana had seen many of New York's different personalities. She had sat in the tents in Bryant Park during New York Fashion Week, drunk cocktails in the bar at the Gramercy hotel. She'd been to fancy art gallery openings in SoHo, eaten quail in the Upper East Side restaurants. But Brooklyn was not on her radar. Never had been.

They got a cab across the bridge and were dropped off by the famous waterfront promenade. They bought hot dogs and supersize milkshakes from a vendor and ate and drank as they strolled down the sidewalk. There were skateboarders in the street, chic, contented blondes pushing all-terrain buggies, couples flirting in the shade of a tree. If a city could transform you into anyone you wanted to be, then Brooklyn was doing a good job of taking her away from being Diana Denver.

Her conversation with Adam flowed quickly, easily. It was as if they wanted to compact everything they should have said over the seven years they had known one another into one evening. Listening to his stories, Diana was shocked by how superficial their acquaintance had been before now. How you could know someone so well, but know absolutely nothing about them at all. She had no idea that he had sailed the Atlantic. She had known about his rather playboy love of polo but was surprised to learn he was a five-goal player. He could play the saxophone, had produced a short film that had been shown at Sundance. He wanted to own a dog but was worried that he travelled too much. He collected Ernest Hemingway first editions and Northern Soul vinyl. In another life he wanted to be a war photographer; in this life he wanted to expand his hotel group from a 250-property portfolio into something to rival the Starwood chain.

'Are we going to see Casa Adam?' she asked, wondering what sort of house he lived in. Diana had always been fascinated by property. It was like holding a mirror up to its owner, a revealer of secrets.

'I'm just over here,' he said, pointing away from the promenade. They walked to a quiet, pretty street banked with expensive-looking brownstones that seemed to have been polished red, stopping at an impressive five-storey terrace that was wider and better restored than the rest.

'Fancy a drink?' As they came through the door, he flicked through some post and pointed towards the kitchen.

'Nothing sweet. All that milkshake is swirling around like sugar going round a candy-floss machine.'

'Martinis it is, then.' He rummaged around in his fridge and cupboards before handing her a glass replete with olives and lemon twists.

'Great place, Adam,' she said, appreciating the modern art and the stylish Danish furniture.

'You've not seen the best bit yet. Come with me.'

She followed him up three flights of stairs. On the top floor, the stairs opened on to a huge master bedroom. She felt anxious until she realised he was not stopping, but was twiddling with a French door that led on to a huge roof terrace. She gasped as Manhattan glittered before her – an incredible skyline of white lights and the soaring silhouettes of skyscrapers.

'You know, when you brought me to Brooklyn, I was surprised. I always thought you were the sort to live in the heart of things, not on the edges. But now I get it. Now I know that sometimes you've got to be on the outside looking in to really know somewhere.'

'Absolutely,' he said, smiling as if they were both in tune with one another. 'I've learnt that from travelling around a lot, checking out hotels. Take Venice. You get the best views of the city from the islands in the lagoon, not from properties on the mainland. You want to see the Matterhorn? You go to Zermatt, not up the mountain itself.'

251

As they sipped their martinis, Adam pointed out Governors Island and the Statue of Liberty, a faint pinprick of light in the darkness. Finally, when her heels were hurting and she felt as if she could stand no more, Diana kicked off her shoes and sat down on a huge stripy cushion propped against the chimneypot.

'Julian was really proud of the job you were doing out here.'

Adam snorted. 'He said that?'

He cut the conversation short, and Diana realised that he didn't want to talk about Julian tonight. If she was totally honest, neither did she. Adam had been right when he said at the beginning of the evening that they should forget, even if it was just for a few hours.

'Have you made up with Rachel yet?' he asked, sitting down beside her.

'I forgot how great she is. I think it got lost in everything else that's been going on over the past few years. I know I can't make up for the time that we've lost, but I'm going to try. I think I might try and get to Thailand when Charlie goes back to school in the autumn, although something tells me she is enjoying life back in London.'

'Do you think she'd come back?'

Diana shrugged. 'There's a guy in Thailand I think she cares about. He's flown over to be with her now, actually. I think they have one of those relationships.'

'What relationships?'

'When you're together but you don't even realise it yet.'

'How's the martini?'

'I should have known you'd be able to mix a good one,' she said, noting that it was sharp and dry, not salty and oily.

He mixed her another, and then another, and they joked that they should just bring the bottles of gin and vermouth up here and pour one into the other.

They were sitting side by side, so sometimes she didn't even look at him whilst he was talking, and it was easy to forget where she was and who she was with. It could have been a balmy evening on their sailing boat, when she would lie in the crook of Julian's arm on the deck, listening to a Nina Simone CD with a bottle of excellent red from the Somerfold cellars. Every now and then a wave of sadness would hit her, and then Adam would distract her with a joke or a glamorous story.

As the night wore on, it seemed perfectly natural to rest her head on his shoulder as they talked. She had no idea how long it was there, but at some point their heads turned at the same time, and then their lips touched, and suddenly they were tasting each other. Vaguely she heard the smash of a martini glass being knocked over, and the whisper of the words *I'm taking you inside*.

He scooped her up in his arms and she arched her back with delight. A voice in her head was telling her to stop, but it was being drowned out by a giddiness that engulfed her like champagne. It was wrong, she knew that, and yet it didn't feel it. The way their bodies meshed together, the way his lips slotted into hers, felt perfectly natural, as if it had always been this way.

He put her down in the bedroom and her hand threaded around his neck to pull him closer. Drawing away again, she unfastened the buttons on his shirt, sighing as she felt his fingers slide down the long brass zip that ran from her neck to the base of her spine. He peeled the fabric off her shoulders so that the dress fell to the floor with a soft whisper. Her bra was unclipped and his palms pushed her wispy chiffon shorts over her buttocks and down her thighs.

'Is this all right?' he whispered.

She arched her neck and groaned as he kissed the soft patch of skin behind her ear. Standing there naked, she felt wonderfully, frighteningly exposed. She could feel his breath on her skin, the featherlight touch of his lips on the curve of her shoulder, his hardness pressing against her belly.

The back of his hand brushed her nipple. She closed her eyes and gasped, knowing she was being admired, explored. He guided her hands to touch him, and she felt him harden even more beneath her fingers.

White heat ripped around her body. She fell back on the bed and, without even thinking about what she was doing, parted her thighs, watching him kneel between them. He was naked too now. He lifted her foot and licked it, then snaked tiny kisses up her leg, towards the tiny, neglected strip of pubic hair.

He spread her thighs wider, and as his tongue connected with her clitoris, arrows of lust fired around her body. His lips moved upwards, to her belly, her breasts, her neck, until he kissed her lips once more and she could smell herself on him and all she wanted, right there, right now, was to feel him inside her.

He lowered his hand to help ease himself into her, fulfilling the wish she need not vocalise, and she cried out with the sweet, exquisite pleasure of being woken from a deep and sexless slumber.

They moved in motion. He cupped his hands around her thighs to rock more deeply into her. He was rough and yet exquisitely tender, rolling her over until she straddled him. She arched her back as he held her hips, not believing that her body could feel like this. She ran her hands over her breasts, over her hard nipples, and down the curves of her body. She wanted to touch herself, feel the skin that seemed to tingle beneath her fingertips. And just as she was about to explode, he curled his finger into her, stroking her secret, throbbing nub until her stomach contracted tighter and tighter, then detonated shock waves to every nerve ending in her body, lust, loneliness and grief colliding in one fireball of desire.

The orgasm finally shrank to a stop. She lay back on the soft pillows, regulated her breathing, and tried to work out what the hell had just happened. But all she could think about, all that she knew for sure, was that it was the best sex she had ever had in her life.

34

Ross hadn't been doing his hacking by the pool, as Rachel had imagined. In fact, the Blue Parrot Inn didn't have a pool, or anything else much. Its sole attraction seemed to be the Coke machine in the lobby.

'Why's he staying here?' whispered Liam. 'I mean, you get to stay at Round Hill; what's Ross got against luxury?'

'I think he was trying to go under the radar,' said Rachel as they let themselves into the room. The half-drunk hotelier had just shrugged and pushed across the key when Rachel had waved five dollars under his nose. Ross, it seemed, had paid a week in advance and asked not to be disturbed by cleaners.

The hotel was on the run-down side of Montego Bay, not far from the place where Ross had been attacked, and Rachel was glad of Liam's presence – and even more reassured by the thought of Yohan within screaming distance. She couldn't quite believe they were here. Dinner on the terrace of the Round Hill had seemed infinitely preferable to venturing out again, but Liam's arrival had galvanised her, spurred her on. Besides, it had been impossible to relax when she felt so deeply unsettled by Ross's attack. How could they sit and have a relaxing swordfish supper when Ross was in a coma, and they were no nearer to finding out why Julian had died?

In stark contrast to Rachel's suite, Ross's room was cramped and dingy, with cigarette burns on the furniture and a grille over the window, but it wasn't as bad as the lobby's sticky carpets had suggested. Ross had certainly kept it neat and tidy – his army training, Rachel assumed – with his shirts neatly folded in drawers and his shoes at right angles to the bed.

Rachel crossed to the desk. Pens laid neatly on the top, a can of Coke, and a newspaper, also folded. No sign of his notebook – presumably he'd had it on him when he was mugged that night. There was also a small room safe, not big enough for anything larger than a Kindle or a wallet. Rachel gazed hopelessly around the room.

'There's nothing. No laptop. No notebooks. Nothing,' she said with frustration.

'Maybe he had it all on him when he was mugged,' suggested Liam, handing her a can of cola.

'Maybe. Diana called from New York. Left me a message. She'd just met with Simon Michaels, CEO of Denver Chemicals, who said that Julian wanted to sell the division.'

'Had he found a buyer?'

'I don't know. You worked in a fancy law firm. What's the going rate for a pharmaceuticals company these days?'

Liam scratched his head. 'It depends how big it is. I've hardly been keeping up to speed, but I do know there's been some pretty major acquisitions in the last few years. A small boutique firm could sell for a billion dollars or more depending on whether it had anything interesting in the R and D pipeline. One of the bigger players? Their valuation could be over fifty, sixty billion.'

'It's a lot of money. And of course a company is worth a whole lot more if it's got a potential blockbuster diet drug on its hands.'

'But it's not just about selling off the division,' said Liam.

'What do you mean?' frowned Rachel.

'Denver Chemicals is only one part of the company. I'm not that familiar with the corporate structure of the Denver Group, but it's a publicly traded company. A high-profile failure in one of the divisions can make the City lose confidence in a company in a second.' He clicked his fingers. 'It only takes a little wobble to send share prices spiralling downward.'

'So none of the Denver Group shareholders are going to be happy to see Rheladrex fail?'

'Absolutely.'

Her train of thought was disrupted by the hotel owner, who was scratching his stomach and rattling a bunch of keys.

'You finished up here?'

Rachel nodded and took one last look at the scene, then went outside to the car, where Yohan was waiting for them.

'Yohan, the Sydon Medical Clinic.'

'Yeah, man. I know it. But it closed down now.'

'Can we see it, please?'

'Rach, it's late,' protested Liam.

Yohan seemed in agreement. 'It's not in a good part of town, Miss Rachel.'

'Yohan, please. It's important.'

He turned the car around, and she could see his reluctance in his dark eyes in the rear-view mirror.

They headed a few miles out of the city, following an old pick-up truck with a Rastafarian band playing music from its open-top boot. After a while the truck turned off and they were left alone. The houses had thinned out and the tropical foliage grew thicker, and all they could hear was the sound of exotic birds and the wind rustling through the palm fronds. The road became dusty, more of a track. There were burning oil drums on the grassy verges.

Eventually they arrived at a near-derelict building less than half a mile from the hotel. It had been name-checked in Megan Hill's report about Rheladrex clinical trials, although looking at it now it was hard to believe that any sort of research had been carried out there.

'Look at this place,' said Rachel, astonished.

'I'm not sure these are places for collecting scientific data as we know it. It's a numbers game. Get people to sign up, test the drug,' said Liam.

'Yohan, park up here.'

'Miss Rachel, it's not a good idea.'

There was a lone street light outside the clinic that cast a silvery phosphorous glow over the building.

Without listening to Yohan, Rachel got out of the car. Liam followed her.

'There's no one here. There's not been anyone here for months by the looks of it,' he pointed out.

She went to a door and tried to push it open but it was locked up with an old iron padlock.

'Shit,' she hissed, pulling out a packet of cigarettes from the bag that was slung across her body. She went to light one, but Liam took it out of her mouth.

'We're going back to the hotel.' His mouth was set in a determined line and he didn't look as if he was going to take no for an answer.

'There's got to be someone around here who knows something.'

'Rachel, get back in the car. We can't be wandering around places like this at night, with or without Yohan. What's it going to solve?'

'Something is wrong, Liam. Julian didn't kill himself because he was distraught over Madison. This is linked to Rheladrex, I know it.'

'Why? What proof have you got? None,' he said fiercely.

The clinic was on the side of a hill, and they had a view across Montego Bay. Hurricane season was starting, and there were distant storm clouds on the horizon – pitch-black thumbprints against midnight blue.

'I'm going to find out the truth,' Rachel said with determination.

'I know you will. But I don't think you're going to find it in Jamaica.'

She knew he was right. Montego Bay was nothing but a dead end, an abandoned clinic and an old friend in a hospital bed.

'We should go back to London. Ross's ex-wife is here. Diana is covering the medical fees. You can't do anything more.'

'You're coming to London?'

'Well I've not come halfway around the world for a can of Red Stripe.' He smiled softly. 'A week. I'll stay a week. The Rachel Miller I know will find what she's looking for in a week, and if she does, then she's coming home with me.'

He put his arm across her shoulder. She wanted to nestle into his warmth, wanted him to take her home. But Yohan sounded the horn. It was dark, it was late. It was time to get back to Round Hill. What a shame her sister had booked them into separate rooms.

35

When her eyelids fluttered open, Diana had no idea where she was.

She was naked, lying on her side in a bed that felt firmer than usual, although the sheets were just as crisp as those in the Somerfold master suite. And then she saw him: a firm, muscular back, broader than her husband's. More tanned, the hair fringing the top of his neck longer than Julian ever wore his. Memories of last night came flooding back. She knew that what had happened on that rooftop, in this bedroom, was wrong on every level, but lying here in this strange bed, in a city she knew but was not her own, felt like an out-of-body experience she would remember for the rest of her life.

Adam was asleep, his breathing still heavy and deep. She reached out and touched him to check that he was real, stroking a mole on his back with her fingertip and drawing an imaginary line to another one between his shoulder blades. Light began to flood through the French door that led on to the roof terrace, a door that Diana was convinced they didn't lock last night. She supposed that was quite a reckless thing to do in a wealthy street in New York, and yet there had been no break-in. Reckless things didn't always have negative consequences, she reminded herself as she watched Adam stir, twitching at first, then moving on to his back, his eyes fluttering open.

Her heart thumped with anticipation. That he was still here was already a bonus, she told herself. Not that he had anywhere else to go – after all, this was his bedroom, his home.

He stared at the ceiling for what seemed like an eternity before he spoke.

'Have you got jet lag?' he asked, his voice husky with sleep.

'I've got something,' she smiled, acknowledging that her blood felt like jelly.

'That will be the famous martini hangover,' he said, sliding one hand behind his head. He still didn't turn to look at her, but his arm rested against hers and he didn't attempt to move it. She knew how easy it would be to hook her leg over his, how easy it would be to initiate sex again, but she daren't, as much as she wanted to feel intimate and close to him once more.

For a moment everything felt suspended in time, and part of her wished they could stay like this for ever. Then he flung back the duvet and swung his legs out of bed, and her heart felt as if it might shatter into a million pieces. She watched him, beautiful from the back, tall, muscular and yet compact, like a Greek statue.

He grabbed his shirt and boxer shorts that had been discarded in last night's encounter and put them on, which heightened her disappointment even more. She doubted that Adam was normally the sort to put on clothes from the night before. Nor was he the modest type, so she could only assume that he didn't want her to see him naked.

'I'll make some breakfast. How do pancakes sound?'

She nodded, and waited until he had left the room before she got out of bed herself. Her chiffon knickers were still on the floor. She picked them up and noticed that they were ripped, which sent another surge of lust around her body. Part of her was embarrassed, ashamed for feeling like this. It had been a careless, drunken encounter, but unlike those she had had in her more wanton youth, she wanted it to happen all over again.

She could still taste him in her mouth, smell the lingering scent of their blended sweat. Last night had been a revelation. It was shocking and exciting that her body could feel all the things it had done, and it had been wonderful and terrible in equal measure. Oh yes, she knew it was forbidden to sleep with her husband's brother – and so soon after his death, too. But the truth was, Diana felt liberated. Overnight she felt a woman again. Sexy and desired and beautiful.

Julian's infidelity hadn't just been a blow to her marriage; it was a snub to her personally. Couples' therapy had brought their relationship back on track, months of individual and joint sessions where they talked about the problems and frustrations in their lives. But the sex had never recovered. Not that it had ever been as good as last night, even in the early days, when they used to meet in car parks after work and steal kisses in the lifts. On one occasion they'd had sex in the boardroom. It had been fantastic, wild, abandoned, but the heel of her shoe had scratched a ten-inch mark down the Biedermeier walnut table, almost giving Julian a heart attack and making him paranoid for weeks that they had been caught on CCTV. Then later on in their marriage, sex had been something with an end in sight. Having a baby. It was a reproductive process, not two people wanting to bring pleasure to one another.

She took a white towelling robe off a hook on the back of the door and put it on. When she went down into the kitchen, Adam was standing at a clean, unused-looking stove, flipping pancakes. She watched him for a moment, the unlikely chef at work. His shirt, which was only half buttoned up, stopped at the base of the boxer shorts, showing off his long legs, sprayed with fine light brown hair. He had good feet – always a potential turn-off – and his shirt sleeves were rolled back, showing off firm, muscular forearms.

For a second Diana imagined herself as one half of a young married couple in some glossy, glamorous sit-com. Part of her yearned for that nice, comfortable normality. So far her life had been full of extremes. She had been the struggling single mother, and then the pampered wife in her gilded cage. But New York had always been her city of dreams, and now here she was in the middle of one: a sexy man cooking breakfast for his girl in his stylish, bright Brooklyn brownstone.

She hadn't imagined that Adam would be a good cook. Okay, pancakes with blueberries and maple syrup was not exactly beef Wellington, but they were hot, fluffy and delicious.

They made small talk about the weather, and she noticed that he was eating quickly and looking at his watch, which he seemed to do a lot when she was around.

'I should go and jump in the shower.'

261

'You have to go?'

He nodded as he finished his fresh orange juice.

'You mean I should go.' She was not naïve. She knew the etiquette of these situations.

'No,' he said matter-of-factly. 'It's just that I've got back-to-back meetings in the city.'

She opened her mouth to speak, but she didn't know what to say. *About last night*... She almost winced at the trite, inadequate cliché on the tip of her tongue.

Instead, silence filled the room.

'You are very beautiful,' he said finally. He was looking at her, really looking at her, and it made her feel as desirable as she had done last night.

'I can sense there's a but,' she said softly.

'The problem with having a big brother like Julian was that he always got there first. First to ski a black run, first to learn to sail, first to work at the company and make my father proud. I was always swimming in his slipstream, always racing to catch up. Sometimes it didn't matter. I became a better skier, a better sailor, but there were other things where he had got there ahead of me and it meant I could never go there. I couldn't be head of the company, I couldn't be with you.'

Tears prickled in her eyes.

'Julian isn't here any more,' she whispered.

She saw his eyes close momentarily, as if he was wrestling with a host of emotions he didn't understand. When he opened them, he looked more steely. He stood up, and took his plate to the sink.

'I have to go. I can give you a spare key. You can return it to me in London.'

'When are you going back?' she said with as much dignity as she could muster.

'I fly back tomorrow on the jet. Do you want a lift?'

Of course it was tempting to say yes. The back seats of the Denver corporate plane converted to a bed.

'No, my flight back to Heathrow is for this evening,' she said, lying about her flexible ticket.

He came round to her side of the table, cupped his hands

around the back of her head and kissed her hair right at the crown. As his lips lingered, she wondered what he was thinking. It was not a kiss that said rejection, but nor was it one that held any definite promise.

'Let's talk when we get back to London,' he whispered. She nodded, not daring to think how this was all going to pan out.

36

Tempting as it was to stay at the Round Hill resort, Rachel and Liam left for Heathrow the following afternoon. The weather had turned by the time they got back to England, making Rachel wish even more that they had stayed a day or two extra for the seafood BBQs, the tennis, and the snorkelling in the electric-blue Caribbean sea. Then again, their trip to Jamaica had not been without its awkward moments. She and Liam had got on well, falling back into their easy companionship that had prompted half a dozen people to ask whether they were on their honeymoon, so from that point, she was glad to be back on safer, less romantic ground.

'Look at this place,' he said as they rounded the corner and Somerfold appeared.

Rachel knew that Liam was from the sort of upper-middle-class family that had friends with country piles. He never boasted about his background, although he couldn't help the occasional reference to things in his past that gave clues about the sort of world he was from. The public school and Cambridge education, the gap year in South America, the nostalgic mention of a holiday cottage in Dorset. But even he couldn't help but look impressed.

'Don't get too excited, this is where I'm staying,' she said, bringing the hire car to a halt.

'A boathouse, but not as we know it,' smiled Liam, grabbing their bags from the boot.

'Actually, Diana did mention I could move up to the big house.'

'Promoted?'

'More like the end of the Cold War, although I'm still on icy ground. What do you think? Want to stay here, or play lord of the manor?'

'This place is great,' he said, looking around the Lake House as they stepped inside. 'Let's stay here.'

Her heart fluttered. 'I'm glad you said that. My mum is up at the house a lot, and she might start asking difficult questions.'

'You mean she might take me to one side and assess my prospects.'

She tried not to read too much into his comment, but it still made her smile to herself.

'Someone's been in here,' she said, glancing around the place.

'It's certainly tidier than your usual style,' said Liam.

'All my stuff's gone . . .'

Rachel began to panic. She certainly felt vulnerable in the Lake House sometimes. At night, if the blinds were not drawn, the large glass window surrounded you with blackness and made you feel as if you were floating in space. Sometimes it was incredibly relaxing – like one big personal flotation tank; on other nights she felt quite afraid.

'You settle in,' she said distractedly. 'I'm going up to the big house. I want to speak to Mrs Bills. See if she knows what's happened.'

She stuffed her hands in her pockets as she marched up the path. It was drizzling, certainly not the weather for the little denim shorts she had been wearing since Jamaica. A disturbing thought flickered in her brain. Had she been burgled, she wondered, remembering that Diana had once commented that Julian sometimes worked in the Lake House. Had someone been in there, rifling through the place, looking for something she had not yet identified?

She confronted the housekeeper as soon as she saw her. 'Mrs Bills, has someone been in the Lake House? My things have gone missing,' she said, aware that she was nearly panting.

'Mrs Denver said you were coming to stay at the main house. I packed up your belongings and put them in the Green Room in the west wing.'

'So it was you,' she laughed, with a sense of relief.

'What did you think had happened?' the older woman asked with surprise.

'Nothing, nothing,' she said with a wave of the hand. 'Actually, there's been a change of plan. My friend has come to stay with me, so I think it's best if I stay in the Lake House until he goes.'

'I'll get Mr Bills to bring your belongings back down, then.'

'Don't worry, I'll do it. Where is Diana?'

'She's just landed at Heathrow, so she's due back in the next couple of hours. Your mother went to pick her up. Your friend, will he want something to eat?'

'That would be lovely,' she said, remembering that they had both slept through breakfast on the plane.

Rachel ascended the stairs to the Green Room, a beautiful space on the top floor. It had a four-poster bed, soft jade-green silk wallpaper and a vase of fresh flowers on the windowsill. The sight of her old canvas duffle bag on the velvet chaise longue made her laugh – it was like a crude interloper in an oasis of luxury. If someone had broken into the Lake House, they would have found slim pickings indeed, she thought, looking at her old biker boots and a wash bag that had seen better days.

Rubbing her eyes, she realised how tired she was. Jamaica had been a dead end, and Liam's seven-day deadline to return to Ko Tao was certainly tempting, especially on a day as grey and miserable as today. Her bare forearms had become flecked with goose pimples. Somerfold must be an unwieldy place to heat even with the Denvers' extravagant budget, she reflected.

Her thoughts turned to the Lake House, with its four exterior walls constructed largely of glass. When it was hot, it was as toasty as a greenhouse but she could only imagine how cold it would be when the weather dipped. In fact, that evening, it was going to be freezing. It would be the perfect excuse to cuddle up in bed with Liam, but she supposed he would welcome that cold-weather survival tactic like a hole in the head.

When Diana had first shown her around the house, she had pointed out a storage room on this floor. 'It's where we chuck all the winter stuff,' she had said at the time. Deciding that it would be a good idea to take some blankets to the Lake House, she went to find it.

Rachel's storage place in her Ko Tao apartment was a broom cupboard overspilling with rucksacks, flippers and boxes of nostalgia but this place was more like Selfridges. She could see shiny leather boots, furry moon boots and smart skis stored in a rack. There were coats, parkas, boxes of mittens and expensive candles, hotel slippers unused in their cellophane and a tall pile of cashmere blankets. There were Vuitton trunks and leather suitcases. On the top shelf was a row of handbags clearly not in current rotation, but Rachel was fashion-savvy enough to recognise one as a Birkin, another an expensive Goyard.

A large jewellery box contained brooches, bangles and earrings – obviously not Diana's expensive baubles; in fact this place was clearly some sort of relegation zone, a halfway house between her proper dressing room and the nearest charity shop. Rachel picked up a silk embroidered wrap and put it round her shoulders. This was her sister's life, a life she admitted she knew very little about these days. They had been so close as teenagers, but now every item of Diana's belongings was alien to her.

She knew she should not be rifling through her sister's stuff; she had come here for blankets, that was all. But it was impossible not to. Rachel had never been very materialistic, but this was still a treasure trove, a pirate chest of shiny possessions that she had never had or would have the chance to own, and she couldn't help but think that if her sister didn't want these delicious things, then maybe she could have some of them.

A cream vanity case caught her eye. She pulled it off the shelf and flipped it open. It was crammed with sunglasses, combs, eye masks and all sorts of pointless paraphernalia. As her hand ploughed through the stuff, she felt something hard. She tugged hard and retrieved a purple hardback book, knowing before she had a chance to flip it open what it might be.

Diana had been an enthusiastic diary keeper as a child and teenager, recording her thoughts and feelings almost obsessively in those flowery notebooks. Rachel had read them a few times – it had started when she had wanted to know the truth about her sister and the fifth-form heartthrob Paul Jones, but had become a bit of an addiction, like slipping into another world that was both familiar and more exotic than her own.

Feeling a surge of anticipation and guilt, she sat down on the bed and opened the book.

6 January. Still feeling woozy from the painkillers, but feeling worse inside. It's been three weeks, but my brain can't seem to grasp what's happened. How could I lose my baby? Why me? After everything that has happened? Don't I deserve some luck? A chance? The nurse told me it was nature's way; that there might have been something wrong and this child – she was being nice, trying to get me to see it as a positive – could have been handicapped or worse, but it doesn't feel like that. I don't feel lucky. I feel cursed. The doctors can take away my baby, but why can't they take away the pain? Julian came in late again yesterday. I don't know how he can carry on working as if nothing has happened. He reached across the bed to me, but I pretended to be asleep. I don't want him touching me right now – not his fault, I know, but it's how I feel.

Rachel felt cold. She didn't want to be this person, reading her sister's diary, intruding on her most intimate thoughts. Diaries weren't meant to be read, not really. They were a way for the author to sort out the day's events, to make sense of the thoughts in their head, unburdening themself to an imaginary friend or a better self, perhaps.

But then something might be relevant here, she told herself. She had spent two whole days going through Julian's possessions, but she had not yet been through Diana's. It hadn't occurred to her that it might be useful. Now she leafed through the book, skimming the pages, looking for anything that might be important.

28 January. Walked to the far edge of the wood and back, killed two hours. Omelette for lunch, trying to diet: again! Didn't even have Mrs Bills for company tonight, so watched TV in bed. I miss being pregnant. I miss the baby's kicks in my belly.

Then, later:

12 March. Jules staying at the NH house again, so alone once more. Took a bath, then had a salad in the kitchen. Went for a ride – Clarissa was skittish. Tried to pick up the knitting as Ruth recommended, but I'm all fingers and thumbs. Besides, knitting reminds me of baby things. Blankets and booties. Things I don't want to think about. Chances of getting pregnant again near zero as my husband feels the need to keep out of my sight.

There were pages of it. Mostly it was a list of each day's events, which were revealing only in their repetitiveness. Rachel had always assumed that her sister's life was exciting, glamorous, but there was page after page of emptiness and dissatisfaction with life, with her husband.

14 May. Third night Julian has spent in London. He says that work is busy but I'm not so sure. Anne-Marie definitely sounds embarrassed when I speak to her. Am I being paranoid, or does she know something that I don't? I keep asking myself if it's happening again. Those whores, those slags who think it is okay to sleep with another woman's husband. I can't go through that humiliation a second time. I don't want to start hating him again, but sometimes I can't help it.

Rachel frowned. Diana's anger shivered off the page. Whores? Slags? This was astonishing. Firstly because she had never known her sister to use such language, and also because Diana had painted a picture of Julian being such a supportive husband in the aftermath of her miscarriages.

16 May. Julian finally home. We tried to have sex. I think he was drunk. I needed to know if he still wanted me. But it hurt so we stopped. I don't feel like a wife, a lover, a mother. I feel a failure. I hate it. I hate this. I hate him. Sometimes I wish that he would go to London and just stay there.

And then the entries stopped. It would have been a week before Julian's death. Rachel closed the diary and let out a long breath. 'Shit,' she whispered, her hands trembling as she put the book back in the vanity case.

There was a pile of blankets behind her. She scooped them up, and shut the door behind her. She didn't want to dwell on what she had just read. In fact she wanted to forget it.

37

Somerfold was suspiciously quiet when Diana returned home from the airport. No music blared from the guest bedroom, there was no sound of heavy footsteps running around upstairs, no loud voice booming into a mobile phone, nothing in fact to suggest that her sister had moved in from the Lake House.

'Where's Rachel?' asked Diana when Mrs Bills came into the kitchen from her living quarters across the courtyard.

'Is she supposed to be here?' said Sylvia, throwing the keys to the Range Rover into the pot by the Aga.

'I invited her to move up here.'

'And she turned you down?'

'It seems so,' said Diana, ignoring her mother's very deliberate *tsk* sound.

'She has a friend staying with her,' said Mrs Bills, who had been waiting for her moment to interrupt the conversation. 'I don't think she wanted to intrude.'

'Which friend?' asked Sylvia briskly. 'Is this the diving boy you said was coming over?'

'He's called Liam and he's her business partner,' replied Diana patiently.

'And he's very handsome,' said Mrs Bills, looking unusually hot under the collar. 'I took some sandwiches down there and he was getting changed. Broad shoulders, swimmer's physique,' she added, trying to make her interest in him appear suddenly anatomical.

'Why don't we go down and see them?' said Sylvia.

'That depends if you're in a hostile mood or not.'

Her mother started to stutter some platitudes, but Diana

wasn't listening. She was too busy looking around the kitchen, glancing into the rooms beyond it. She didn't like to admit to herself what she was hoping to see – a huge bouquet of flowers from Adam. A welcome home. A declaration . . .

Of course there was nothing. Just a slightly wilting arrangement of peonies she recognised from before she went to New York. She tried to mask her disappointment. She'd had Adam down as a flower person, but then again, these were different, difficult circumstances.

'So he's not her boyfriend, then?'

Sylvia and Diana were sheltering under a golfing umbrella as they walked to the Lake House.

'Just friends, apparently.'

'Aren't they always?' said Sylvia with undisguised disapproval.

'Mum, I told you. We've all got to make an effort with each other.'

'I still don't understand why she is here. I mean, I am glad she has finally paid her respects to Julian, and she does seem genuinely upset about what has happened, but why has she been to America, to Jamaica . . . It's almost as if she wants to go on holiday at your expense.'

'Rachel is only doing things I have asked her to. She's being supportive.'

'Hmmm,' said Sylvia, sounding unconvinced, as they reached the door of the Lake House.

'Just spend a bit of time with her, Mum. And then make your mind up.'

Rachel hadn't seen them approach, and for a moment Diana stood outside the window, watching her sister and her friend. They were playing some sort of board game at the table at the window overlooking the lake. They were both laughing, and she could tell by the way they looked at each other that there was a special connection between them.

Sylvia knocked, and Rachel turned with a look of surprise and then anxious pleasure.

'This is Liam, everyone. Liam, you've met Diana before, and this is my mum.'

272

'You have a tattoo,' exclaimed Sylvia.

'Me?' asked Rachel, glancing quickly at Liam.

'What is it?' asked Sylvia, looking as if she had never seen one before.

Rachel stroked the tiny dolphin that was peeking round her T-shirt.

'It was a present to myself when I started free-diving.'

'She's really good,' added Liam, taking the umbrella off Sylvia and standing it up in the corner. 'Got one of the best teachers in South East Asia, who reckons she should compete internationally.'

Sylvia smiled politely, and Diana felt the frostiness around the room.

'So who fancies some lunch?' said Rachel quickly.

Diana put her hand in the air. 'I can send Mrs Bills down with something.'

'No, she's already brought us a sandwich once this morning.'

'We do have people to do these things,' said Sylvia quietly.

Liam put a hand on her shoulder. 'I can go to the shops. Sylvia, do you fancy joining me?'

His smile was so impossible to resist that Diana half wished he had invited her to go with him instead.

'So how was Jamaica?' she asked when Liam and Sylvia had left.

Rachel described the abandoned clinic, Ross's injuries, Detective Henry's hunch that he had been beaten up more than the average. It didn't seem to add up to much.

'Tell me about New York,' she said when she had finished.

Diana could feel her cheeks flushing. She got up and stood by the open window, hoping that the breeze might cool her down and disguise her embarrassment. She was desperate to tell her sister what had happened. Rachel might not be able to sort out her own love life, but she had always been a sage counsel on other people's dilemmas.

Diana had slept with Adam, but more than that, she had feelings for him. Was that so terribly wrong, or was it a sign that she could stop living in the past, a sign that she could love again and have a future without Julian in it?

Cowardice stopped her from speaking her thoughts out loud.

Instead she described the meeting with Simon Michaels.

'I got the sense that Michaels wasn't that happy about the company being sold,' she concluded.

'So he had a beef with Julian?' asked Rachel.

'I didn't say that.'

'And what did Adam think?'

Even the mention of his name made her heart thud harder.

'He didn't really say. I think he felt it was all a bit of a wild goose chase.'

'Perhaps I should phone him,' said Rachel.

Diana felt territorial at her sister's suggestion. 'No, I'll call him,' she replied, knowing that it might be a good excuse to speak to him again. 'But maybe he has a point.'

'So *you* think we're on a wild goose chase?' said Rachel, looking hurt.

'I know how hard you're working on this,' Diana said kindly. 'But what I don't understand is that if Julian was trying to build up some sort of case about Rheladrex, whether it was for or against, with or without Madison Kopek, then where is all the stuff about it? He was organised. He would have collected files and papers. He wouldn't think about nixing the pharm division's pet project without any sort of thought process behind it.' Julian's laptop had been returned by the police, and she knew that Rachel had already been through its files and found nothing relating to Rheladrex.

Rachel was the type to always have a ready answer for everything, but right now she looked flummoxed.

Outside, there was the grumble of the hire car returning, and Liam and Sylvia came in, each holding a bag from the village stores. They were laughing over some shared joke and went straight into the kitchen, where Diana could hear him teaching her mother how to make a Thai soup called tom ka kai.

'I think Liam's a hit,' she grinned.

'Liam's always a hit with the ladies,' replied her sister with a bittersweet smile.

It was quite a makeshift meal. No place mats, no matching cutlery, none of the other accoutrements Diana was used to when she hosted a lunch or simple supper. But it was quite delicious, even though the village stores had apparently never even heard of lemongrass let alone stocked it, forcing Liam to improvise with a bottle of Jif and a garlic bulb.

Although it was drizzling, Rachel pulled the double door all the way back, and it was soothing to watch the rain bounce off the surface of the lake.

Liam asked Sylvia all sorts of questions about the girls. Sylvia was a woman who loved attention, and she was only too happy to talk. Their early Sheffield upbringing was whitewashed from history. Instead, she recalled an idyllic Devon childhood that Diana hardly recognised: Sylvia coping admirably as the loving single mum, summers spent looking for clams and scrambling over rocks like some scene out of an Enid Blyton book. In return, Sylvia lightly quizzed Liam on his own background. Diana recognised the school he had been to as a top-flight day school that she had considered for Charlie before Julian had insisted he go to Harrow.

Sylvia announced that she was fairly certain she had met Liam's mother at a charity event for the English National Ballet, which Liam reluctantly admitted was quite possible.

He seemed so different from other boyfriends Rachel had brought home. Boys with vague ambitions to be rock stars or poets, even the ones who seemed to be well into middle-age. Diana was relieved to see her mother thaw. She had always felt very mixed emotions about how unequivocally Sylvia had taken her side after the *Sunday Post* scandal. But she had been right when she had said that Sylvia just needed to spend some quality time with her daughter. To remember all the wonderful things about Rachel, not just the incident involving her newspaper.

'So, Rachel, Liam tells me you're thinking of opening a hotel together. I think it's a marvellous idea,' said Sylvia, finishing off her generous glass of Chablis.

'Perhaps,' Rachel said vaguely.

'I've never been to Thailand,' Sylvia continued pointedly.

'You should come,' encouraged Liam. 'January is perfect weather. We can go to Ao Nang Park, and it's never too late to start scuba diving.'

Sylvia laughed coyly. 'What do you think, Rachel?' she asked, turning to her daughter.

'I think we should get your flights booked before you change your mind,' agreed Rachel.

It was impossible for Diana not to feel warm and fuzzy about what was going on before her. She had no idea if Sylvia would have softened to this extent without Liam's presence, but he had certainly helped. This man was good for her sister. Rachel had never been lucky in the romance department, never been a flirt. Diana remembered Paul Jones, a good-looking fifth-former in the school they had both attended. Rachel had known him from the swimming team and had started talking about him with increasing regularity, telling Diana and her friend how she had challenged him to a fifty-metre butterfly race, offered to train with him before school. Diana had liked him too. Most of the girls at their school did. But she had realised that men didn't want a rival, a mate – they wanted a cheerleader. So she had gone to watch school football matches, cheered him on in the swimming team. She had felt guilty when Paul Jones had finally asked her out, trying but failing to convince herself that Rachel didn't like him anyway. Not like that.

Her sister deserved to be lucky now. She deserved a friend, not a rival.

'You two should go into London. Have a night out rather than sit here day in, day out. There's a new restaurant that's just opened in Covent Garden. Sister restaurant to Casper's in New York.'

'I read about that on the plane. Hottest table in London. Which means impossible to get into.'

'I'm sure I could call reservations for you . . .'

'Would you?' asked Liam, looking hopeful.

'Of course. I'm sure there's a Denver hotel you could stay in as well, if you really wanted to make a night of it.'

Rachel flashed her a panicked expression, and she knew immediately that it had been a suggestion too far.

'We should go,' said Diana finally. 'I'm exhausted.'

'Forget you're on New York time,' smiled Liam.

She wanted to tell him that it was impossible not to think

about New York, but instead she just got up to thank him for lunch.

On the way back to the house, Sylvia linked her arm through her daughter's.

'That was nice,' she said contentedly.

'Go back and tell her,' replied Diana.

'She knows,' said Sylvia quietly. 'It was a lovely lunch. Everyone could tell that.'

Diana nodded. She had a feeling that they had turned a corner. That life might just be beginning to get better.

38

Rachel wasn't sure if the tight cobalt-blue Roland Mouret dress that Diana had lent her was the right thing to wear to meet the investigating officer in charge of Julian's case, but she didn't really have much choice. On her sister it was respectably knee-length, but when you were five foot ten it hovered mid-thigh, making her feel like a seventies game-show hostess.

She glanced up and saw Detective Inspector Mark Graham coming out of the station.

'Inspector!' she panted. 'Can I have a word?'

He turned around and for a moment looked her up and down as if he was pleasantly surprised by the sight before him. Rachel couldn't help smiling. As a student, she would have practically punched a man if he'd wolf-whistled at her in the street.

'Sorry, hi,' she gasped. 'I'm Rachel Miller, Julian Denver's sister-in-law. Julian Denver – the suicide victim. Big house. Near Holland Park tube.'

'Yes, I know,' he said, frowning.

'I think Diana – his wife – I think she mentioned that I wanted to speak to you.'

'She mentioned it,' confirmed the inspector, moving away from her. 'But I'm just leaving for the day. If you'd like to make an appointment, I'm sure—'

Rachel ran ahead of him to block his path.

'With respect, Inspector, I tried that. You've been avoiding my calls.'

'Avoiding your calls?' he asked with an amused arch of his brow.

'I've phoned three times and you haven't got back to me. Please,' she said, trying to bat her eyelashes.

'Are you okay? Do you have something in your eye?' he said, offering her a tissue from his pocket.

'Look, do you have five minutes? I just need to ask you a few questions.'

'Back to the day job, is it?' he asked, motioning back to the station.

He found them a small room and left her in it while he went to fetch two plastic cups of coffee.

'Day job? How do you know I used to be a journalist?' she asked when he sat down.

'Because I'm a police officer looking into the death of a high-profile industrialist, Miss Miller. It pays to know who you're investigating.'

'So I'm a suspect now?'

'You sound a little paranoid, or is the caffeine fix making you jumpy?'

'Or perhaps you don't like me because of my former career.'

Mark Graham started to laugh. 'Your type have caused the Met a great deal of trouble over the last few years, you know that.'

'It takes two to tango and all,' she said, remembering the brown envelopes of cash she had paid to bent coppers in the past. 'So. We both know that inquests can be shy of reporting a suicide verdict, but what do you think?'

'You don't waste any time, do you?'

'I live in Thailand now. I have an apartment with a sea view and I want to get back there,' she said, almost convincing herself that this was true.

'Well, it wasn't a kinky sex thing and we haven't referred it to the Murder Investigation team, so there's your answer,' he said, sipping his coffee.

His words reminded her of Megan Hill and an observation she had made in Washington: *Three people are dead: Madison, her brother and Julian Denver. And they all have a connection to Rheladrex.*

'So it wasn't foul play?' She had to ask the question, otherwise what had she sent Ross to Jamaica for?

Mark Graham took her remark seriously.

'Julian Denver was an extremely wealthy man, one with lots of enemies if you believe the rumours, and that makes us consider all options. But as far as we're concerned, cause of death was ligature strangulation. No third-party involvement. Not unless the investigative journalist in the family thinks there's something else here?'

'It's driving Diana crazy . . .'

Graham began to nod, as if he was beginning to understand her motives for being here.

'What is it, Miss Miller? What's your involvement here? Life insurance policy won't pay out if it's suicide?'

Rachel shook her head vigorously. 'It's nothing to do with money,' she said tartly. 'My sister is grieving. It's hit her pretty hard, I think, and all this uncertainty doesn't help.'

The policeman raised an eyebrow. 'Is that a criticism of our investigation?'

'Just an observation.'

Graham stirred his coffee and put down his spoon.

'So is that all?'

'Just humour me and answer a few questions.'

He had a doubtful expression on his face.

'Why was Julian on his knees? Diana told me she found him on his knees.'

'It was a short-drop hanging.'

'Short drop?'

'The victim dies by cutting off the oxygen supply to the brain. All it needs is sufficient pressure on the neck.'

'And you're sure he did it himself? Someone couldn't have broken into the house and killed him? Can a murder be dressed up as suicide?' She could feel her mouth running away with her.

He gave her a doubtful look.

'Well, can it?' she pressed.

He picked up his spoon and began playing with the foam at the bottom of his cup.

'I know it's hard, Rachel. People don't want to think that someone they love would do something like this. But there's nothing to make me think anything other than that Julian took his own life. A locked house, no sign of entry, forced or otherwise,

280

complete surveillance coverage – yes, we've been through it – and no one unusual in or out of the house. In theory, of course, someone could dress a murder up as a suicide, but it would be very, very difficult. I've seen it happen once in my career, and that was a professional hit, although we could never formally confirm that. In this instance, the only other person in the house was your sister, but unless she forced him into the noose, which I don't buy, then yes, we're looking at a suicide.'

She took a pen and a scrap of paper from her bag and scribbled her number on the back of it.

'Out of business cards, I'm afraid. If you come up with anything that might help my sister make sense of this, you will give me a call?'

He gave her a sideways look as he handed her his card.

'Why do I get the sense you're doing a bit of detective work on your own?'

'Me?' she said innocently. 'I'm just a diving instructor these days, Inspector.'

'Then a piece of advice. Look after your sister, wait for the inquest and then go back to your Thailand room with a view. It's a better place for you there, I promise you.'

She met Liam outside Covent Garden tube station. Long Acre was packed with tourists and the night air hummed with music and conversation.

'I can't move in this thing,' said Rachel, wriggling in the blue dress as they moved away from the main thoroughfare. It was Liam's cue to say that it looked hot, sensational; instead he muttered something about Mark Graham thinking it must have been his lucky day.

'I hope you don't mind me inviting a friend along. I just thought she might be useful,' he said as they approached Casper's on a quiet corner of Covent Garden.

Rachel's heart sank. She had been thrilled when Diana had suggested they should have a night on the tiles. Could have kissed her, in fact. Lately she had been wondering if life experience beat the optimism out of you, but still she harboured a faint hope that Liam might see the error of his ways and proclaim his undying love for her, and dinner *à deux* in a glamorous, exciting place seemed the perfect opportunity to do that.

Her thoughts had been full of Julian's suicide from the moment she had heard about it. Madison, Diana, Rheladrex, Ross McKiney; sometimes it was impossible to think of anything but those things, but still Liam crept into her consciousness unbidden. What she couldn't believe was that she had spent three years in his almost constant company, and although she had acknowledged how handsome he was, realised that she was a little bit in love with him, she hadn't done anything about it. And now it was possibly, probably too late.

'Of course I don't mind,' she lied, pasting a broad smile on her face. 'I know you want to see as many of your friends as possible whilst you are in London.'

Modelled on a belle époque French bistro, Casper's was exactly the kind of restaurant Rachel had enjoyed coming to on expense account when she worked in London. The sort of place where 'French peasant food' set you back fifty pounds for moules frites and a tarte aux pommes. It was hot and exclusive and impossible to get into unless you were press or connected.

'Your guest has already arrived,' smiled the pretty waitress as she showed them to their table.

Sitting in a plum booth in the corner was a beautiful, fragile blonde in an impeccably tailored suit that screamed *investment bank*.

'Rachel Miller, may I introduce Alicia Dyer?' said Liam.

Ooh, get you with your fancy ways, thought Rachel, but she held her tongue and smiled.

'Hello,' she said simply.

Alicia was beautiful – that was if you liked the willowy blonde type with big tits and flawless milky skin, of course. Rachel immediately felt dowdy and invisible next to her.

'So you two work together?' Alicia smiled, glancing at the menu.

'We run the diving business in Ko Tao. And you?'

'We were at Cambridge together.'

One of those, thought Rachel. Keen to get their Oxbridge credentials in from the get-go.

'And then we were *together* together, which all seems a bit of a lifetime ago, doesn't it?' she said, flashing an orthodontically perfect smile Liam's way.

'You went out?' Rachel said, laughing nervously, trawling through her mind for his previous references to girlfriends. It was a topic they had never particularly lingered on, another good sign, she had often thought. There had been a Helen and an Emma, and an Ally who had obviously broken his heart, not that Liam had ever expressed it in so many words.

Ally. *Alicia.*

Rachel felt as if she had been punched in the stomach. A bottle of champagne arrived and the waiter started to pour. She raised her hand to refuse a glass and then gestured for him to top her up.

'So Liam called me and said his friend wanted the skinny on the Denver Group,' said Alicia, flipping back her hair.

Rachel's mouth felt dry. She longed for something smart and witty to say, but the words had deserted her. She felt as if she had suddenly been dropped into the middle of a gladiatorial ring, without sword or shield, and she was clearly going to come off worst.

'My sister is – was – Julian Denver's wife, you see, and, well . . .'

Alicia gave a sympathetic nod. 'I'm sorry,' she said.

'I thought it might be useful to talk,' Liam said. 'Al works in mergers and acquisitions at Goldman Sachs. You must know all about the Denver Group.'

'Not really,' laughed Alicia. She ordered a steak and salad.

'You're an analyst.'

'For my sins,' she smiled. 'Listen, I'm no expert on Denver, but I might have picked something up along the way. What's your interest? Getting a handle on the company for your sister? I assume she'll have inherited some of her husband's shareholding.'

'Something like that,' said Rachel, taking a sip of champagne. She felt nervous. She had always worn her smarts on her sleeve and had never been ashamed of her cleverness or tried to hide it, but it was impossible not to feel intimidated by Alicia, who had almost certainly had numerous Superwoman profiles written about her. 'What do you know about the pharmaceuticals division?'

Alicia pouted and shook her head. 'Not much, I'm afraid. Not my sector, but Liam mentioned you were interested, so I asked around discreetly.' She leant in slightly. 'I've heard there are problems in the division. They deal mainly in generic drugs, have few medications still under patent, and an unimpressive R and D department, although their new weight-loss drug has got people talking.'

'So Rheladrex has made the company more attractive, more valuable.'

'Without question. If it's as successful as they are hoping, you're talking about a twenty, thirty billion valuation all of a sudden.'

'And without it?'

Alicia shrugged. 'It's hard to say. They might even have trouble finding a buyer. Acquiring companies want to see value and potential for growth in a target buy. Not one that brings little to the table.'

Rachel had stopped drinking and begun listening to what the other woman had to say.

'And what about the Denver Group as a whole?'

'No big news there. The value dipped after Julian's death, though the markets rallied when Ralph was installed as interim CEO. But there won't be any stability until an official appointment is made.'

'Who is favourite for the job?'

'Elizabeth, the daughter, of course.'

Rachel tried hard not to curl her lip. 'She's highly regarded, isn't she?'

'Difficult, but brilliant,' replied Alicia. 'To be honest, no one really knows why she wasn't made CEO in the first place. I don't want to speak ill of the dead and all that, but I never got the sense that Julian Denver's heart was in it. A huge company like Denver needs a very strong figurehead, a Warren Buffett, a Branson, a Ratan Tata. And quite honestly, the City never felt Julian was quite of that calibre.'

'Come on, Ally, there's no need to talk like that,' said Liam diplomatically.

'Rachel wants the truth, doesn't she? And as a woman, she will know, as I do, that in this world tradition and pig-headed stupidity go hand in hand. Elizabeth was the eldest child but Julian was the eldest son, and Ralph Denver pushed for him to be head of the board. Tradition, you see, that's the way it is for these men.'

'But didn't the scandal undermine his position?'

Rachel wasn't sure she wanted to hear the answer, given her involvement.

'Yes, but by the time Ralph announced his retirement, the brouhaha surrounding Julian's indiscretions had died down and he got the job.'

Even with Diana's connections, they had only been allotted a two-hour time slot for dinner. The rest of their supper was more convivial. Rachel found out what a lot of Liam's old Cambridge friends she had never met or even heard about were now up to. Alicia in turn asked a few perfunctory questions about their life in Ko Tao.

When it was almost time to leave, Liam excused himself to go to the gents'. While he was gone, Alicia laid a hand on Rachel's arm and told her to take care of him. Rachel didn't like to correct her. Liam didn't want or need her protection, but it was interesting that she too thought they were together.

'He's one of the good ones,' said Alicia with a note of regret. 'Sometimes I can't even remember why we decided to break up. Here, let me give you my card, and I'll take your details in case I hear any more about Rheladrex.'

Liam helped them both on with their coats, a minor tussle for who should have his attention first, and they began to leave the restaurant.

'Rachel. Rachel Miller. Is that you?'

For a minute she couldn't place the loud shriek above the clattering plates and the conversation of the diners. Then she froze. The face was familiar. 'Becky Moore? Crikey, I didn't recognise you.'

'Rebecca Mitchell now,' she said, holding up a glittering wedding ring. Becky had been an intern on the showbiz desk when Rachel had first joined the *Post* and had been her wing man on all those nights hanging around in clubs trying to catch a story they could sell. She had spent some time on the entertainment pages at the paper, then moved sideways into celebrity magazines, where, if Rachel was up to date, she was now editor of one of the more popular titles.

'Should I see you outside?' asked Liam.

Rachel was loath to leave him alone with Alicia, but there was no way she could ignore Becky, so she nodded.

'So how the hell are you?' said Becky, looking Rachel up and down. 'Looking very tanned and yummy.'

'Well, I'm living in Thailand now,' smiled Rachel. 'I have a diving school. That's my partner over there,' she added, pointing out Liam. Becky's jaw almost hit the floor.

'Gorgeous!' She slapped Rachel's arm. 'Where did you find him? I want one too!'

'Business partner,' she smiled, correcting her. 'We're opening a hotel, too.' Rachel had never been boastful – in fact she hated the sort of people who exaggerated everything – but she wanted to impress Becky, wanted her to see that she hadn't crashed and burned after the hacking debacle.

'Well, it's good to see that you've made a go of things. You're better off out of newspapers,' said Becky, waving her hand. 'It's changing; the media as we knew it has gone. There's no advertising, circulations are dropping and everyone's reading everything they want to on the internet or their phones. Newspapers are a dying breed, magazines aren't that much better. I think I might just go and open a chocolate shop.'

It was good seeing her old colleague; it brought back so many fun memories of a time when they were both hungry and driven. They'd had some brilliant times together.

'Come on then,' urged Rachel. 'Tell me some news. I've been on the other side of the world for the last three years. Who's doing what?'

Becky rattled off a few names, a few snippets of gossip that meant very little to her. 'And do you remember Lydia on the picture desk? Big girl with bad eyebrows? She's moved to France.'

'Don't tell me,' said Rachel. 'To open a chocolate shop?'

'Nope. To get away from that shit of a husband.'

Rachel frowned and shook her head. 'Mild-mannered Stuart? He was the blandest man I ever met.'

'Yes, well bland, old mild-mannered Stuart was a bigamist.'

Rachel almost choked. 'A bigamist?'

'Well, almost. For the last three years he's had a girlfriend tucked away in Reading. Bought her a flat, went down on one knee, got her in the family way, the whole nine yards.'

'Incredible.'

A waitress tapped Becky on the shoulder to indicate that her table was ready. 'I should go,' she said quickly. 'How long are you in town for? How about a nice long boozy lunch?'

'Not sure yet. But that would be lovely.'

'I'll Facebook you,' she said, already moving away from her.

Liam was standing on the pavement under a street lamp.

'Where's Alicia?'

'She had to go,' he said as they started walking off in the direction of the tube.

'She's pretty,' said Rachel after a minute.

'Yes, she is.'

'And clever.'

'That too.'

'Why did it finish between you two?'

'Just because she's pretty and clever doesn't mean that we were right for each other,' he said without looking at her.

'Is she why you came to Thailand?'

'Not really.'

'Not really?' said Rachel with a jolt. 'That's a change from "I wanted out of the rat race", as you've always insisted.'

Liam glanced up and frowned. 'No one thing made me change course. It was a few things. I hated my job, I looked at the partners above me and I knew I didn't want to be that person, sitting it out till sixty-five, waiting for retirement before I could actually start living. Yes – Alicia and I ended our relationship, but it was just another excuse to leave, not the whole reason.'

'Why didn't you tell me?'

'About what?'

'About Alicia.'

'Does it matter?'

She folded her arms across her chest and fell silent.

'So what did your friend have to say?'

'She was telling me about a friend whose husband turned out to be a bigamist.'

'Double life, eh?'

She nodded, and as she did, it was as if a penny dropped. Suddenly she could hear Julian's voice in her head. It was that hot night in Italy. His lips were on her neck, and he was whispering in her ear. She had tried so hard to block that evening out of her memory, but fragments of it were crystal clear

'I want you, Rachel.' That was what he had said. 'I know you want me too. No one needs to know.' He had whispered it urgently, his hands on her, his breath coming quickly. 'We can do this all the time,' he'd said. 'I have a place we can go.'

'*I have a place we can go,*' she repeated softly.

Liam turned to face her. 'What did you say?'

'I have a place we can go,' she said again. It didn't even occur to her that Liam might misinterpret her words.

She didn't want to confess Julian's attempted seduction to him. Not yet. 'Yesterday, Diana was wondering why Julian didn't have any printouts, details, information about Rheladrex,' she said quickly.

'Because he wasn't arsed about Rheladrex and he was just after a shag?' said Liam cynically.

'Perhaps he *was* collecting information about it – he just didn't keep it at work or in the house.'

'So if it existed, where would he keep it? You've checked his office, both houses.'

'Julian had mistresses,' she said quickly. 'When you're a billionaire adulterer, how do you keep them under the radar? You're not going to want to check into hotels. You probably have a little pied-à-terre somewhere for your extracurricular activity.'

'Not being a billionaire adulterer, I wouldn't know the form, but it's possible. But how do you track down his mistresses to find out? We're only aware of one of them, and she's dead.'

'I certainly know of one other. Susie McCormack. The lover who was exposed by my paper. Perhaps it's about time we revisited old news.'

39

Olga Shapiro seemed concerned that it was only Diana's second visit in three weeks. This was not apparently the sign of a committed patient and she could not be helped, really helped, unless she devoted more time and energy to therapy.

Diana squirmed on the soft grey felt sofa as she spoke, feeling compelled to make her excuses. She did not enjoy being a bad pupil. At school, she was never anywhere near the top of the class, but she always tried hard enough not to get into trouble, getting Rachel or clever friends to help her with homework, never disrupting any lessons, never breaking the rules.

'I live in Oxfordshire. Sometimes it's not easy to get into town,' she explained, stroking a thick strand of brown hair between her fingers.

'If it's a problem, I could recommend somebody closer,' said Olga, folding her slim hands on to her lap.

Diana shook her head. She liked Olga. In another life she could have been a third Miller sister, someone more sensible and serious than Rachel, someone smarter than herself. She wondered what had gone wrong with her life that she had no one with whom she could share her innermost secrets. The secret she was keeping about Adam Denver.

'So how are you feeling?'

'Well some days I can't even get up in the morning. But other days have been much better. I've even had fun,' she said, feeling a spark of guilt.

Olga nodded, as if she was pleased with her progress. 'Tell me about them.'

Her question took Diana by surprise. She had always thought

that she would be in control of her sessions with a therapist, that she could drip-feed someone only the information that she wanted to reveal. But the intensity of Olga's gaze had backed her into a corner.

'I've been spending time with my brother-in-law. I've enjoyed his company.'

A flashback. Adam's warm naked body, his mouth on her nipple, his tongue inside her, their sweat on the sheets. She felt her cheeks betray her, burning hot, glowing pink.

'Do you want to tell me more about that?' pressed Olga.

Diana could only look down at her feet.

'It's natural to enjoy the company of those closest to your husband,' said Olga, encouraging her to say more.

Meeting Olga's gaze, Diana wondered how much her therapist had worked out. If she was as clever as she thought, it was probably obvious to her.

'I have feelings for him.' She felt a huge wave of release just saying the words.

She waited for Olga to say something, but when the therapist remained quiet, Diana knew that she had fallen into a trap. A silent confessional booth, where once you had entered, you were expected to admit everything.

'We had sex.'

She knew what Olga Shapiro was thinking. *I told you to go fly a kite with a friend, you silly woman, not jump into bed with your brother-in-law.*

'How did it happen?' she asked.

Diana wanted to tell her everything, as if she was single and carefree and gossiping with friends or some glamorous character on *Sex and the City*. She wanted to tell her about the rooftop in Brooklyn. How beautiful and sexy he made her feel. How she finally understood what all the fuss about orgasms was about. How she had stopped feeling sad and lonely.

'We met up in New York and it was wonderful,' she said simply. She glanced up, expecting another smile of encouragement. Instead, Olga Shapiro's face had a stern, disapproving blankness.

'You and your brother-in-law are joined in grief. You have experienced loss and you each represent Julian to one another.

You have an emotional attachment and sometimes that can spill over into a temporary physical connection.'

Diana frowned. 'I don't think you understand. I didn't think it was Julian that night. I didn't want it to be Julian. I felt like a woman again. It felt like a fresh start. I felt reborn. As if I could carry on living.' She could feel herself gushing, but it was impossible to hold back her emotions. She wanted to defend their night together, defend her relationship with Adam.

Olga appeared unmoved. 'Loss creates a need for affection. You miss a sex life. You miss the support of someone who cares for you. Your brother-in-law has stepped into that role . . .'

Diana could feel her eyes narrowing. The woman didn't understand. Sex had never been important to Diana. It was something that she associated with failure – she didn't need a therapist to tell her that. She could remember very little about Charlie's father; she couldn't even picture his face, beyond a vague recollection that he had been cool and good-looking. They had met in a club in Ibiza and had sex on a little fisherman's boat that had been moored in the harbour. She had been drunk and high on vodka cocktails, a couple of Ecstasy tablets and a holiday recklessness that made girls like her do things they shouldn't. He was going home the next day, so they hadn't even exchanged numbers. That was what he had told her anyway, but maybe she hadn't been a good enough screw. Failure.

She had always had irregular periods and didn't realise she was pregnant until she was almost three months in. She had made an appointment at the abortion clinic, the date in her diary there like a big scary full-stop, but before she went, she had spoken to a girl who'd terminated her pregnancy a few weeks earlier. The girl had talked about the searing cramps, the clotting and bleeding afterwards, and when she had described what a baby looked like at eleven weeks, Diana hadn't been able to go through with it. Of course she was glad of that decision now. Charlie was the most precious thing in her life.

After Charlie had been born, after she moved to London, she had avoided sexual relationships because of the fear of where they might lead. Men thought she was frigid and casual boyfriends gave up on her before it became anything more serious; no matter how beautiful they thought she was, she wasn't worth the effort. Until she met Julian. Julian changed everything. She went on the pill a week after they started dating. They made love in hotels, in deluxe villas, under the stars. They made love everywhere, and this time she wasn't scared where it all might lead. She was aware that she was not a practised lover, and this was often a source of much concern. She had no real idea whether what they were doing in their sex life was too much, or not enough. Was she being slutty allowing him to do certain things to her, or was it all too vanilla?

She had got her answer soon enough when she had found out that Julian was unfaithful. It had been easy to blame it on herself, easy to believe that she simply hadn't satisfied him sexually. And the existence of Madison Kopek had only reinforced that sense of failure. But that night in New York Adam Denver had made her feel anything but a failure.

'Have you spoken to your brother-in-law about your feelings?' asked Olga.

'Not yet.'

'Then you should. Perhaps you should encourage him to speak to someone in the way that we are talking,' said Olga efficiently.

Diana almost laughed out loud. Adam was the least likely person to seek solace in a shrink's chair.

'When someone leaves us, dies, it can feel like a betrayal,' continued Olga. 'Sexual contact with your brother-in-law is a way of compensating for your loss.'

'Why does this all have to be about Julian?' said Diana, feeling her temper fray. 'Why can't it be about two people who like each other? I know the circumstances aren't ideal, but this man feels right for me.'

Olga Shapiro twisted her silver pen between her fingertips.

'I am not here to tell you who is the right man for you. I'm not here to tell you when is the right time to start dating again. What I can say is that your brother-in-law might feel like a safe option right now, but what has happened between you two might not be helpful. It's not going to heal your pain.'

Diana fought the urge to shake her head. There was nothing safe about Adam Denver. He was exciting, unpredictable and she knew what people would say if word of their romance got out. But she couldn't help the way she felt about him or the way he made her feel.

'So what are you saying?' she asked, feeling tears well. She had come to see Olga Shapiro to find answers, get solutions. Wasn't that what everyone wanted from therapy? She wanted Olga to approve of her relationship with Adam. After all, it had been the therapist's suggestion to seek out the people that made her happy; it was why she had gone to Dorset that day with him. It was why they had flown a kite.

'I am saying that when people are at difficult points in their life, it doesn't help to add more issues, more problems, more challenges . . .'

'Adam isn't an issue,' said Diana, more sharply than she'd anticipated. 'I didn't choose for this to happen. I didn't want it to. But I care about him and I think he cares for me. I think we make each other happy and how can that be a bad thing? Can't you see we make each other happy?'

Her pale hands were trembling and she couldn't stay in this claustrophobic room a second longer.

'I should go,' she said quickly.

'We need to talk this through, Diana.' Olga's voice was firm and commanding, but Diana had already blocked it out and left the room.

40

Susie McCormack, now Susan J. Mack, had come up in the world. Her Docklands flat was small, but smart, modern and expensive, all cream throws and minimalist leather upholstery, plus it had a killer view of the eastern stretches of the Thames estuary. It was Susan herself, however, that most impressed Rachel. Her hair fell to her shoulders in artful shining waves, her teeth were as white as a chat-show host's and, dressed in a crisp white shirt and tailored pants, she looked every inch the mover and shaker she now was.

'It's good to finally meet you,' Susan said as she showed Rachel into her lounge.

'Likewise,' said Rachel thinly, thinking that the young woman didn't even know the half of it. Susie McCormack hadn't been the easiest person in the world to track down. Although Rachel had turned a blind eye to the paper running the story about Julian and his eighteen-year-old mistress, she hadn't been involved in the research and actually hadn't paid much attention to the story when it appeared; all she cared about was the fact that Julian had been caught with his hand in the cookie jar. She racked her brains now: had they found him with this girl in some tucked-away shag pad? She just couldn't remember. And there was no point in looking it up: Denver had done a pretty good job of exorcising the whole business from the web. According to Diana, the company lawyers sent any website recounting the story threatening letters until one by one they simply took it all down for the sake of a quiet life.

Rachel had trawled Facebook trying to find her, but she had eventually turned up on the business networking site LinkedIn as Susan J. Mack. At first Rachel hadn't believed it was her. Susie McCormack had been a teenage wannabe model from the rough end of Battersea. Susan J. Mack was an account director for a prestigious financial PR consultancy.

Looking at her now, it was hard to believe that she was only about twenty-three. What was most amazing was her sudden jump in confidence, a transformation from doe-eyed Lolita with a penchant for too-tight jumpers to a self-possessed woman who could have slipped effortlessly into one of Diana's society dinner parties without turning a hair.

But then perhaps Rachel, like everyone else, including Julian, had underestimated Susie McCormack.

When the tabloids had fallen on her like hooting jackals, Susie had simply batted her eyelashes and played the simpering hair-twirling innocent, just an ordinary girl who had fallen in love with a wealthy older man. Who could blame her? Julian was handsome, rich and, seemingly, immoral. Susie was cast as the injured party, a slip of a girl seduced by a philanderer, but clearly there was much more to her. Much more.

'Of course I heard about you from Julian,' said Susan. She smiled as she perched elegantly on the edge of a sofa. 'I don't think he was your biggest fan at that point.'

'I imagine not,' said Rachel, sitting opposite the woman. 'So I understand you're working for a lobbyist now? That's impressive.'

'Not as impressive in reality, let me tell you.'

It had to be well paid, however, unless . . . Rachel wondered for a moment whether there was another older, wealthy lover paying for all this. *Don't be a traitor to your sex, Rachel*, she scolded herself. Why couldn't a woman – and a woman clearly suited for a job charming powerful men – earn a decent living under her own steam? She'd had enough men dismissing her own rapid climb up the media ladder as a clear case of sleeping with the editor; she should really know better.

'Talking of which,' said Susan, glancing at the slim gold watch on her wrist, 'I should have been at work thirty minutes ago. You were lucky to catch me.'

'Of course,' said Rachel. 'As I said on the phone, I'm looking into Julian's death, trying to find out what pushed him to . . . well, do what he did.'

Susan nodded, looking down at her lap. 'It was quite a shock,

I have to say. I know I was only young, and as things turned out, I was horribly naïve,' she said haltingly, 'but I did . . . I did care for Julian.' She looked straight at Rachel, her expression defiant. 'You thought I was a gold-digger, didn't you? Everyone did, I don't blame you. But Julian was my first love, that's the truth.'

'But you knew he was married?' asked Rachel carefully.

'I'm not particularly proud of that part of it. But think back to when you were that age. What would you have said, what would you have done if a handsome, charming billionaire came along and promised you the earth?'

Rachel thought back to her own teenage years. Stranded in Ilfracombe, with its chip wrappers and run-down arcades, she'd had no more chance of meeting a billionaire than flying to the moon. Of course, there had been that one awkward episode when Mr Ferris from the newsagent's had touched her bottom . . . but he hardly counted. He had a bad back and was paying off a loan for a caravan in Rhyl.

'Where did you go to meet Julian?' she asked.

'Well, we couldn't go to any of his houses, of course. So he'd book hotel suites if he could get away.'

'Did he have anywhere special he used to take you? An apartment, perhaps?'

Susan glared at her. 'I wasn't a kept woman, if that's what you mean. I've told you, I was in love with Julian. I didn't need him to buy me a flat or jewellery or things like that. All I wanted was to be with him. Besides, the relationship didn't last very long. Little more than a summer. Your newspaper made sure of that. And Julian certainly wasn't going to fight for me. I understood that he would have to go back to his wife – for the sake of his family if nothing else – but the thing that hurt the most was the way he just dropped me like a stone. He rang me the day before it was in the paper, you know? I think he'd had a tip-off and he was ringing to warn me. He told me he didn't care, that we could still see each other, but that was it. I never heard from him again.'

Rachel never thought she would have any sympathy with a husband-stealer, but there was something about Susie that made her feel some compassion. She had been young. Very young and very impressionable.

'Well I'm pleased you've made something of yourself. It can't have been easy after all the tabloid attention.'

'I didn't work for a year,' Susan said matter-of-factly. 'Not unless you include the offers of pole dancing.'

'I thought you got some money from the newspaper.'

'You'd know that,' she said tartly. 'You'll also know that I wasn't one of those kiss-and-tell girls. I didn't go to you. Your news team tracked *me* down. Had me over a barrel. They said they'd give me a few thousand quid if I posed for some photos. Thought I might as well, seeing as they had me anyway.'

She hooked her handbag over her shoulder and made for the door.

'I have one question for you, Miss Miller. Why didn't you expose his other affairs? For all his claims about a "moment of madness" in those carefully worded press statements, I wasn't the only one.'

'Which ones?' Rachel asked cautiously. She had heard whispers, of course, all from good sources, but she'd never found any other names.

'I was at a party about a year ago – this was when I'd finally turned my life back around – and a lady came over to speak to me. She was beautiful, a redhead in this gorgeous dress, you'd guess she was the wife of a lawyer or a banker – she looked a lot like your sister actually; anyway, she came up and told me that she knew how I felt. I asked her, "How I feel about what?" and she said, "Julian Denver".'

'Who was she?'

'She gave me her card. I kept it. You never know when Julian Denver's other ladies might need one another.'

'Do you have it?'

Susan sighed, as if Rachel had truly overstayed her welcome, then disappeared into her bedroom, returning a few moments later with a business card.

'You can't have it,' she said quickly. 'But you can take down the details. I can't tell you anything about Julian's secret assets. I assume that's what you're here for, tracking down his love nests. But perhaps she can tell you more than I can.'

41

The Limelight Club in Bishopsgate was one of the most exclusive private clubs in London. It had stunning views over the City, an executive chef who had just been poached from Alain Ducasse in Paris, and on any given day it would see Forbes 500 chief executives, senior bankers and an assortment of other City power-players pass through its revolving doors. Most importantly, it accepted women as members, unlike many of London's more established clubs, like White's or Boodle's in the West End.

Patty Reynolds stood by the window in a meeting room on the top floor known as the Snug.

'I know we'd all have preferred lunch in the restaurant – but these walls have ears,' she said, instructing a waiter to leave a platter of sandwiches on the table.

Diana looked around the cosy space. Greg Willets and Michael Reynolds were reclining in two leather club chairs. A third chair was conspicuously empty.

Patty noticed her line of vision. 'I did invite Elizabeth, but she was too busy to come.'

'Is that what she said?' said Diana.

'What's wrong?' asked Greg Willets, sniffing out the gossip.

'She's challenging Julian's will,' said Michael, putting down his *Financial Times*.

'And what's Adam got to say about that?' asked Greg, sipping some mineral water.

'You can ask him after the meeting,' said Patty, nodding towards the door.

Diana turned, and her heart raced as she saw Adam striding through the door in a smart grey suit. Their eyes connected and she felt a flood of butterflies turning somersaults in her belly.

The empty chair was opposite her, and she shifted her position so that she was only looking at Patty.

'The reason we're here is to discuss Julian's memorial service. Adam, I think even you will agree that perhaps the funeral didn't have enough of Julian's soul in it.'

'I think Elizabeth is quite far down the line with arrangements. Does she know about this?' Adam looked slightly fearful about the repercussions of what Patty was proposing.

'Leave it with me. We can make some suggestions here today and I can pass them on to Elizabeth.'

'Suggestions?' said Greg. 'You know as well as I do that Elizabeth will disregard anything that doesn't come as a three-line whip.'

'Perhaps you should give them to Ralph,' said Diana diplomatically.

'I said I'll deal with it.'

'Okay, okay,' said Michael, putting up his hand. 'Let's remember why we are here. And it is possible to work with Elizabeth on this, rather than against her.'

Everyone nodded in agreement.

'Diana, what do you think the day should be like?' said Patty.

She felt nervous speaking first. Everyone else around the room was so confident, so sure about everything that came out of their mouths. Diana never had been.

'I'm bothered about the guest list,' she said tentatively.

Patty looked at her with encouragement.

'I looked around the funeral and there were too many people that Julian didn't really know or care about,' she continued haltingly.

Patty started scribbling notes. 'We should all suggest a dozen people that Julian really liked. Get Anne-Marie Carr involved too. Di's right. Everyone knows how successful Julian was in business, but what about all the other things he did, like that Atlas Mountains trek for charity? How much did he raise, Greg?'

'One point one million.'

'We could make a slideshow of all his adventures,' suggested Diana.

'I've got lots of photos from when we did the Paris–Dakar rally,' said Greg, sitting up straight in his chair.

'There's plenty of that stuff,' agreed Adam.

'It shouldn't just be a load of showing-off,' said Diana carefully.

'I can tell some horror stories about his cooking,' smiled Michael. 'Remember when he dragged us fishing to Iceland, Greg, and said he was going to whip us up a Scandinavian delicacy. What did he give us?'

'Harkarl.'

'What's that?' smiled Diana.

'Fermented shark.'

'It is a delicacy,' said Greg.

'Not served with soggy chips,' roared Michael.

They were all laughing and a little misty-eyed.

Diana thought of the music that had been played at the funeral. The aria sung by the world-famous soprano had been beautiful, stirring and appropriate, but it hadn't been the sort of music Julian really loved. She remembered how he used to listen to U2's 'One' over and over again when he'd had a particularly stressful week at work; how Bruce Springsteen's 'Born to Run' would blare out of his iPod when he went for a jog around the lake; the heavy-metal music he was nostalgic about from his youth – his old denim jacket covered in Metallica and the Scorpions patches still hung in the storage room, never allowed to be thrown out.

To people in the City Julian had been the king of the world, but in his own space he was just a regular guy who liked football and middle-of-the-road rock. He loved cars and watching *Top Gear*; he liked going to boxing matches with his friends, and fishing for salmon in crystal-clear waters.

What a life he had led, she thought with bittersweet sorrow. She wondered if he had remembered all those things as he tied the climbing rope around his neck. She wondered how long it had taken for him to die; whether there had been a point when he'd thought about all the wonderful things his life had been full of, wonderful things he could do again, and wanted to stop what he was doing. Or had it been too late by then? Had he been past the point of no return, so that he couldn't come back to the people who loved him?

'What do you think, Adam? You were closest to him.'

Diana didn't dare look at him.

'Do you remember John Duncan?' said Adam.

She shook her head.

'Worked in the post room. Single dad. Died about ten years ago. Well, his kid Luke got in touch yesterday. He said that Jules had turned his life around. Apparently Luke got into drink and drugs after his dad passed away. Jules paid for him to go to rehab, to go back to college then on to university. He's just qualified as an architect.'

'I didn't know that,' Diana whispered.

'Apparently he wrote to you too.'

'I haven't had a chance to open all my post yet.'

'You should. I think you'll find a lot of stories like that.'

After an hour, they had a long list of things they all agreed would give Julian the memorial service he deserved, after which they all dispersed.

Diana found herself standing on the street alone with Adam.

'I'm glad we did that,' said Adam finally.

Diana nodded. 'I didn't know you were coming.'

'Well, Patty called me this morning . . .'

The conversation stopped still.

'Here's your house key,' Diana said, rooting around in her bag. She handed it over to him and he put it in his back pocket. It was as if she were handing over a future she hadn't yet lived.

'Do you want to go for lunch? None of us really ate much in there.'

'I'm not hungry.' She looked at him and then away. She didn't want to spend the rest of the afternoon with him. Not today. Not when they had just spent an hour talking about Julian. 'Are you coming to the Boughton fair on Saturday?'

'Am I invited?'

'Actually, I've got a surprise for you.'

'Sounds intriguing,' he said, his eyes dancing with hers.

His smile gave her confidence. 'Perhaps you should come and see it before Saturday.'

'Now this really is curious. What is it?'

'Remember you encouraged me to invest in that café? You said I needed a project.'

'You've done it?' The caution that had been evident in his expression just a few minutes earlier dissipated.

'We've just tarted it up really, changed the menu. The grand opening is the day of the fair. I'm picking Charlie up from school on Friday. Maybe you could come after work on Thursday to see it.' She felt bold, brazen saying it. Were her intentions so blatant? That she wanted to be alone with him?

She held her breath until he answered.

'Okay. I'll see you then. It's the place on the green, isn't it?'

And she smiled with relief.

42

'Want to meet to get the train home?' asked Liam on the other end of the phone. He was in London to see friends for lunch and they had a loose arrangement to travel back to Somerfold together.

'I've got things to do,' she said distractedly.

'Want any company?'

'No. I'll be fine.'

'What are you doing?' he pressed.

'If you must know, I've tracked down one of Julian's other mistresses.'

'Bloody hell.' He whistled slowly. 'So he really did get around a bit.'

'Thanks for that insight, Liam.'

'Where are you going?'

'St John's Wood.'

'Then I'm coming with you. I'm only in Marylebone.'

'Don't be silly,' she protested.

'Rach, I don't like you going off alone. Not after what happened to Ross.'

Rachel grinned to herself. She usually hated other people bossing her around, but she couldn't help admit there was something flattering about Liam's concern.

'So you want to be my white knight, do you?' She knew she was flirting, but what the hell.

'I'll meet you at St John's Wood station in twenty minutes,' he said gruffly, and hung up.

*

Marjorie Case-Jones, the society beauty who had given Susie McCormack her card, had been understandably jumpy on the phone when Rachel had called her, but the name Julian Denver had opened doors. Literally.

The Case-Jones residence was an impressive detached house on one of the area's prime residential streets. The iron gate swung open as they announced themselves. 'Mrs Case-Jones? I'm Rachel Miller, we spoke earlier. This is my friend Liam Giles.'

The woman seemed to soften when she saw Liam. Not for the first time, Rachel realised the power of a good-looking man at your side.

'Come through,' she said quietly.

The kitchen was situated at the back of the house. It was an impressive space with double-height ceilings and glass and marble at every turn. Certainly no cooking was ever done here; it was spotless, and the ridiculously over-the-top appliances – a chrome coffee machine built to serve a thousand people a day, a matt-black range with at least ten industrial burners – were there for aesthetic effect, not practical reasons.

'Do sit,' said Marjorie, indicating a row of ironically distressed fifties bar stools. She herself took a seat on the other side of the breakfast bar.

Rachel could see that Susie McCormack had been right: there were striking similarities between Marjorie and Diana. Marjorie had vivid chestnut hair as opposed to Diana's dark elegant locks, but both shared exquisite pale, delicate features.

There was an open bottle of wine and two glasses on the counter – Rachel noted that the bottle was a little over half empty already. Dutch courage? Or was this standard operating procedure for rich housewives at three in the afternoon?

'It was quite a shock to hear Julian's name when you called,' she began. 'I mean, obviously I'd read all about it – terrible to think of him like that – but I didn't expect to get a telephone call, not after so long.'

'When was the last time you saw him?'

'Oh, I saw him on and off quite regularly,' said Marjorie. 'It's the nature of the circles we move in, a very small world. My husband gets invited to the same parties, which can be a little awkward. It's not easy keeping up pretences.'

'What does your husband do?'

'He's in business. Nothing you have probably ever heard of, but successful all the same.'

Rachel glanced around the room and had to agree with her.

'I couldn't believe it about Jules,' Marjorie said slowly. 'We see our husbands go off to work each day, we have no idea what they really do, how much pressure they are under. How well do we know the people we love? you might ask yourself. My husband certainly knows very little about *my* life. Regarding some aspects, I'd like to keep it that way.'

Rachel understood what she was implying. 'Mrs Case-Jones, I assure you I'm not here to embarrass you or make your relationship with Julian public. Nothing you tell me will ever leave this room, I promise.'

'You promise?' laughed Marjorie. 'Oh, you're good. I know what you did, Rachel, I know the whole story. Do you really think we didn't discuss every last detail about Julian's newspaper disgrace at every dinner party for about six months? The girl who betrayed her sister says "I promise"? Ha!'

Rachel noticed too late how Marjorie was slurring some of her words and how her left eye was drooping slightly. Clearly this half-finished bottle was not her first.

'So if you don't trust me and you have no love for Diana, why are you speaking to me?'

'Because I loved him,' she said simply. 'And I can't help but think that if I'd pushed him a bit more to do the right thing, he might be alive today.'

'Do the right thing?' asked Liam cautiously.

'We talked about running away together. We both knew we could make each other happy. If you love someone you should be with them, simple as that. You shouldn't let golden handcuffs get in your way.'

'He wouldn't divorce Diana?' said Rachel.

Marjorie shook her head violently. 'No. It wasn't going to happen.'

'How long did your relationship go on for?'

'Maybe eighteen months. It started a couple of years ago. It ended when Diana lost the last baby.'

'How often did you see each other?'

'Whenever we could. The sex was good, so good, but we really liked each other too. We could talk, confide in each other. I'm not sure Julian had a great deal in common with his wife. I think she came along at the right time. A time when he thought he should settle down, have a family. I think he liked that she had a child already. He wanted to protect her, look after her. I think a shrink might say he had a saviour complex.'

'You say you loved Julian, but was the feeling mutual?'

'I thought we had a future together.'

'Why do you say that?'

'He bought a house for us. We were both sick of all the rules we had to follow to not get caught. Assumed names at hotels, never entering a building at the same time – it took some of the fun away, to be honest. So he got us a place where we could meet.'

Rachel's heart gave a little leap – her hunch had been correct. 'Where?'

'Highgate, of all places,' said Marjorie with a laugh. 'He loved it up there. The expanse of the Heath, the view of the city.'

'He bought it?'

Marjorie nodded. 'Handed me the keys all tied up with ribbon. That was typical of Julian. Big sweeping gestures. Declarations of love . . . Didn't turn out that way, though, did it?'

'What do you mean?'

'I was ready to leave my husband. Julian said I could live in the Highgate place when I did. But when Diana got pregnant and passed the twelve-week point where she usually miscarried, he cooled off the relationship. He wanted me to play the little mistress, tucked up in the cottage in Highgate, but he made it clear that it wasn't going anywhere more serious. I ended it, thinking he would come running back. But he never did, and now he never will.'

'And what about the house?'

'Of course he didn't put it in my name. But I still have the keys.'

'Could I borrow them? I'm looking for something that Julian had, something I think he might have tucked away somewhere.'

Marjorie laughed. 'It was a tucking-away place all right. I mean, it used to be me.'

She stood up and left the room, returning a few moments later with a piece of paper. She slid it across the counter.

'That's the address, and these . . .' she held up a set of keys, 'these will get you inside.'

43

'This isn't what I was imagining at all,' said Liam, shutting the door of the cottage behind him and looking around the small, low-ceilinged room.

Rachel couldn't help but agree. Julian's little house was in a quiet back street near the cemetery. It looked cute enough from the outside, with wisteria scrambling around the door. But inside it had the unloved air of a house that hadn't been occupied for some time.

'I thought it was going to be all chrome and leather,' said Liam as they looked into the rather ordinary front room with its corduroy sofa and pine bookshelves.

'Well he was hardly going to have anything too flashy, was he?' said Rachel. 'This was supposed to be discreet. Besides, I think he was only interested in the bedroom.'

They went upstairs into the master suite. The bedroom covered most of the first floor, with high windows offering a view out across Parliament Hill and the Ponds. It had cream curtains and crisp baby-blue sheets on the king-sized oak sleigh bed, along with evidence of a woman's touch in the generous en suite. Marjorie? she wondered. Of course, perhaps Julian had changed the decor every time he acquired a new mistress – even though for all they knew, Marjorie Case-Jones was the only one he'd brought here.

'Oh yes, now this is more like it,' said Liam, coming up behind her. 'A proper little shag pad.'

'Is it?' snapped Rachel. 'Does it fit nicely with your image of him? Does it tick all the right boxes?'

Liam put his hand on her arm. 'I'm sorry.'

She nodded, and exhaled sharply. 'I'm sorry too. It's been a long day and I guess I just hate finding all this stuff out.'

'Julian's secret life.'

She nodded sadly. 'He wasn't my favourite person by a long chalk. But he was my sister's husband. My nephew's father. How can you live with someone, look them in the eye each day, knowing you have another life, another lover? It's just all lies. Marriage. It's one big lie.'

'Not always,' he said quietly. 'Not in most cases.'

'All right,' she said, sniffing hard. 'Let's do this room by room. I'll start downstairs. You take up here. I'm not sure I can bear to find balled-up lingerie at the bottom of the bed.'

She clomped back downstairs and got to work. It didn't take long; the house wasn't that big. She found nothing of any note; everything was where it should be: pots and pans in the kitchen cupboards, brooms and mops under the stairs, DVDs in the cabinet by the TV. As she'd expected, the books on the shelves were pulpy boy's own novels by George MacDonald Fraser mixed with a few sports and movie biogs: the real Julian, she supposed, compared to the 'acceptable' Julian she had seen in the Notting Hill bedroom. Reading Diana's diaries, she had got the sense that her sister was living in a gilded cage. But did the same apply to Julian? Had he boxed himself into a hole he didn't want to be in?

She was just walking back into the hall when she heard a muffled call from upstairs.

'Rach, I think you might want to see this.'

But Liam wasn't in the bedroom or the bathroom.

'Where are you?'

'In the loft,' came the reply.

She followed the sound to a door in the corridor she had assumed was a cupboard. Inside was a set of steep stairs, and at the top, another bedroom, which had been converted into a study of sorts. *More of the real Julian*, she thought as she walked in. An acoustic guitar was propped in one corner, and there was another TV with an expensive-looking games console, plus a pile of games cases strewn in front of it. There was also a desk covered with piles of papers – it looked as if Liam had been going through them.

'In here,' he said – she could just see his feet and his bum sticking in the air. He was leaning into a storage cupboard built into the eaves of the house.

He threw her an A4-sized book. Actually no, it was professionally bound with a plastic cover, but it was obviously a business report. In fact, it was more than that. Much more.

' "Controlled Test of Rheladrex. Report number six." This is it,' she gasped.

She sank to the floor and sat cross-legged to speed-read it. Much of it didn't make sense, much of it was in impenetrable jargon. But one paragraph in particular stood out.

'Dr Adriana Russi, formerly of Denver Chemicals, confirms that there were problems in clinical trials – before and after approval.'

Dr Russi's number was written beneath the text in biro. Another name and cell number were scrawled on the cover page. Rachel could make out the word *Maddison*, spelt with a double D and with a heart over the I.

'Well there's someone you should probably speak to,' said Liam, typing something into Google on his iPhone.

'You're right. I wonder where that area code is, though? I don't recognise it.'

Liam looked up as if he regretted what he was about to say.

'It looks like Adriana Russi lives in Rome.'

44

Under any other circumstances, Diana would have leapt at the opportunity to fly to the Eternal City. She adored its energy, its history, its passion. It wasn't just a city for lovers; a market trader in the Campo de' Fiori could sell you a bag of ripe peaches with such zeal and delight it could make you feel as if they would somehow transform your life. And perhaps for a few moments those sweet, succulent fruits actually would. The food seemed more flavoursome in Rome, the light softer, its nights more sultry and full of magic. It was a city that made you feel alive, which was why it felt wrong to be here, right now, looking for the reasons why Julian had died.

Diana had had incredibly mixed feelings about Rachel's discovery of the report into Denver's wonder drug. When she had found out about Madison Kopek, she had thought she would welcome any explanation about her husband's suicide that did not involve a relationship with another woman. But the truth was that there was no comfort in *any* reason, and that was something she hadn't truly appreciated when she had persuaded Rachel to look into his death.

Rachel hadn't said out loud that she thought Julian had been murdered. It was something Diana had extrapolated from her sister's suspicions about Madison's death, Ross's attack, Julian's investigation into Rheladrex and the urgency with which she wanted to talk to Adriana Russi.

Diana wasn't completely naïve. Julian had been the head of a multi-billion-pound company and the stakes were high. He had taken decisions that made – or cost – millions, decisions that affected people's lives, not always in a good way. She knew

311

that Rachel might not be too far off-base with her theories. But *murder*? The very idea of it haunted her thoughts and her dreams. Only last night she had woken up drenched in sweat, and for a few seconds had believed that she was still in her nightmare, a patchwork of bloody images that didn't quite knit together. It was too gruesome a notion to fit into her world, even one that had been rocked by suicide.

They had checked into the Exedra hotel, chosen by Rachel for its rooftop pool overlooking the city, although Diana had a feeling they were not going to be in the hotel long enough to check out its facilities.

'Dr Russi *does* know we're coming?' she asked as Rachel hailed a white taxi and instructed the driver in wonky Italian to take them to Trastevere. It had only just occurred to her.

'Of course she does,' said Rachel, settling into the back seat. 'How do you think I know her address?'

'I didn't like to ask.'

Rachel glanced up with irritation. 'She just might be a bit cagey.'

'Cagey?'

'Sounded a bit paranoid on the phone. Not surprising really.'

As the taxi grumbled through the crazy, traffic-clogged streets, past a statute of Julius Caesar and over the green-grey river that snaked through the city, Rachel buried her nose in Julian's Rheladrex report as if she were doing last-minute swotting for an exam.

'I've started therapy.' Whether it was something to fill the silence, a way of exchanging information or a hope that it would lead subtly to a discussion about Adam Denver, Diana had no idea why she said it.

'Good,' said Rachel, looking up from the report.

'You think so?' Rachel's approval was suddenly important to her.

'I just hope you haven't told her anything that you haven't told me.'

Adam's name was there, on the tip of her tongue, but then the taxi ground to a halt, almost flinging them forward off their seat and taking all discussion off the agenda.

'We are here,' said the driver.

Adriana Russi's apartment was in a tall, crumbling sandstone building opposite a bustling market and a row of cafés where people spilled out on to the streets at small wicker tables loaded with tiny espresso cups and bowls of pasta.

They searched for an empty table at the quietest bar, slipping a waiter a ten-euro note to find them somewhere. Rachel sent Dr Russi a text, and after twenty minutes, a forty-something woman with dark blond hair cut into a bob approached them. She was plain-looking, but she made the best of herself in pale chinos, a neat blue Oxford shirt and loafers. If it wasn't for the deep lines around her eyes, she could have been an Ivy League college student rather than a professor.

'Mrs Denver?' she asked in perfect American-accented English.

'Yes – this is Diana. I'm Rachel Miller, her sister.'

Dr Russi took a seat overlooking the street and looked around. Diana wasn't sure if she was seeking out the waiter or someone else.

'Thank you for meeting us.'

'I couldn't say no to the chief executive's wife, could I?'

'So you worked for the pharmacovigilance department of Denver Chemicals?' asked Rachel after they had ordered coffee. It was thick and black and almost stuck to her lips as she sipped it.

'You know that,' said Dr Russi, not unkindly.

'We know it but we don't exactly know what it means.'

'I am sorry about your husband,' said Dr Russi, directing her attention to Diana.

'News travels this far?' said Diana quietly.

'People are always interested in their former employers.'

'So you met Julian?' asked Rachel quickly.

'I did.'

'Was it about Rheladrex?'

Dr Russi fell silent.

'Do you know why I left Denver?' she said finally.

'Can you tell us?'

'I would if I hadn't signed a confidentiality agreement when I joined the company and a gagging clause when I left.'

313

At that moment Diana could understand the buzz of Rachel's job. It was a series of puzzles you had to unlock, a game, a cat-and-mouse chase where you used your skill to tease out of people what you wanted. Diana had always relied on her looks for that purpose, but seeing Rachel in action made her wish more than ever that she had her sister's smarts.

'Diana is the CEO's wife. A member of the Denver family,' began Rachel pointedly. 'They sign off every pay cheque, every redundancy, every contract, every arrangement . . .'

Dr Russi looked uncomfortable, but then softened.

'Rheladrex was an enormously exciting drug for the company. Everyone has heard about the obesity problem in America, but it was the global opportunities that really excited every single pharmaceutical lab in the world. I mean, did you know that there are as many overweight people in China as there are in the States? This one drug had the potential to transform the company. Generate profits that it could then plough back into revitalising research and development.'

'What made it different to other anti-obesity drugs on the market?'

'Its effectiveness. The fact that you could use it long-term,' said the doctor bluntly.

'And was it safe?'

She paused. 'Rheladrex jumped through all the appropriate hoops to get approval,' she said cautiously.

'Adriana, please talk to us. We know that Julian supported you.'

'How much do you know about clinical trials in the pharmaceutical industry?' she said after a moment.

'Not as much as you do.'

'Drugs trials are generally conducted by or on behalf of the companies manufacturing them. Is it any wonder when trials then tend to produce results that favour them?'

She didn't wait to hear their reply.

'Of course, no one wants a drug to be unsafe. Thousands of drugs don't make it to market and of those that do, possible side effects are always put on the literature that accompanies the medication.'

'You mean all the tiny writing on the leaflet that we never take any notice of?' said Rachel cynically.

'Perhaps you should,' replied Dr Russi. 'Then again, perhaps you would never take so much as an aspirin if you believed it. But medication is about risk management. Is the tiny chance that I might suffer a side effect worth the benefit this drug might bring me? For most people, it is.'

'You were going to tell us about your role at Denver,' said Diana. 'What is pharmacovigilance exactly?'

'When a drug is approved by the FDA, it still has to have a period of review. That's what I did. I monitored drugs. We particularly looked out for adverse side effects.'

'And you found some with Rheladrex?' said Rachel, leaning her elbows on the table.

Dr Russi nodded. 'I had my reservations about it from the start. I felt it was too close in compound structure to another diet drug that was pulled off the market over a decade ago. So I wasn't entirely surprised when we started to receive reports of heart and respiratory problems amongst people who had taken the drug for longer than nine months.'

'I thought you said it was supposed to be an obesity drug suitable for longer-term use,' said Diana, getting drawn into the story.

'Perhaps not,' replied Dr Russi.

'So why didn't you report it to the FDA?' asked Rachel.

'Let's just say I encountered resistance from my superiors.'

'Simon Michaels?' asked Diana.

'He wasn't directly involved, but perhaps he would have been informed about it.'

'Surely they can't do that?' said Diana, aghast.

'There are ways of burying the truth,' said Adriana obliquely. 'Twisting the definition of regulatory requirements to meet your purposes.'

'What happened next?'

'I was asked to leave.'

'Fired?'

'I was given a financial incentive to bring my period of consultancy to an end,' she said diplomatically. 'It all left a very

315

bad taste in my mouth. I left America and came back to Italy, which is where I am from.'

'What was your connection with Julian Denver?'

'I had very little awareness of him whilst I was working for Denver Chemicals. Obviously you know the name of the CEO of your company, but beyond that we had no contact. I was settled back in Italy, actually, doing some academic work at one of the universities, when Julian got in touch with me.'

'When was this?'

At first she looked reluctant to tell them.

'Six weeks ago. He flew to Rome to meet me. He knew I'd been working on Rheladrex in the pharmacovigilance department and had heard I had left the company, learnt I'd been paid off. I don't know how, but he seemed to know about the potential side effects of the drug. He said that someone he knew was taking it and had died. He wanted to know what I knew; he wanted to know all the risks.'

'So you told him?' said Rachel.

'He was the CEO of the company. I couldn't not. I told him that we were potentially sitting on a ticking time bomb that could cause fatalities, irreparable damage to people's lungs and hearts, not to mention billions in potential payouts. I told him that I felt the senior management at Denver Chemicals were underreporting the adverse effects to the FDA.'

'What did he say?'

'He talked about pulling the drug.'

Diana felt her heart surge. The image of Julian, a hero – flying across Europe to do the right thing blotted out all thoughts of him as the unfaithful husband.

'Just like that?' asked Rachel.

'Voluntary withdrawal.' She nodded.

'And is that usual?'

'When you have a drug with known adverse side effects, there are a few things you can do,' said Dr Russi carefully. 'You can carry on marketing it and wait until you get pulled up by the FDA or one of the other pharmaceutical regulatory bodies.'

'And what happens then?'

'Sometimes the FDA asks you to put a black box warning on

316

the drug – it's an alert that goes on the packaging. That's the strongest warning they require and signifies that medical studies indicate that the drug carries a significant risk of serious or life-threatening side effects. Or you get ordered to pull the drug off the market. Voluntary withdrawal does happen, but not very often.' She sipped her coffee.

'What did Julian think?' asked Rachel.

'Julian was cynical about black box warnings,' said Adriana. 'Yes, they decrease usage, but millions of people will still take the drugs. Julian had a grave moral dilemma about keeping such a drug on the market. He said that saving lives was more important than making money. We weren't sure how dangerous Rheladrex really was, but something was wrong with it and he didn't want to take the risk. Before I was fired, I copied a lot of my reports, took them home. Just in case. I gave them to Julian, and when he'd read them his mind seemed to be made up that the drug was too dangerous to stay on the market.'

Adriana reached into her handbag and pulled out a five-euro note, which she put under her saucer.

'I should go.'

'Please, stay,' pressed Rachel. 'This is really helpful.'

'Honestly – I want to put all this behind me, not get dragged back into it,' she said softly. 'I tried to do something commendable, but when it didn't work, I took the pay-off from Denver. I'm not proud of that, but it now means I can do lower-paid jobs that might make a positive difference. The sort of difference Julian wanted to make.'

'Do you think Julian's opinion might have put him in danger?' said Rachel quietly. Diana felt her lungs tighten.

'I hope not. Because then I am also in trouble,' said Adriana, rising to her feet. 'Now I really must go.'

Diana watched her disappear down the busy street, then closed her eyes tightly, as if she wanted to block out what the woman had told her. When she opened them again, Rachel was on the phone.

'Who are you calling?' she asked.

'Adam.'

She inhaled, but no oxygen seemed to draw inside her.

317

'What are you calling him for?'

Rachel was shaking her head as she stabbed the digits on her phone.

'Julian wants to pull the most profitable drug the company has ever had, and weeks later he is found dead.'

'But what do you expect Adam to do? Fly back to New York and accuse Simon Michaels of being a murderer?'

'No,' she said, her tone hard. 'But having heard all that, we can't just sit back and do nothing.'

45

Beach Blanket Babylon in Notting Hill was one of Rachel's old haunts, and she was glad that it hadn't changed a bit. It had been almost fifteen years since she had first come here as a bright-eyed student who was impressed with everything the capital had to offer, but even now she still found it delightfully atmospheric, with its little nooks and crannies and flamboyant baroque decor.

She had come here every Friday night with her friend and colleague Carl Kennedy, a journalist almost as flamboyant as the restaurant's interiors, to gossip and bitch about their fellow workers, PRs, rival papers and each other's often non-existent love life. Tonight it felt serendipitous that she had agreed to meet Carl for a social catch-up dinner at the exact time when her investigation into Julian's death seemed to be getting somewhere. Back in the days when they had worked together, he had been her sounding board. Alistair, their old editor, used to say that Carl was in possession of a unique mind, which was certainly more polite than some of the other hacks in the office, who used to joke behind his back that he was 'on the spectrum'.

'Darling, I knew you'd be here first!'

Rachel almost didn't recognise Carl when he walked in. His hair was shorter, neater, and he was wearing a tweed jacket, jeans and an enormous pair of trainers that looked as if they belonged on Justin Bieber.

'You look fabulous,' he said, kissing her on both cheeks. 'Although I was rather hoping you'd turn up in that little black wetsuit of yours.'

'How have you seen me in a wetsuit?' she said, hitting him with the cocktail menu.

'I have to say, the Giles-Miller website is a very well-put-together marketing tool. Sexy bloke, sexy girl teaching you how to scuba-dive. I pop in occasionally, see what you're up to.'

'I feel like I'm being stalked.'

'Alleviating tedium I think is a more correct way of describing it. Opportunities for titillation in rural Norfolk are rather hard to come by.'

Rachel cracked up laughing. It was as if the years had fallen away and nothing had changed between them.

'So what have you been doing? I can't believe you left the paper.' They had kept in sporadic email touch, through which she had found out that Carl had left London and joined the family business.

'Cut loose,' he said, surveying the wine list. 'You know everyone had to reapply for their jobs. I was apparently deemed disposable.'

'Sorry, I just can't picture you sitting on top of a tractor, Carl. Wellies would ruin the line of your suit.'

'Yes, that's pretty much the attitude my father took when I had to go crawling back to him cap in hand. So I've been given an executive role.'

'Don't tell me you're running the farm?'

'God, no. My two brothers went to Cirencester. I leave all that to them.'

'So what do you do – milk the cows?'

Carl pulled a sour face. 'I see the warm climate of Thailand hasn't taken the sharp edge off your humour, young lady.' He reached into his pocket and pulled out a shiny business card.

'"Carl Kennedy",' she read. '"Innovations Director". What's that mean?'

'Expanding the business. I thought some glamour needed to be injected into potatoes.'

'So what have you done?'

'Crisps, darling, crisps,' he said.

'Crisps?'

'You see, we had two thousand acres of potatoes sitting there, so I came up with the brilliant wheeze of using them for a higher purpose. We're now turning them into a rather wonderful little brand of boutique crisps. We've sold zillions of them, TV ads, celebrity endorsements, sides of buses, the lot. Surely you've heard of Sausage Sizzler Tatties?'

'They haven't made it as far as Ko Tao, I'm afraid.'

'Well, I'll put South East Asia on my five-year plan. Speaking of which, darling, what brings you to this side of the globe?'

Rachel shrugged. 'Julian, of course.'

Carl nodded. 'I did hear. All very strange, too, I thought.'

'Strange? What do you mean?'

'Well I met him once, do you remember? That godawful awards thing. I have to say, he didn't strike me as the sort of person to do what he did.'

Rachel nodded. That was pretty much her conclusion too, and suddenly she wanted to tell Carl everything. She had spent the last month wondering who she could trust, wishing she didn't have so many secrets to hide, but right here was someone she could share it all with.

'I don't think it is as cut and dried as you read in the papers.'

'Do tell,' said Carl, steepling his hands together.

'You sure you want to hear all this?' she asked.

'Are you kidding? The inside track on one of the hottest stories in the news?'

Rachel took a deep breath and did as she'd been told.

'Ross McKiney is in a coma?' said Carl finally, when she had brought him up to date. His serious expression took the wind out of her sails. 'Talk about a run of shitty luck. I'm glad I've moved into potato farming. PI work seems far too hazardous.'

'For the first time in my working life, I'm scared, Carl.' She breathed a sigh of relief that she had finally said it. There was no one else to confess to. Liam would worry; Diana was neurotic enough as it was.

'You know, crisps, scuba-diving, I think it's a better life for us, Rach.'

'I'm not giving up,' she said with a flood of determination. 'After everything that happened with Malcolm McIntyre, I can't back off again, let someone off the hook.'

'And who is the someone?' he whispered dramatically.

That was the one thing Rachel hadn't yet figured out, the one thing that made her head spin as she went to sleep at night.

321

Suddenly she realised that they were only ten minutes' walk away from where it had all happened, and that the keys to the house were still in her handbag.

'Come with me,' she said, pushing the cocktail menu to one side and grabbing his hand.

It was clear that no one had been in the house since she had last left; in fact it looked as if no one had lived here for months, rather than weeks. It was surprising how quickly a home could drain of life. Dust was beginning to settle on the marble mantelpiece in the hallway, and there was the beginnings of a silvery cobweb in the door to the cloakroom.

'Remind me why you have brought me here? Tell me you don't want me to conduct a seance, because I only did that once and I've not stopped seeing red eyes staring at me from my bedroom wardrobe ever since.'

Rachel turned on the light – a vast crystal chandelier – to try and make the place look less intimidating.

'I want you to look over the house. You always had that funny ability to see all the different angles, spot things that other people can't see.'

'I think you're referring to my incredible powers of lateral thinking. Beautiful place,' he said softly as he looked around. 'You know, fifty, sixty years ago you could have picked this place up for a song. I bet this building was multiple flats, maybe even a squat.'

'Times change. You wouldn't get change out of forty million for it now.'

'Look at this. Fingerprint-access locks, video surveillance. This is state-of-the-art,' said Carl. 'If there're cameras in this place, does that mean you have security film?'

She had got hold of a copy of the video surveillance footage on her first day in England.

'Yes, and most of it's static shots of the stairs where nothing happens for three hours. In the dark. James Bond it ain't.'

Rachel left Carl examining the doors in the study and wandered back into the kitchen. Forty million pounds. And that was just one of the assets that Julian had bequeathed his wife. What would she do with forty million? she thought idly. She'd have a pretty good go at trying to spend it, that was for sure. Yachts, jets, Caribbean islands, tanned muscular waiters bearing cool towels and cocktails – that would be a start.

In many ways, she could see that Julian had done Diana a huge favour. She had hated his narrow little dinner-party circle with his superior friends like Greg Willets, and now she was free of them. She never had to eat another canapé or make polite conversation about so-and-so's divorce or face lift. She could go anywhere she chose. If Julian had lived, the money would still be there in the bank, the Denvers would still be as wealthy, but Diana would be obliged to live this uptight, predictable and frankly deathly dull life.

'Tight as a gnat's arse, this place,' announced Carl, joining her in the kitchen. 'I'm not surprised the police didn't think anyone could get in. As far as I can see, there aren't any blind spots on the CCTV camera. There wouldn't be with a security system this sophisticated. My only thinking is that if it was foul play, then it must have been someone already in the house.'

'You mean Diana?' She thought about her sister's diary. Which she had tried to put out of her mind since she had read it.

Carl shrugged. 'It's possible.'

'Of course it's not possible,' she blustered. 'Why on earth would she want to kill her husband?'

'For the forty-million-pound mansion, the country retreat, the billion-dollar shareholding . . . Perhaps she was still just bloody pissed off with him for shagging that model.'

'I don't think she would have waited all this time to do it, do you?'

'There's the possibility that she did it in conjunction with someone else. Someone who manipulated her into helping them get rid of him. You used to say she was the soft, timid sort.'

'Diana's not a murderer,' said Rachel defensively.

'But Julian Denver had enemies. Enemies who wanted to bring him down and who didn't care who got caught in the crossfire. Look at Susie McCormack. It's not my proudest moment that we probably wrecked a teenager's life for the sake of a story. But the person that shopped her didn't worry about that. They just wanted to nail Denver.'

She stopped thinking of her sister for one moment and looked directly at Carl.

'What do you mean, shopped her?'

Carl looked embarrassed, as if his mouth had run away with him.

'You remember how Alistair told us he wanted sleaze stories, how fat cats misbehaving were suddenly hot again? So we needed to find industry figures, unfaithful bankers, so-called society family men who were, well, no disrespect to Julian, hypocritical sleazebags.'

Rachel didn't react, just let him talk.

'I mean, he wanted the whole news team working on it, but the pressure was on me because of the sorts of people I knew: society people, country people, exactly the sort Alistair was after, in fact. One day he called me into his office and told me he was counting on me.' Carl did a note-perfect impression of their editor's rich Scottish baritone. 'So I did my best. Put the feelers out, mined the most well-connected and wealthy people I knew for gossip . . .'

'And?'

'I came up with nothing. Zero. I don't know whether the wealthy socialites had got wind of the *Post*'s appetite for their blood, but it was almost as if they had shut down completely.'

Rachel frowned and leant forward. 'But you did find something. You were the one who found out about Julian's infidelity.'

She could remember his face that day, the day he had come to her, offered to buy her a drink, then told her that he'd found out about her brother-in-law and his affair with an eighteen-year-old girl. He'd shown her the pictures of them together, said he was warning her in advance, 'as a friend'.

'So what are you telling me, Carl, that you didn't break the story on Julian?'

Carl pulled a face. 'I did, yes. But not quite in the super-sleuth way I led everyone to believe,' he said, shamefaced.

Rachel sank on to a chair. 'Tell me,' she said, the anger coming off her in waves.

Carl sighed, then nodded, as if he'd been dreading this moment for years but knew it was inevitable.

'I told the news team that I'd heard rumours about Julian, that I'd followed him until I saw him with Susie, then took photos.'

Rachel remembered those photos. She could still picture them as if they were lying on the table in front of her. Julian and Susie, embracing, kissing. Wrapped around each other like two teenagers. The Denvers had threatened to sue, of course, claiming that the *Post* couldn't prove that Julian was having an affair with Susie or anyone else. When the paper had produced a sworn affidavit from Susie attesting to their sexual relationship, they had tried to have her branded an evil opportunist or a naïve fantasist. Either of which could have been true, but by then it was academic – the photos and the story had run.

'So that's what you told the editor,' said Rachel, her lips tight. 'What was the real story?'

'I never heard any rumours about Julian,' said Carl quietly.

'I don't understand. So how did you know about Susie? And how did you get photos of them together?'

'The photos were sent to me,' said Carl, his eyes full of regret. 'Brown envelope, anonymously delivered to the office and addressed to me. There was a note that came with them that simply said "Julian Denver and a blonde who is not his wife." Just in case I hadn't grasped the point.'

'Those photo weren't yours?' she said incredulously.

'I didn't lie about the whole thing, Rach,' said Carl quickly. 'The only thing I lied about was how I got to hear about it in the first place. Once I was tipped off, I got a pap to trail Julian and we took our own set of photos of them together.'

'But why lie at all?' said Rachel, trying to grasp the significance of the tip-off. 'Why claim the first photos were yours?'

Carl snorted. 'You remember what it was like. The *Post* was struggling, there were strong rumours of redundancies and a recruitment freeze. I was worried about my job – we all were. It was no secret that Alistair was under pressure to downsize the staff and make more use of stringers.'

He stared down at the table.

'I had to make myself look good, and finding out about Julian through my supposed network of contacts looks a lot better than the story landing on my desk signed, sealed and delivered, doesn't it?'

Rachel wanted to scream at him, to tell him he was just trying to justify his lies, but she knew that what he was saying was true. That old cliché about being only as good as your last story was right on the money, or at least it had been back then. That was why so many of them had been sucked into phone-hacking, eavesdropping on email conversations and listening to message services. You had to keep coming up with the goods or you were out; that was the culture, and it was one the editors and management were happy to perpetuate, because they weren't taking any risks themselves and were reaping all the rewards as exclusive after exclusive splashed across their front pages.

She looked at her friend, the wealthy potato crisps entrepreneur, and tried to remember him as he was back in that newsroom. The truth was, Carl had needed a scoop more than the others. He'd always been an outsider on the *Post*. Posh, sexually ambiguous, bouncy and eager to please rather than jaded and cynical. She understood, of course she did. Hadn't she been there herself, desperate to succeed as the new girl, as the only young woman on the team? And she had pulled just as many stunts, played all the cards she could. Still, it didn't stop her feeling angry, betrayed.

'You should have told me,' she said. 'You know that, don't you?'

Carl nodded. 'It's easier to lie to yourself, come up with excuses, isn't it? Once I had my own set of photos, I convinced myself it didn't matter how I'd found out. And it didn't really matter where things came from, did it?' he added, looking at her with a hint of accusation. 'Not to us. But now he's dead, and you think he had enemies – I just thought I had to tell you.'

Her head was a whirl of emotions: guilt, anger, disappointment and, above all, confusion. If they hadn't come from Carl, then who had sent those photos, and why?

She voiced her question out loud.

'You have to ask yourself, who had the most to gain from Julian's infidelity, from his disgrace. If you ask me, the answer points straight back to the family, and whoever within it wanted the top job.'

46

Susie McCormack wasn't pleased to see her, but then Rachel hadn't really expected her to be. That was why she had sneaked in through the service entrance at the back of Susie's office building and come up the stairs, walking past the receptionist with studied confidence. The bored-looking blonde girl at the desk barely gave her a glance. Clearly there were a lot of busy women in heels striding in and out of the headquarters of Leith and Brody Consultant Media Group.

Quite a mouthful for a PR company who put policy and mission statements into pithy little sound bites, Rachel had thought as she looked for Susie's office.

She needn't have bothered – she bumped into her target coming out of a meeting room, followed by a group of important-looking men in grey suits.

'Rachel?' said Susie, with a glance over at the man immediately to her left. 'I, er, I didn't know our meeting was so soon.'

'Everything all right, Susan?' said her companion, clearly having picked up on Susie's distress, despite her laudable efforts to take Rachel's intrusion in her stride.

'Yes, yes, I must have forgotten to put it in the diary.' She forced a smile and glanced at her watch. 'Shall we go through to my office now?'

'Yes,' said Rachel. 'Why don't we do that?'

Susie led her to a glass-fronted room and closed the door.

'I hope you've got a bloody good excuse for barging into my workplace like this. Was an appointment not good enough for you?' Her face had drained of colour but her cheeks were bright

327

red with anger. Rachel thought she looked like a lollipop – a big red and white head on a tall, skinny body.

'Can I get you some coffee?' said Rachel, walking to the machine in the corner of the room. Susie was rattled, unusually rattled, and in Rachel's experience that was usually a sign of guilt.

There was a pointed silence as the two women's eyes locked. Rachel silently counted the seconds: Susie looked away on the count of six.

'The story with you and Julian. You do know that he was set up, don't you?'

'Yes, I do,' she said, her eyes still blazing. 'Set up by your newspaper.'

Rachel shook her head slowly. 'No, it didn't happen like that,' she said evenly. She explained how Carl Kennedy had been sent the photos. 'Remind me how you met Julian, Susie. Don't miss out a detail.'

Rachel had a theory. A theory that had developed like a television picture on an old TV set coming into focus. She had no idea if it was correct or just a series of convoluted ideas born of her own desperation. But she had a feeling that she was about to find out.

'We met in a nightclub in Chelsea,' said Susie tartly. 'Don't you remember? It was all there for you to read in your newspaper. It went from there.'

'What were you doing in a Chelsea nightclub? You were eighteen years old. I thought the Clapham Grand or the Fridge in Brixton would be more your style.'

'Well I wanted to better myself, didn't I?'

'And you thought you'd do that by meeting a rich man.'

'I grew up in Battersea in a crappy council flat and those Chelsea lights used to wink at me from the other side of the river. *That* was where I was going to get to, whatever it took. At first I thought I could do it by working hard at school. So I did; I was heading for A-levels and uni, all that. But then one day I was window-shopping in the King's Road and some guy drove past me in a Porsche, tooted his horn at me. That was the moment I realised I was kidding myself. What was I going to do? Get some pointless degree, clock up a load of debts that I'd never be able to pay off and sit there and watch all the best jobs go to people with contacts and pedigree?'

'So you decided to cheat.'

Susie curled her lip. 'Call it that if you like; I prefer to see it as an alternative career path. I had my looks; that was my gift. I won't apologise for using them. Look at your sister, she did exactly the same thing.'

Rachel was about to object, say that Diana's marriage was a love match, but in the circumstances, that would sound a little hollow. Besides, Susie was right: their mother had spent most of Diana's childhood telling her how she was going to meet a handsome prince who would carry her off to his glittering castle. A-levels weren't exactly valued in their house either.

She still had a sense that Susie was holding something back. The younger woman's eyes were shining, as if tears were forming but she was desperately trying to stop them.

'Susie, you know what I am doing,' she said more kindly. 'I'm investigating Julian's death. You know as well as anyone what sort of man he was. Do you think he was the type to commit suicide?'

'No one knows what goes on in people's lives, do they?'

'If you want to help, now is the time to tell me what you know. Anything. Anything at all. I think he had enemies, I think someone wanted to hurt him.'

A single tear finally glistened down Susan McCormack's perfectly made-up cheek.

'Susie, please tell me. You told me about Marjorie Case-Jones. You want to help him, I know you do.'

Susie glanced around as if she were looking for an escape route. 'I can't,' she said quietly, looking out of the window.

'Yes, you can,' said Rachel in a softer tone.

Susie perched on the edge of the desk and squeezed the bridge of her nose.

'Julian wasn't the first wealthy bloke I went out with, not by a long chalk,' she said finally. 'I knew I wanted to meet a rich man and I knew the places to go to find them: Raffles, Chinawhite, Boujis. But I learnt quickly that they might not want the happy-ever-after ending that I did. Most of them were just after a quick fuck with some gullible pretty girl who would open her legs for a champagne cocktail.'

Susie blinked hard and composed herself.

'One day I met a woman at the bar of some club, I don't even remember where. She had lovely clothes, expensive jewellery, she was obviously rich and connected. She seemed to take a shine to me and gave me her card, said we should meet for lunch.'

'You went?'

'Of course I went. That was what I was there for – to make contacts, to network.' Susie smiled to herself, as if she was remembering a secret joke. 'She seemed so keen, I thought maybe she fancied me herself, and part of me didn't even object to that thought because there was something about her. Something magnetic that made you want to please her.'

'Who was this woman?' asked Rachel.

'As if you didn't already know.'

'Elizabeth Denver?'

Susie gave a curt nod. 'After a couple of weeks of lunches and nights out to these dazzling parties, I think Elizabeth knew every-thing about me: how old I was, where I was from, what I wanted from my life. That's when she told me she had a job for me.'

'She wanted you to seduce her brother,' said Rachel, filling in the gaps.

'She said she hated his wife and wanted to break them up. She made it sound like a noble gesture. Painted the wife to be quite the Wicked Witch of the West.'

'So you went along with it.'

'Elizabeth said that if I managed to pull it off, she'd give me fifty thousand quid. *Fifty thousand quid!*' she repeated, her eyes lighting up. 'I mean, that was two years' wages for most people, more where I come from. So Elizabeth got me a ticket for an event Julian was going to and, well, I can't say he offered much resistance to my charms.' She smiled. 'By the end of the night I'd given him a blow job in the back of his Bentley. The next day, he sent me a necklace.'

'So it was just a job?' said Rachel, trying her hardest to hide her shock.

330

'Of sorts,' Susie said honestly.

'Did you know what Elizabeth had planned? Did you know she was going to shop you to the newspapers?'

She shook her head. 'I don't think I really stopped to think how it would all pan out. I'd been given the fifty grand by this point and I was sleeping with Julian. I mean, I might even have done it for free if I'd known how handsome and charming he was going to be.'

'You liked him?'

'I did,' she said quietly. 'It was hard not to fall a little bit in love with Julian Denver. He was different from all those other men from the nightclubs, you see. He was smart, generous. And he never once talked about his wife, not like some I'd met. They treated you like a whore, made it clear from the start that they were married and this was just sex. Julian wasn't like that. He made you feel special.'

She puffed out her cheeks and turned to the window as if she were getting emotional once more.

'We saw each other for about a month. I lied to him – told him I was twenty-one. We had a good time together. Then Elizabeth came to see me and said that the tabloids had got hold of the story.'

'You didn't send those photos to the paper, then?'

She shook her head emphatically. 'No way! I was terrified; I thought my dad would kill me when he saw what I'd been up to.'

'Surely you realised you might end up in the papers if you started dating rich men like that?'

'Why?' said Susie, turning back round. 'It wasn't as if I was going after footballers or celebrities. Julian was just a rich businessman. Sure, I knew he was in the newspapers occasionally, but he was hardly Tom Cruise, was he? I was never interested in doing kiss-and-tells – I just wanted a nice life for myself, that's all.'

'So what did Elizabeth do?'

'She encouraged me to co-operate with the paper. She said that the story was going to run, run big, so I might as well go along with them.'

'How did she know it was going to run big?'

Susie snorted. 'I heard a rumour she was sleeping with the editor.'

Rachel couldn't find her breath. 'She was having an affair with Alistair Hall?'

'I don't know about that. But she certainly had him where she wanted him. The story was going to be a splash, so I thought I might as well make a bit of money out of it. But I wasn't stupid, I knew I had more leverage than that. I told Elizabeth that I could let it slip that she had orchestrated the whole thing.' She laughed at the memory – as if she had outwitted the great Elizabeth Denver. 'She had more to lose than I did if the truth came out. So I played hardball, got a few little sweeteners added to the deal.'

'Sweeteners? What like?'

'Elizabeth used her connections. I did as I was told, sat tight for twelve months, living off the *Post*'s money, waiting for everyone to forget my name. Then Elizabeth got me a job with a PR firm in Dublin. I started going by the name of Susan Mack. No one recognised me. No one asked too many questions because I had a powerful mentor. And four years on' – she waved a hand around her office – 'here I am, on a six-figure salary, under my own steam. And now I don't owe anyone anything.' She looked at Rachel, daring her to say different.

'Do you still see Elizabeth?'

Susie shook her head. 'I'd served my purpose; I was a liability as far as she was concerned. And by then, I was glad to get away from her. She scared me, if I'm honest. If she could do that to her own brother, what would she do to me if I dared to cross her?' She raised her eyebrows. 'But then she called again a couple of weeks ago. To talk about you.'

'Me?' Rachel sat forward, her attention focused on the other woman.

'It was just after Julian's death had been in the papers. She reminded me that I couldn't breathe a word about our little arrangement. Made a few veiled threats and said I might get a call from you. She knew what you were doing, that you were asking questions about Julian's life.'

Rachel frowned. 'If Elizabeth threatened you, why are you telling me all this now?'

'Julian was always kind to me, and I screwed him over.'

In more ways than one, thought Rachel.

'That's why I'm talking to you,' said Susie. 'Because I think he deserves justice. Elizabeth is dangerous. She got away with stitching her brother up. I hate to think what else she might be able to get away with.'

47

'So finally, this is what's on the menu for Saturday,' said Dot, perching her glasses on the end of her nose to read from her scrawled notebook.

Diana put down the pile of blue and white gingham tablecloths and sat down to listen. They had been working non-stop all afternoon and she was glad that Dot had suggested a breather.

'Quiche. Two types. The classic Lorraine and a petit pois, tomato and asparagus.'

'Petit pois. Get you, going all fancy,' teased Diana as she sipped a glass of water.

'We've got a leek and potato soup and bread from that supplier you recommended in London.'

'Poilâne,' said Diana, almost tasting the delicious sourdough from one of her favourite ever bakeries.

'Never heard of it, but if you say it's good then I believe you. Then we've got the main event. The cake,' she said, making a dramatic drum-roll noise. 'I'm doing a classic sponge but tarting it up with lavender cream and some edible flower petals. I'm calling it the Diana cake – sweet and lovely – and I'm not taking no for an answer.'

'In which case, I'm honoured.'

'We've got Ron's date and walnut loaf, plus his flourless chocolate cake, using that chocolate you also recommended.'

'Valrhona,' said Diana, thrilled that Dot had taken some of her suggestions on board. She herself was not a chef or a baker – far from it – but she had eaten in enough fancy restaurants, met enough chefs to know that even simple food could be elevated to something special by using the very best ingredients.

'I'm also doing a batch of his macaroons, in raspberry, pistachio and coconut.'

'Great – I've got just the boxes for those,' said Diana, holding up a lilac cardboard container which she thought would look lovely wrapped with white satin ribbon.

'And not forgetting the courgette and ginger cake, of course. Gosh, do you think that's enough?'

'Dot, it's plenty.'

'But what if it's too much?'

'Do stop panicking.'

'I wish we'd never told anyone we were relaunching the café on the day of the fair. I feel under pressure. I've got no extra staff – just Bet, who helps out at the weekend – so if it is busy we're stuffed and if no one comes it's just going to be embarrassing.'

'Charlie finishes school tomorrow, so I'm going to rope him in. And Mrs Bills is a wizard in the kitchen. And if no one does turn up, then we can lock the door and eat a lot of cake.'

Dot grinned, then wiped her forehead with a tea towel. 'I'm going to finish up in here. It'll be a long day tomorrow. Whatever was I thinking of, letting you rope me in to all this?'

'It's good for you,' said Diana softly.

'Good for both of us.'

Diana watched her leave and smiled. Dot had become an unexpected but treasured friend in a very short space of time. Diana had thought she wouldn't care if the café was a success or not, since it had only started off as a distraction. But now she didn't want it to fail, didn't want to let Dot down.

She draped a blue and white cloth over every table and went to fetch a box that had arrived by courier that morning. At Diana's request, an interior designer friend had sourced two dozen beautiful old medicine bottles at Lots Road antique auction and had them delivered. She filled the bottles half up with water and arranged a small bunch of freesias in each, tying the necks with pieces of distressed string.

Other bits of work had also been done in the last week, to her specification. The wooden floors had been freshly sanded, and the shutters had been fixed and painted the soft sage green that always reminded her of the Ile de Ré. Mr Bills and some friends had brought down an old dresser from Somerfold. The interior of the café was still a long way from where she would ideally like it to be, but for now it was shabby-chic and cosy.

It was almost nine o'clock and the sun was beginning to fade in the sky. She switched all the lights off and lit a row of candles on the dresser. The place looked beautiful, she admitted to herself. She hoped Adam was going to like it as much as she did.

Her tote bag had been stuffed under the counter. She fetched it and pulled out a bottle of champagne, stashing it in the fridge to chill. She felt a little guilty that she had not cracked it open with Dot that evening, but she wanted to share the moment with someone else. With him.

Touching up her make-up in the antique mirror on one wall, she glanced at her watch with a quiver of excitement. He should be here any time, she calculated, working out the distance from London in hours and minutes.

She had no idea what she was going to say to him, and that was half of the strange, nervous excitement she was feeling. For the past few weeks she had felt like a small boat lost at sea. At times, most of the time, she felt as if she was about to capsize and get sucked under the water, but perhaps there was another way to turn. Perhaps the answer was to allow herself to be swept away on a tide of uncertainty, not to constantly fight the tumult of questions and confused emotions that had been running riot in her mind since Julian's death.

She helped herself to an elderflower cordial and spruced up the little bundles of flowers. He was late now. She looked around the café, wondering if there were any more jobs to be done, but it really did look perfect.

Her mobile phone beeped, registering that a text had arrived.

Still in London. Meetings going on for ever so going to have to give tonight a miss. Sorry for late notice. See you on Saturday. Looking forward to it. Adam

Somewhere in the back of her mind a little voice told her it was for the best, but inside her chest, her heart felt as heavy as a lead anchor. She blew out the tea lights, trying with each puff to blot out her disappointment. It was fine. He was busy. It was a long way to come from London. She would keep the champagne for Dot tomorrow.

48

Postman's Park had always fascinated Rachel. When she had first arrived in London she had lived in a flat-share in Clerkenwell, and had often strolled there on sunny days to lounge on the grass with a makeshift picnic, enjoying the relative peace of this quiet oasis, the roar of the traffic circling the heart of the City and the jagged remains of Roman Londinium temporarily muffled by the trees and the walls.

She walked over to the sloping shelter against the wall of a block of flats bordering the park to the east. The Memorial To Heroic Self Sacrifice: the thing that made this particular park special and which always sent shivers down Rachel's spine. Fixed to the wall behind a row of benches was a series of ceramic plaques, each one commemorating the heroism of individuals who had died trying to save other people – the idea being that their sacrifice would never be forgotten. They were poignant, such as 'Edmund Emery of 272 King's Road, Chelsea, passenger. Leapt from a Thames steamboat to rescue a child and was drowned, July 31 1874.' Or they could be strange: 'Frederick Alfred Croft, Inspector, Aged 31. Saved a lunatic woman from suicide at Woolwich Arsenal Station but was himself run over by the train, Jan 11, 1878.' But they were always bold and brave.

Rachel had often sat here by the wall, reading about these faceless people's deeds, wondering if she too would leap into the Thames or dash into a burning building to save the life of, as one plaque put it, 'a stranger and a foreigner'. She supposed not, but then that would probably have been the answer all these ordinary people would have given before they were faced with a life-or-death situation. You just never knew until it was right there before you, did you?

She heard Elizabeth approach before she saw her, the sound of her heels clacking against the stone path. She was dressed in a tight black skirt and a sky-blue top, her hair scraped back into a bun: just another businesswoman wandering through the City. But was that all she was? Had Susie McCormack been correct? Was she a killer too? Rachel almost smiled at the irony; she had always sneered at scenes like this in pulp thrillers. If you suspected someone was capable of murder, why would you arrange to meet them in some out-of-the-way place where no one could hear you scream? Postman's Park was not exactly the middle of nowhere, but this early in the morning it was all but deserted.

'I hope this isn't a waste of my time,' said Elizabeth by way of introduction. 'You do realise the litigation involving Julian's will is in the hands of our solicitor? I won't discuss it with you, Rachel.'

'It's not about that,' said Rachel. 'Not directly, anyway.' She indicated a wooden bench and they both sat down.

'So what is it? I haven't got all day,' said Elizabeth, glancing at her watch. 'What's so important I have to rearrange my diary?'

'You had an affair with Alistair Hall.'

Rachel watched Elizabeth's reaction carefully. There was just the slightest tic in her left eye, a recognition that Rachel's blow had hit home, but the other woman recovered her composure almost immediately.

'Is that it?' she laughed. 'You dragged me out here to discuss old love affairs?'

I very much doubt love had anything to do with it, thought Rachel.

'No, Elizabeth,' she said. 'I dragged you out here because I wanted to discuss the way you slept with Alistair so you could conspire your way into destroying Julian's reputation.'

Now that one really did hit home. She could almost see the cogs whirring inside Elizabeth's head as she tried to work out where Rachel was going with this and, more importantly, how much she knew.

'Destroy his reputation?' she scoffed. 'He did that himself,

338

Rachel, you know that as well as anyone. I didn't force my brother into bed with that girl; he went of his own accord.'

'But you provided him with the girl, didn't you?'

Elizabeth stared at her, the fury evident in her eyes, and now Rachel could see what Susie had been talking about when she had said that Elizabeth was dangerous.

'Why are you doing this, Rachel?' she said. 'Is it guilt? Don't you think you've caused enough damage to this family without throwing around accusations like this?'

'Why? Because you destroyed Julian's reputation, because you almost broke up his marriage and because you screwed me over too.'

'You? What's any of this got to do with you?'

'For four years I have tortured myself with the thought that I didn't try to stop that bloody story. Did I do the right thing? Should I have let Julian get away with it? But all the time you had Alistair Hall in your bed and in your pocket. I wouldn't have been able to stop it any more than I could stop a meteor hitting the earth.'

Elizabeth waved a hand in the air in a manner that suggested she thought the idea was ridiculous – or beneath her attention. *Yeah?* thought Rachel. *Well screw you too.*

'I'm going to expose you,' she said evenly.

Elizabeth snorted out loud. 'Run another of your sordid little stories in the newspapers? Reveal me as some sort of evil Svengali? How do you think that's going to go down with Diana? Do you think she wants her husband's infidelities raked up again?'

Rachel refused to be intimidated. 'The trouble with people like you, Elizabeth, is that you're so used to getting your own way, you think everyone can be bought off. But there's one type of person you can't threaten – someone who has nothing to lose.'

She let that sink in for a moment.

'I have no career any more, no credibility with anyone. What exactly are you going to threaten me with?'

Elizabeth shifted in her seat, but her discomfort was only momentary. She was used to getting her own way. There was always a deal to be struck.

'What is it you want?' she said finally. 'You must want

something, otherwise why engineer this ridiculous cloak-and-dagger meeting?'

'I want the truth!' cried Rachel, her loathing for this woman finally getting the better of her. 'I want to hear you admit what you have done!'

Elizabeth glared at her. 'I thought that was obvious. I want to be the head of my family's company, as I always should have been. Just because I had the misfortune to be born a girl, somehow that meant I wasn't worthy of being in charge of Denver. It didn't matter how good I was, how hard I worked, Julian was the golden boy. Everything was always handed to him on a platter.'

'So you set him up.'

'Oh grow up!' shouted Elizabeth. 'This is big business, Rachel. Do you really think people in power – politicians, CEOs, all those billionaires – do you think they never tread on a few toes? Do you think your precious Julian never did any of those things? No, he did whatever was necessary too. He would outmanoeuvre, he'd stab his friends in the back, foul means to achieve a fair result.' She curled her lip into a sneer. 'And you, Rachel – you too. Don't pretend you don't know what I'm talking about. The phone-tapping, the long lenses, the illegal hacking of emails, all in the name of the story. You call it public interest; others call it a gross invasion of privacy.'

'Don't turn this back on to me,' said Rachel. 'We're talking about you, Elizabeth.'

'Really? And I suppose you think we're so very, very different, don't you?'

Rachel shook her head in impatience. She was sick of being played with.

'Yes, we are different, Elizabeth,' she said. 'I would never go to the lengths you did. Never in a million years.'

Elizabeth's smooth forehead crinkled into a frown. 'What do you mean?'

Rachel sat forward. 'Did you kill your brother?'

Elizabeth's eyes fluttered wide open. 'What? What the hell are you talking about?'

'Answer the question.'

'No, I did not,' she spluttered with horror.

If she had been on the jury in a murder trial, she would certainly have been convinced by that performance. Still, she couldn't let Elizabeth deflect her.

'I know about Rheladrex,' she said. 'I know that Julian wanted to withdraw it from the market.'

'Rheladrex. The diet drug? Being withdrawn?' Elizabeth shook her head. 'Why, when it's doing so well?'

'Either he told you about it or you found out. You knew what the implications would be for the company's share price and the sale price of Denver Chemicals.'

Elizabeth held up a hand. 'Stop this nonsense, Rachel. I honestly have no idea what you're talking about. There is certainly nothing wrong with our share price; in fact Denver is in better shape than ever. And the sale of Denver Chemicals is going ahead . . .'

She looked down at the ground, as if she were trying to make sense of it all, then swung her gaze back to Rachel's face.

'You really think I killed Julian?' she said incredulously.

Rachel nodded slowly.

'I did *not* kill my brother,' she said, her voice shaking. 'How could you even think that? Just because I'm *ambitious*?'

'How could I think it?' said Rachel. 'You set Julian up in a sting that almost ruined his whole life. You use people like they're just pawns to be sacrificed to your ambition. And you want me to believe you wouldn't simply dispose of someone if they got in your way?'

Elizabeth rubbed her hand across her mouth. Her nostrils were trembling and her cheeks had turned scarlet.

'What do you want, Rachel?' she asked finally. 'People like you always have a price.'

'Let's talk money.'

Rachel almost laughed at the look of relief that flooded across Elizabeth's face. Finance was her business. If Rachel was prepared to settle this with money, Elizabeth felt back on solid ground – she could see a way out.

'Okay, I have a solution,' she said. 'You're a good investigator, Rachel, you've proved that these past few weeks.'

Flattery now? thought Rachel, enjoying the moment.

'You know as well as I do that the media is screwed,' continued Elizabeth. 'So do you know where a lot of the very best investigators – detectives, hacks – end up these days? In private security work.'

She let that idea hang in the air for a moment.

'As it happens,' she continued, 'I am about to make an investment in one such firm. I think with a few introductions and a little pressure I could get you a senior position there, maybe even an equity partnership. If the company takes off in the way I think it will, that would be a very lucrative career move for you. More lucrative than running diving courses in Thailand, I dare say.'

Rachel nodded, as if she were thinking the proposition over. 'That's a generous offer,' she said slowly. 'But it's not the sort of transaction I had in mind.'

Elizabeth frowned, momentarily confused. 'Then what do you want? A cheque?'

'This challenge to Julian's will,' she said. 'You mentioned it earlier. I understand that you're the one behind it, correct?'

'Yes. So?'

'I have to say I wasn't surprised. You didn't want your brother to be CEO; you sure as hell wouldn't want his poor adopted son to inherit the company, now would you?'

'Where is all this leading, Rachel?'

Rachel raised her eyebrows. 'Drop the challenge,' she said flatly. 'That's what I want. No cheque, no job, just pull out of contesting the will. You know as well as I do that you probably won't win anyway, so you might as well turn the situation to your advantage.'

'And what's in this for you, exactly?'

'Nothing,' said Rachel, shrugging. 'Well, maybe it's to do with that guilt you mentioned earlier. Maybe I can do something good for someone else, for Julian's son.'

'His son?' sneered Elizabeth. 'That little bastard brat? He's nothing to do with my family and never will be.'

Anger rose up inside Rachel. 'Either you drop your challenge to Julian's will or I will go public with your little scheme to set up your brother with a teenage girl. I told you before, Elizabeth,

I have nothing to lose, but you? My guess is that if Denver's shareholders ever heard the true story of how you so recklessly tried to destabilise your brother's career – not to mention undermining the reputation of the company – they would have you out of the building and out of the company so fast it would make your head swim.'

Elizabeth glared at her for a moment, but Rachel could tell she knew she was beaten.

'All right,' she said, standing up and smoothing her skirt down.

'Great. And whilst we're at it. That security firm you mentioned you're investing in? Get my friend Ross McKiney a job with them. He's a good investigator. One of the best.'

'You have a deal,' Elizabeth said grudgingly.

'Excellent,' said Rachel with a smile.

'Smile all you want,' said Elizabeth, her eyes narrowing. 'But know this: you've just laid down your only hand. You might have won this time, but nobody plays this game better than me. No one.'

Rachel watched her walk out of the park, her heels still clacking even after she was out of sight.

49

'Charlie. Table five wanted two slices of the courgette and ginger cake, two cream teas and a soup. How are we doing with the order?'

Diana smiled as she watched her son, freshly arrived back from boarding school, throw a tea towel over his shoulder grumpily.

'Mum, this is supposed to be my summer holiday. I'm a student, not Gordon Ramsay.'

'Stop complaining,' she grinned, hitting him with a dishcloth. 'Me and your auntie Rachel had a paper round and two waitressing jobs at your age. Just because you go to a fancier school than we did doesn't mean you're not going to get to work when your mother says so.'

'And get Rachel to make another batch of lemonade while you're in the back. We've run out!' shouted Dot after him.

Diana and Dot had seriously underestimated how popular they were going to be. Ever since they had opened the café at eleven thirty, at exactly the same time as the church bell had chimed to indicate the beginning of the village fair, there had been a queue snaking out of the door. Dot had apparently pulled an all-nighter to prepare an array of delicious-looking cakes and scones, but it wasn't even three o'clock and they looked in serious danger of having nothing left to sell. An entrepreneur who appeared on a *Dragons' Den*-type programme had once told Diana that a major cause of business failure was stock control, and she hoped that they hadn't bitten off more than they could chew.

But no one could deny it was a roaring success. It was a

beautiful afternoon and people must have come from far and wide to the fair.

She felt a tap on her shoulder and then a voice.

'I wonder if you've got any of the Diana cake. I've been told it's the best in show.'

Spinning round, she saw Adam standing right behind her. He smiled and the corners of his eyes crinkled.

'You came,' she said, wiping her hands on her pale blue Moschino dress.

'You asked.'

She didn't like to mention Thursday night. The café glowing like a romantic French bistro for the evening she had planned together.

'This is seriously impressive, Di.'

'I didn't do much,' she lied. 'Put a few flowers in jars. That's all.'

'That's not what I've heard.'

'What *have* you heard?' she asked, filled with pride.

'I've heard you've transformed the Blue Ribbon top to toe.'

Diana smiled. 'Dot's Bakery: we're changing the name. It's what everyone around here calls it anyway, and I thought we could do lovely little spotty cake boxes, maybe merchandising like aprons and mugs.'

'And dozens of franchises across the country?' smiled Adam. 'I like it.'

Diana couldn't deny it had crossed her mind. Secretly she liked the idea of making a big success of a business, so that for once people wouldn't look down on her, dismiss her as a gold-digger, the secretary who'd snagged the boss. Also, in some small way it would be keeping Julian's memory alive – and Diana realised that she did want that very much, despite her feelings for Adam, which were making themselves heard at that very moment.

'Do you want some lemonade? Rachel's made it. It's rather good.'

Adam nodded.

'I'll just grab two cups and we can sit outside. I can get Charlie to cover for me . . .'

She realised she was rambling and stopped.

'Take your time.'

The door of the café tinkled open, although she could barely hear the bell over the din inside.

'Diana. Diana Denver.' It was the vicar, and he looked hot and exasperated. 'There you are, my dear. They are shouting for you in the marquee,' he said, lowering his voice from its sermon level. 'Judging is about to start. I have to say, there is a tomato out there the size of a watermelon . . .'

Diana glanced at Adam and winced.

'Go,' he mouthed, and then winked at her.

She hoped that he would follow her out of the shop towards the marquee, but as she turned back to look at him, he was already sharing a joke with Charlie.

Rachel was making her eighth batch of lemonade. One cup of sugar, one cup of water, one cup of freshly squeezed lemon juice to make the syrup, then a further four cups of water and plenty of crushed ice to dilute. She had varied the recipe throughout the day, even adding a few secret ingredients she had found in Dot's cupboards, although she preferred it herself straight up, with a little grated zest and mint. She had shared a private grumble with Charlie earlier on in the afternoon, not quite believing that she had been roped into helping out with the café. As if she wasn't doing enough for Diana, she thought, feeling momentarily irritated, then stopped her uncharitable thoughts.

Dot bustled in and helped herself to the pitcher of lemonade that Rachel had just made.

'You know, this stuff is getting better and better as the day goes on. You should set up shop when you get back to Thailand.'

'Cheers. I'm not doing badly for someone who can't boil an egg successfully.'

'Speaking of Thailand. Where's that handsome boyfriend when we need him?'

'He's gone into London. He leaves for Bangkok tomorrow. He said he'd be back by now actually.' She smiled brightly, trying to hide her disappointment.

Rachel understood that Liam's time in England was limited

and that he had had more friends and family to see, but she was still confused and upset at his no-show at the fair. He had known how hard Diana had worked to revamp the café and how much Rachel had wanted the day to be a success for her sister's benefit if nothing else. Besides which, despite Rachel's chores in the kitchen, it was the sort of perfect English afternoon that she wanted to share with him. The sort she knew she would miss in Thailand's relentless sunshine.

Her mobile phone was buzzing in the pouch of the spotty apron that Dot had lent her.

'My phone. I had better get this.'

She could hear a faint voice at the other end, but the noise in the café was so loud, she could barely make out what it was saying. She went outside, which wasn't much better, so she stuck a finger in her ear.

'Is that Rachel?' The voice was at first unfamiliar. 'It's Alicia. Alicia Dyer. I just wanted to let you know that Liam is on his way.'

'Liam's been with you?' she said, feeling her mouth dry.

'Didn't he tell you?'

'Of course,' she lied.

'Sorry we didn't get to say goodbye at Casper's last week. But as promised, I asked around. I was going to pass the message on through Liam, but I thought I had better tell you myself. Anyway, word was definitely out that Julian wanted to sell the business. All the big players were after a meeting with him to angle for the instruction; in fact a partner at our place was certain he knew exactly the right buyer. Bit of a lost cause, though, as Julian had a tight circle of investment people he liked using. It's a shame we didn't meet before. I mean, I didn't know Liam had such a connection to the Denver family.'

'Julian's dead, Alicia. I don't think Liam's connections could help now. Not that they ever would have.'

'Of course not,' she said with embarrassment.

Rachel ended the call and sank down to the kerb, reeling. She kept hearing Alicia's words. *Liam is on his way . . . Didn't he tell you?* She had no idea if the woman was being deliberately toxic, and she had certainly gone out of her way to help Rachel. But still she felt duped and betrayed. Liam had said he had to go into London to run some errands, meet friends, and, well, meeting Alicia did, strictly speaking, fall into that category. But she felt sure that Liam would have mentioned who he was going to see if it had been anyone else other than Alicia. And he had no reason to cover his tracks unless there was some romantic element to his visit, an element that he wanted to hide from Rachel because he thought it would upset her.

She looked up and saw Adam Denver walking out of the café, which was strange as she hadn't seen him go in. There was something about him that made him look like a film star on the set of a Working Title movie. Squinting in the sun she waved at him and he came ambling over, his hands thrust in his jeans pockets.

'Shouldn't you be judging cauliflowers?'

'Your sister's the local celebrity around here. No one knows me from Adam.'

She gave a short laugh and he came to sit next to her on the kerb.

'Excellent lemonade, by the way.'

She was only half listening to him. All she could think about was that Liam and Alicia had rekindled their relationship and the very idea of it made her feel sick.

'Did I taste vanilla?'

'What?'

'Vanilla. In the lemonade.'

She started to laugh. 'I went a bit off-piste.'

'It was great. Inventive. Are you okay?' he said after a moment.

'I'm fine.'

'Come on, Rachel. What's wrong?'

'Why are men arseholes?' she said, turning to him.

'Ah. Boyfriend trouble.'

'I haven't got a boyfriend,' she snapped.

'Whatever it is, believe me, it's not as important as you think it is. Nothing that can't be sorted by talking to someone.'

'I didn't expect you to be an agony aunt.'

'I'm here if you need me.'

'As I said, there isn't a problem.'

'Well let's toast that with a Pimm's.'

'And hold the lemonade,' she said grumpily. 'I'm sick of it. I want to mainline on pure alcohol.'

He went to the drinks tent and came back with two plastic tumblers stuffed with cucumber and mint.

'I don't drink,' Rachel confessed, taking a refreshing sip of the peculiarly British beverage and pushing all thoughts of Liam out of her head. 'I haven't done since I was arrested, but the last few weeks have been hard.'

'Well alcohol isn't the answer,' he said, taking the Pimm's out of her hand and putting it on the pavement.

She turned to look at him. 'You know I was thinking of going to see Julian's grave before I went back to Thailand. Where is he buried?'

'In the grounds of the church near my parents' house. I can take you there if you like.'

She nodded. 'It's something I have to do. You know there were aspects of Julian's life I didn't like, didn't approve of. But I think he was a good man. Decent. Away from the affairs and the infidelity, he was moral.'

'People are complicated,' said Adam softly. 'No one is just good or bad.'

'I need a list of Denver Group shareholders,' she said snapping into work-mode. 'People with significant holdings in particular. Can you get that for me?'

'It might take a few days, but yes, of course.'

She looked up and saw Liam walking towards them.

'Finally. Here he is,' she muttered, feeling suddenly anxious.

'Someone you know?'

'My business partner.'

'Ah, Liam. The bronzed diving hunk. I heard about the mercy dash from Ko Tao.'

'Does Diana tell you everything?' He saw her annoyance and touched her arm.

'Sorry, I didn't mean it like that. I meant that he sounds like a very good friend.'

'Well, not everyone thinks I'm the Wicked Witch of the West.'

'No one does, Rachel.'

'Yeah? And who was it called me a bitch not so long ago?' She was joking and he knew it.

'I'll leave you to it,' he said, getting up to leave.

'Don't go,' she said, putting her hand on his arm.

Adam nodded as if he completely understood. 'I'd better go and get us all another drink then.'

50

'Jim the butcher wants to know if you'll join him for a do-si-do,' said Dot, her face flushed with exertion. For a sixty-eight-year-old, Dot had certainly thrown herself enthusiastically into the country dancing, not to mention the liberal amounts of cider and Pimm's that had been on offer at the village fair and the 'after-show' party – the annual barn dance at John and Elsa Deacon's farm. Diana looked across at Jim, saw his shy glance towards her friend.

'I don't think Jim wants to do the do-si-do with me, Dot,' she smiled. 'I think he wants to do it with you.'

A happy smile played across Dot's lips. 'Do you think so?' she whispered.

Jim seemed to be hopping from foot to foot, like he was waiting for an answer. It was sweet: well into their seventh decade and they were still acting like twelve-year-olds, still unsure of the opposite sex, but still hoping for that dance with someone special.

'Jim's been sweet on you for ages, Dot. Didn't you see when he was selling the raffle tickets, he pretended not to notice when you took six tickets instead of three?'

'That's slander!' said Dot with mock-offence, and Diana giggled. Dot cast a quick look across to where Jim was still standing on his hot bricks.

'Don't you think he's nice? You know he lost his wife four years ago, just eighteen months before Ron.'

Diana smiled kindly. 'Dot, none of that matters. All he wants is a dance.'

Dot shook her head, her expression suddenly turning serious.

'See, grief doesn't end, you know, at least that's how it is with me and Ron. It changes, it softens, and then it doesn't keep you awake so much at night. But it always stays with you. I don't want anyone to replace Ron, I just want someone to talk to at night.'

'And someone to do the do-si-do with,' smiled Diana, making a shooing gesture with her hands. 'Go! Before someone else snaps him up.'

'How am I looking?'

'As tasty as your courgette and ginger cake.'

Dot looked momentarily unsure of herself. 'When do you think is the right time to move on? You know, thinking about other men . . . like that?' Her cheeks turned even redder. 'Sorry, it's the Pimm's, I shouldn't have asked you that. Too soon after Julian.'

Diana put a hand on her arm. 'When you're ready,' she said simply. 'That's the answer, Dot. I know that Ron would want you to smile again.'

'Thanks, lovey,' said Dot, and set off across the floor, her hands extended towards her new beau.

Diana felt herself torn as she watched them dancing. She was happy for Dot, of course she was. It was the beginning of something. That excitement of the first few minutes, hours, days, when all that was between you was hope. She had often thought how entire industries were built on that window of time. Expensive lingerie shops, high heels – all designed to make someone fall in love. But at the same time, she felt horribly guilty. When *was* the right time to move on? In her case, it had been three weeks after she had buried her husband. She had jumped into his brother's bed with barely a second thought; what did that say about her? What did it say about her relationship with Julian? She had tried to put it down to grief, to her emotions playing tricks on her, but the truth was, she was attracted to Adam. She wanted his hands on her flesh, his breath on her neck, she wanted him rearing above her . . . She shook her head. It wasn't right, she knew that. She should be deep in mourning, wearing black like Queen Victoria, weeping and wailing. Dr Shapiro had warned her about the stages of grief, about the

352

possible need for emotional connection with another person, but she hadn't referred to it as a 'horny' stage.

She glanced across the barn to where Adam was sitting on two hay bales with Rachel and Liam.

He was here. That was something. But they hadn't had a chance to talk. Not like he'd promised in Brooklyn. The judging of the flower and vegetable show had taken over two hours, the presentation of the trophies another one. Then Adam and Liam had got roped into the clearing up, and since the barn dance had started, he'd sat around drinking with Rachel and Liam, making jokes, laughing, avoiding Diana if the truth be told. Not in an obvious way or even a deliberate way – he wouldn't be here if he really didn't want to see her. But she could sense that there would not be a repeat performance of that night in New York. Not tonight, anyway.

As she took a sip of the warm cider that the bar had been serving all evening, she felt her phone vibrate in her pocket. She answered it, and heard an unfamiliar voice with a heavy foreign accent.

'Mrs Denver. It's Yohan Clarke. I'm calling from Jamaica.'

It took a second for her to place his name.

'Yes, Yohan, how are you?'

'Good, and how is Miss Rachel?'

'Home safe and sound. Thank you for your assistance out there.'

'I am ringing to tell you to expect a call from Officer Henry of the Montego Bay police force.'

She felt on sudden red alert.

'Is there a problem?'

'Not really. He thinks they have found Ross McKiney's assailants. They made an arrest about half an hour ago. Three men with a history of robbery and violent assault.'

She had heard that Yohan had ears around the island, and his connections were now obvious.

'That's good news, isn't it?'

'Perhaps,' he said cautiously. 'Do you want me still to keep an ear open on things around here?'

'If you think it's necessary.' For a moment she had the

353

uncharitable thought that Yohan was trying to extract more money out of her. She'd paid him well for his assignment looking after her sister and Liam, but Rachel herself had described Jamaica as a dead end. 'Yes, go ahead.'

Across the dance floor she could see that Adam had asked Rachel to do-si-do. It was difficult to watch them, but she knew she wasn't the only one. Liam had been left on the sidelines and she could see his eyes following Rachel across the room. Diana picked up two glasses of cider from the table at the side and walked over to him.

'So, how are you enjoying the fair?' she asked, handing him a drink.

'It's been fun,' he said, then grimaced at the glass in his hand. 'Mind you, you could strip doors with this.'

'A bit of hard liquor is sometimes not a bad thing,' she said quietly. 'So you're going back to Thailand tomorrow?'

He nodded, his mouth turning down, and she saw him glance across at Rachel. Diana's heart squeezed at that look. How she wished she had a man who looked at her like Liam had just looked at her sister.

'You're going to miss her, aren't you?'

'She'll be back soon,' he said, staring into his drink.

'I'm sorry for dragging her away. You know, out of all of us, I think she wants to know what happened to Julian the most.'

'She's dogged all right. Look, I'm glad you got things sorted between you. It tore her up, the rift in the family. I can understand why you blamed her, but sometimes her ambition just gets the better of her.'

'It wasn't that.'

Liam looked puzzled.

'Julian tried it on with her. That's why she hated him, turned on him.'

Now it was Liam's turn to look off-balance. Anger, concern and embarrassment flickered across his face.

'She didn't tell me that part.'

'She wouldn't. She was too loyal for that.'

She looked at him, feeling quite certain that Liam was the sort of discreet and decent man you could trust with your secrets. 'I hated my husband too sometimes,' she said softly. 'Hated him but still loved him. I had the choice to leave years ago, but I stayed because I couldn't go. That's what love is, isn't it? You love someone in spite of everything, not because of it.'

Liam nodded, looking over at Rachel again. 'Maybe.'

'You know, I was always jealous of Rachel.' She said it with a small laugh, the alcohol making her careless.

'She always said you were the one who had everything.'

'Yes, I was the pretty one – our mum never stopped telling me that. But Rachel has something I never had: she's happy with who she is. Always has been. Confident, too; this cast-iron belief that she could rule the world. Not that she's that bothered if she makes it or not. She just wants to have fun trying.'

Liam smiled and looked over again at Rachel, who was skipping in a line with the vicar.

'Tell me about this hotel she wants to buy in Thailand. At first I thought it was bluster for the benefit of my mother. But then I remembered what she's like.'

'Then you'll know she's not just after a hotel. It's a full-blown resort she wants – Racheland,' replied Liam.

They both started to laugh, but their hearts weren't in it.

'I'm sorry about everything that's happened. It can't have been easy for you these past few weeks. I hope it's helped having Rachel around.'

'It's not been easy, but I've learnt a lot, about other people and about myself; about life, too. I've learnt that if you love someone, you have to tell them. Because one day they might not be there any more and you'll regret that there were things you wanted to say to them and didn't.'

'Good advice.'

Diana nudged him. 'Ask her to dance before Adam monopolises her for the rest of the night.'

She knew she wasn't being entirely altruistic. She wanted to monopolise Adam herself; in fact, as the music stopped, she knew that now was the time to break up their little party.

'Come on, let's go over. Besides, I've just had a phone call and I've got something to tell her.'

51

Rachel needed to think, and inside the Deacons' barn wasn't the place for it. The music was loud and her head was spinning. A few sips of Pimm's and a sneaky half a lager did that to you when you had been on the wagon for three years.

She went outside, listening to the strains of 'Come on Eileen' fade into the background, and sat down on a stone wall. It was almost eleven o'clock and pitch black, with just a thin crescent moon spilling watery light over the village. Lighting a cigarette, she blew a perfect smoke ring, watching it float off into the air then disappear like the tiny feathery seeds on a dandelion clock.

'Can I bum a cigarette?'

She swivelled as she heard the voice behind her.

'Dexy's not doing it for you?' she said, smiling softly at Adam.

'Just needed a cig. Thought I should come out here before I set fire to a hay bale. So how's your friend Ross? I heard Diana say they had caught the muggers.'

She nodded. 'The cop in Jamaica just called me, and Ross is out of a coma, so things are getting better.'

'When are you going back? I assume you're not on Liam's morning flight to Bangkok.'

'I've not tied everything up here yet.'

'Or perhaps you're not missing Thailand as much as you thought you would.'

'I do miss it. I miss the green water, the smell of the breeze. I miss my clients, I miss my life.'

'I know how you feel. Neither here nor there. I've made six transatlantic flights in four weeks.'

'Bravo, you've beaten me. I've only managed four and a rather nice helicopter flight to Jersey.'

She blew another smoke ring.

'That was pretty good.'

'You have a go.'

'I can blow a smoke ring. I had a very misspent youth.'

'All right, let's see who can blow the longest chain of them . . .'

'Hang on, you started before me.'

'Stop it,' she said, almost choking.

Adam snorted with laughter and pushed her off the wall, and soon they were giggling so hard they didn't hear the footsteps behind them.

'Rachel, I'm going.'

'What?' she said, registering the voice.

'I said I'm going.'

'Oh, right,' she said, stubbing out her cigarette. 'Why so soon?' *Off to call Alicia?* she wanted to ask him.

'I have to pack.'

'I'm heading in,' said Adam quickly, as if he had detected the tension between them.

Rachel had been glad of Adam's company all afternoon. Alicia's phone call had upset her so much, had Adam not been there, she knew she might have said something to Liam she would regret. He was still her business partner. At some point she was returning to Ko Tao to work with him.

But this time she let Adam leave them alone.

'He's not as bad as people make out,' said Liam when Adam had gone back inside the barn.

Rachel perched back on the wall.

'He's fun.'

'I'll say.'

She had to mention it. It had been bugging her all day and she didn't want to leave it like this, let him go back to Ko Tao without airing her annoyance.

'You didn't tell me you were meeting Alicia today.'

'How did you know about that?' he said, frowning in the darkness.

'She called me.'

He hesitated.

'You don't have to lie,' she said quickly.

'About what?'

'You were about to lie to me.'

'I wasn't,' he said sharply.

'Well, I hope you had a fun afternoon. I'm surprised you didn't stay on for a fun *night*.'

Liam shook his head slowly. 'If you must know, I met her to try and raise some finance for the hotel.'

Her stomach did a back-flip, but she wasn't going to show it.

'Really?' She couldn't stop the words coming out as a confrontation.

'While I've been in England, I've spoken to my dad, my brother-in-law, Alicia. They've got the most money out of everyone I know. I've been pitching the resort to them, thinking that one of them might be interested in investing.'

She felt a wave of emotion. He'd been doing that all along. Was he doing it for her?

'We can't have your ex-fiancée investing in the business.'

She could have kicked herself. Why couldn't she just be grateful for what he had done rather than criticise him?

'We were never engaged.'

'Still.'

'Well who else are we supposed to get three quarters of a million quid from? Because that's how much it's going to cost us.'

'I'm not asking Diana, if that's what you're hinting at.'

'I never asked you to speak to Diana. In case you'd forgotten, you're the one who wants the hotel. I was simply doing my best to make it happen.'

'Well you could have told me you were meeting Alicia.'

'You sound like you're jealous.'

'Don't be ridiculous,' she barked. 'We're friends. I thought we made that clear the other night on the beach.'

He looked at her and she was sure she saw a flicker of contempt in his gaze.

'Can you remember what you were like when you came to Ko Tao? You were all wound up, snap, snap, snap, like a little crocodile.'

'I never knew you had such a great first impression of me,' she said sarcastically.

Liam continued. 'It took you about six months to calm down, and when you did, you were a different person. Happier, more relaxed, better company. You were the real you, not this person. Angry, shouty, stressed, ungrateful . . .'

'I've got a lot on my mind,' she said, as if she was talking to a child.

'Are you coming home?' he said flatly.

'I'll get someone to drop me off later,' she said sulkily.

'I meant Ko Tao. You said you'd stay in London for two or three weeks when Diana came out to Thailand to get you.'

'Well, I might be a little longer,' she said without looking at him. She could feel the conversation spiralling out of control. She just wanted to stop it, take it back to the easy-going companionship that used to exist between them.

But you spoilt that, she told herself. *You spoilt that on Sairee Beach.*

'Are you ever coming back, because if you're not, you had better tell me now.'

'I'll be back, Liam, but I want to finish the job here.'

'Job? Rachel, this is a fantasy,' said Liam angrily. 'Julian was found locked inside a house, the alarm on, CCTV showing no one going in or out. Now unless you've suddenly started to suspect that your sister is secretly a homicidal maniac with the ability to subdue a grown man twice her size, I'd say this idea that Julian was murdered is wearing a bit thin.'

'But all the evidence . . .'

'*What* evidence, Rachel? Okay, so Madison was pregnant when she died and maybe it was Julian's kid but we don't know for sure. Maybe she was run off the road in Maryland – maybe not. But then why haven't all the other people making complaints about Rheladrex been silenced too? And Ross, perhaps he could have been beaten up for getting too close to the test clinic, I'll give you that one – if the detective in Jamaica hadn't called Diana to say he'd caught the culprit.'

He took a thin cardboard wallet out of his back pocket and gave it to her.

'What's this?' she said without even looking at it.

'A plane ticket back to Samui for a week's time.'

She glanced down and saw something written on the back of it.

'And that number. It's for Kroll,' he added. 'I know some people in London who have used them. They are one of the best investigative and security services in the world. Give it to Diana. Tell her to call them up and let them take over the baton. If anyone's going to turn something up, it's them.'

'You're telling me to give up,' she said incredulously. 'You're saying I'm not good enough to get the job done.'

'You're good enough to do anything, Rachel. You don't need me to tell you that. What I *am* telling you is that I don't think this investigation, or however you'd describe it, is helping anyone, least of all you. It's not about Julian or Diana any more. It's about you, trying to prove something to the world. And you don't need to do that. You never have.'

'Don't tell me what I need to do.'

He stepped away from her, rubbing his handsome face.

'Are you still okay to give me a lift to Heathrow? It's an early flight, so I understand if you're too tired or hung-over,' he said flatly.

'Yes, yes. Of course,' she stuttered.

Liam's face softened. 'Thank you.'

'Could you do me a favour?'

'What is it?' he said, going immediately on guard.

'I haven't really had a chance to scroll through all the security footage. I thought that while you were on a twelve-hour plane journey, you could take a look; in fact I left it on your bag in the bedroom . . .'

Liam shook his head. 'You're incredible.' She knew he did not mean it in a good way.

'I just thought you might as well make good use of the time.'

'You're obsessed, you know that?' He was beginning to walk away.

'Where are you going?' she said, getting up to follow him. Her breath felt shallow with panic.

'Back to the house.'

'You can't walk. It's pitch black.'

A car stopped and tooted. The window of the Mercedes was lowered and they saw Mr Bills smiling at them. Diana was in the back seat.

'Want a lift back, you two? Party's almost over.'

Liam nodded, and they both got into the car in silence.

52

Diana sat in the doctor's waiting room with a dog-eared magazine in her lap. Why did all the worst things in life always involve waiting rooms? Root canal, long train journeys, even a waxing session required you to undergo the ritual of sitting in silence, flicking through three-month-old copies of *Country Life.* They'd even made her wait on her own at the hospital before a nice young policewoman – God, she couldn't have been more than twenty-six – came in to officially inform her that the paramedics had been unable to revive her husband, even though she had known the second she had opened the library door that he was dead.

Someone behind her coughed all over her, and she shifted uncomfortably in her chair, pulling a hand sanitiser out of her bag and wiping her hands discreetly just as her name was called by the receptionist. The last thing she needed was a bout of the lurgy when she was feeling so rotten already. She had heard of the two-day hangover, of course, but this was ridiculous. It had been three days since the village fair and still she felt weak, curdled and nauseous.

She knocked on the door and pushed it open. She knew Dr Minas well. Her miscarriages and their aftermath had been dealt with by her obstetrician, but Dr Minas had provided support and had been sympathetic and helpful throughout her ordeals.

They made polite conversation, after which Diana reeled off her symptoms, told the doctor about the fair, speculated about the fruit punch and the hotpot she had sampled at the barn dance, then sat patiently as the doctor scribbled a few notes on the pad in front of her.

'And how are you generally? I was sorry to hear about your husband,' she said with feeling.

'I'm seeing a therapist to talk some things through. Was,' she corrected herself as she recalled her last meeting with Olga Shapiro. 'At first it was as if there was this black fog hanging over me the whole time. It's a lot better now.'

'I wouldn't be too hasty giving up therapy if it was working for you. These things take time, even when you think you're on an upswing.' More scribbled notes. 'And are you sleeping?'

'I can sleep for twenty-four hours and then not sleep for two days.' Diana gave a nervous laugh. *I sound like a crazy woman*, she thought.

'Could you be pregnant?'

Diana's eyes opened wide. *Pregnant?* Immediately her mind pictured her with Adam, almost as if she were watching it on a dim TV screen.

'Is it possible?' repeated the doctor.

Clothes torn from each other, strewn on the floor, Adam climaxing inside her. They hadn't exactly been thinking about birth control or anything else.

'How quickly can symptoms appear?' Diana asked slowly, anxiety creeping upon her.

'It varies from woman to woman and from pregnancy to pregnancy,' said Dr Minas. 'When was your last period?'

'I can't remember exactly . . .'

Those words sounded so odd. When she and Julian had been trying for a baby, she had thought of nothing else, she had known every last detail of her menstrual cycle, when her peak ovulation time was, what her optimum temperature was, which foods she should be eating, everything. Diana's cycle had never been the most regular of beasts, but to miss a period? Surely she couldn't have *missed* one? But no – she genuinely couldn't be sure. In the foggy haze after Julian's death, she couldn't be sure of anything. Nothing had mattered except getting from day to day.

'Well,' said the doctor briskly, 'shall we do a quick test now? I'm sure you're familiar with the procedure by now. You can go into the toilet there.'

But Diana sat there, rooted to the spot. She didn't want to

know. Her mind couldn't cope. *Pregnant?* It just couldn't be happening.

Dr Minas reached forward and put a reassuring hand over hers.

'It's normal to feel mixed emotions. And I imagine it's particularly bittersweet in your case, given the circumstances.'

Julian. She was talking about Julian, of course. She assumed that Diana was pregnant with her dead husband's baby, not his brother's – why wouldn't she? Anything else was unthinkable, repugnant.

'Come on. Let's try it,' said the doctor with a kind smile. 'Just a quick pee, then we'll know one way or the other.'

Diana's hand was shaking as she took the sample cup and went into the adjoining toilet. She sat down on the lid, putting her head in her hands. *Breathe*, she urged herself. You can do this. What if she *was* pregnant? Why now? After all those times she and Julian had been disappointed, it would be the cruellest irony possible. Julian's brother. His *brother*. She bent her head lower, worried that she was going to be sick, breathing in through her nose, trying to clear her head.

'Everything all right in there?' called the doctor through the door. 'Just relax, maybe run the tap if that helps.'

Diana could see that she was trapped – literally, in fact. There was no way out except through the doctor's office.

'Come on, Diana,' she whispered to herself. 'Be brave.'

The doctor was right, of course. There was no hiding from it – she had to know one way or the other. If she was pregnant, it wouldn't just go away like the hangover she'd come here about. Quickly she flipped up the lid and mechanically went through the motions, carrying the sample out to Dr Minas. With a reassuring smile, the GP dipped a cardboard strip into the urine and waited, looking at her watch.

'It's positive,' she said, smiling.

No, no, no. Diana couldn't draw a breath. She felt as if she had pins and needles all over her body.

'Really?' she croaked finally. 'Is it definite? I mean, are these tests a hundred per cent accurate?'

'A blood test is the most accurate,' smiled the doctor, nodding at the cardboard strip, 'though false positives do happen.'

'But in your medical opinion, am I having a baby?' she said, stuttering.

The doctor clearly saw Diana's pale face and leant forward to touch her knee.

'I know there's going to be conflicting feelings. But this is what your husband would have wanted, especially as you'd both tried so hard for a baby.'

Diana nodded dumbly. 'How far gone am I?'

Dr Minas raised her eyebrows slightly and Diana saw a look of understanding pass across her face.

'Well, we'd need to do a scan to tell you that. But these instant urine tests are usually effective from the first day after your missed period.'

The one question Diana wanted to ask she knew would have to go answered. However understanding Dr Minas was, she couldn't bring herself to say it: 'Could I be pregnant by the man I had sex with ten days ago?'

'After you conceive, the body produces a hormone called hCG,' explained the doctor. 'Around two weeks in, there's enough hCG in your system and that's what the tests are picking up.'

'Two weeks?' she said slowly. 'Are you sure?'

'Could be as little as a week. As you'll know, a woman conceives when the egg and the sperm fuse to become a zygote. The zygote travels to the uterus – which can take up to nine days – where it implants itself, and the body starts producing the hCG. As I said, it varies from woman to woman. It's not an exact science, I'm afraid. We won't know for sure until we have a proper scan.'

The tears were rolling down Diana's face now, plopping into her lap.

'Oh my dear,' said the doctor. 'Whatever is the matter?'

'I'm sorry,' said Diana, taking a tissue from her. 'It's just as you said – it's bittersweet, that's all.'

But Diana felt as if she had been plunged into a living nightmare.

365

53

Rachel stared listlessly at her computer screen. In theory, she was trawling through the hours of security footage from the Notting Hill house. But in reality, all she could think about was Liam. It had all ended so badly. That moment outside the barn on Saturday should have been exactly that. A *moment*. Liam had been racing around London trying to raise the money for her hotel venture, and that had to count for something. She should have thanked him, kissed him, told him how she really felt, given it one last shot to find out once and for all what they meant to each other. Instead she had insulted him, abused him. Told him to go back to Ko Tao where girls in bikinis were snaking round the block for him.

A sharp tap at the door jolted her out of her thoughts. She turned to see Adam Denver grinning through the glass, and suddenly she felt a little better.

'Adam! What the hell are you doing here?' she said, opening the door of the Lake House and welcoming him in.

'Sorry, did I startle you?' he said, clearly amused at her reaction. 'I didn't realise you'd be deep in thought.'

'I was just doing some work,' she said, snapping her computer shut.

'Yeah, yeah,' laughed Adam. 'Work that involves looking at expensive shoes, I'll bet.'

'So are you here to see Diana?'

'No, not today. I was in the area, thought I'd check you were all right out here in the woods now that you're all on your own again.'

Rachel glanced around the little room. Actually, the Lake House did feel lonely without Liam. She hadn't realised how much she had enjoyed having him in the next room, or humming to himself as he shaved, or leaving his dirty running shoes next to the door for her to trip over. Not that she was about to tell Adam that.

'I'm managing,' she said. 'Some of us independent young women don't actually need a man all the time, you know. We can choose the TV channel on our own.'

'Believe it or not, I always had you down as a very capable woman. This place is great, isn't it?' he said, walking to the window and staring out over the lake.

'Have you never been here before?'

'Julian got very excited about building these things and then grew bored of them pretty quickly . . . Do these windows open?'

'Sure, give it a tug.'

'Wow, you can dive straight into the water from here.'

'Tempting, isn't it?'

'Yes, I remember Jules saying that when he showed me the plans. I don't think he ever did it.'

'No. Funny, it was the first thing I thought when I saw it, but I have never got round to it either.'

'Better late than never,' he said, drawing the window right back so that a soft early evening breeze floated into the room.

'What do you mean?'

'Go on. If anyone should do the inaugural dive from the living room into the lake, it should be you.'

'Stop it, it's late,' she chuckled.

'It's not even seven o'clock, and it's still twenty-five degrees out there,' he said, leaning out and peering down into the green water. 'How deep is it?'

'Don't know exactly. At least ten feet. Maybe more.'

'You've checked?'

'Well, yes, sitting here with the sun on me, I've often—'

Adam turned and pulled his T-shirt over his head.

'Adam!' she gasped. 'What the hell are you doing?'

'What do you think?' He laughed, undoing his belt.

'This is crazy,' she said as he wriggled out of his jeans, unable to keep her eyes off his shapely bum.

He looked back at her. 'Sometimes crazy can be good, Rachel.'

He opened the floor to ceiling doors, and with a whoop, plunged into the water.

'Adam!' she cried, then broke out into a belly laugh. She ran to the window and looked out just as he surfaced, his dark hair slicked back.

'Wow! It's lovely,' he called, his arms spread wide. 'And I can't touch the bottom either!' He turned and did a somersault, the water glistening off his back like a pale fish. 'Come on,' he laughed as he came up for air. 'I thought you were the champion swimmer. What are you, chicken?'

'No,' she shouted back, feeling herself rise to the challenge.

'So jump in, then,' he grinned.

Shaking her head and laughing, she peeled off her jeans, but kept her T-shirt on. She thought about jumping straight in, but part of her wanted to do it with more panache than Adam, so she stood on the edge and executed a perfect dive into the lake.

The shock of the cold water pushed the air from her lungs.

'Show-off,' he shouted, lifting his hand and splashing water all over her.

'It's bloody freezing.'

'It's pretty good, isn't it?' grinned Adam, his face bobbing in front of her.

'Why didn't I do this weeks ago?' Rachel laughed.

'Ah well, sometimes you need a partner in crime.'

Rachel pulled herself deeper with strong strokes of her arms. She loved the tingling sensation of the cool water on her skin, and that incomparable feeling of freedom. She swam out towards the middle of the lake, going deeper still until she touched the bottom, maybe five metres down. Serge would scoff at this, she thought. She counted to ten, then kicked for the surface.

'Where have you been?' said Adam when she reached him. 'I was worried.'

Rachel shook her head. 'Don't worry, I'm a very accomplished free-diver.'

'Wow, you free-dive?'

'I could show you a few moves.'

Adam slapped his hand against the water, sending a shower into Rachel's face.

'Hey!' she giggled, flipping water back at him.

'Don't take me on, Rachel Miller,' laughed Adam. 'I'm the king of water fights.'

Suddenly they were in a frenzy of slapping and splashing, both of them laughing and shouting.

'Okay, okay,' coughed Adam finally, holding up his hands. 'I surrender, you win.'

They swam to the edge of the lake, clambering out under a willow, slipping on the mud and the moss-covered rocks and sitting down heavily on the bank.

After a minute, shivering, they ran back to the house.

'That was fun,' said Rachel. 'Thanks.' She went into the bedroom, retrieved two towels and threw him one.

'Sounds like you haven't been getting much fun out here.'

She tipped her head to one side, to let the water drain out. 'No, not a lot.'

'Well, all work and no play makes Jack a dull boy. Why don't we keep going? I've got the car here, it's a lovely evening; let's go and find some more fun.'

'Adam, no. I've got things to do.'

She didn't recognise her own voice. She was usually the first one to suggest a spontaneous night out, and yet here she was saying no to the one man who had always intrigued her.

'Nothing that won't wait a few hours, surely?'

She looked out across the lake, lazy sunlight twinkling off the surface, insects zooming and diving through the haze. It *was* a nice evening, she thought. And it *was* stuffy in the Lake House. And if she had to look at any more CCTV footage, she thought she might scream.

'All right,' she said, standing up, suddenly feeling bold. 'I'm in your hands, Adam Denver.' She paused, letting the words hang in the air. *I can flirt too, you know*, she told herself. 'But I'd better get changed first, otherwise I'll leave a puddle on your leather seats.'

'I don't mind,' he said, squinting up at her. Rachel could feel his gaze on her body, her soaked T-shirt clinging to every curve. *Well, let him look*, she thought.

He stepped over to her – was he going to make a move? Lean in for a kiss? Instead, he plucked a leaf from her hair.

'Are you going to keep those on?' said Rachel, staring at his wet boxer shorts.

'That's what all the girls say,' he teased.

'I mean, I can go and see if Liam's left anything . . .' she stuttered.

'Another man's pants?' He smiled. 'Don't worry. I'm sure I can go without for one evening.'

All Rachel could do was blush furiously.

54

Diana stepped away from the window, wrapping her arms around herself. It was a warm evening, but she still felt cold. From the Peacock Suite she had a good view of the lake and the road leading away from Somerfold; she could still see the back of Adam's Aston Martin disappearing around the last curve. She tried to take a deep breath, but it was ragged, shaky. She had seen him. She had seen *them*. Together. Adam and Rachel. *Together*. She had seen them swimming in the lake, she had seen them run out of the water half dressed, she had seen them disappear into the house for almost ten minutes and then leave for who knows where. Suddenly the spell seemed to break. Diana's hand flew to her mouth and she bolted for the toilet, bending over the bowl, heaving up her meagre lunch.

How could he? How could *she*? Rachel was her sister, for God's sake. And to think she'd bought all that crap about how Julian had forced himself on her when clearly her instincts had been right first time – Rachel had led him on in Tuscany, her jealousy pushing her to grasp at the one thing that made Diana happy. And now she was doing it again, trying to take Adam away from her.

She grabbed a fistful of toilet roll and wiped her mouth.

What a mess, she thought, remembering that she had woken up that morning feeling unusually positive. She had spent the previous day in her bedroom with the curtains closed, crying on and off, unable to deal with the horrific possibility that she was carrying Adam Denver's child. Was it God's vengeance on her for her moral slip? Was Julian punishing her from beyond the grave for failing to provide him with a baby of his own? Or was it just all a terrible, terrible mistake she'd have to live with? Mrs Bills had tried to coax her out, but she had complained of a migraine and hadn't touched the food that had been left outside the door on a tray.

But this morning, with the sunlight pushing through the curtains, Diana had felt the dark cloud lift. Was it really so bad? She had a new life inside of her, someone to love and cherish, someone else to care for. And just because it hadn't been planned didn't mean that the child would not be welcomed. Adam would have remembered they had been so drunk, so reckless in New York that they had not used a condom. He would guess that the child might be his. He wanted a child, a family. He had told her so himself that day in Dorset. And although he had been cold and uninterested in her since New York – she felt sure that he was as confused as she was – perhaps a baby was what he needed to make him confront his feelings. To the outside world it would look as if the baby was Julian's last gift to her, a miracle life springing from the ashes, while Adam could play the part of the caring uncle until the time arrived to come clean to their family and friends about their relationship. In many ways it had panned out perfectly.

There was only one person in the world she wanted to share her thought process with, and that was Rachel. Rachel, who had been so strong and wise when she had found out that she was pregnant with Charlie. Rachel, with her slightly skewed moral compass, who would not judge her for having sex with Adam Denver. So Diana had set out down towards the lake. She suspected that Rachel might be feeling lonely now that Liam had gone back to Thailand, so she had brought along a bottle of fizzy raspberry lemonade; not quite the bottle of rosé they used to share in the old days when they could giggle over boys, but it would be nice to sit drinking it with the windows open all the same.

She heard the splashing and laughter before she saw them; along the path, a line of trees blocked the view of the lake's edge, but immediately she sensed she wasn't going to like what was waiting down there. Careful not to be seen, she crept forward, ducking so that she could see between gaps in the branches. Her heart lurched as she saw Adam, that familiar bare chest, those same muscles that had strained and twisted above her. He waded to the edge of the lake, naked save for a pair of dripping, clinging boxers. And then Rachel walked into view, squeezing the water from her hair, also practically undressed. It was as if Diana were watching it on television, but she couldn't turn it off, could not tear her eyes away as Adam splashed over to her sister, his hand reaching for Rachel just as he had done to her that night in New York.

That was when she ran, sprinting up the path towards the house, desperate to get as far away from both of them as she could. As she passed a clump of trees, she startled a group of birds – crows, starlings, she didn't have time to see which as they exploded into the sky, their wings dark, their cries menacing. She threw an arm up to protect herself, tears rolling down her face now, her only thought to get to the safety of the house. She burst inside, pushing past Mrs Bills on the stairs, and closed her bedroom door behind her, falling on to the bed, her mind full of questions.

How long had it been going on? Why hadn't she seen it before? Was this the first time, or had it been happening under her nose for weeks? Had he fucked her before their own night together in New York? Was this just a game of conquest for Adam – just like his brother? And what did it mean for the baby? Her fantasies of handsome, caring Uncle Adam bouncing his secret child on his knee, then sneaking into Diana's bed at night, had all dissolved the moment she had seen him reach for Rachel. Or was it all her sister? Was this revenge? Spite? Did Rachel secretly hate her? Was her investigation just an elaborate way to ingratiate herself with Adam and prove that she'd been right about Julian all along?

'Come on, breathe,' Diana whispered to herself, slowly clawing back some control. She sat up and rubbed her face. *Don't let them win*, she told herself fiercely. She walked over to the window, looking down towards the Lake House. Were they lying together right now? But to her surprise, she saw Adam's car appear, climbing up from the lake and out along Somerfold's drive to the main road. It was then she had run for the toilet.

373

What now? she wondered, walking unsteadily from the bathroom. What could she do? Tell Adam about the baby, force him into taking responsibility? Clearly it wasn't something he wanted – he'd already moved on. 'To my bloody sister!' she hissed out loud.

She snatched up her phone from the bedside table. She wanted – no, needed – to talk it through with someone. But who was there she could call? She didn't really have friends like that. There was Patty Reynolds, but she had also been Julian's friend – how would she react to the news that Diana was pregnant with Adam's child? Unable to settle, Diana paced the room. *God, what a mess, what am I going to do?*

She was just about to throw down her phone when it buzzed in her hand. She looked down: an email. It was from Simon Michaels in New York.

She read it carefully. It had been sent to both Diana and Adam, saying that Michaels had asked around the appropriate departments but no one had heard of Billy or Maddison Kopek. Something struck her as odd about it, so she read it again. When she scrolled down to the bottom of the message, she saw that Simon was replying to an email that Adam had sent him asking about Maddison Kopek. She remembered asking him to send that email. They had been standing on the sidewalk in New York before their night of passion.

She read it again. Maddison Kopek. That was what was strange. Maddison spelt with two Ds, which was very unusual. Everything from Madison Avenue to the American girl's name was usually spelt with one.

It jogged something in her memory. Rome. That was it. Julian's report on Rheladrex that had taken them to see Dr Adriana Russi. She had a copy of the report in her case, she was sure of it. Rachel had given it to her to read before they had flown out there.

The case was in the storage room on the top floor. She went upstairs, noticing the bags of Julian's clothes she had stuffed in here in a fit of anger, and retrieved the report, leaning against the wall as she read it. There it was. Maddison Kopek, with a phone number written next to it. The flowery, girly writing suggested it had been written by the young woman herself.

Her mind was a swirl of thoughts. Adam had referred to Madison as Maddison in his email. Was it a slip of the hand, an incorrect spelling, or had he seen a copy of this report?

Bile rose in her throat.

Adam, say you're not involved in any of this.

Her next thought was Rachel. She was in the car with him. Who knew where they were going? She felt a sudden shiver of fear for her sister and knew she had to contact her. Why? To warn her? She didn't care if Rachel thought she was checking up on her, she just had to tell her what she knew. She had a horrible sinking feeling about it.

Her phone was still in the Peacock Suite. She ran to the stairs, taking them two at a time.

Almost as if she was moving in slow motion, Diana saw her toe miss the edge of the step, her ankle turning over, her arms pinwheeling. She knew what was about to happen, but was powerless to stop it, as her weight pitched her forward, her body momentarily seeming to pause in the air. And then she was falling, down, down, and the hard wooden floor was rushing up to meet her.

Rachel arched her back and let her hair fly back in the breeze. She had changed into a cotton dress, but she hadn't had time to dry her hair. This was much nicer anyway, letting the warm air do its work. She loved convertible cars, she decided, watching the countryside go by in shades of green, the long shadows of late afternoon stretching across the fields, cutting across the roads. She reflected how almost everywhere looked good in the summertime, but that the rolling hills of Oxfordshire looked better than most places she had ever been – even the paradise islands of the South China Sea.

'Why are we going to Oxford?' she asked, shouting over the noise of the engine.

Adam tapped the side of his nose. 'Ask me no questions . . .' he said with an enigmatic smile.

'Come on, I hate surprises!' said Rachel, but Adam just shook his head.

They parked on the far side of the Cherwell, crossing the old stone bridge with the wooden punts gathered beneath. As the dreaming sandstone spires of Magdalen College rose up next to them, Rachel couldn't believe she had once dismissed these ancient, student strongholds as stuffy and old-fashioned.

'It's amazing here,' she said. 'Like a medieval town. No wonder it still has such magic.'

'Actually, I used to hate Oxford,' said Adam. 'I mean, hate it with a passion.'

'Really? But it's beautiful here, how could you hate it?'

He waved a hand along the high street. 'Take your pick. All the students with their look-at-me scarves weaving about on their stupid bikes, all the crumbly old buildings, the crowds of Japanese tourists wanting to snap every inch of the place. I wanted to bulldoze the lot.'

Rachel laughed. 'What's your problem with it?'

'Oh, it's embarrassingly shallow,' said Adam. 'Because Julian and Elizabeth were offered places here. It was clear from a pretty early age that that was never going to be my educational trajectory. "Good at sport", that was the euphemism they used to describe thickies like me at school.'

Rachel wondered for a moment if Diana had ever felt the same way about her. She had always been the one to do well at exams – it had actually rather irritated her that so little was expected of Diana, but perhaps she had felt stupid by comparison.

'It's funny, you don't strike me as the sort of person who would be affected by your siblings' success. You always come across as confident in your own skin.'

He glanced at her. 'We all have our crosses to bear, don't we? Now you, I bet you went to Cambridge.'

'Why do you say that?'

'Well, you obviously don't know this town, but you still have that Oxbridge thing, that inner confidence they all seem to come out glowing with.'

'I can see you haven't quite lost your dislike of the place,' laughed Rachel. 'Anyway, I didn't go to Cambridge. I was offered a place actually, but I turned it down.'

Adam laughed. 'I never believe people who say they turned down Oxbridge. It's a bit like "I could have been the lead singer in U2, but I left the band to concentrate on gardening."'

Rachel giggled. 'Well *I* did, but my heart was set on London – that was where everything seemed to be happening. Not that I could really afford to study anywhere.' She stopped short of saying 'not like some people who have everything laid out for them by their rich parents'; she couldn't really blame Adam for the accident of having been born a Denver. 'I got a job in the Green Room restaurant in Soho to pay the rent. Actually, that's how I got into journalism.'

'How come?'

She pulled a face. Nowadays she wasn't exactly proud of her

behaviour. The restaurant on Dean Street had been at the centre of the mid-nineties Cool Britannia surge, its tables and bars buzzing with celebrities and hedonists, and she had paid attention: who was snogging who, who was popping off to the toilets every five minutes, who had spent a year's wages on vintage champagne and had to be poured into a taxi. A lot of the staff made a few quid on the side ringing it in, tipping off the tabloids, but Rachel had taken it one step further and had actually written up the stories, taken photos on the sly.

'It's a long story,' she said.

'Ah, well, that's perfect timing,' he said, leading her down a side street and out into a wide cobbled square.

'Bloody hell!' gasped Rachel. 'What's that?'

In front of them was a tall domed building standing right in the centre of the square. That was impressive enough, as were the many arches and pillars covering it, but the most arresting thing about the building was the fact that it was entirely circular.

'That is the Radcliffe Camera,' said Adam. 'It's actually part of the Bodleian Library, one of the oldest in the world.'

'It's like an enormous stone cake,' said Rachel. 'And I mean that as a compliment.'

Adam smiled. 'That's the Palladian style, actually. The building was started in 1737. There are over half a million books in there and in rooms underneath the square.'

Rachel gave him a sideways look. 'Are you sure you're not academic?'

They sat down at a table outside a café to the side of the square and Adam went inside for a jug of Pimm's. They watched as the last of the light slid across the square and up the yellow walls of All Souls College, and Rachel told the story of her arrival in London and her climb up the rickety ladder of Fleet Street, then Adam told her how he'd ended up as head of the hotel division.

'I've always preferred hotels to houses. I suppose it's because we spent so much time in them as children and they seemed to be magical places – like ice-cream sundaes could just appear in your room, or if you wanted a book, they'd go out and get you one.' He raised one eyebrow. 'Well, they would when we were staying in them, anyway.'

He looked over at the library.

'I went to art college for a year. Mum and Dad didn't know what to do with me. Thought I needed a bit of time to mature before I started working for the company. I got hooked on architecture: I loved the idea of design for living, that form could also have function. And to me, hotels seemed to be the epitome of that. They were pleasure palaces, constructed entirely with a single purpose: to service the guest.'

'I had no idea you were such an idealist, Adam Denver.'

They left the café and wandered out into the winding streets of Oxford, just enjoying the warm evening, the yellow light spilling from Dickensian pubs and restaurants on to the worn flagstones of the pavements. It was impossible not to get caught up in the romance of it all, and Rachel found herself stealing a glance here and there at her companion. He was handsome, that went without saying, but he seemed to be surprisingly sensitive too. Some people just didn't fit the stereotype.

As they passed another equally impressive circular building, this one surrounded by railings upon which the heads of stone giants appeared to be impaled, Rachel could see a crowd gathered.

'What's going on here?' she said, tugging at Adam's arm. 'Let's go and see.'

As they approached, she could see it was a walking ghost tour. The guide was dressed as an undertaker in a long black coat and a top hat. His skin looked pale – Rachel suspected artificially so, as was the voice, which was a Christopher Lee-type baritone. They paid their money and joined the back of the group, following it through dark narrow back streets and passageways.

'This is actually quite creepy,' she whispered, as they stopped by a college gate to listen to a story about a spectre who had risen from the chapel grounds.

'I thought you Fleet Street hacks were tough as nails,' Adam hissed back.

'*Ex*-Fleet Street hack, remember?'

She was making light of it, but as the tales of murders and torture continued, she became increasingly uneasy and nudged Adam.

'I'm not sure I want to be here any more.'

She didn't mention Julian, but she didn't have to. Adam simply nodded and they drifted away from the pack, back towards the main drag.

'I feel a bit stupid,' she said sheepishly.

'Don't be silly,' he replied. He took her hand and wrapped his arm around hers, a gesture more of reassurance and solidarity than intimacy. 'Listen, you came here to find out why Julian killed himself; it's only natural that it's going to get to you after a while.'

'I know, I just feel like an idiot getting freaked out by a man in a top hat.'

He glanced across at her. 'D'you want to talk about it? The investigation, I mean? It must be hard having to keep it all to yourself.'

'Not tonight,' she said softly.

'In which case. Can you smell that?'

Rachel sniffed the air. 'Fish and chips!'

Adam grinned impishly. 'I will if you will,' he said.

'Only if they have mushy peas.'

They each bought cod and chips and walked back up the road, eating as they went.

'I'd have had you down as a health freak,' said Rachel.

'Me? I'd better have a stern word with my PR.'

Rachel giggled. 'Why didn't we do this sooner?' she said.

'Do what? Eat chips?'

'No, spend time together, get on as friends.'

'I always got the impression you thought I was a knob,' grinned Adam.

'You *are* a knob,' she laughed, throwing a chip at him. 'Just not a total knob.'

He looked at her for a long moment. 'Come on,' he said, taking her hand. 'I want to show you something.'

He led her through a maze of back streets until Rachel had completely lost her sense of direction.

'Adam, where *are* you taking me?'

He stopped outside a honey-stone building with a crest carved over the door. 'Here.'

'What's this? Whose is it?'

380

He took a set of keys out of his pocket and jangled them. 'Mine.'

'Yours?'

'Well, the company's. Oxford has a huge tourist industry but very few hotels actually in the town centre.'

Rachel looked up dubiously at the dusty windows. 'It's a hotel?'

'No, not yet. The lawyers tell me that it won't be too difficult to get the planning permission, but I'm still a bit nervous.'

'You? Nervous?' She smiled.

'Come on, I want to show you inside,' he said, rattling a key into the lock and opening the door.

Rachel had been expecting something grand, like most other hotels she'd seen, but it was just a normal hallway.

'You're disappointed,' said Adam.

'No, actually. I quite like that it could just be a house from the street and then you open the door and – it is. Like it's your home away from home.'

'No ordinary home, though,' he said, leading her down the corridor, past what looked like a cosy drawing room and up to a wooden door. 'What do you think?'

'You should be asking Diana. She's the one with the interior designer's eye.'

Adam ignored her and opened the door.

'Oh wow,' said Rachel.

It was an old library, with floor-to-ceiling polished wooden shelves, some still stacked with books, and brass-handled ladders on castors for reaching the topmost shelves.

'What is this place? I mean, what was it?'

'A private museum,' said Adam. 'One of those Victorian gentlemen who brought things back from his travels. Things like this, actually.'

He gently turned her by the shoulders and Rachel was brought face to face with a full-sized stuffed bear. She let out a little shriek.

'Wimp,' he laughed, and she swatted his arm.

They walked through the maze of rooms, each one with a feature of interest – a Zulu shield and spear, an alabaster sculpture of a winged horse, a polished fossilised shell the size of a chair. Adam explained that he was planning on using the artefacts to decorate the rooms in the finished hotel, and his eyes lit up as he discussed it.

'So you like it?' he asked.

'I love it. I'd stay here in a heartbeat. How many bedrooms has it got?' she asked before stopping herself. *Jesus, Rachel!* she thought, flushing. *What the hell are you doing asking him about bedrooms?*

'I reckon we could get thirty-five bedrooms out of it, and one penthouse.'

'Penthouse?'

'Follow me,' he said, taking her hand. He pushed at an open door with his toe and it creaked back on its hinges.

'What are you doing?' Rachel said nervously. She could just make out the inside of the room; it was a dark, intimate space, crowded with boxes.

'This was the curator's quarters,' he whispered, as if he feared waking up the old chap's ghost. 'This way.'

Without letting go of her hand, he led Rachel up a winding iron spiral staircase.

'Isn't this wonderful?' he said. There was no other word to describe it. They were standing on a circular gallery, a sort of mezzanine looking down on the rest of the quarters, and above them was a glass dome through which they could see a dark expanse of star-spangled sky.

'It's . . . beautiful,' she whispered, her head tilted back. 'Truly.'

He was standing behind her and she could feel his breath on her neck. He stroked her hair and it felt as if his fingertips had seared her skin. She moaned softly, a voice in her head willing her to turn around, a thought that thrilled and exhilarated her, but his hands were already on her, doing it for her. And when they were face to face, he took the final step forward and kissed her softly, tenderly.

She could almost hear herself purring with pleasure.

As their kisses got deeper, he pushed her against the wall. 'Why have we never done this before?' she said between short, desperate gasps.

'You've always been a very tricky customer,' he murmured.

'I'll show you tricky,' she whispered, finding this game, this banter the most natural and easy thing in the world.

His lips brushed down her neck whilst his hands pulled up her short cotton sundress, exposing her thighs and her knickers. He pushed himself against her, and she felt his hardness, reminding her that he had nothing on beneath the denim. Smiling slowly, she undid the button of his jeans and teased the zip down slowly. His cock sprang free and she sank down to meet it. He groaned with pleasure as she took him in her mouth, her hand guiding him in and out.

She stood up, leaving him hungry for more, and he cupped her face and kissed her deeply, pulling at her lips, probing his tongue into her mouth. Rachel reached around him, pulling him in tighter, running her fingers up through his hair. She wanted him. She wanted him more than anything.

'Please,' she growled as her phone began to ring.

'Don't answer it,' he mumbled, pushing the thin spaghetti strap of her dress off her shoulder.

She had no intention of answering it right now, she wanted to turn it off. But as she pulled it out, the phone slipped from her grasp and clattered down on to the iron walkway.

'Bugger,' she muttered, bending to retrieve it and bashing her head against his.

'I'll get it,' he said, rubbing his forehead, but in the confusion Rachel kicked the mobile and it bounced down the stairs, end over end, still ringing, then hit what sounded like a plate at the bottom.

'Shit!' she cried, chasing down after it.

'Rachel, don't . . .' called Adam, but she was already retrieving it from a pile of shattered pottery.

'Bills' read the caller ID. Rachel frowned and stabbed at the 'speak' button. What was Diana's housekeeper doing calling her at this time? In fact, what was she doing calling her at all? Rachel only had her number in her phone because Diana had been paranoid about prowlers in the grounds at night and insisted that everyone should have everyone else's numbers.

'Mrs Bills? Is that you?' said Rachel, raising the phone to her ear. She could hear Adam's frustrated groan from directly above.

'Yes, Miss Rachel, it is me. I had to call, I'm sorry, but it was an emergency . . .'

The woman began to sob, and Rachel immediately felt her stomach turn over. Had the prowlers finally come?

'Calm down,' she said, trying to keep her voice steady. 'Tell me what's happened. Where are you?'

'I'm in the hospital; the ambulance brought me here with Miss Diana.'

'Ambulance?' she repeated dumbly, looking up towards Adam. 'What's wrong?'

'It's Diana, she had a fall. A bad fall, she hit her head. Oh Lord, there was blood everywhere!' The housekeeper began to cry again.

'Okay, Mrs Bills, I'll get there as soon as I can. But is Diana all right? Is it bad?'

There was a pause, and Rachel held her breath, crossing her fingers as she did. *Please, please, please*, she thought, *not another one, please.*

'I think she will be okay, just a few stitches,' said Mrs Bills, then her voice went quieter, as if she was worried about being overheard. 'But the baby, Miss Rachel,' she said. 'Diana only wants you to know, but they think she might lose the baby.'

56

Diana was aware of people in the room before she even opened her eyes.

'Charlie?' she said, turning towards the figure at the side of the bed. She winced as her eyes opened; the light was so bright, and even that small movement made everything ache.

'Not Charlie, love. He's still at his friend's,' said Mrs Bills, putting a concerned hand on her forearm. 'Thought it was best we didn't tell him until we know what's happening. Your mum is on her way over here from London, though.'

'Rach, is that you?' It was all coming back to her now. Rachel and Adam in the lake, the car disappearing from view, the email, the rush down the stairs . . . 'I fell?'

Rachel came to the side of the bed, crouching down and holding her sister's thin hand.

'Only landed on your head,' she smiled, 'so nothing vital anyway. Mrs Bills called the ambulance straight away and they brought you here. You've got concussion, some stitches . . .'

Diana reached up to touch the dressing on her head. It felt huge.

'Don't worry, only five stitches,' whispered Rachel. 'And just inside the hairline, so no one will see.'

Mrs Bills slipped discreetly out of the room and closed the door.

'Di, Mrs Bills said you might have lost the baby.' There was a concerned crease between Rachel's eyebrows. It was the first time Diana had seen her sister look anything but vibrant and youthful. 'I don't understand,' she said softly.

'I'm pregnant, Rach. I was. We just have to wait for the scan . . .'

Rachel gasped and drew a hand to her chest. Her eyes pooled with tears and Diana knew she could tell her no more. Not yet.

She could remember the rest of the evening now: talking to the nurse, the guilty, whispered confession that she was pregnant. She knew that she had to break her silence, even though a part of her wanted to keep it hidden, wanted to brush it under the carpet. And then the added panic when Mrs Bills told her that she had called everyone to inform them about the fall, even Ralph and Barbara Denver, who were at their villa in Provence and were chartering a plane to get here as they spoke.

'Where were you this evening?' she began haltingly. 'I saw you at the lake with Adam.'

She watched Rachel colour, ever so slightly.

'It was just a silly bit of kids' stuff, jumping into the lake, then we went into Oxford for a drink.'

'Is there anything going on between you?' she asked finally. She gripped the edge of her sheets, not wanting to hear the answer, not wanting to look her sister in the eye as she replied.

Rachel hesitated. 'Don't be daft, he's just a friend.'

Diana felt her body relax and reached for her sister's hand, not wanting to think too hard about whether she believed her or not.

'Good. I mean, I'm relieved, because I need to tell you something about Adam.'

57

She found Adam in the waiting room, where he was feeding coins into a machine to retrieve a plastic cup of coffee.

He jumped when he saw Rachel coming towards him.

'How is she?' he asked, looking genuinely concerned. 'I was just coming up . . .'

'You are not going to see her,' said Rachel, jabbing her finger in his face.

Coffee spilled on to his T-shirt. He looked completely bewildered and put down the cup before he spoke.

'What the hell is going on, Rachel? Is everything all right?'

'It will be. But first I want you to tell me everything you know about Julian and Rheladrex.'

'Bloody hell, Rachel, can't you just forget about Rheladrex for one evening?'

'Why do you think Diana is in hospital?' she asked, glaring at him. She didn't stop to let him answer the question. 'She found out about you. She was coming to phone me and she fell down the stairs.'

'Found what out about me?' he said, flicking the coffee drops off his T-shirt.

'Julian's report on Rheladrex,' said Rachel simply, watching his reaction carefully. A tiny widening of the eyes, then a rapid recovery of his studied cool. 'You knew about it, didn't you? You read the report.' She could barely speak. She didn't know which was trembling more, her hand, which was curled into a fist, or her voice.

'That's how you knew she was called Maddison. Double D, and I don't mean her cup size.'

'What are you talking about?'

'Don't you dare deny it, Adam. You asked Simon Michaels if he had heard of Maddison Kopek. But you knew all about her before Diana and I ever told you anything. Julian had got there first. He told you what was up with Rheladrex, showed you the report, and yet you pretended you knew nothing about the drug, the tests or her death.' She squeezed her eyes tightly closed, not wanting it to be true.

Adam looked down at a point on the floor, unsmiling, not speaking.

'Julian showed me the report, yes,' he replied softly. Rachel hadn't thought he would admit it so readily. 'He was confused. He didn't know who to talk to about it, said he needed someone impartial. Of course, he thought that person might be me. I mean, what do I have to do with the company? What do I care whether it succeeds or fails, right?' His sarcasm was obvious.

'And what did you tell him?'

'I told him to sit tight,' replied Adam more evenly. 'Not to do anything rash. Certainly I didn't want him to pull Rheladrex off the market. It would have been madness. Do you know how much a successful sale of the company would have netted us? I'm family, I loved Julian, but I'm also a shareholder. We can't have the CEO being so cavalier with the company's interests.'

'So what did you do? Kill him?'

'What?' said Adam, incredulous. 'I wouldn't kill my own brother.'

'How do we know that?'

'I knew this would happen,' he said, looking towards the ceiling. 'I knew our paranoid family hack would let this run out of control. I knew she would go seeing things where there was nothing to see, cause more trouble within the family . . .'

'Is that why you've been keeping tabs on me, Adam? Come to Jersey, come dancing, come to Oxford, share your burden with me. You just wanted to know what I knew, what I had discovered in the investigation. I can't believe I was so gullible.' *And I can't believe I almost had sex with you*, she added to herself. She just wanted to shower, to scrub him off her. She could still taste him in her mouth, feel his sweat on her hands, see a tiny spot of her lipstick on his ear lobe.

'Rachel, don't be ridiculous,' he said, stepping forward. 'What happened in Oxford happened because I like you, because I'm attracted to you.'

'Save it,' she snapped. 'They *are* right about you. What they say in the papers, in the Denver boardroom. You are the playboy brother; it is all a game to you. And you're everything a player should be: charming, handsome – and weak.' She spat out the last word.

'See it from my point of view, Rachel,' he said, his voice pleading.

'Oh, I do, Adam. I really do. And it isn't pretty.'

She willed herself to think. Of course it looked bad that Adam had known all about Rheladrex. And whilst she could believe that his greed and his warped morals had made him want to stop Julian from pulling the drug off the market, he had neither the cold-heartedness nor the balls to do anything about it.

'Just tell me: who else knows about the report?'

She knew the answer even before he had said it.

'I gave a copy to Elizabeth,' he said sheepishly. 'She is in line to be CEO after all. She needs to know, she needs to be up to speed on all this if legal action starts against Rheladrex.' He looked at Rachel curiously. 'What's wrong? Why shouldn't I have told Elizabeth?'

She felt cold with fear. Images were flashing on to her retinas. Julian. Elizabeth. A coffin. Elizabeth sitting in the boss's chair with a wintry, triumphant smile.

Adam grabbed her shoulders and shook her as if she were in a trance.

'Rachel, tell me. What's wrong?'

She shrugged him away violently. 'Just go,' she said, putting her hands up in front of her, wanting to block him out of sight.

'All I did was read the report. All I did was tell Liz.'

'That's all,' she said quietly, feeling so out of her depth, she thought she was about to drown.

58

Diana gripped her mother's hand and looked anxiously at the blank screen to the side of her bed.

'Just relax, my love,' said the nurse as the sonographer busied herself with the equipment. 'You won't feel a thing and it will only take a few minutes.'

'It's going to be okay,' said Sylvia, looking as nervous as her daughter felt.

As the technician inserted a wand-type instrument inside her, anxiety gripped Diana so severely she could hardly draw breath, but suddenly grainy black-and-white images began to appear on the little monitor.

'Is that it?' Diana whispered, although she couldn't make anything out.

'No, not yet,' said the woman distractedly. 'Just need to get our bearings.'

The door of the examining room opened, and Diana could see Rachel peering into the room. She locked eyes with her sister. There was so much at stake, so many questions, so many answers she didn't want to hear.

'There we go,' said the sonographer. 'I can see it. Just do a quick check of everything, take a few little measurements . . .'

She could feel Rachel by her side, stroking her shoulder. The sonographer looked up and smiled.

'Would you like to see?'

Diana nodded. Her heart was thumping so hard, she wasn't sure if the noise was coming from her own chest or the medical equipment. The woman turned the monitor towards her and then clicked a button, freezing the image in the centre of the screen.

'See here?' she said, pointing with her pen. 'Can you see the curve of the spine? And here, the shape of the head?'

Diana gasped. She could – and were those tiny legs? The woman clicked the button and the picture started moving again. 'Can you see baby moving?' she said. 'And right in the middle, there's the heart beating.'

'The heart?' croaked Diana. *Her baby?* 'So . . . so what does that mean? It's an actual baby? It's all right?'

The sonographer laughed. 'Yes, an actual baby. And as far as we can tell, it wasn't at all hurt by your fall; it looks completely healthy.'

Diana squeezed her eyes closed and willed herself to connect with Julian. His soul, his spirit. She just wanted to say sorry. Sorry that she couldn't have given him his own child; sorry that she had conceived with his brother.

'I'd say you were about eight weeks,' said the sonographer more slowly.

'Eight weeks?' whispered Diana, snapping her eyes back open. 'Are you sure?'

'You can't tell too much from early scans. But I would say around eight or nine weeks, yes.'

She was eight weeks pregnant.

She shook her head in disbelief. She counted back the weeks, working out the approximate time of conception. A moment flashed into her head, although it felt so long ago it was as if it belonged to another lifetime. It had been a matter of days before his death. Julian had come back from London, slipped into bed and had initiated sex. It had been painful, uncomfortable, and she had been certain that he hadn't come inside her. But obviously it had been more successful than she'd thought. She started to tremble, fat tears clouding her vision.

She covered her face and began to bawl. 'It's his,' she sobbed. 'The baby's his.'

It wasn't Adam's baby. It was Julian's. He was alive. Julian was alive, and he was inside her.

59

Rachel looked around the Admiral Nelson pub in Victoria and decided it was quite appropriate that she should be here. It was an authentic copper's pub that sold a decent pint of draught bitter and had scampi fries and pork scratchings behind the bar, an almost extinct type of watering hole; *the Last Chance Saloon*, she told herself ruefully as she waited for Inspector Mark Graham to arrive.

The past few days had gone by in a blur. Rachel had moved her stuff up from the Lake House to Somerfold and had tried to share Diana's bittersweet joy about her pregnancy. Realising how difficult it must be for Diana anticipating the arrival of a child who would never know its father, her priority was to support her sister. But despite her fears that Diana might fall to pieces, Rachel had instead witnessed a surprising show of strength, a renewed sense of purpose that she herself was sadly lacking.

Rachel knew why she felt so helpless and defeated. There was no end in sight, no light at the end of the tunnel. She had discovered that Julian had been having an affair and had wanted to withdraw a controversial drug from the market. But she was still no clearer about whether those two things had anything to do with his death – or nothing at all.

The plane ticket to Thailand that Liam had given her felt as if it was glowing with temptation. The flight departed in less than forty-eight hours. If she wasn't on it, would she ever go back to Ko Tao, she wondered, or would she be stuck in London chasing her tail, like a lost soul trapped in the underworld, as everyone else, even Diana, moved on?

'To what do I owe this pleasure?' asked Graham, sitting down on the banquette next to her and disturbing her thoughts. 'You've got ten minutes.'

'You don't mess around, do you?' said Rachel, watching him compose a text message.

Graham looked up and smiled at her. 'Listen, I have a wife and four kids to get back to and I'll catch earache off all of them if I'm home a minute later than I have to be.'

'Then I'll be quick. I need you to interview Elizabeth Denver.' Rachel sipped her Diet Coke and observed the policeman.

Graham put down his phone and frowned. 'I've already spoken to Elizabeth Denver.'

'And what did she say?' she asked, searching his face for some sort of clue to how his investigation was going.

'Wait for the inquest,' he replied flatly.

'Look, you were right about me. I've been looking into this myself . . .'

'You surprise me,' he said sarcastically as he unfastened a couple of buttons on his suit jacket.

She didn't want to tell him about Julian's affair with Madison Kopek, but she knew she had to give him something to keep him interested. There was no one thing that pointed directly to Elizabeth's involvement in her brother's death. If this was a story, if she was presenting it before the editor and the newspaper's legal team, she would have nothing concrete to show them. But Elizabeth had been ruthless enough to destroy her brother once, and Rachel just knew that she was capable of doing it, more efficiently, more literally, again.

'Julian was looking into a new drug produced by Denver's pharmaceutical division when he died. He wanted to pull it off the market and it's my belief that there were people in the company who didn't want that to happen.'

'Like who?'

'Like his sister, Elizabeth Denver. She knew all about his plans. She is a big shareholder in Denver, with ambitions for the top job, and she won't have been happy about it. Pulling the drug would have had serious repercussions for the potential sale price of the pharmaceutical division, which would then impact on the share price of the company.'

She stopped, reminding herself of Albert Einstein's definition of insanity: doing the same thing over and over and expecting different results. It was something that now struck a chord. However many times she voiced her fears about Rheladrex, there was no guarantee that it would bring her any nearer to finding out the truth about Julian's death. As Liam had pointed out, she was beginning to sound like a fantasist.

'Look,' she said more reasonably. 'I know that no one could have got into Julian's house that night. I get that it was probably suicide. But I just don't trust Elizabeth Denver and I can't help thinking that she was involved in this. Have you been through her emails, her phone records?'

'Looking for what?'

'Elizabeth wanted Julian out of the picture. There are ways to have that done.'

'You think she killed him? Or had him killed? Is that what you're saying?' said Graham incredulously.

'I don't know. I don't know anything any more,' she said, throwing her hands in the air.

'Have you thought about seeing someone about this?'

'Yes! You,' she said, sitting more upright. 'I mean, Elizabeth won't speak to me. I've called her a dozen times, and each time it's gone to voicemail.'

Understandable, she thought. The last time she had seen Elizabeth Denver was when she had blackmailed her to stop her contesting Julian's will.

'But you can do something. You can speak to her in an official capacity. You should also confirm cause of death with the pathologist who did Julian's post-mortem. You said yourself a murder could be dressed up as suicide. It would just have to be a professional who did it and Elizabeth Denver has the power, the resources to order that. I mean, what if an assassin came down the chimney or something . . .'

'I mean speak to a therapist,' said Graham slowly.

She hesitated in disbelief. 'Me? See a therapist?'

Graham nodded. 'Just because Julian was not direct family doesn't mean to say you are not grieving. I know you had quite a complicated relationship with your brother-in-law,' he said diplomatically. 'Because of it you are probably trying to work through a lot of emotions, a lot of guilt. I understand how this is a difficult time for you. I understand that letting go is hard.'

'I don't believe it,' she whispered.

Inspector Graham looked at her sympathetically. She knew she looked a mess. She hadn't washed her hair since the lake swim with Adam Denver, she had an angry red spot on her chin and her jeans hadn't been cleaned in a week. She had never been one for high levels of personal grooming – the last time she had had a professional blow-dry had been for Diana's wedding – but she knew there was no excuse for her tramp-like appearance. No wonder Graham thought she was crazy.

'Forget it,' she said, holding up her hand. 'You've got a wife and four kids to get back to, I know. Just go.'

'Rachel, please. I know you're trying to help.'

'I have to leave,' she said, getting up.

She left the pub, regretting her impulsiveness almost immediately. She shoved her hands into her jeans pockets and started walking down the street. It was getting dark and there was a chill in the air. The roads were jammed, the bus lanes clogged with traffic, but despite the noise, London seemed cavernous and lonely. She quickened her pace, glad that she had checked herself into a hotel in Victoria, glad that she didn't have to trek all the way back to Somerfold.

She was running out of options, she thought miserably. Rachel Miller had never been somebody who liked to fail at anything. Looking back at her childhood, she knew it was the real reason she had given up competitive swimming. Boys and a social life had just been a convenient excuse. She had given up because she was never going to be the best and she had known when and how to bow out gracefully.

She was in the hotel lobby when her mobile rang.

Liam's name flashed up on caller ID and her heart galloped. She hadn't wanted to admit to herself how much she was missing him. Hadn't wanted to admit that his departure, his rejection of her had in some way contributed to her sexual misadventures with Adam. At least that was what she had been telling herself.

'Liam,' she said with surprise. It was a moment before she

worked out that it was almost 3 a.m. in Thailand, and the thought unsettled her immediately. 'Is everything okay? It's late.'

'I couldn't sleep.'

Her pulse beat with hope. Had he been lying in bed thinking about her?

There was a lag on the line.

'So I looked through the security tape you asked me to.'

'Oh.' She wasn't sure if she was disappointed or flattered.

'Something struck me as odd.'

She reverted instantly to business mode. Suddenly she wasn't thinking about Liam in bed, but sitting in front of a computer screen, wearing his intelligent black-framed glasses, his sharp brain in full throttle.

'Did you find anything? On the footage, I mean?'

'There was a lot of it.'

'You've been through it all?' she said with surprise.

'I've had bad jet lag.'

'I'd say it was a fairly good cure for insomnia.'

'So you've been through it too?'

'Yes,' she confirmed.

'And you were looking for someone coming into the house.'

'To see if it was foul play, yeah.'

'I just wondered if we were looking at this from the wrong angle.' He paused before he spoke again. 'What if no one came in?'

'I don't understand.' Rachel frowned.

'What if someone was already in the house?'

'You mean the catering team?' replied Rachel. 'I've already asked Diana about them. She was horrified at the thought that they could have had anything to do with it. The owner is a good friend of hers. She'd used them many times before.'

'I don't mean the caterers, Rach,' said Liam. 'I mean the guests.'

'The *guests*?'

'I know it sounds crazy, but just hear me out. Are you near a computer?'

'I'm at a hotel. I'll just go to my room.'

She ran up the stairs, pushed her key card into the room lock and went inside. She flipped open her laptop and logged into her mail.

'I'm sending something through now.'

A few seconds later there was a ping.

'Okay,' said Rachel into the phone, clicking on his message. 'I'm opening the file.'

Immediately she could see a grainy screen-grab from the footage. It was time-stamped 19:48 and was a reasonably clear picture of an attractive blonde woman.

'Do you know who that was?' asked Liam.

'I've never met her, but I identified all the guests with Diana. The blonde came with Greg Willets.'

'Well, she never left the party.'

'Never left?'

'I've looked at everyone coming in and cross-referenced them with everyone leaving. Everyone who came in also left. With the exception of Greg's girlfriend.'

Rachel cursed herself for not having looked at the footage that way.

'Are you sure?' she said, scrabbling through her bag to see if she had her own copy.

'Pretty sure. I've been through the relevant bits a couple of times now. I've ticked all the guests in and out – and I can't see this woman leaving the house. Her partner, Greg, left at about a quarter to twelve, when most guests seem to go.'

The disc was in her bag. She pushed it into the laptop and it whirred to life.

'I'm going to go and look at it now. Thanks, Liam. Thank you, so much.'

There was a long silence. It was as if he was about to say something and then stopped himself.

'What?' she asked quietly.

'Just show it to the police and come home.'

'You know I can't do that.'

'Rachel, I'm not messing about here. Will you please fucking come home.'

She rarely heard him swear and it shocked her.

'I can't. Not yet,' she said, feeling tears well up in her eyes.

'I didn't think so,' he said, his voice softening again.

Another long lag.

'Are you alone?'

'Of course I am.'

'Right then—'

'How's things? How's Sheryl?'

'We're all busy.'

'You should get a good night's sleep then.'

'Good night, Rach.'

'Good night, Liam.'

She ended the call, and bit her lip so hard it drew blood.

'Darling, how are you?'

Patty Reynolds breezed through the door of Somerfold like a rainbow. Her smile was a broad red slash of lipstick, her hair was freshly highlighted, her green dress Diana recognised as one of Erdem's most beautiful summer numbers.

'All the better for seeing you,' said Diana, feeling suddenly dowdy in her cashmere jogging bottoms and white T-shirt. 'Where's Michael?'

'Just finishing up a call outside. Here he is now.'

Michael came through the front door, his round face beaming. He embraced her, his soft arms wrapping her into a friendly hug. Just being in the Reynoldses' presence made Diana feel safe and warm.

'Come on, come through. Mrs Bills has made supper,' she said as her friends followed her to the kitchen.

The farmhouse table was set beautifully, and a shepherd's pie was bubbling in an orange Le Creuset dish on a serving tray.

'Look at that,' said Patty, handing Mrs Bills the huge bunch of flowers she had brought with her. 'It's our calorie intake for the week.'

'I'm eating for two now, remember,' said Diana with a grin.

She saw Patty's eyes cloud with joyful tears.

'Now then, I've had a doctor friend of mine prepare a document for you,' Patty said, reaching into her large leather tote. 'It's a list of five of the world's top obstetricians, in London, Switzerland and New York. All of them specialise in identifying

398

early-stage pregnancy problems. We are not taking any chances with this baby. I know there's no real link between stress and miscarriage, but even so, I have suggested to Michael that you stay with us for a while.'

'I can't go to Switzerland for an obstetrician's appointment,' smiled Diana.

'Then they can come to you,' Patty said flatly.

'Let's not talk about it this evening,' Diana replied gratefully. She wished that Patty the Powerhouse had been around more in the last few weeks. Perhaps she would have helped her make fewer bad decisions and wrong turns. She thought of Adam and puffed out her cheeks. She didn't want to see him again, but he was still family and they had to talk it over, clear the air. He had been the first one to send flowers when he'd heard about the baby – no doubt when he had learnt that she was eight weeks gone. He had called twice; both times she had let it go to message, not knowing what on earth to say to him. When he had emailed her to suggest lunch, she had relented – she couldn't avoid him for ever – and he was due round the next day. It was not something she was looking forward to; perhaps she could persuade Patty and Michael to stay over and make the gathering more of a social occasion. She would make sure that Rachel stayed away from the house. She wanted company when Adam came round, not a *ménage à trois*.

It was an enjoyable supper. Michael especially was on top form and kept her distracted with stories about his eccentric circle of friends, who included a shark hunter, a hot-air balloonist and a beekeeper.

Over crème caramel, Patty leaned forward and broached the elephant at the table.

'So, are you going to tell me what your sister has been up to over the past few weeks? I saw Greg Willets for lunch today. Apparently the three of you went out for lunch to discuss Julian's *private* life.'

They hadn't mentioned him all evening. Sometimes she was just desperate to hear his name, but tonight it had been fun talking about the future rather than the past with people who had loved Julian as much as she had.

'I've been conducting my own private inquest into his death,' she said honestly.

'Is that why she called me the other day?' said Michael with surprise. 'She was asking all sorts of questions about Julian although she didn't really specify what it was all for. What have you discovered?'

'I discovered how much I love my sister,' she said quietly. 'I've discovered how much I've missed her, how proud I am of her, how I never want her not to be part of my life again. I discovered that you can't blame people and look back; you can only make amends and move forward.'

'I think that's sensible,' said Patty, nodding slowly. Her phone was buzzing furiously. Looking irritated, she picked it up and went into the hallway to take the call.

'Just let Jules rest,' said Michael quietly when she had gone.

'I know,' whispered Diana, and for the first time she actually believed that that was the right thing to do. Nothing Rachel had discovered would bring Julian back. But living as happily and without drama as she could might mean a better, quieter, safer life for herself, Charlie and the baby. Elizabeth Denver had even called her the previous day to ask about her welfare, to send her congratulations about the baby and to explain, quite guardedly, that the challenge to Julian's will had been a little bit hasty. She wasn't sure if things were finally going right, but at least they weren't all going wrong.

'So how was Greg?' she asked, dipping her spoon into the cold, wobbling custard.

'A little worried about business, I detected. Although he didn't admit that to me directly.'

'Really?'

'You know what investment banking is like, up one minute, down the next. Now that he hasn't got Julian around feeding him deals, feeding him business, I think he's worried whether his company will survive.'

'I thought Greg's company was doing well,' Diana said with concern. She knew very little about what Greg actually did. It was the same with all of Julian's friends in the world of finance – she didn't know a junk bond from James Bond. But from what

400

she understood, Greg's company was a boutique investment bank working on smaller deals than some of the more established players. He had worked hard establishing his business over the past five years, ever since his world came crashing down when he lost his high-flying job with Lehman Brothers. Like many of their alpha-male acquaintances, he was an ambitious man and would not take any more failure well. She made a mental note to go and see him in the next week or so. People needed protecting, even the ones who seemed as if they could look after themselves.

Patty bustled back into the room.

'So, who wants an Irish coffee?' said Diana.

'I'll make it,' said Michael. 'Without the whisky for you, young lady.'

'Why don't you stay over? Adam is coming for lunch tomorrow.'

'Oh, we can't,' said Patty with disappointment. 'Michael has a very early flight to Namibia, so we should get back. Are you all right by yourself here? I mean, where is Rachel?'

'She's in London, back tomorrow, I think. And yes, I'm fine. Mr and Mrs Bills have been wonderful and my mother is here more often than not. What are you going to Africa for, Michael?'

'Extreme sand-dune surfing,' he grinned.

'He couldn't find any hobbies closer to home,' said Patty, rolling her eyes.

'Not these dunes.'

'There's always an excuse, isn't there?' replied Patty sharply.

Diana frowned. It was not like her friends to bicker.

'You should come,' said Michael.

'Are you talking to me?' laughed Diana.

'You'd be hard pushed to find more spectacular scenery. It might be the break you need.'

'I'm pregnant,' she smiled, delighting at the word. 'I don't want to go dune surfing. But I know someone who might.'

'I hope you're not talking about me. I don't want to get sand-blasted in the name of fun,' said Patty more softly.

'No. My sister. She'd love it, and she needs a break after everything I've put her through.'

'Everything she's put *you* through,' said Patty, raising a brow.

'She doesn't belong in London; she belongs in places like Ko Tao and Namibia,' said Diana, remembering the first time she'd seen Rachel in Thailand, gleaming, relaxed and happy.

'What about Julian's investigation?' asked Patty.

'It's over,' said Diana quietly. 'It's time to move on.'

60

Rachel picked up the phone and ordered room service. The menu changed to a skeleton one after 11 p.m. and as she knew that it was going to be a long night, she ordered everything she fancied to keep her going as long as possible. A cheeseburger, a club sandwich, a Caesar salad, French fries, a milkshake, a pot of coffee and an interesting-looking 'trio of desserts' that sounded like something from one of Diana's dinner parties.

She blinked hard. Not only was she tired, but she had watched the footage of Greg Willets leaving again and again until it made her head spin. Perhaps there was a perfectly reasonable explanation for it. But what? She had fast-forwarded the footage from all three security cameras and it looked as if Liam was right. Greg's girlfriend had certainly not left with him. Nor was she seen leaving at any other time during the party. It was as if she had vanished into thin air.

Swigging at a glass of tap water, she opened her notebook and noticed that Greg's number was one of the first things she had written in it after their lunch meeting in the City. She picked up her mobile and debated whether to call him. But what was she supposed to say without it sounding like an accusation? No, she would go through the tapes one more time before she ruffled any more feathers. She had to think this through, think about what it all meant.

Greg's companion couldn't just have vanished. The security cameras were angled towards the doors of the property to monitor entrance and exit of guests, which meant that the blonde must either have slipped out undetected or had not left the house at all. She felt a cold shiver all over her body, recalling her meeting with Carl Kennedy in Notting Hill, remembering something he had said: *If it was foul play, then it must have been somebody already in the house.*

At the time she had shamelessly thought of Diana, but what if it was someone else? She felt suddenly nervous. She went to the loo and splashed water over her face. What did she really know about Greg Willets other than that he was Julian's best friend? They had met many times – holidayed even on trips to Ibiza and Tuscany. Then again, what did anyone really know about anybody else?

Think, she willed herself.

There was a knock at the door and she jumped. She peered through the spyhole, unchained and unbolted the door and opened it. A member of the hotel staff wheeled in a dumbwaiter laden with food. She tipped him generously, chained and bolted the door behind him and returned to her laptop.

There was no pithy Wikipedia entry for Greg Willets. Instead she had to do her own research. There were some details on LinkedIn, more still on financial newspapers and potted CVs from seminars he was appearing at around the globe. His company, Canopus Partners, was apparently a boutique investment bank, as opposed to a bulge bracket bank such as Goldman Sachs or J. P. Morgan. According to its own website it had a thirty-person team in London and a small outpost in New York. Greg Willets was listed as its founder, along with a brief history of his career and a flattering, unsmiling black-and-white photograph. There was a section listed 'News' which provided details of deals the firm had advised over the past twelve months, including an item about the Denver Group – selling their paint division to a German chemicals company for seventy-five million euros. A Companies House search was also revealing.

Greg Willets was successful. Everyone in their circle thought so. He had all the trimmings – a house in Chelsea, a place in Monaco and a vintage Ferrari, although he had won that off Julian in a poker game. And yet Canopus Partners did not look in particularly robust health, with current assets of under half a million pounds and heavy liabilities. Rachel was savvy enough to know that this was not particularly damning. Financial people were clever. Money was hidden offshore. She made a note to find out more about Greg Willets, but still, where would it lead?

His girlfriend had disappeared in the house. But did that mean Greg had had anything to do with Julian's death? If Julian had been murdered, his killer needed a motive. Certainly it seemed to benefit Greg to have his friend alive, so that he could throw business his company's way.

She went to the minibar and emptied it of all the miniature cans of Coke, pouring them into a tooth glass.

There was a notepad by the bedside cabinet. She tore off all the individual squares of paper and placed them around the table. On each square she wrote down a fact that she had learnt during her investigation. Julian wants to pull Rheladrex. Julian dies. Elizabeth Denver wants CEO job. Adam Denver sees Rheladrex report. Sale of Denver Chemicals going through. Julian helps Greg's business. Greg's girlfriend in the house?

'What's the motive?' she asked herself out loud, staring at the notes.

Two bits of paper stood out. The sale of Denver Chemicals, and Julian giving Greg business.

She flipped back to her laptop and reread the Canopus website. The list of their areas of expertise wasn't particularly narrow, but pharmaceuticals seemed to feature prominently. What if Julian had got Canopus to advise on the sale of Denver Chemicals? Alicia Dyer had said that her company was probably not in the running for the business, as Julian had his favoured bankers to deal with. Was that Greg Willets and Canopus? It was possible. Probable.

And if Julian *had* handed Greg the Denver sale, what did that mean? It meant a lot of money for Greg, that was for certain.

She sighed, crumpling up a ball of paper and throwing it in the bin in frustration. Her knowledge of the Denver Group and how these sorts of deal worked wasn't up to joining the dots. She needed to brainstorm with someone who knew more than her. But who? Elizabeth Denver? She'd know the answers to all of these things, and more. But Rachel didn't trust her. There was

Adam – but she didn't trust him as far as she could throw him either. And there was Greg himself.

She had only meant to close her eyes for a second, but when she awoke, there was a crack in the curtain and pale morning light poured through. Her head was resting on the table and dribble from her mouth had trickled on to her patchwork of notes. She blinked hard and sat up, shrugging back her shoulders and stretching her arms in front of her. It was almost eight o'clock. She was tired and stiff, but noticeably less anxious than she had been the previous night.

She looked at the damp spread of papers; they were still no clearer than they had been last night.

One thing she had learnt from her days on the newspaper was that she often had all the pieces she needed for her story; it was just a case of putting them together in the right way. And that was what had led her down an illegal path of phone- and email-hacking. The need to prove and connect the dots.

The prospect of speaking to Greg Willets was no more attractive than it had been the night before, although she knew she had to confront him at some point.

Who is smart and clever and knows about the Denvers? she asked herself, wondering if she should try Alicia Dyer one more time.

She flicked through her list of contacts, her finger stopping at two names she knew and respected. Patty and Michael Reynolds. Patty was known as one of the sharpest minds around. Michael was another of Julian's inner circle. Both were close friends of Greg and the Denvers. Both were financial whiz-kids.

She ordered some breakfast to wake her up – a full English, with a Virgin Bloody Mary with extra Tabasco sauce. By the time it had been delivered to her room and she'd wolfed it down, it was past nine, a perfectly respectable time to call even if it was a Saturday morning. Michael was usually the more jovial of the two, so she decided to try him first. She didn't know him well, although she had always liked him: his sense of humour, and his upper-crust English manners.

'Hello.'

'It's Rachel. Rachel Miller.'

'Hello, Rachel.' His voice lacked the frostiness of many of Julian's friends she had spoken to. His disapproval had been registered the first – and only – time they had spoken after she had arrived back in London. 'You're going to have to be quick. I'm on a plane. Just about to take off, in fact. Stewardess giving me rather dirty looks as we speak.'

'Do you know if Greg Willets was handling any deals for the Denver Group?' she said, jumping straight in.

'This isn't really the place to talk about things like that,' said Michael carefully.

'Just yes or no. Specifically the pharma division.'

'There was talk of that, yes,' he said, lowering his voice. 'I've got a small but significant shareholding in the company, as you probably know, so I've been keeping an eye on it all. Encouraged Jules to sell the division, in fact. Was Greg involved in the transaction? Possibly. Canopus have some expertise in that sector, although it would be an incredible coup to get the business.'

'Why do you say that?'

'A bank like Greg's handles deals up to a hundred million, maybe two hundred. The Denver Chemicals sale would be worth billions. The fees alone on a transaction that size could be fifty, sixty million. I dare say he could do with the business. I know it's somewhat fashionable to banker-bash, but it can be tough for some of those guys too,' he said.

Rachel suddenly had lots of questions.

'Darling, the stewardess is about to slap my wrists with a hot towel. I'd better hang up.'

'When do you land? I can speak to you then.'

'I'm flying to Namibia, so try me tomorrow.'

'Michael, please. Just five more minutes.'

'What do you want to know?' She could almost see him frowning.

'I want to know how M and A deals work.'

'Well we can't cover that in ten seconds. Why don't you speak to Patty? Do you have her number? She's driving down to Greenfields this morning. Give her a ring.'

He hung up. Slapped down by a hot towel perhaps, although

407

Rachel doubted very much that that happened to first-class passengers.

Patty's mobile number was in her book. She tried calling, but it went straight to message. No doubt Patty was still on the A3, heading south to their rural retreat. She should go and see her. Patty Reynolds was sharp as a whip but could be gossipy and indiscreet under the right circumstances – a face-to-face meeting was definitely better than a phone call. She couldn't recall the exact address but remembered its New Forest location, having wangled an invitation to Michael's fiftieth about five years ago, after they had all been in Tuscany together.

She grabbed a piece of cold toast and stuffed it into her mouth as she started to pack. Her phone beeped and she picked it up hoping it would be Patty returning her call, but it was just the device running out of juice. She sent a quick message to Diana to tell her where she was going, then switched off her phone to conserve the battery. She had to check out. She had to get going.

61

It was a grey and miserable day when Diana got out of bed and flung back the curtains. Although it was morning, swollen black clouds hovered over the grounds and the lonely-looking Lake House, making it seem like dusk. Diana watched as fat droplets of rain hit the window; it was the first storm she'd seen this summer, but she welcomed it. The lawn was beginning to brown, the earth crack, and a good downpour would clear away the muggy heat that made shirts and dresses stick to you. She heard a distant rumble and smiled. A few days earlier, she knew, she would have seen a sudden squall like this as a black omen and would have been plunged into a depression, but now? Well, nothing could get her down. She touched her hand to her belly, trying to remember how long it was before you felt that first kick. In previous pregnancies she would never have dared think such a thing; it was unlucky, tempting fate. But this time she had an overwhelming feeling of well-being, a premonition that everything was going to be fine with this baby. Julian's baby. Her child. How could that not make her smile?

She turned as her bedside telephone rang.

'Hello?'

There was a pause, then a slight echo of her own voice.

'Diana?' said a male voice. 'Is that Diana?'

'Yes. Who's this?'

The pause again.

She felt a growing sense of dread in the pit of her stomach, but at the same time, she wasn't panicking. She felt strong, in control. She could deal with this. Her hand slipped down to her belly again. She could deal with anything now.

'It's Liam. Liam Giles.'

'Liam,' she said with relief. 'How are you? Safe trip back to Thailand, I assume.'

'I'm trying to get in touch with Rachel,' he said without preamble. His voice contained the same anxiety she had felt a few moments earlier.

'She's in London. Have you tried calling her?'

'I spoke to her last night.'

'What's wrong?'

'Probably nothing,' he said. 'She's just not answering her phone.'

'It's still early. You know Rachel. Given the choice, she'd stay in bed till lunchtime, or have things changed that much?'

'I just hope she's not done anything stupid . . .'

Her smile vanished. He was starting to worry her.

'Tell me what's wrong, Liam.'

He waited before he spoke.

'She gave me a DVD of the CCTV footage from the night of the party before I left, and when I went through it, I noticed that one of the guests never left the party.'

'Never left the party?' she queried.

'I sent the footage to Rachel, and she identified the person as Greg Willets's guest.'

'Can you send the image to me?'

'Sure. Are you near a computer?'

There was an iPad on the dressing table. She switched it on, and within seconds she was looking at the picture that Liam had sent her.

'That's right. Her name was Eva,' said Diana, recognising her instantly. She had barely spoken to her all evening. She was blonde, foreign, with an incredible gym-toned body, and she had not seen her since. But then it wasn't unusual for Greg's girlfriends to be seen once or twice then never again.

'What are you thinking, Liam?'

'I just don't want Rachel going places alone. Not after what happened to Ross.'

'You mean we don't know who to trust?'

'I think you should get in touch with the officer in charge of the investigation. I think the police have missed this. And I don't want her seeing Greg, or anyone else for that matter, by herself. If you can't make that happen, I'm going to be on the next flight back from Thailand to bring her back home.'

'You love her, don't you?' she said softly.

'I won't ever let anything happen to her.'

'Don't worry. I'll look after her until she's back home with you, where she belongs.'

Liam's call had distracted her from Adam's arrival, but it had also given her another thing to feel unsettled about. She tried Rachel's mobile but like Liam was unable to get through.

The rain had faded to a gentle drizzle by the time Adam's Aston Martin pulled up at the front door. She was glad it wasn't blazing hot, glad that the weather didn't remind her of their day out in Dorset. How stupid she had been, she told herself. How could she have let herself be seduced like that?

She watched him jump out of the car, shocked by her lack of feeling as he approached. She thought about all the emotions he had dredged to the surface in New York. All that passion, desire and belonging. Had they ever really been there? Or had they just been a mirage, conjured up by her own sense of stupidity and loneliness?

'Hello, Di.' He kissed her lightly, awkwardly on the cheek. It was the first time she had seen Adam do anything awkwardly.

'I'm glad you came.'

'I didn't want things to be uncomfortable between us.'

'Neither do I.'

'I meant what I said in New York.'

Is that what you say to all the girls? Including my sister? she wanted to shout. But it wasn't worth it. As he said, they didn't want things to be uncomfortable between them. He was still part of her life; he was still going to be her baby's uncle. She didn't want to jeopardise that with insults and recriminations. Besides, she didn't blame him for being attracted to Rachel; not like Julian, who she could never forgive for what he had done.

'Adam, these are strange times, and perhaps things have happened that wouldn't happen under normal circumstances.'

411

The trace of a frown appeared between his brows, and it almost made her laugh. She had been expecting relief, but instead he looked mildly irritated.

'Absolutely. So you don't want to talk about it . . .'

She shook her head.

'Do you fancy going for a pub lunch? Or we could go to Dot's Bakery,' he said hopefully.

'Actually, I want to talk to you.'

Adam had the look of a man cornered. A reluctant boyfriend pressed into discussing the future by a partner who had not yet realised that their relationship had passed its sell-by date.

'Okay.' He shrugged, with an awkward smile. 'Let's grab some coffee.'

They walked into the conservatory, which was the brightest place in the house, even managing to capture some light despite the grey cloud cover.

'I wanted to talk to you about Greg Willets,' she said, before telling him everything that Liam had discussed with her.

When she had finished Adam looked confused.

'I don't understand why he thinks Rachel is in danger. Why he doesn't want her talking to Greg . . .'

'Rachel had a theory that someone might have killed Julian, you know that. She had the *why* – Rheladrex. She just couldn't work out how they would have got into the house.'

'Greg was his best friend,' said Adam with disbelief. 'They started off working for Denver on the same day; Dad got Greg a job, in fact. He'd come in for work experience during university and impressed everyone that much. He's a very good friend of the family, my dad, Elizabeth, a good friend of mine, in fact.'

'Why did he leave Denver?'

Adam shrugged. 'He was attracted to investment banking. Thought there was more money in it, I suppose, than being a salary man at Denver.' He shook his head. 'I don't believe it. Check the film again, I'm sure you'll find an explanation.'

'Did Greg have anything to gain from Julian's death? Last night Michael Reynolds said his business might be in trouble.'

'Diana, Greg just wouldn't do a thing like that.'

'One thing I've learnt over the past few weeks is that you never know what people are thinking,' said Diana softly.

'Elizabeth's the person to talk to,' he said finally. 'She knows more about business, Denver, investment banking than anyone.'

'Call her,' she ordered. 'I don't want my sister in any danger. For all we know, she could be on her way to see Greg Willets.'

'Stop being so dramatic.'

'I thought you cared about Rachel,' she said sharply.

He looked embarrassed, and she knew she had him.

'Don't worry, Adam, I know something happened between the two of you.'

'I didn't mean it to,' he said finally.

Confirmation of what she had suspected was like a punch in the stomach.

'Of course not. Have one sister, have them both.'

'Diana, please. I knew you were pissed off about New York. We should talk about it.'

'What is there to talk about? That you just can't keep your cock in your trousers? That you wanted to have something that Julian couldn't have? Not now, not then. His wife. His sister-in-law who had the guts to turn him down.'

She saw the flash in his eyes. The look of being caught out.

'That's it, isn't it? Thing is, you don't even realise it yourself. You probably thought you were attracted to me, to Rachel. But really it was all about you and your ego.'

Adam was shaking his head slowly.

'Don't worry. It doesn't matter. Save your explanation and just make the call to Elizabeth. At least this way you might be able to redeem yourself.'

He reluctantly picked up his phone and went to stand by the window. Whilst he was calling Elizabeth, Diana tried to ring Rachel again. She was still unable to get through, but she felt some relief that her sister had sent her a message to say that she was going to see Patty Reynolds. She texted her back asking her to contact her immediately.

62

Rachel had heard about microclimates, but this was ridiculous. London seemed to be in the grip of a summer storm, people holding newspapers as they sprinted for shelter, the rain sending spray into the air, the whole city brooding under dark clouds. But as she drove south-west along the A3, it was as if she were moving not just from the outer suburbs of London into Surrey and Hampshire, but from winter straight into summer. The sky ahead of her lightened, the clouds parted and bright blue sky poked through. She saw two rainbows in the space of half an hour and by the time she had arrived at the southern reaches of the New Forest, the sun was slanting through the trees, her car was dry and the Beaulieu river sparkled in the light.

There was no mistaking the Reynolds's place. On the outskirts of Beaulieu, it was set back off the main road, and she could see the slate roof of the Queen Anne manse gleaming in the sunshine even from a distance. The iron gates were open, so she drove straight towards the house, which loomed like the sort of place you'd only usually see in TV period dramas, surrounded by ladies in crinoline dresses.

There were no cars on the drive, and the doors of the quadruple garage adjacent to the property where Patty could have parked her car were closed. It was an awfully long way to come if no one was home, thought Rachel, looking around for signs of life.

She rang the bell and was relieved when Patty finally came to the door. Her ash-blond hair had been swept back off her face into a ponytail. She was wearing a short white Lacoste tennis dress, trainers and some sort of expensive wraparound sunglasses dangling on a lanyard. Rachel looked her up and down. Patty must have been pushing fifty, but her figure was still pretty sensational, only her slightly veiny hands giving away her age.

'Rachel Miller,' she said, looking startled. 'What on earth are you doing here?'

'I did call,' said Rachel, aware that she was intruding on the woman's day.

Patty wiped a bead of sweat off her brow with the palm of her hand.

'I haven't picked up my messages. I've been playing tennis. Everything's fine?' she asked with alarm. 'Diana is okay, I mean?'

Rachel nodded. 'She's fine. I just wanted to pick your brains about something. I spoke to Michael before he took off and he suggested I talk to you.'

'He did, did he? Determined not to give me a weekend's peace,' she said with annoyance.

'I'm sorry. If this is inconvenient, I can come back later.'

Patty hesitated, and then beckoned her inside.

'Don't be silly. You've come all this way.'

As Rachel stepped inside, she gave the place a 360-degree sweep of her gaze.

'I forgot how fantastic this place is. Through my sister I've seen a lot of nice places, but if I had to choose one, I think yours would be up there in my top three. It's truly . . . grand.'

'You came to Mike's fiftieth, didn't you? Disappeared with a member of the jazz band, if I remember correctly,' said Patty, taking a slug of water from an Evian bottle.

Rachel smiled thinly as she recalled that particular evening. She had been thrilled to wangle an invite to the Reynoldses' fancy party, but since she had known very few people there, she had ended up chatting to the drummer from the jazz band that had played after dinner. They had liberated a bottle of Dom Perignon from the catering supplies and played strip poker in the tennis pavilion, which had culminated in very vigorous and noisy sex that had apparently been overheard by some of the guests. He had gone on tour to Germany the following Monday and she had never heard from him since, but she could still remember the evening with hot embarrassment.

It was typical of Patty Reynolds to have remembered too.

415

'Well, thank you for your comments about the house,' said Patty more kindly. 'I still pinch myself whenever I wake up here.'

'Pinch yourself?'

'The house I grew up in was smaller than the garage,' she smiled.

'Really?' said Diana with surprise.

'I'm not from Julian or Michael's sort of background. Actually I think it was the making of me. I went to the sort of school that rewarded success in football and woodwork, not academic achievement, but I always used to tell myself that it didn't matter, because one day I would make my own money and buy a place by the sea.'

'Well, what a place.'

'You can see the Isle of Wight from our grounds; that was the only place my parents ever took me on holiday. I look at it now and remind myself how far I've come. Drink?'

'Diet Coke if you've got it.'

Patty produced an organic cola from her enormous Sub-Zero fridge.

'So what did you want to know?' She smiled, and Rachel felt more at ease. 'I assume this is about the investigation you've been doing into Julian's death. I wondered when it was my turn for a proper interrogation.'

'Can I be blunt?'

She smiled. 'We don't know each other well, Rachel, but well enough for you not to ask that question, surely.'

'I think there was a multi-million-dollar motive for Julian to be murdered.'

Patty didn't look surprised by her remark.

'You could probably say the same about any billionaire businessman found dead in unusual circumstances.'

'In the weeks before he died, Julian was about to pull a potential blockbuster drug off the market. Doing so would have devalued the market price of Denver Chemicals, which was for sale. It's still for sale; in fact the wheels are already in motion for finding a buyer.'

'So what do you want to know from me?' asked Patty, frowning.

'Do you know if Greg Willets's company Canopus was advising on the deal?'

She was silent.

'If you know anything, Patty, please tell me.'

'Probably,' she said after a moment.

Rachel began to speak her thought process out loud. 'And if Greg was handling the deal and the market value of the company suddenly plummeted, what would happen?'

The older woman shrugged. 'The sale price would be reduced or the whole thing might fall through.'

'And what happens to the investment bank in that situation?'

'They work on commission essentially. You can spend months on a deal and if it falls through – *nada*. So if anything went wrong with the Denver Chemicals deal, that would impact on Canopus's fee, which could run into tens of millions on a multi-billion-dollar transaction.'

'Ballpark on the investment banking fee with a blockbuster drug still on the market?'

'I heard they were after thirty to forty billion sale price. Commission fees around one per cent . . . You're talking thirty million.'

'That's a lot of money,' whistled Rachel. 'Would it have an impact in other ways?'

'It would catapult Canopus up the M and A table, that's for sure. They're quite a small outfit at the moment. A deal like this would push them into the elite bracket, and more business of that size and quality would undoubtedly come their way.'

It was all falling into place.

'What's this about, Rachel?' said Patty, her brows creasing with intrigue.

'I think Greg came to the party with Julian's killer.'

'What on earth are you talking about?'

'He came with someone who didn't leave the party.'

Patty put down her water bottle. 'Rachel, Julian committed suicide . . .'

'He was killed,' she said, shaking her head slowly. 'As was his friend Madison Kopek. It was all about Rheladrex. Rheladrex couldn't be pulled off the market because it would jeopardise the deal, and Greg wasn't going to let that happen.'

'Rachel, please. Listen to yourself. Greg Willets was as distraught as anyone when Julian died.'

She had already noticed the car keys on the blond wood countertop, recognising the Ferrari fob even from this distance. A cog in her brain began to turn.

'Patty, who told you the Denver Chemicals sale price was around thirty to forty billion?'

She didn't hear the woman's reply. Her head seemed to vibrate, her vision started to swim. Vaguely she registered that she had been hit, with force, on the back of the skull, and then she fell to the floor.

63

Elizabeth Denver had been riding at Hanley Park when she had received Adam's call and had grudgingly agreed to meet them for lunch in a pub halfway between the family seat and Somerfold.

'What's all this about?' she snapped, ordering a glass of tap water from the bar and coming to sit next to Diana and Adam by the roaring fire. She was still in her jodhpurs and a slim-fitting tweed jacket and did not look as if she would be staying long.

'Did Greg Willets have any reason to want Jules dead?' said Diana without preamble.

Elizabeth put down her glass without it even touching her lips.

'Simple answer, Elizabeth,' said Diana with more steel than she had ever felt. 'Yes or no.'

Her sister-in-law looked completely taken aback. 'What's wrong?' she asked quietly.

'Just tell me,' Diana repeated.

Elizabeth tucked a strand of hair behind her ear and fell quiet. Diana wasn't sure if she was thinking or had been stunned into silence.

'We think it has a connection with Rheladrex,' said Adam, speaking up.

'Rheladrex?'

Elizabeth was a smart woman, and Diana could tell just by looking at her that she had realised the implications.

'Greg's company Canopus was going to handle the sale of Denver Chemicals. I suspect we all know about Julian's report into Rheladrex, his concerns about it. A Chinese firm had been identified for Denver and it was Rheladrex that they were most interested in. A sale price of forty billion had been mentioned. It was a big deal for the parent company to lose. A big deal for Greg to lose,' added Elizabeth.

'Is it still going ahead?' asked Adam, fixing his full gaze on his sister.

Elizabeth lifted up a hand. 'Hang on. Don't make me out to be the bad guy here. Julian's gone. Rheladrex stays on the market, although we will fully co-operate with any regulatory board when matters come to a head. That's if we still own the company.'

'You still want the deal to go through?' asked Diana in horror.

'Of course I do,' she snapped. 'My job is to make money for the company.'

'At what expense?'

Elizabeth looked incandescent. 'No one knows anything concrete about Rheladrex. Not yet. The buyers are doing their own due diligence and nothing has been thrown up there. It's not the evil drug you think it is, Diana. And the success of Denver depends on it.'

'Have you been dealing with Greg on this, then?' asked Adam.

'Yes,' confirmed Elizabeth.

Diana and Adam looked at each other.

'Greg had a motive to kill Julian, Liz.'

'We all had a motive,' said Elizabeth, looking around the table. 'It doesn't mean that any of us did it.'

'There's something you should know, something odd,' said Diana, and she began to tell her about Greg's guest Eva not leaving the party.

Elizabeth didn't say anything after she had finished speaking.

'We should talk to Greg,' said Adam eventually.

'As if he's going to admit anything,' scoffed Elizabeth with her usual superior expression.

'Phone him,' pressed Diana.

Adam picked up his mobile and made a call, but there was no reply.

'He's probably out fucking Patty Reynolds,' said Elizabeth under her breath.

'Sorry?' said Diana, unable to believe what she had just heard.

Elizabeth looked up. 'Well Michael's gone to Africa, hasn't he? And whilst the cat's away . . .'

'Patty and Greg?' replied Diana after the implication of what her sister-in-law had revealed fully registered.

'Come on, you've heard the rumours,' said Elizabeth dismissively.

'No I have not,' she gasped. 'Their marriage is the strongest out of anyone we know.'

Elizabeth snorted with contempt. 'Look at Patty, look at Michael and ask yourself why she isn't going to fool around with someone a decade younger.'

'But they love one another. Michael is a great guy . . .'

She felt a wave of fear and was desperate for reassurance. Her first and only thought was to speak to Patty. Picking up her phone, her fingers like putty, she called her friend and was surprised when the older woman answered.

'Patty, it's me.' She had no idea what to say next.

'Is everything okay, Di?'

'Yes,' she said, composing herself. 'I'm just trying to track down Rachel. She said she was coming to see you this morning.'

'No, she hasn't arrived. Michael phoned me from the airport to say she might drop by, but she's not come. I hope everything is all right.'

'I'm sure it is,' Diana replied, feeling cold.

Patty began to make small-talk but Diana just wanted to end the call.

When she put down her phone she noticed that Elizabeth looked serious.

'What's wrong, Liz?' she asked instinctively.

'Nothing,' she said slowly.

'Liz, tell me, what are you thinking?'

'You know Patty helped Greg bankroll Canopus to get it started,' said Elizabeth finally. 'She has a vested interest in making that company work.'

Dread filled Diana's throat.

'Try calling Rachel again,' said Adam quickly.

She tried, but there was still no reply. Rachel's message to say

421

that she was on her way to Hampshire had been sent almost three hours ago. Surely she must be there by now?

'I want to go to Patty's house,' said Diana with a desperate need to do something other than sit in the pub.

Adam nodded.

'But Jules killed himself,' said Elizabeth, shaking her head. Diana felt a wave of solidarity with the woman. Her sister-in-law was not her favourite person, but right now she looked as confused and crushed as she herself felt.

Adam glanced at his watch. 'Hop in the car. It shouldn't take us more than an hour and a half if I put my foot down.'

'An hour and a half?' said Elizabeth, taking control. 'We're ten minutes' drive from Dad's and the helicopter's there.'

'We'd better get moving then,' said Diana, beating them both out of the pub.

64

She thought she had been out cold for only a few minutes, but really she had no idea how long it had been. Rachel blinked hard, seeing the world at first in a soft, blurred focus; then, as her vision sharpened, she could make out Patty and Greg arguing a few feet away from her.

She closed her eyes once more, trying to listen to what they were saying. At first it was hard to concentrate. She was aware that she was lying on the floor; her hands and feet had been bound and sticky black gaffer tape had been stuck over her mouth.

'What are we going to do?' Patty's voice was quivering with panic. 'That was Diana on the phone asking where Rachel was. Believe it or not, she's not completely stupid. Her bloody sister must have told her where she was going.'

'Ask her,' hissed Greg as Rachel felt her heart pump with fear.

'Leave her whilst I think,' snapped Patty.

But Rachel could hear Greg striding towards her, felt him tapping her with his foot to wake her up.

She stayed motionless, pretending to be unconscious.

He lifted her up, propping her against the kitchen units. He pressed his fingers against her eyelids to pull them back, and she blinked hard in the light, so he knew she had come round.

'What have you told Diana?' he growled, pushing his face so close to hers that she could see the lines and blemishes on his skin. He ripped the tape off her mouth and waited for her reply.

'I haven't told her anything,' croaked Rachel, her lips sore and stinging.

'Don't fucking lie to me,' he roared. 'She's just called Patty.'

Rachel gulped hard. 'I said I might come and talk to her, but that's it.'

Greg shook his head. 'You're way off base with this, you know,' he said, wiping a line of dribble from his mouth.

'Which is why you smashed me over the head with a tennis racquet and tied me up,' she said, noticing the glimmer of metal sports equipment where she had been standing with Patty.

She coughed and her whole abdomen ached.

'Don't make this worse than it is already, Greg.'

He looked at her, his dark eyes blazing. 'You're the one who made it something it doesn't need to be,' he said grimly. 'Just like Madison Kopek.'

'So you killed her too,' she whispered, suddenly imagining Pamela Kopek surrounded by photos of her dead children.

'She went poking her nose into places she shouldn't,' he sneered. 'Must have been one hell of a good fuck to make Julian go chasing after Rheladrex.'

'How did you know?'

'He told me. Told me he wanted to pull the drug and I thought he'd lost his mind.'

She could feel her hands shaking behind her back. She knew her phone was in her back pocket, but she was sitting on it. Maybe if she could just reach it, she could do something, but she had to stall for time until she worked out what to do.

'Julian was your friend,' she said quietly. 'All he tried to do was help you. If the Denver Chemicals deal had fallen through, there would have been others . . .'

She thought she saw a flicker of regret but then his gaze hardened into a look of venom.

'Do you know how this business works, Rachel? How much time and effort goes into brokering deals? Weeks, months, sometimes years. Wining, dining, licking their arses. You can imagine how hard it was finding those Chinese buyers who were willing to pay such a premium. And do you know how much I would have got if it all came to nothing? *Nothing.* I worked my balls off to get where I am today. I came from nothing and I crawled back from nothing. I was fucked by Lehman's, everything

I had gone, vaporised, and I wasn't going to let that happen again.'

'Stop it,' said Patty, putting a hand on his shoulder. He shrugged her off angrily.

'Who was the blonde with you at the party, Greg? Where did you find her? How did she do it?'

'Eva? Though I doubt that's her real name. Striking girl, Kosovan. Saw some terrible things in the war, or so I'm told. It made her very hard, ruthless. That was ballsy, even for me, coming to a dinner party with a contract killer.'

'She hid in the house, didn't she?' whispered Rachel.

'No idea where. Didn't ask for the details; I just paid her fee. I assume she hid, waited and chose her moment.'

'And how did she leave?' She didn't particularly expect him to answer but Greg was in full flow now.

'It was another waiting game. Wait till the police come, the forensics team, wait until there's activity in the house and she could stroll out without anyone really noticing. All in a day's work, apparently.'

'That's enough!' screamed Patty.

'What have you got to do with all this, Patty?' growled Rachel. She was afraid, scared what would happen next. She knew that these two were cornered enough to do something rash.

Patty walked away, out of her line of vision.

'That smart mind of yours wondering what to do next?' said Rachel defiantly. 'I thought you'd have both had the brains to sort all this out another way. Did you really need this deal that much, Greg? Enough to kill Julian and Madison?'

His eyes darted away from her. 'I needed those fees,' he said desperately. 'The company was about to go under. Five major deals have fallen through this year. I couldn't afford another one.' He seemed lost in his own world. 'Can you imagine a CEO blowing the whistle on his own company?' he said scornfully. 'Who does that? Willingly confesses that Rheladrex was fatally flawed? Just because some stupid little trailer-park trash was bleating about her dead brother.'

'You got Ross beaten up too, didn't you?'

'I didn't know how much he knew, so I paid two Jamaican

425

scumbags a thousand bucks to scare him off. I regret that. Probably a little excessive, but I hear he'll live.'

'The only thing you regret is that it drew more attention to Julian's suicide,' she replied with a grimace. 'In fact that's it,' she said, remembering the meeting with Greg in that fashionable City restaurant. 'That's why you told me about his mystery blonde in the first place. You wanted me to find Madison because you knew how it would look. Julian had a girlfriend and she was dead. You wanted us to think he killed himself because he was so cut up about it.'

'You're right.' His smile was faint but there was no disguising the look of quiet triumph. 'I guess I'm not quite the idiot you believe me to be.'

Patty had walked back into the room. She looked more composed than she had a minute earlier and had changed into jeans and a top.

'You should take her on the boat,' she said brusquely.

'Why?' he queried.

'Come on, just move her.'

Patty grabbed Rachel's T-shirt and pulled her up. The woman was strong and she stumbled to her feet. Patty slapped tape on her mouth again, then cut the rope around her ankles so that she could walk and pushed her forward.

'Call Eva,' she instructed. 'Tell her where we are. Get her to advise us what we should do.'

Rachel shuddered. She tried to call out, but the tape was too tight.

The grounds of the house were not overlooked. Greg dragged her across the grass and down to the water's edge, where a boat with a shiny walnut hull was moored. Suddenly all Rachel could think about was those plaques in Postman's Park. All those people trying to do the right thing. All those people killed trying to save someone else. It had turned out to be Julian's fate, and now she shivered with the thought that she too was going to join the ranks of the dead.

Well she wasn't going to let it happen, she thought defiantly. She slipped one bound hand into her back pocket. She could just feel the phone with her fingertips.

'Jump on,' ordered Patty.

Rachel was determined not to cry, but she was quaking in fear. She lifted one leg over the side of the boat, then the other. Her eyes scanned the vessel and she spotted a knife – the sort that sailors carried for cutting rope. She knew that if she could just get hold of it she had a chance. She knew she was stronger, taller and fitter than either Greg or Patty, and she wondered if she had a chance of overpowering them, because she knew that as soon as Eva got here it would all be over.

She fell back on the deck deliberately in close proximity to the knife.

'Get up,' said Greg, jumping on to the boat and hauling her to her feet. She had the knife between two fingers but she dropped it and it clattered to the deck. Greg turned and saw it, the silver blade glinting in the sun.

'Naughty girl,' he whispered, his lips so close to her ear that they touched her skin. 'Don't go getting any clever ideas now.'

There was a small cabin below deck and he pushed her down three stairs so that she landed on the floor with a thump. She had fallen on her face. Her cheek throbbed violently, and as Greg locked the door behind her, she cried out in pain. For a moment she lay motionless, her eyes squeezed closed. She thought of Thailand and the lapping jade waters. She thought of Liam and all the happy times they'd had on their boat. She thought about the fruit punch they served in her favourite bar, and how tasty the curries were at the beach shack next to their office. And as she realised that she would probably never experience any of those things again, a tear trickled down her cheek, landing on the deck in a small, clear watery circle.

Don't give up, she willed herself. Snapping her eyes open, she pulled herself to her feet and looked around for anything that could cut the rope free from her wrists. Sweat was beading down her neck and her breathing was shallow. There was nothing. No knife, no scissors, no sharp edges on anything. She remembered how she had once interviewed a man who did magic tricks. She had got him drunk and he had confessed that the way he got out of handcuffs was to dislocate his own thumb. She was tough enough to do that, she thought, exhaling sharply.

Suddenly she heard something – a gentle whoop-whoop coming closer and closer. The boat started swaying angrily on the water and she realised that a helicopter was coming in to land on Patty's estate. Adrenalin fired around her body as the noise, a growling flutter of blades and wind, grew louder.

In the corner of the cabin she could see a thin cupboard. She turned around and backed towards the door so that she could open it with her hands. Spinning back around, she could see that it was stacked with fishing tackle. She kicked at it, jumping out of the way as rods rattled to the floor. The gleaming hook of a fishing gaff shone in the low light. Lowering herself to the floor, she took a minute to feel for the hook with her fingertips. She knew that she could slit her own wrists if she made one false move, but she had no idea who was in the helicopter. If it was Eva, she would be dead within five minutes if she didn't escape.

She pulled hard against the hook, gasping as she heard a rip. Her hands dropped to the floor, and for a split second she wasn't sure if they had been severed from her body. Shaking the rope off her wrists, she grabbed the gaff and rammed the long wooden end against the locked door of the cabin. 'Come on,' she hissed as it refused to open.

She could tell that the helicopter had landed. Tears streamed down her cheeks as she smashed the door harder and harder until finally, it burst open and she saw a face. She lifted the gaff, prepared to strike, and then she recognised who it was standing in front of her. Diana. Her sister had come to get her. Her sister was here to save her.

'Rachel, it's me. It's okay. It's going to be okay,' she said, and they fell into each other's arms.

65

Diana drove down the long winding drive towards Hanley Park and parked the car – one of Julian's favourites – outside the Doric pillars. She was welcomed into the house by Concepción, one of Ralph and Barbara Denver's maids, who kissed her on the cheeks, talking excitedly about 'baby', and led her out to the back of the house, where the long green lawns disappeared to the horizon.

She could see Ralph in the distance, in a cream panama hat and a blue blazer with brass buttons, looking as if he were about to go and watch tennis or a regatta. Her father-in-law turned and waved, and then walked towards her slowly, with difficulty.

His face was tanned – she knew they had spent most of the time since the funeral in Provence – but it could not disguise his world-weariness. But as they embraced, Diana felt more warmth and feeling in his touch than she had ever done before.

'Come and sit,' he said, leading her to a wrought-iron table and chairs in a shady spot under the branches of an ancient oak tree. 'How is Rachel?' he asked quickly.

'Having a long, well-deserved sleep,' she smiled.

'She's one ballsy girl, your sister.'

'We wouldn't want her any other way.'

Ralph's expression hardened. 'You know, Greg Willets and Patty Reynolds are going to pay for what they did. I will make sure of that.'

She saw the steely ruthlessness in his eyes and she had no doubt in her mind that he would. Diana did not consider herself a vindictive person but she knew she was feeling her own maelstrom of emotions about Patty Reynolds and Greg Willets. She could see them now, running along the bank of the Beaulieu

River away from the helicopter. Adam had called the police immediately and chased after them, and although they had disappeared into the woodland that adjoined the Reynolds's property, they had been picked up by uniformed officers within the hour. Diana was sure she would never forget those few excruciating seconds before she opened the cabin door of the boat praying that she would not find her sister dead inside. But it hadn't worked out that way. Not this time.

She took a minute before she spoke again. 'I believe Denver Group is holding a selection committee meeting in a fortnight to formally appoint the new chief executive.'

She was up to speed with everything. Anne-Marie Carr was going to give her full daily reports on all the major events happening within the company, and Diana had been surprised at how interested she had been in her first missive.

'I need to tell you something,' she said slowly.

Coming over here, she had wrestled with what she was about to say.

'It's not easy to do this,' she began. 'But please believe that what I'm about to tell you is the truth. Believe me when I say that I want the right thing for your family. For you, for Charlie, for Julian.'

Ralph frowned. 'What are you talking about?'

'I know that Elizabeth is the favourite to take over the CEO job, and I don't think that's right.'

She couldn't pause for breath, she couldn't look him in the eye. Part of her felt traitorous saying this. Without Elizabeth she felt sure that her sister would not be tucked up soundly asleep; in fact she hated to think what might have happened to her. But she also felt quite strongly that people had to account for what they had done.

'As you know, I got Rachel to look into Julian's death. I did it because I had to know the truth. Rachel did her job, she did a great job, but she found out more than she'd bargained for, more than she wanted to know.'

She closed her eyes, knowing that what she was about to say could blow the Denvers even further apart. The words were right there, settling on her tongue. Elizabeth's involvement with Susie

McCormack. The plan to seduce Julian so that he would be irrevocably tarnished, so discredited that Elizabeth would get his job. But did she want to put his family through any more pain?

Tears were prickling at her eyes.

'I'm sorry. I shouldn't be telling you this,' she whispered finally.

'Don't worry. We know what Elizabeth did.' Ralph's low baritone was so soft she could hardly hear it.

'You do?' she said incredulously.

He looked up and met her gaze directly. 'Knowledge is power, Diana. How do you think I built such a successful business?'

He took off his panama hat and put it on the table.

'After the scandal, we had that girl, Susie McCormack, investigated. Tracked, if you like. My team became aware of communication between Elizabeth and Susie, communication that suggested that they had been involved in the scheme together. If you ever wondered why our daughter didn't get the CEO job on my retirement, then there is your answer. Sometimes you can be just too ambitious, too ruthless, and that leads to recklessness and mistakes. She is a brilliant executive but she will never get the top job. Not while I am alive anyway.'

'Did you ever think she was involved in Julian's death?'

'Not for one moment,' he said, his eyes burning a little more brightly, as if Diana had crossed a line. 'As a parent, you know that your children will make mistakes. But there are some things that you just cannot accept them doing. Some things your mind, your instinct as a parent will not let you even countenance.'

Diana looked to her left and saw two tears running down Mr Denver's crêpey cheeks, one slightly ahead of the other.

'I had one motto when I ran the business. Learn from your mistakes, but always look forward. Never back. A new CEO will be appointed for the Denver Group, and for the first time ever, that person will not be a member of the Denver family.' He gave Diana a small smile. 'Perhaps it's not a bad thing to have some fresh blood whilst we wait for the next generation.'

'Next generation?'

'You know how proud we all are of Charlie. He is growing up into a very fine young man indeed.'

431

He had stunned her into a relieved and happy silence.

'You are still part of this family, Diana. If my daughter made you feel that you weren't, then I apologise for that. I was angry when I heard what you had asked Rachel to do. Of course I wanted to know how my son died, but I was too scared to look myself. I didn't *want* to look, because I knew that whatever we found, the blame would come back to me.'

'Back to you?'

'Did the stress of running the family business kill him? Was his depression some hereditary fault of mine? Did I not protect him enough, guide him enough? I was sending myself mad with those questions.'

'It's not your fault, Ralph. None of it.'

He looked sad, defeated. 'Yes it is. That man. Greg Willets.' He almost spat out the words. 'I was taken in by Greg Willets as much as everyone else was. I gave him his first job. And then he killed my son.'

He puffed out his cheeks. His eyes were so misted Diana could barely see the pupils. She stood up and walked around to him, putting her hands lightly on his shoulders.

'It's okay. We'll get through this. We're family. Family stick together.'

66

Dot came out of the bakery kitchen holding an enormous six-tiered coconut cake. It was covered in frosting and sparkles and had one big candle protruding out of it like a rocket.

'Are we all supposed to start singing "Happy Birthday"?' grinned Charlie, slurping his vanilla lemonade.

'I'm only going back to Thailand,' grinned Rachel, feeling herself getting quite emotional. 'What's all this for?'

'I want to remind you how fantastic Boughton is so you come back and see us all as often as possible,' said Dot bossily.

'Cake always works as a bribe for me,' said Rachel, sticking a knife through the creamy stickiness.

'A cake feels like a celebration and I don't feel like celebrating,' smiled Sylvia sadly, hooking an arm through Rachel's. 'My little girl is going halfway around the world again.'

'Well, your big girl is loaded so there shouldn't be any problem with you all getting plane tickets at least twice a year to come and see me.'

Rachel squeezed her mother's arm and rested her head momentarily against her shoulder. She half expected Sylvia to pull away but when she did not Rachel almost laughed out loud with contentment. She wasn't sure whether she'd ever have a close and unconditional bond with her mother but right now she at least felt as if Sylvia finally accepted and liked her youngest daughter for who she was. And it made Rachel feel unusually proud.

'When are we going then, Mum?' said Charlie. 'Liam said that the best diving is about now. And I'm old enough to get my PADI certificate.'

'How about next month, before school starts?'

'Really?'

'Truly,' grinned Diana. 'Who's up for it?'

Everyone put their hand in the air.

'Hang on. I've got a surprise for you,' said Charlie. He retreated to a corner of the café, where he fiddled around with a laptop before calling Rachel over. 'You've got a phone call,' he said.

Rachel walked across hesitantly and almost stepped back in shock when she saw Ross's face on the computer screen.

'What the hell's this?'

'Skype, you idiot,' grinned Charlie.

She put on a pair of headphones and sank into a chair, her fingers brushing the screen. Ross's face was still bruised and scarred, but he was awake, propped up in bed, and the twinkle in his eyes told her that he was on the mend.

'All right, Rach? What trouble have you been getting into this time? You see, I can't turn my back for a minute.'

'Ross . . .' She was lost for words. 'I've got you a job,' she said finally. 'A great one, actually. All sorted out by Elizabeth Denver, would you believe, but I'll save it for non-alcoholic beers when I see you.'

'Well I'm on a plane home tonight. Will you still be there?'

'I think so, I hope so,' she grinned.

'Let's talk later. I believe you're having a party.'

Rachel was still smiling five minutes later. Diana put her arm around her shoulders and gave her a gentle hug.

'There's something I want to do before I leave,' said Rachel, turning to her sister. 'Come with me.'

Rachel drove the Range Rover north. Even before they were on the road towards Hanley Park, Diana knew where they were going.

The church was quiet when they arrived. Somewhere in the village they could hear the sound of a lawn-mower, but other than that it was still. The two sisters linked arms as they walked up the path towards Julian's gravestone.

Rachel crouched and laid a little bunch of purple and yellow freesias from Dot's café on the soil.

'I hope I didn't let you down,' she whispered.

'You didn't,' said Diana, touching her shoulder.

They turned and walked back to the car. At the gate, Diana stopped and fished an envelope out of her handbag.

'Open this when you get back to Thailand,' she instructed.

Rachel looked at her and laughed. 'You expect me to wait that long? You remember what I was like on Christmas Eve.'

Diana held back the envelope playfully. 'Well I'm not giving it to you unless you can exercise some self-control.'

'All right, on the plane then?' she asked hopefully.

'Nope,' said Diana, remaining firm. 'Do it when you're with Liam.'

'With Liam?'

'No peeking. You promise?'

'Tell me!'

'No.'

'All right, then, I promise.'

Diana handed over the envelope and gave her sister a squeeze.

'I am going to miss you so much,' she said, clutching her tightly.

'I can stay.'

Diana shook her head as if she knew it was time for Rachel to move on.

'I'm going to be busy here. I've got things to do.'

'The café?'

'That's one thing. I'm going to get a lot more involved with Denver too, and I want to set up a foundation in Julian's memory to help disadvantaged kids go to university. He paid for the son of one of his employees to study architecture, and I know he would have wanted to do more of that, so I thought I could roll it out to hundreds of kids who might benefit from our money.'

'You're one of the good ones, Di. Don't ever forget that,' said Rachel, feeling all warm inside.

'Stop getting sentimental,' Diana grinned, tapping her shoulder. 'This isn't goodbye. You've got us for a whole month in August, and believe me, you're probably going to be sick of the sight of me by then.'

'No I won't,' replied Rachel. 'We won't even have started making up for lost time.'

'You're right. We won't,' she grinned as they got in the car and headed back to Somerfold.

67

It was funny how things could seem so alien so quickly, thought Rachel, as she arrived outside the Giles-Miller Diving School. Six weeks ago this had felt like home. Now it felt like a postcard. A snapshot of someone's honeymoon. The palm trees, the beach, the hot, shining sun were things she had forgotten. She hadn't been joking when she had told Diana that she would stay in England. There were so many things about it she loved and it was not just her family. Liam had been right when he had predicted she would get sucked back into it. Life as a reporter was like that. It was seductive, exciting. It suited her and perhaps that was the secret to happiness – working out what fit.

Taking a deep breath, she bounded up the two steps into the ramshackle building, feeling nervous as she heard the sound of laughter coming from inside. Part of her wanted to turn back but she knew it was too late now. She saw Sheryl first, in shorts and a T-shirt, and tried to shut off the disappointment that Liam seemed to be having fun without her.

'Rachel, you're back!' grinned the Australian girl, bounding over to hug her.

Caught in her grip, Rachel glanced over Sheryl's shoulder, wondering if Liam had disappeared into the back room. But when someone came out, she was surprised to see that it was Jeff, who she had almost forgotten was now one of her employees.

'Is Liam here?' she asked, feeling apprehensive.

'He's at the boat, I think. Does he know you're here?'

'No.' She smiled, willing her courage not to desert her. 'No, he doesn't.'

It was just a couple of minutes' walk to the jetty, and she felt tongue-tied all the way there. She recognised him from a distance, his tall, muscular figure on deck cleaning the boat, his back still turned to her until she was standing right on the edge of the water.

Her dreams and nightmares had been full of boats for the past forty-eight hours, which wasn't surprising after her experience at the Reynolds's house. But watching their own boat bob gently in the water, backlit by a beautiful golden setting sun, she felt her resolve strengthen.

'I wanted to know if you were taking any more divers out today,' she said, trying to keep her voice as clear and steady as she could.

He spun round, and as she watched his face break into a wide smile, she felt her heart slowly melt.

'You're back. You used the ticket,' he said, jumping on to the jetty.

'You sound surprised?' she said, feeling like a teenager.

'I thought you'd want to stay longer.'

'Well I couldn't wait.'

'For what?' he asked hesitantly.

'I need to tell you something.'

As she steeled herself, she could feel the line of her mouth growing firm and a crease appearing between her eyes. She must have looked really serious, because Liam's own face became concerned.

'What's wrong?'

She took a breath, her speech prepared, her mind clear. She felt suddenly emotional. She was tired from the flight, but she knew she had to do this.

'I know we kissed. And I know you turned me down. I tried to pretend that it didn't matter, but I know now that it does matter. It really matters. Because I think we are just right together. Me and you. And if two people who are so right together *aren't* together, then it makes me wonder who the hell should be.'

Liam opened his mouth to speak, but she held her hand up to stop him.

'Let me finish, because if I don't, I'm not sure I will ever say it. I loved being back in London but I love something else more.

437

You make me so happy, Liam. You're right, I was a snappy little crocodile when I came to Ko Tao, and then I wasn't and that difference was you. I can't bear the thought of losing you or of you not being in my life any more. And right now, just looking at you is making my heart beat so fast that I could fall off this jetty into the Gulf of Siam. And I know I don't look like Diana or Sheryl or Alicia Dyer. I know I will never be posh or well-spoken like your friends in London. But we fit. And I just think that two people who fit together like us should be together. In life. In love . . .'

She had barely noticed that he had walked right up to her.

'Just stop talking for one minute so I can kiss you.'

And the kiss was sweet. So sweet. As if it was nectar, as if she was coming home.

'So you've changed your mind, then?' she said eventually, her heart almost jumping out of her chest.

There was silence. All she could hear was the lapping of the tide against the hull of the boat.

'Everything I do is because I love you,' he said, holding her face between his hands. 'I had that disgusting fifty-baht curry the first night we met because I didn't want to let you get away. I set up a business with you because I came here to make my life better and I knew that if I spent every day with you in it, then I couldn't not be happy. I've been single in Thailand for three years not because I'm mourning for Alicia or any other girl in London, but because I don't want to be with anybody else but you. And when I turned you down on the beach that night, it was purely because I thought we wanted different things, not because I wasn't hopelessly in love with you.'

'You told me we should stay friends.'

'You'd just heard about Julian.'

'That didn't change the way I feel about you.'

Liam shook his head, his blue eyes shining. 'For three years I have listened to you dissing love, dissing marriage, keeping your distance from everyone, anyone, because you didn't want to get hurt. When something happened between us, I didn't think you wanted what I wanted, so I said that we should stay friends because I was protecting myself.'

'What do you want?' she said, hardly daring to breathe.

'I want to be with you. In life. In love. Till we grow old. Forever.'

She melted into his arms and it was as if they would never be apart. She could taste salt water from the tears that were leaking down her face, but it didn't matter because Liam kissed them off gently and wiped her eyes with his thumb. Then he cupped her face in his hands once more and kissed her again properly.

'Marry me,' he said finally.

She nodded. 'It can be a family affair. Right here on the beach. Diana was thinking of coming out with Charlie this summer anyway for a month before the school holidays finish.'

'Well let's do it then,' he grinned.

Her pulse was racing with excitement as she started to make plans.

'Actually, Diana gave me something. She said I wasn't allowed to open it until I was with you.'

'Go on then, do it now.'

She opened the envelope. Inside was a key.

'What is it?'

'I'm not sure.'

There was also a card, which she handed to Liam to read out.

'"Here are the keys to the Sunset Bungalows. The property is yours. I agree with you that it's a very good business investment indeed. The title deeds will arrive separately. Your sleeping partner. Diana."'

'She's bought the bungalows. For us.'

'What a wedding present.'

'What a sister,' she smiled, as they walked hand in hand down the beach.

Acknowledgements

Many thanks as usual to the terrific team at Headline. And to Eugenie Furniss, Neil Rodford and Lianne-Louise Smith at Furniss Lawton and James Grant management for all they do.

To Suzanne and Cath for all their probate advice (with added cocktails), and Sean and Crispin for their banking expertise. That's what you get when you sit next to me at the quiz. Continued thanks to my family, especially my wonderful boys John and Fin – I promise not to bring work on the next holiday.